Praise for
Whose Voice the Waters Heard

On the brink of "a day that will live in infamy," two young lives cross paths in Hong Kong. When a world at war threatens the gentle love between a best-selling author and his beautiful Irish wife, they seek a REAL refuge. Robert Vaughn knows war, love, and the Lord, and in *Whose Voice the Waters Heard*, he weaves an intriguing tale that links all three. It's like eating a piece of sweet cake . . . you just want more.

> — Oliver North, former U.S. Marine and host of the nationally syndicated program "Common Sense Radio with Oliver North"

Vaughan's latest novel of World War II confirms his status as one of the very best American authors of his generation, especially when he writes of men and women in wartime. This is a novel illuminated by Christian faith and written by a veteran of our armed forces.

> — Greg Tobin, former editor-in-chief of Book-of-the-Month Club, Inc. and author of *Conclave*

Whose Voice the Waters Heard is an epic, full-bodied novel bringing back one of the most stirring and perilous times of our history. A masterful treatment of WWII, teeming with colorful characters. One of those rare novels which blends accurate history with colorful fiction. First-rate writing that entertains and instructs—exactly what a historical novel *should* do!

> — Gilbert Morris, bestselling novelist and teacher

If you enjoy meeting and getting to know interesting, even heroic and inspiring people whose paths cross and recross during the Great War, then you are in for a treat when you pick up *Whose Voice the Waters Heard*. Robert Vaughan is a truly gifted storyteller with a knack for involving you in the situations and scenes of the naval war in the Pacific—from Pearl Harbor to Japan's surrender. Not only did I like the characters and their stories but I also absorbed the feeling and the pace of life aboard the combat ships. A thoroughly entertaining book. I recommend it highly!!

> —C. E. Gurney, Rear Admiral, U.S.
> Navy (retired)

Whose Voice the Waters Heard gives an excellent view of the people, places, and events of the Pacific arena during WWII. It took me back to my own time on board a submarine in those eventful days.

> —W. J. Isbell, U.S. Batfish (SS310)

It is not by coincidence that the title of Robert Vaughan's latest book *Whose Voice the Waters Heard* is from the Navy Hymn. His novel is itself a hymn of men and women at war, extolling the virtues of honor, patriotism, and a deep and abiding commitment to faith.

> —Ken Cumbie, Chaplain,
> Commander, U.S. Navy

Vaughan captures the human side of war. Love, racism, ambition, crime, and heroism mix together in extraordinary effort and sacrifice. On the high seas and on the home front, exciting events weave together in the great adventure of the "greatest generation," as the very globe shakes from the most explosive events ever in human history. Be warned: once you pick up this book you will set aside all else for the duration.

> —Frank S. Virden, Captain, U.S.
> Navy (retired)

WHOSE VOICE
THE WATERS HEARD

WHOSE VOICE THE WATERS HEARD

A WWII NOVEL

Robert Vaughan

THOMAS NELSON PUBLISHERS®
Nashville

A Division of Thomas Nelson, Inc.
www.ThomasNelson.com

Published in Nashville, Tennessee, by Thomas Nelson, Inc.

Publisher's Note: This novel is a work of fiction. All characters, plot, and events are the product of the author's imagination. All characters are fictional, and any resemblance to persons living or dead is strictly coincidental.

Library of Congress Cataloging-in-Publication Data

Vaughan, Robert, 1937–
    Whose voice the waters heard : a WWII novel / Robert Vaughan.
        p. cm.
    ISBN 0-7852-6315-2 (pbk.)
    1. World War, 1939–1945—Fiction. I. Title.
PS3572.A93W48 2003
813'.54—dc21

2003000250

Printed in the United States of America

2 3 4 5 6 — 07 06 05 04 03

This book is dedicated with great affection to my brother,
Phillip Clinton Vaughan

"O Christ, whose voice the waters heard,
And hushed their raging at Thy word"

From *The Naval Hymn*

1

New York
October 22, 1941

Patrick Michael Hanifin was six feet tall, thin, with red hair and the barest suggestion of freckles. He looked a little like the young actor Van Johnson, and most women found him good-looking, though not classically handsome. After graduating *summa cum laude* from Boston College with a degree in music, Pat did his graduate study at the New England Conservatory of Music. Now, sitting on the windowsill of a seventh-floor suite at the Algonquin Hotel, he was sipping a Coca-Cola as he looked out at the city. Pat had an apartment on Lexington Avenue, but was visiting his parents in their hotel suite. Though they lived in East Chatham, New York, they had come to the city for a few days.

Below him on Forty-fourth Street, a delivery truck was parked in front of the hotel, and cars were maneuvering around it with difficulty. As a result, traffic was beginning to back up, and the honking horns of impatient drivers echoed back from the canyonlike walls of the buildings.

Pat's father, Sean Hanifin, came into the room. Sean was only fifty, but his white hair made him look a bit older. He was a big, barrel-chested bear of a man with massive shoulders, muscular arms, and a noticeable belly-rise. His bushy beard seemed to add to his overall bulk.

"Did you see section seven of Sunday's *Times?*" he asked, dropping the paper on the coffee table. "*Gossamer Wings* is number three."

"Yes, I saw that. Congratulations."

"Have you read it?" Sean asked.

Pat took a swallow of his drink and smiled. "Not yet, but I've been meaning to get around to it."

"You've been meaning to get around to it, huh? Well, I'm glad everyone isn't like you. If they were, my books would never sell."

"Sure they would, Pop," Pat replied. "Don't you know there are people who buy best-selling books and never read them? They just put them on the bookshelf in the living room so everyone can see how cultured and well-read they are. And what do you care? You get your royalties from the sale whether the book is read or not."

Sean laughed. "I suppose you have a point there," he said. "Oh, and I appreciate your agreeing to play the piano at the reception. It means a lot to your mother."

"I don't mind. It's good to be able to play a little classical music now and then."

"If you would audition for an orchestra somewhere, I'm sure you could get in," Sean said.

"Yes, for thirty-five dollars a week," Pat replied. "I'm making twice that at the club."

"I sent you to college so you could play for drunks?"

"The Emerald Club is a supper club," Pat said. "There's more eating than drinking."

"I suppose so. But you'll never become a classical conductor by playing silly little songs for a bunch of tone-deaf gluttons and drinkers. Besides, how can anyone hear your music over the sounds of gnashing teeth and mindless conversation?"

Pat chuckled. "I play forte, Dad. Forte." He made a vigorous piano-playing motion with his hands.

Katie Hanifin came into the room then, fussing with an earring.

Slender, with shoulder-length red hair, high cheekbones, and blue-green eyes, she still revealed a great deal of the beauty that had drawn Sean to the young Irish immigrant twenty-four years earlier.

"Sean, an' would you be lookin' at yourself now. When are you going to get dressed? Or is it a pub we're going to, and not a fine reception?"

"I've got plenty of time," Sean replied.

"Sure'n didn't Mr. Pendarrow himself say that he wanted you there early for publicity photos?"

"You are a slave driver, Katie O'Malley," Sean said. "I'll get dressed now, if it'll make you happy."

"Aye, that it will. Patrick, do you know what music you are going to play?"

"I've got it all planned."

"And will you be playing 'Clair de Lune'?"

"Sure now, an' what kind of a son would I be if I didn't play me own mither's favorite?" Pat replied, perfectly mimicking his mother's thick Irish brogue.

"Don't you be makin' fun of your poor immigrant mother, now," Katie scolded, a smile in her voice.

The phone rang, and Sean grabbed it as he was passing by. "Hello." He listened for a moment, then said, "I'll tell him." Hanging up the phone, he looked at his son.

"John Henry?" Pat asked.

"Yes. He's waiting in the lobby."

Pat finished his Coca-Cola, then reached for his jacket. "I've got to go."

"Go? And where is it you're going?" Katie asked.

"I promised John Henry I'd have lunch with him today."

"But the reception?"

"Don't worry, Mother. Mr. Pendarrow doesn't want any pictures of me. I'll be there in plenty of time."

The reception given by Sean's publisher, Pendarrow House, was to serve two purposes. One was to honor Sean for having yet another book on the best-sellers list. The other was to wish him bon voyage for his upcoming trip.

Sean's latest novel, *Gossamer Wings*, was about a group of passengers crossing the Pacific on a huge, four-engine flying boat that Pan Am called a Clipper. As part of the publicity for the book, Pendarrow was sending Sean and Katie on just such a trip.

Sean was paying for Pat to come along too. They would be leaving shortly for San Francisco, where they would catch the *China Clipper* for Hong Kong. Katie was a little apprehensive about such a long flight over water, but Sean and Pat were very much looking forward to it.

"You're sure I'm not intruding?" John Henry asked as the cab stopped in front of the Flatiron Building on Fifth Avenue, where Pendarrow House had its offices. "I mean, after all, this is your father's reception."

"No, you're not intruding," Pat answered. He paid the driver, and then started toward the building with John Henry right behind him. "They welcome drop-in guests. In fact, they've been known to stand out in the street and snare the unsuspecting passerby, luring him up with false promises of wild debauchery. Publishers' receptions are so boring that most people use every excuse they can to avoid them."

John Henry laughed as he followed his friend through the revolving doors.

John Henry Welsko was a Virginian, a graduate of the College of William and Mary, and the son of a very wealthy tobacco farmer. He had the double name that was common among his peers in the South, but along with John Henry came the surname Welsko. And neither his father's wealth, nor the fact that his great-grandfather had served as a brigadier general on Gen. Thomas "Stonewall" Jackson's staff could overcome the latent prejudice against a last name that ended with a vowel.

John Henry had further alienated his peers by getting a degree in business rather than the more genteel and acceptable disciplines of philosophy or the fine arts. After all, one went to college—especially a school like William and Mary—for cultural betterment. One did not go to college for something so crass as to make a living.

John Henry then compounded his sin by leaving Virginia to come to

4

New York, where he intended to work in the stock exchange. However, he found that he could earn more money by keeping books for the Emerald Club than he could by interning for the New York Stock Exchange.

By coincidence, both John and Pat had been distance runners in college. When they began comparing notes shortly after they met, they realized they had actually run against each other a few times. The comparison did not bode well for John Henry, who sometimes described himself as "two inches shorter and ten seconds slower than Pat."

For his program, Pat replaced his normal Cole Porter, Sigmund Romberg, and Rogers and Hart with the works of Vivaldi, Beethoven, Bach, and Debussy. Against this background, publishers, publicists, editors, authors, and others drifted about the room, nibbling the hors d'oeuvres, talking, and laughing loudly. In other words, these "listeners" were just as non-attentive as Pat's regular audience, the guests at the club. Only when he played "Clair de Lune" did they grow quiet enough to hear the music, and then only because Katie insisted on it.

Yokohama, Japan
Sunday, October 26, 1941

Diane Slayton stood in the doorway of the Kokusal Odori Presbyterian Church of Yokohama, handing out pew sheets to worshipers as they arrived for the Sunday morning service. Her father, McKinley Slayton, had been pastor of this church for ten years. Just last week he had announced to his congregation that he would be returning to America before the end of the month. The Church World Missionary Headquarters had pulled him from this ministry because of "deteriorating conditions between the governments of the United States and the Japanese Empire."

From his chair at the front of the church, McKinley watched as his daughter met each arrival, smiling and greeting them easily in their own language. Twenty years old, tall and willowy, with long blonde hair, Diane was lithe and very pretty—and completely unaware of her own beauty. McKinley found her like her mother in so many ways that it was sometimes unnerving.

His wife, Anna, had died of pneumonia three years ago. Shattered by her death, McKinley had almost returned to the States then. He was begged to stay not only by the missionary group that sent him, but also by every member of the church. Even Diane had asked him to stay.

McKinley stayed, telling himself that he was doing God's work. Sometimes though, he wondered if he hadn't done Diane a disservice by denying her the right to grow up in America. She had never tasted a malted at the corner drugstore, listened to American music on a juke-box, attended a high-school football game, or gone to a prom. She had never had a Saturday-night movie date or a Sunday-afternoon ride in the rumble seat of a jalopy.

Diane did not lack for schooling, however. She was tutored in Yokohama, then attended an all-American boarding school in the Philippines. As a result of her privileged education, she was well-read in classical literature, spoke and read five languages, and was exceptionally fluent in Japanese. She had absorbed Japanese culture and was proficient in flower arranging and calligraphy and even the tea ceremony. She also enjoyed discussing Japanese literature and theater with the most ardent devotee.

After graduating from high school, Diane returned to Yokohama. McKinley offered to make arrangements for her to return to the States to attend college, but Diane didn't want to leave. And in truth, her father didn't want her to, so he didn't press the issue.

As Diane continued to greet the arriving parishioners, a staff car belonging to the Imperial Navy came to a dignified stop in front of the church. Diane didn't have to see the passengers to know who they were. This would be Comdr. Yutaka Saito and his family.

Commander Saito walked up the steps, followed by his wife, Hiroko. Their daughter, Miko, was nineteen and was Diane's best friend.

Miko had once confided to Diane that her father's career in the navy had suffered because of his Christian faith, but it was not so much an issue of religious intolerance as it was of social nonconformity. Despite the social separation his religion caused him, Saito refused to abandon the faith he had found when he was a student at UCLA.

Diane had a great deal of respect for Saito and the other parishioners of her father's church. Christians made up less than 1 percent of the population and were a small and nearly invisible minority in a nation where it was extremely difficult to be different from those around you. To be a follower of Jesus Christ, and to owe supreme obedience to Him, was contrary to Japanese culture.

As they came up the steps, Diane smiled at them and greeted them warmly. Saito, as was his custom, merely nodded, his expression never changing.

"Although my father is a Christian, he follows the code of the Samurai," Miko had explained, when Diane asked why she never saw her friend's father smile. "It is not his way to show emotion."

Miko made no effort at all to hide her emotions; she laughed easily and was completely open in expressing her feelings for friends. She was crying now as she climbed the steps to the church.

"I have been sad for the entire week, ever since learning that you are going to leave," she said.

"I have been sad as well," Diane said.

Miko smiled through her tears. "Then, stay. I know your father must go back to America, but you could stay with us," she said brightly. "Father, can Diane not live with us?"

"I think . . . such an arrangement would be difficult," Saito replied, choosing his words carefully. "Come, now. We do not want to be late for the service."

Miko bowed slightly in acquiescence, then dipped her head toward Diane. Diane returned the gesture and, as Miko and her family went into the church, turned back to the job at hand, passing out the church bulletins she had run off on the mimeograph machine the day before.

Just before Miko entered the church, she turned back toward Diane. "You will not forget Miko?"

"I will never forget you, Miko," Diane promised.

From the top of the steps Commander Yutaka Saito watched the exchange between Diane and his daughter, and though neither of the young women noticed it, his expression softened slightly. He knew something that neither of the young women knew—in fact, something that very few people in all of Japan knew.

Despite the ongoing peace talks in Washington, war between the United States and Japan was now a virtual certainty. Saito knew this because he had just been given his sailing orders. He would report for duty aboard the aircraft carrier *Kaga* as part of a fleet that would depart for Hawaii. Their mission: to bomb the American fleet at Pearl Harbor.

With the Japanese fleet, North Pacific
Tuesday, December 2, 1941

On board the Japanese carrier *Kaga*, Comdr. Yutaka Saito lay in his bunk looking at a small photograph of his wife and daughter, wondering if he would ever see them again. He could feel the throb of the ship's engines as it beat its way through the North Pacific at a speed of twenty-four knots. The fleet was in these waters—far, far north of the normal shipping lanes—in order to keep their presence, and their progress, secret.

Unable to sleep, Saito got out of bed and made his way through the ship to the hangar deck. Maintenance men swarmed around the airplanes under the blaring lights.

On the floor of the deck was a beautiful plaster-of-paris relief map of Pearl Harbor, and though Saito had already studied it many times, he decided to look at it once more. He walked around it so he could approach the model from the north, the same way their approach would be made when the time came. He stood there several minutes, scrutinizing every detail.

After climbing the ladder to the flight deck, Saito had to stand still until his eyes adjusted to the darkness. Once he could see where he was going, he walked across the deck, passing the hulking shadows of the attack planes already in position. Then he saw a guard come to attention at his approach.

On the bow, he stood with his legs spread and his hands on his hips, riding the pitching deck as the ship plowed through the rough seas. Saito savored the splash of water on his face as some of the waves broke high enough to spray onto the deck. He licked his lips and tasted salt and squinted into the blackness ahead of him. His thoughts broke loose.

If he could take off now and fly far enough, fast enough, could he get a glimpse of the future? Would he be able to see the results of the adventure he and his country were about to undertake? And if he could see it, could he return to govern his life by what he had seen?

With a slight shake of his head, Saito cleared his mind of such thoughts, then started back across the flight deck to the hatch leading down into the pilots' compartments. He didn't believe that anyone could see into the future, though many went to the fortune-tellers to try to learn what their future was to be. Saito wouldn't do such a thing. Even if it were possible, Saito didn't think he would want to know what lay ahead.

Royal Savoy Hotel, Hong Kong
Wednesday, December 3, 1941

So far the trip had been longer, more tiring, and more boring than Pat could have imagined. He actually found himself wishing that he hadn't come along. But his parents had given him this trip as an early Christmas present, and he was very careful to show them his appreciation.

Sean Hanifin considered travel an essential ingredient for writing. As a result, young Pat had traveled all over the world with his parents. As a boy, he went hunting with Ernest Hemingway. Miró entertained him with drawings on the backs of envelopes. And as Pat was learning the piano, he sometimes found himself sitting on the piano bench alongside such friends of his father as Vladimir Horowitz and Sergei Rachmaninoff.

But all that had been when Pat was much younger. This was the first time in quite a while that he had gone anywhere with his parents. Now he found himself in Hong Kong, sitting on a padded sofa that made a circle all the way around a column in the hotel lobby. He was reading a newspaper when he happened to look up to see a man coming through the front door, accompanied by a very pretty, young, blonde-haired woman. The arrivals were so laden with suitcases and parcels that they could barely move. The woman dropped some of her load, and Pat jumped up and hurried to her aid.

"Thank you," the woman said, as he gathered up the suitcase and bundle.

"I would have thought a bellboy would help us from the cab," the man complained, "but there was no one there."

"There's the bell captain's desk. I'm sure if you asked, he would get someone for you," Pat suggested.

"Thank you, young man, I shall. Diane, you wait here with the luggage."

"All right, Dad."

"Did he call you Diane?" Pat asked.

"Yes."

"A pretty name. And you called him Dad. That is good too."

"It's good that I called him Dad?"

"It means he isn't your husband, or fiancé, or anything like that."

Diane laughed.

"Are you and your father visiting Hong Kong?"

"We're passing through. We have passage to the States on the *China Clipper*."

Pat smiled broadly. "So do I! We shall be traveling companions." He stuck out his hand. "I'm Pat Hanifin."

"I'm Diane Slayton."

At that moment Diane's father returned. "I am assured that a bellboy will be with us shortly," he reported.

"Good," Diane said. "Mr. Hanifin, this is my father, the Reverend McKinley Slayton. Dad, this is Pat Hanifin. He'll be going to the States with us."

"I'm pleased to meet you, Mr. Hanifin," McKinley said. "Have you been vacationing in Hong Kong?"

"Yes, I guess it was a vacation of sorts. My father's publisher paid for a trip for him and my mother. I just came along for the ride."

"Your father's publisher?" Diane echoed. "Wait a minute . . . *Hanifin?* Would your father be Sean Hanifin?"

"Yes."

"And he will be on the flight as well? Oh, how exciting! I love your father's work."

"Sean Hanifin?" McKinley asked, a look of confusion in his face. "Is that someone I should know?"

Diane laughed. "He is an author, Dad, a wonderful writer. He wrote *Becalmed* and *Conversation in the Shadows*, among others. His latest is *Gossamer Wings*. I haven't read it yet, but I intend to." To Pat she added, "You'll have to excuse my father. We have lived in Japan for the past fifteen years, and I'm afraid he hasn't kept abreast of things literary."

"You've lived in Japan for fifteen years?" Pat echoed, obviously impressed.

"Yes," McKinley said. "I was pastor of the Kokusal Odori Presbyterian Church of Yokohama. And my daughter is right, I'm afraid. My reading has been limited to theological tomes and letters from the mission office. I apologize."

"No apology is necessary. Besides, my father is the author, not I. However, we do have several copies of *Gossamer Wings* with us. If you'd like, Miss Slayton, I'll be happy to have a copy sent to you as soon as you are checked in."

"Oh, that would be lovely."

At that moment a bellboy arrived with a cart, which had a wobbling, squeaking wheel and a barely legible sign declaring it to be "Property of the Royal Savoy." The bellboy, who was well into his seventies, handled the suitcases and bundles with little show of effort. Once the cart was loaded, he began pushing it across the lobby.

"Well, we must get checked in now," Diane said. "I'm sure we'll be seeing each other again."

"Yes, I'm sure," Pat called to them, as Diane and McKinley started after the bellboy.

2

Hong Kong
Wednesday, December 3, 1941

A long, slow-moving swell rolled across Kowloon Harbor and lapped against the hull of the *China Clipper*; a Boeing 314, it was one of many huge, four-engine flying boats that the Pan American Airways System called Clippers. On the flight deck of the *China Clipper*, a tall, slender, fine-featured man sat alone in the cockpit, busy with his pre-flight check. Captain Ken Cooley looked up to ascertain the cause of the gentle rocking and, seeing that it was only the wake of the ferry, returned to the task at hand.

One at a time, he caged and uncaged each of the gyro instruments on the panel in front of him. After tapping every gauge with his finger, making certain none of the needles was sticking, he pulled the old course heading and magnetic variation from its holder just under the magnetic compass and replaced it with the new one he had just prepared.

"Hand me up the nine-sixteenths deep socket," one of the mechanics said.

Ken heard the voice through the open window to his left, and, looking outside, he could see the cowling stripped away from number two. The mechanic was working on the twin row of cylinders that encircled the big fifteen-hundred horsepower Wright-Cyclone engine.

"The crew that flew in here wrote up a mag drop. Did you take care of it, Charlie?" Ken called through the open window.

"Yes, sir. I've put in a new coil and retimed the magnetos, and I'm replacing both banks of spark plugs. You won't be having any trouble with this baby; you can count on it."

"Oh, believe me, we *will* count on it," the captain said. "We'll be a long time over water." He got up, rebuttoned his jacket, put on his hat, and then exited the aircraft to ride the hotel launch back to shore. Behind him, Charlie and the other mechanics and service personnel continued to work.

For five years Pan American had been operating a trans-Pacific passenger service. Twice a week the big flying boats would arrive in Hong Kong from San Francisco, and twice a week they would depart Hong Kong for the return trip.

Ken was part of an aircrew of six. His first officer and copilot was Mark Harrington. Second officer and navigator was Elliot Meeker, a balding, somewhat overweight man who had been a navigator for the merchant marine.

The oldest member of the crew was Gordon Travers, the flight engineer. During flight, Gordon sat in front of a control panel, monitoring gauges and operating the engine controls. It was his job to keep everything working properly, and the airplane even had access panels through which he could crawl to service the engines in flight. Gordon was perfect for this task, because the former Texas cowboy and oilfield roughneck was a somewhat undersized man . . . lean but leathery and tough.

Jason Peabody was the purser and chief steward, and though he had only been flying for a couple of years, he had worked for the White Star Line and was highly regarded by Ken for his thoroughness and concern.

While Gordon was the oldest, Betty Bridges, the stewardess, was the youngest. A tall, sloe-eyed, slender brunette, Betty charmed the passengers not only with her beauty, but also by the way she had of relating to each person, making each one feel as if he or she were the absolute center of her attention. Ken liked to hear Betty talk. She had a cultured way with words, a nonspecific accent that was rich in tone, like an announcer on a classical radio station.

After dusk that evening, Sean Hanifin sat rocking on the veranda of the Royal Savoy. The huge white-and-gold hotel fronted Kowloon Harbor and covered six acres of beautifully manicured lawn and gardens. Built in a style known as British Colonial, the hotel was famous for its elegance and service and was a favorite of the international set. It featured several lighted croquet courses and frequently hosted the Hong Kong Croquet Championship.

This was not Sean's first visit to Hong Kong, though it was the first time he had ever visited it under such elegant conditions. In his youth he had worked as an able-bodied seaman on board a windjammer, one of the huge, square-rigged sailing ships that mounted one last, valiant challenge of sail to steam.

Whether running before a Cape Horn gale, or riding a trade wind, the windjammers were unparalleled in size and power. Averaging 350 feet in length, they were more than twice as long as the wooden clipper ships that preceded them, and nearly as fast. Thousands of square feet of sail were spread from the steel spars of the four towering masts, and during the fifty years of their active lives, the vast holds of the windjammers carried millions of pounds of cargo around the world.

From 1910 until the end of the Great War, Sean had sailed from London to Belfast, to Boston and New York, then around the Horn to San Francisco and on to Hong Kong in the four-masted bark *American Roamer*. Nearly thirty years later, as a haunting echo, he could sometimes hear the music of a windjammer at sea—from the organ notes of wind as it spilled from an acre of flying sail, to the harplike sound of shrouds and straining backstays, to the banjo twang of halyards and the timpani of heavy blocks slamming against steel spars. When the ship rolled, the scuppers would go awash and the heavy seas would crash against the hull, swirling from fo'c'sle to deckhouse to poop deck, while strake and frame groaned, and storm-driven canvas thundered.

It was during those long voyages when Sean, inspired by the power and magnificence of the sea, realized that he wanted in some way to chronicle the wonder of God's creation. He began writing, with no real plan in mind beyond responding to the divine discontent that drove him.

In 1917 an Irish family booked passage from Belfast to the States on board his ship, and Sean fell in love with their twenty-two-year-old daughter. It was Katie who, without telling Sean, submitted a collection of his short stories to Northern Lights, a small publishing house in Boston. Sean was upset with his young wife, until he received a letter of acceptance. The result was *Sea Tales*, a collection of short stories. Although he didn't get a great deal of money from the publication, it emboldened him to leave the sea and attempt to make a living as a writer. Thus it was that in 1920, Sean, Katie, and their small son, Pat, moved to Paris, where, for the next few years, Sean supported his family by writing articles for the *Boston Evening Transcript*.

In addition to reporting for Bostonians what M. Pierre Garneau said in his address to the assembly of Paris street cleaners, Sean also continued to write fiction, publishing short stories in *The Paris Review* and a second book of short stories for Northern Lights called *The Longitudes*. It was in Paris that he met other young artists, writers, and musicians who were taking advantage of the creative muse that seemed so prevalent in the cafés and coffee shops. There, Sean counted among his friends such people as Ernest Hemingway, Gertrude Stein, Pablo Picasso, Joan Miró, Vladimir Horowitz, and Sergei Rachmaninoff.

Unexpectedly, *The Longitudes* began to be noticed back in the States, receiving several favorable reviews. It also brought Sean to the attention of Paul Tobin, an editor for Pendarrow House. "I have read with interest your wonderful collection of short stories," Tobin wrote. "Would you be interested in submitting something to Pendarrow?"

Pendarrow House was a large and very respected company, which published some of the giants of literature. Sean sent them *Becalmed*, his first novel, and Pendarrow House published it. Critics raved over his "compelling characters, vivid description, crisp narrative, and gripping story." It became a best-seller, and Sean Hanifin moved to the forefront of America's novelists.

Flipping through the pages of *Time* magazine, Sean read by the light of a yellowed overhead globe around which moths fluttered and insects buzzed. He was dressed for comfort in khaki pants and a flowered sport shirt that hung loose.

A young woman started to approach him but, seeing that he was reading, hesitated and stood a few feet away, holding a book.

Sensing a presence, Sean looked up. "Something I can help you with, daughter?"

"Mr. Hanifin, I was wondering if you would autograph my book," the young woman said, holding a copy of *Gossamer Wings* toward him.

"Of course I will."

"I apologize for intruding upon your privacy. It's just that, well, I saw you here and I thought . . ."

"It's no bother at all," Sean said. He took a pen from his shirt pocket. "What's your name?"

"Diane. Diane Slayton."

Sean wrote "To a lovely young lady in a romantic setting. Best wishes to Diane Slayton." He signed his own name with a flourish, then handed the book back to her.

"Thank you," she said. "I must tell you that I've read all your books, and I love your writing. That's why I was so thrilled when I learned that we would be returning on the same flight, and so pleased when your son had this book sent to me."

"Oh, so you got the book from Patrick, did you?" Sean asked.

"Yes, we met him as my father and I were checking in."

"Well, you want to be careful with that one, daughter," Sean warned. "He has a way with the ladies. Of course, he gets that from his father. The apple never falls far from the tree, you know."

Holding the autographed book against her breast, Diane smiled once more, then turned and hurried away.

"'Tis the shameless rascal of a man you are, Sean Hanifin," Katie said from the shadowed corner of the veranda.

"And what did I say that was shameless? Would you be for telling me that, woman?"

"Teasin' the poor girl with your nonsense about apples and trees," Katie said. "'Twas outright flirtin'."

"You wouldn't begrudge an old man the right to flirt with a pretty girl now, would you, my dear?"

Katie chortled. "Flirt with the young, pretty ones all you want," she replied. "As long as it's myself you come to when reality sets in." She moved out of the shadows and stood behind him with her arms draped across his shoulders.

He picked up one of her hands and kissed it.

"Katie O'Malley, you are my fantasy and my reality," Sean said. "Always have been, always will be."

Katie laughed. "'Tis blarney you're feeding me. Sure'n I don't know why I ever fell for the likes of you, a poor sailor-boy with no money and no prospects for some."

"Because you were smitten with my manly good looks and gentle-manly charm."

"Aye, an' that's the truth of it, God help me for my foolishness."

At that moment Capt. Ken Cooley, who had been strolling through the hotel garden, stepped onto the porch. Seeing the Hanifins, he nodded toward them. "Good evening, Mr. and Mrs. Hanifin. Beautiful evening, isn't it?"

"Aye, Captain, that it is, thanks to the good Lord for providin' it to us," Katie agreed.

"Captain Cooley, you aren't anticipating any delay in our departure tomorrow morning, are you?" Sean asked.

"No, not that I know of. Why do you ask?"

"I just wanted to double-check, especially when I saw all those men working on the plane this afternoon."

"That was just routine maintenance," Ken assured him. "We do that before every flight."

"I was sure that was the case. But I saw you out there as well."

"Well, it's my job to make a last-minute check." Ken smiled. "And I'm happy to say that all is well."

"Good, good. I shall quit worrying then."

"Will the two of you be joining us in the dining room this evening? As you know, it is the custom that passengers and crew eat together on the last meal before departure."

"Last meal?" Sean replied with a little chuckle. "That has a rather ominous sound, don't you think?"

Ken laughed. "Only to best-selling authors, I suspect." He nodded toward the *Time* magazine lying closed in Sean's lap. "Anything interesting in the news?"

"It's like all the others . . . full of stories about the peace talks with Japan."

"Yes, well, I hope they get it all settled," Ken said.

"I would like to hope so as well," Sean said. "But I don't have a good feeling about it."

In the hotel's main dining room, dozens of ceiling fans suspended from long, spindly poles turned briskly overhead. Potted palms and containers of other assorted plants were set about on the mauve-and-black tile floor, while white-jacketed waiters darted to and fro, delicately balancing as many as half a dozen food-laden plates on large trays. Young barefoot boys, most no more than ten, crawled along the floor carrying Flit spray guns. They would slip in and out of the underside of the tables, offering the services of their insecticide for a small coin. There, covered by the drape of crisp, white tablecloths, they squirted citronella on the ankles and legs of the diners. Despite their best efforts, the mosquitoes continued to harass the guests.

Off the main dining salon the Royal Savoy had a more exclusive room set aside for the Pan American passengers and crew. This room was much less crowded and much less noisy. When Ken Cooley went inside, he saw his stewardess standing by the RCA Victrola, shuffling through a stack of black discs.

"Any Glenn Miller records, Miss Bridges?"

"I've already stacked them on the changer, Captain," Betty said. "Just for you."

"Good, good. That should liven up our departure dinner."

Before joining the rest of the crew, Captain Cooley went from table to table, visiting and talking with the passengers. Beyond the tables, through a huge picture window, the diners could see the giant flying boat riding at gentle anchor in the harbor. The Boeing was bathed in the wash of a dozen high-powered floodlights, and its silver-blue paint scheme glowed brightly. Just aft of the nose was a stylized painting, in navy blue, of Pan Am's winged globe. All the way back, on the outside stabilizer of the three-tailed ship, was a brighter splash of color—the red, white, and blue flag of the United States.

Noticing that Pat Hanifin was sitting at the table with the Reverend Slayton and his daughter, Ken smiled. Transoceanic aircraft, like ships, created an artificial atmosphere that quickened the social process. The excitement often gave birth to brief romances, but since an aircraft had a much more closed environment than an ocean liner, the romances were less likely to be troublesome.

Ken joined the crew table. "How goes it, Gordon?" he asked the flight engineer.

"All consumables are aboard, sir," Gordon answered. "All maintenance entries signed off."

"Elliot?"

"Course plotted and weather checked, Captain," the navigator replied. "I'll check weather again tomorrow just before we take off."

"Ah, here's Mark," Ken said as his copilot arrived. "What have you got for me?"

"Weight and balance computed, Captain," he said. "We are well within weight limits, and I have the fuel cross-feed worked out to maintain CG."

"Good, good, then we are ready to go."

"By the way, I see we have Sean Hanifin with us," Gordon Travers said.

"Yes, as well as his wife and son," Ken said. "That's Pat with the young Slayton woman."

"I'll say this for young Mr. Hanifin," Mark said. "He has good taste in women. She's quite attractive."

"Have you heard him play the piano?" Elliot asked.

"Who, Pat Hanifin?" Ken replied. "No, I haven't. Is he any good?"

"He's very good. I heard him playing in the lobby this afternoon. Too bad we don't have a piano on the airplane. He could entertain our passengers."

Mark chuckled. "Looks to me like there's only one passenger he's interested in entertaining. I'll bet you he doesn't get more than a couple of feet away from Miss Slayton for the entire flight."

"I'm glad he's the only single young man aboard," Ken said. "An aluminum box two miles above the ocean is no place for competing suitors."

The others laughed.

"That sounds like a plot for one of Sean Hanifin's novels," Mark said. "By the way, I just read *Gossamer Wings*. It's an adventure story that takes place on board a Clipper."

"A Clipper, huh?" Ken replied. "So tell me, Mark, how does it feel to be a character in a novel?"

Dinner was over, and Pat and Diane were taking a walk across the hotel lawn, strolling under the long, glowing strings of Japanese lanterns. The air was soft and perfumed with many varieties of flowers, colorful by day, fragrant by night.

They stopped to sit on a low stone wall and looked across the bay toward the Clipper, still shining brightly in the floodlights.

"Did you like living in Japan?"

"I liked it very much."

"And you didn't miss being in America?"

"You can't miss what you don't know. I was born in America, but I can barely remember it."

"What do you think you'll miss most?"

"For one thing, the people. They are so polite and kind."

"Not the kind of people you would go to war with?"

"Do you think there will be war between America and Japan?" Diane asked.

"I don't know, but my dad seems to thinks so, and he sort of has an instinct about these things. What do you think? Growing up in Japan should give you a perspective that we don't have."

Diane shook her head. "Actually I don't have any perspective about that at all, because it's not being discussed in the newspapers. Until our church mission office called Dad back, we had no idea of the severity of the situation. I certainly hope there is no war."

"Well, there are talks going on in Washington, so maybe cooler heads will prevail."

Diane pointed to the airplane. "I've never flown before."

"You will enjoy it."

Diane smiled at him. "I know I will enjoy the company. At least, I have so far." She gasped and put her hand to her mouth. "Oh, that must've sounded terribly forward. I apologize."

"Nonsense," Pat said with an easy smile. "One should never apologize for honesty."

Diane slid down from the wall and brushed her hands against the back of her dress. "I'd better be getting back now. Dad will be wondering what happened to me."

"I'll walk you to your room."

As they strolled back up toward the hotel, they saw the pilot and copilot in deep conversation on the porch.

"Aren't those two men our pilots?" Diane asked.

"Yes. They're probably trying to figure out which way we need to fly tomorrow to find the States."

"What?" Diane gasped.

Pat laughed. "I'm kidding," he said. "I'm just kidding."

3

Manila
December 5, 1941

T he leg from Hong Kong to Manila was a picture-perfect, uneventful flight. The plane set down at the Luneta in Manila, then the passengers disembarked and rode the small launch to the dock, where a jitney carried them to the hotel.

Because of Diane's high school experience in the Philippines, she knew Manila very well and offered to take Pat on a taxi tour of the city. He eagerly accepted the offer, promising to repay her in kind if she ever came to New York.

They visited the usual tourist spots along the bay, then Diane asked the driver to take them to the Plaza Dilao-Paco District. Nestled in a small patch of trees and surrounded by flowers stood a statue.

"When I was attending school here, I found this place to be particularly meaningful," Diane said.

"Why? Who is it?"

"It is a statue of the Japanese feudal lord Ukon Takayama, who was exiled to the Philippines in 1641 for refusing to disavow his Christian beliefs."

"They erected a statue to someone just because he was a Christian?"

"You don't understand," Diane said. "In Japan, it takes faith and courage to declare yourself Christian."

"You're Christian. Your father is a preacher. Were you in danger?"

"No," she replied. "We're Americans, and we were expected to be Christian. The Japanese are tolerant, so long as you do what is expected of you. But Japanese citizens are not Christian, and when they declare that they are, they face many hardships. Dad worried constantly about the members of his congregation. In particular about one man, Yutaka Saito, and his family."

"And why was that?"

"Because he is an officer in the Imperial Navy," Diane said. "For him, it is extremely difficult to be a Christian. His daughter, Miko, was my best friend."

"Religious intolerance doesn't seem compatible with your description of the Japanese as being such kind and gentle people," Pat said.

Diane smiled. "Perhaps I should also explain that Japanese society is full of contradictions."

"You say Miko was your best friend. What will you do if there is a war between your countries?"

"Pray that she and our friendship survive."

It was dark by the time Pat and Diane returned to the hotel. After he paid the taxi driver, he offered Diane his arm and they walked up the long, curving sidewalk toward the hotel entrance. As they were passing under the shielding canopy of overhanging acacia trees, Pat stopped.

"Diane," he said.

She looked up at him. "Is something wrong?"

Pat stared at her for a long moment. "No, nothing is wrong. Everything is right." He put the tip of his forefinger under her chin, raised her head toward him, and bent down to kiss her softly on the lips. "I just wanted to do that," he said easily.

Diane stared at him with an expression somewhere between surprise and shock.

"Diane?" Pat asked, concerned that she may have found the unsolicited kiss too forward.

"So," she finally said. "That's what it's like."

"That's what what's like?"

"A kiss. I've read about them, of course, but—"

"Wait a minute! Diane, are you telling me you have never been kissed?"

"This was my first time," she admitted.

"Oh, I'm sorry. I had no right to impose myself on you like that. I had no idea that—"

"Can we do it again?"

Pat paused, then laughed. "Yes," he said. "We can do it again." When he kissed her this time, Diane's arms wound around his neck, and she kissed him back.

They rode in the covered launch with the other passengers to the airplane. Katie sat beside Sean, and Pat sat just on the other side of Katie, right across from Diane Slayton. It seemed to Sean that Pat and Diane were paying even closer attention to each other now than before, though it might just be his imagination. It didn't appear, however, that the Reverend Slayton had noticed it. Right now the good reverend was sitting beside his daughter with his hands folded across his lap and his eyes squinted against the glare of the morning sun.

The boat operator docked the launch against the side of the *Clipper*, and the passengers began boarding. When all were aboard, the purser, Jason, closed the door, then signaled to Betty, who picked up the phone to call the cockpit.

"All passengers are aboard, Captain."

"Very good. Prepare the cabin for takeoff."

Betty and Jason moved through the compartments, making certain that everyone was buckled in; then they took their own seats as they felt the tug take the airplane under tow.

Up on the flight deck, Ken could feel the plane jerk and weave as the towboat pulled it away from the dock. After several feet, the towline parted and the boat moved quickly out of the way, leaving the airplane to bob on the gentle waves of its bow wake.

"Starting sequence for engine number one," Ken said.

"Fuel rich, prop full RPM, fuel pump on, engine primed, inertia starter energized," Mark said, talking through each phase. The whine of the inertia starter built up to a high, keening sound, then the engage toggle switch was moved. The number one engine coughed, belched smoke, and took hold. This sequence was repeated three more times until, finally, with all four propellers spinning, Ken taxied the big flying boat out to the far end of the bay, then turned to head into the wind. He picked up the microphone.

"Manila, this is *China Clipper*, requesting permission for takeoff."

"*China Clipper*, altimeter is two niner niner five. You are cleared for immediate takeoff and departure," the voice in Ken's headset said.

"Roger, Manila," Ken replied. He hung the microphone on the hook and put both hands on the wheel. "Flaps at thirty," he told his copilot.

"Flaps at thirty," Mark answered.

"Mixture full rich."

"Full rich."

"Props to increase RPM."

"Increase RPM."

"Okay," Ken said as he pushed the four throttles forward. "Here we go."

The *Clipper's* engines roared at maximum power as the airplane started across the bay, leaving a long streak of white foam behind it on the water. For forty seconds it skimmed along, splashing so much sea-water onto the windows that from within it looked like a tropical down-pour. Then some of the noise and all the vibration ceased as the plane lifted free and began climbing slowly away from the island, breaking cleanly from the streak of white foam and spilling water from its keel and outriggers.

Ken picked up the microphone. "This is *China Clipper* off at 0645 local. Please advise Guam."

"Will do, *China Clipper*. Have a good flight, sir."

Ken clicked the microphone button two times, breaking the squelch twice by way of acknowledgement, then hung the microphone on its hook. Leaning back in his seat, he looked around the flight deck, smiling broadly. "And once again, skill, daring, and experience triumph over fear, ignorance, and superstition as we get this collection of spare parts and disparate souls into the air."

"How long have we been under way?" Ken asked, awakening from a catnap. Mark was flying.

"Four, plus zero-five," Mark answered.

Ken twisted around in his seat. "How goes it, Elliot?"

"We're on course, Skipper, ground speed one-five-zero, heading two-zero-five."

Ken got up from his seat. "I think I'll go below and visit a while."

"Aye, aye, sir," Mark replied.

Ken climbed down the ladder and stepped into the passenger compartment. Whereas the engines had been a reassuring but loud roar up on the flight deck, down here in the passengers' cabin, the sound was reduced to a manageable drone, about the same level as the inside of a high-speed train. Here, too, were all the amenities of a first-class hotel: plush carpets, wall upholstery, elegant curtains.

Jason had been busy, and the results of the steward's work were on display. On a small table were spread hors d'oeuvres of cold shrimp, caviar, and sliced fruit. Half a dozen passengers were already gathered in the dining salon, enjoying the food. Ken walked over and speared a cold, peeled shrimp with a toothpick.

"Ah, Captain, you've left us in capable hands, I trust?" Sean Hanifin asked, joining Ken at the hors d'oeuvres table and picking up a shrimp.

"I believe things are well under control."

"This is good shrimp," Sean said, popping one into his mouth. He chuckled. "If someone had told me twenty years ago that one day I would be eating boiled shrimp while flying two miles above the ocean, I would have told them that they had read too much Jules Verne. But here we are. We live in a marvelous age, Captain Cooley. A marvelous age indeed."

"That we do," Ken agreed.

"Mr. Hanifin," one of the passengers said, approaching them.

"Please call me Sean."

"Okay, Sean. I wanted to ask you about . . ." The passenger pulled Sean closer to him as Ken moved farther down the table to get a pineapple spear. He took the fruit over to the window and stood there, looking down. The sea was a brilliant blue, sparkling with the sun dance of a million tiny reflections.

After visiting with a few more passengers, the captain climbed the ladder back to the flight deck. As he walked past the navigator's table, Elliot held up his hand to stop him.

"Captain, I'm getting something strange here."

"What do you mean, strange? I don't like 'strange,' especially when we are twelve thousand feet over the ocean and several hours from the nearest land."

"I'm getting a lot of radio traffic that I can't make out."

"Ships?"

"I think so, yes sir. But they're north of here."

"North? There are no shipping lanes north, are there?"

"No, sir."

"Are you sure the signals are coming from the north?"

"I'm positive. I traced them with the DF."

"They aren't interfering with our signals, are they?"

"No, sir."

Ken ran his hand along his cheek. "Well, check in on them from time to time just to see if you can figure out what it is. In the meantime, as long as they represent no problem for us, I'm not going to waste time worrying about it."

"All right, Captain," Elliot said. "But you have to admit, it is curious. There's not supposed to be anyone up there, but clearly there are a lot of someones there."

Pearl Harbor, Hawaii
Friday, December 5, 1941

When the USS *Turner*, DD-363, returned to Pearl Harbor, she was flying the "E" pennant from her mast, emblematic of her superior performance during the training exercise just completed. Many of the destroyer's crew, already in their liberty whites, were standing on the deck as the ship slid by the channel entrance buoys and started along battleship row. There *Arizona*, *Nevada*, *California*, and *Maryland* rode at anchor, rising above the much smaller destroyer like gigantic gray-steel skyscrapers. Fifteen minutes after passing the entrance buoys, *Turner* was lying alongside the pier with all lines secured.

The bosun's call trilled over the ship's intercom speakers. "Now liberty call, liberty call. Liberty commences for sections one and two. Now set the in-port watch."

Even though most of the sailors were already topside, and the ship's executive officer, Lt. Jerry Cornelison, was below deck in his cabin, he could hear the sailors' cheering. He, too, was going on liberty, and his tunic hung from his bunk. Someone knocked at his open door, and when he turned he saw S1c. Tony Jarvis.

"Jarvis?"

"Mr. Cornelison, could I ask you a favor, sir?" Jarvis was holding his white hat in his hand, turning it slowly as he spoke.

"Don't tell me you've already been put on report. We just got here."

"No, sir, it ain't nothin' like that, sir." Tony was a rather stocky man, five-feet-four and 157 pounds. He was an outstanding boxer and had won the middleweight championship in the interservice boxing matches the year before. He was popular with the crew, but the combative spirit he showed in the ring often came to surface in his private life. More than once it had been necessary for Cornelison or one of the other officers of the *Turner* to go down to the police station and bail him out of jail.

"All right, then, what is it you need?"

"I was wondering, sir, if I filled out the papers I need to get married, would you sign 'em?"

"Wait a minute. Didn't I just sign some papers for you to get married?"

"Yes, sir, you did."

"What happened? Did you lose them?"

"No, sir, it's nothin' like that," Jarvis replied. He cleared his throat then mumbled, "Different girl."

"I beg your pardon?"

Jarvis cleared his throat once more and answered again, more forcefully this time. "This here is a different girl, sir," he said.

"A different girl."

"Yes, sir. The last one? Well, that was Elaine. She works over to the Aloha Bar. This here one is Rosie. She works at the Wet Mouse."

"And . . . correct me if I'm wrong, but the XO before I came on board had approved another girl before Elaine?"

"Yes, sir."

"You seem to be going through your women at a pretty rapid pace, Jarvis."

"Yes, sir. Well, but at least I ain't made the mistake of marryin' any of them yet."

"But you want to marry this one, right?"

Jarvis smiled broadly. "Yes, sir!" he said. "This is the one for me. I know she is."

"When is this wedding supposed to take place?"

"I don't know exactly," Jarvis admitted. "I ain't asked her yet."

"Don't you think you should?"

"Yes, sir. Well, I plan to ask her before, uh, we actually get married."

Jerry chuckled. "That's probably a good idea."

"So you'll sign the papers?"

"I tell you what, Jarvis. Suppose you go ahead and ask her. But tell her you want to wait a few weeks. If she says yes, and you still want to go through with it then, I'll sign the papers. But I think you should give it just a little while to see if this is really what you want to do, don't you?"

Jarvis squeezed his hat a few more times as his face drew up in serious contemplation. Then he nodded. "Yes, sir, that's prob'ly the best thing all right. It's just that I thought . . . well . . . Muley is sort of sniffin' around her too, you know what I mean? And I figured that if me 'n' Rosie was already engaged, why, she wouldn't have nothin' to do with Muley."

"Muley? You mean our Muley? Seaman Lewis?"

"Yes, sir."

"Then it seems to me that's something else you need to work out before you rush into marriage," Jerry suggested. "I mean, what if Muley comes to ask me to sign papers for him?"

"You . . . you wouldn't do that, would you, sir? I mean, seein' as I asked you first?"

"Look at it from my position, Jarvis. I can't show favoritism now, can I?"

"No, sir. I guess you're right, sir."

"I'm glad you see it my way. Now, anything else?"

"No sir, nothin' else."

"Then what are you standing around here for? The way I figure it, you've already used up twenty minutes of your liberty."

"Oh, you're right, I have!" Jarvis said. Putting his hat on, he came to attention, then saluted. "By your leave, sir."

"Dismissed," Jerry said, returning the salute.

Turning, Jarvis nearly collided with Dickey Traser, who was standing just outside the door.

"Oh, good morning, Mr. Traser. I almost didn't see you there," Jarvis said.

"Good morning, Jarvis."

Lieutenant, junior grade Dickey Traser was communications officer for the *Turner*. Though Jerry hadn't noticed him, the young officer had been standing out in the passageway during the discussion.

Traser was Dickey, not Richard, not Dick. Dickey's family did not feel constrained by convention. His father was J. Arthur Traser, and if he wanted to name his son "Dickey," then the rest of the world would just have to handle it.

31

"Just how rich is J. Arthur Traser, Jack?" Mary Livingston asked of Jack Benny during one of his radio shows.

"How rich is J. Arthur Traser? He is so rich that when he writes a check, the checks don't bounce, the banks do."

"Did you hear what Jarvis asked for?" Jerry asked.

Dickey chuckled. "Yeah, I heard. How long do you think it'll be before the duty officer has to go pick him up?"

"Oh, I'd say until he and Muley show up at the Wet Mouse at about the same time," Jerry replied.

"You ready for liberty?"

"Ready," Jerry answered.

"Let's go."

Jerry Cornelison and Dickey Traser had planned to share a room at the Royal Hawaiian. It was a great suite of rooms, situated on the ocean-front, seventh floor, with a tremendous view.

While Dickey took a shower, Jerry waited in the sitting room. The window was open, and a gentle breeze lifted the curtain so that it angled out over the floor. For the moment Jerry was slouched in an easy chair, drinking a 7-Up and enjoying the view framed by his propped-up feet. The music coming over the radio was interrupted by the voice of a newscaster.

"In Washington, the Administration's price-control bill is bruised, battered, and buried. The bill, introduced by Tennessee's bright young representative, Albert Gore, provides for a ceiling on wages as well as on prices and rents.

"Also in Washington, Special Envoy Saburo Kurusu continues his talks with the Administration, trying to convince the U.S. to allow Japan free run in the Pacific. In the meantime, Premier Tojo has told the world that it is the destiny of Japan to rule the Pacific, and she intends to have her way regardless of the outcome of these talks. Mr. Tojo said, quote, 'There is a limit to our conciliatory attitude. America must accommodate our demands or deal with the consequences.' End quote.

"Meanwhile, in Manila, Manuel Quezon, president of the Philippines since

1935, won reelection by a majority of 87 percent. Though some Filipinos are advocating dominion status under the United States for the Philippines, especially as they are threatened by the shadow of Japanese aggression, Quezon remains committed to independence for the Philippines in 1946."

After the staccato, nearly breathless voice of the news stories, a softer and more even-toned voice began a commercial.

"Ladies and gentlemen, did you know that actual sales records show that in the army, the navy, and the marines, the favorite cigarette is Camel? With 28 percent less nicotine and five extra smokes per pack, is it any wonder that this is the best-selling cigarette? Camels give you smoking pleasure."

Jerry walked over to the radio and fiddled with the dial until the strains of a steel guitar playing Hawaiian music filled the warm air. He returned to his chair and looked out over the ocean again. From this position he saw a submarine coming into the harbor.

He couldn't see a submarine without feeling just a little jealous of its officers. Both he and Dickey were qualified submariners, but budget restrictions had halted construction on the submarine that was supposed to be theirs. As a result they were assigned to a surface ship. The *Turner* was a good ship, and both men were proud to serve on her and quick to defend her against any disparaging remarks. But she wasn't a submarine.

In addition to having attended submarine school together, they were also Annapolis graduates. Both first-generation navy men, they were drawn together by the fact that neither was fulfilling a family legacy. To the average person, that might seem to be little in common, but many Annapolis graduates were second-, third-, and in some cases even fourth-generation naval officers. Their clique was difficult for outsiders to penetrate.

Jerry Cornelison grew up in Oklahoma. His father, a tenant farmer, dealt with the struggles of the great Dust Bowl and Depression of the thirties by abandoning his family. Jerry's mother found work in cleaning houses and taking in laundry, and she managed to keep herself and her son fed, though barely. Sometimes she would spend hours on her hands and knees, scrubbing floors in return for a bucket of leftovers from her employer's supper table.

Jerry's clothes were badly worn, but always clean. Without complaint, he went barefoot in the summertime to save shoe leather, and sometimes he came to school without lunch.

From the beginning, Mary Cornelison had known that Jerry was gifted and courageous. He could read and write before he started school, and she was determined that he would get the best education possible. Due in part to his mother's encouragement, Jerry had an innate appreciation for learning; his mind was always thirsty for more.

At fourteen, Jerry was on his way home from school when he passed a house on fire. Several people stood on the street in front of the blaze, but the firemen had not yet arrived. From the second-floor window in back, a young girl was calling for help.

Without hesitation, Jerry climbed a tree near the house and worked his way along a limb that stretched almost to the window. He cajoled the trapped girl onto the limb and helped her safely down, then continued on his way. It was three days before the town was able to track him down and give him a medal.

In high school, Jerry's heroics were displayed on the football field, resulting in his selection to the all-state high-school team. But his academics matched his athletic ability, and when he graduated number one in his high-school class, the congressman from his district, remembering Jerry's heroism, arranged him an appointment to the U.S. Naval Academy.

Annapolis not only provided him with a free college education, it also paid him a salary while he was attending school. The midshipmen were advised to save as much of their school salaries as they could, but Jerry used his pay to make life easier for his mother. He continued his sports heroics by making the All-American college football team his senior year. His biggest regret was that his mother died before he graduated; she never saw him graduate or win his commission.

At Annapolis Jerry quickly developed a real affection for the navy. He loved not only the excitement and adventure; he also liked the structure and the sense of belonging. The navy was not just his career; it was his family.

Dickey Traser was like a brother to Jerry. Even though Dickey had the means to attend any college he wanted, there was only one place he wanted to go for as long as he could remember—the U.S. Naval

Academy at Annapolis. From early childhood, and for no apparent reason, he developed a fascination for ships and for the navy. Like Jerry, Dickey had played football in high school, and he continued his football career while at the Naval Academy, though with considerably less success than Jerry.

Despite his personal wealth and background, Dickey was making a career of the navy. For him it was much more than a career. It was his passion.

Freshly showered, Dickey came into the room, buttoning the last button of his tunic.

"Hey, Dickey, there are cold sodas in the ice bucket over there."

"Thanks." He pulled out an Orange Crush and popped the top off the bottle. "So, what movie do you want to see?"

"I haven't given it much thought."

"How about that Fonda picture, *Grapes of Wrath?*"

Jerry chuckled. "You forget, Dickey, I've lived the *Grapes of Wrath*. I don't need to see it."

Dickey looked pained. "Gee, I'm sorry, Jerry. I wasn't thinking."

Jerry smiled at him. "Ah, don't worry about it. We can see it if you want to. You might enjoy some expert commentary from the sidelines."

"No, we'll find something else to do. In the meantime, what do you say we go down to dinner?"

"Good idea. I'm starved."

4

Tony Jarvis walked down the street listening to the music of juke-boxes spilling through the doors of Honolulu's bars. For a moment "Blues in the Night" was strong, then "I'll Be Seeing You," followed by "There, I've Said It Again." The music, the neon lights, and the paid barkers competed for the attention of the hundreds of soldiers and sailors who had come into town to squander their precious money and precious hours of liberty.

Being stationed in Hawaii was the best deployment anyone could have. Whether on liberty from one of the many ships in the harbor or on weekend pass from Schofield Barracks or Wheeler Field, fresh-scrubbed young men in white or khaki uniforms relished their time off in Honolulu.

At one time or another during their tours of duty, nearly all of the soldiers did the tourist things. They took pictures on the beach, usually with Diamond Head visible behind them, or in front of a twisted palm tree, or at one of the island cultural centers. These were photographs to show family and friends back home, for a trip to Hawaii was only a dream for most people.

The difference between Tony Jarvis and most of the other service-men crowding Honolulu's streets was that he took no "vacation in para-dise" photos because he had no one at home to share them with. Tony could trace his roots back only as far as a cardboard box at the railroad depot in Jackson, Mississippi. He had been abandoned in that box along with a note that read *I'm going home to Chicago. Please take care of my baby. His name is Tony.*

The infant was taken to the Baptist Children's Orphanage on Bailey Avenue. He needed a name to follow Tony, so the orphanage authori-ties named him for the box in which he had been left: "Jarvis Fine Pickles."

Tony lived at the orphanage until he was sixteen, when, in order to free up operating funds, the board of deacons declared him competent to live on his own. They gave him a new pair of dungarees, a serviceable pair of shoes, two new shirts, and a ten-dollar bill, and sent him on his way.

Tony didn't hang around in Jackson. The only clue he had to his past was Chicago, so Tony went there and for a year supported himself in menial jobs.

While mopping the floor of a gym one day, he heard the sounds of gloves on flesh behind him. In a well-worn ring, two boxers were working out. The gym manager suddenly approached him. "Hey, you. Mopping the floor."

Tony looked up, hoping he wasn't about to be fired.

"You ever sparred before?"

"Sparred?"

"Yeah, work out in the ring with a fighter, you know?"

"Yes." Tony didn't mean yes, he had sparred before; he meant yes, he knew what the manager was talking about. But the manager mis-understood.

"Good. There's some trunks, shoes, and gloves back in the dressing room. One of our sparring partners didn't show up. I'll give you ten dol-lars to take his place today."

Tony was spending the entire day mopping for three dollars. The thought of ten dollars for a few minutes in a ring sounded very good to him.

To his pleasant surprise, boxing came easily to him. He was graceful, quick, and had a punch that was much heavier than was expected for someone in his weight class. A promoter signed him, changed his name to Rocky Sarducci, and started him on the road to a promising boxing career.

After a string of victories, his manager, Jay Solinger, promised him that another couple of wins over ranked opponents was all he needed to guarantee him a shot at the championship. Tony started dreaming of a real future.

St. Louis, Kiel Auditorium
March 10, 1939

There were four matches on the card for the Friday-night fights, but the main event was a ten-round middleweight bout between Frankie O'Brien, the number-one contender, and Rocky Sarducci, ranked number eight by *Ring Magazine*.

In the darkened bleachers, the burning ends of hundreds of cigarettes and cigars glowed like tiny red stars in the firmament. A huge, billowing cloud of smoke collected under the high roof, gleaming in the ambient light. In the brightly lit ring, two fighters danced around each other, throwing and parrying punches.

The bell rang, and the two fighters returned to their respective corners. At ringside a radio announcer talked into the microphone, priming the listening audience all across America for the main event to follow.

"Ladies and gentlemen, this is Don Dunphy bringing you the Gillette Cavalcade of Sports Friday-night boxing match from Kiel Auditorium in St. Louis, Missouri. To look sharp, feel sharp, and be sharp, always use Gillette Red Blades."

Back in the dressing room, Rocky Sarducci was getting his hands taped. Detached sounds drifted down through the cavernous corridors: the noise of the crowd, the call of the barkers, the warning buzzer, the clanging bell to start the next round of the fight in progress. Rocky could almost follow the action of the fight by listening to the ebb and flow of cheers from the huge crowd. A myriad of smells wafted into the dressing room: tobacco smoke, body odors, popcorn, stale beer, and alcohol and analgesic balms used to sooth sore muscles and ease aching joints.

"How's that?" Sam O'Leary was the trainer. A fighter himself in his youth, Sam now sported a flat nose and cauliflower ears, badges of the manly profession and his only reward for years in the ring. "That too tight?"

"No, it's fine, Sam."

Rocky's manager entered, wearing a long camel's-hair overcoat and a hat with a silk band. He wore two rings, wide gold bands set with large diamonds. A cigar protruded from the middle of his mouth, and he was smoking it the way someone would suck on a straw.

"Rocky's lookin' real good, Mr. Solinger," Sam said. "He's just lookin' real good. I predict he'll take this bum in three rounds."

Jay Solinger said nothing. He just stood inside the door, his head wreathed in smoke, studying Rocky. From above there was a loud cheer, then applause, followed by the repeated ringing of the bell. Finally Solinger extracted his cigar and, holding it between his thumb and forefinger, motioned with it toward the door.

"Take a hike, Sam," he said.

"I'm not finished with the taping."

"Take a hike," Solinger said again. "I need to talk to Rocky."

"Yeah, sure," Sam said. "But make it quick, will ya? I'm not finished, and I don't want to have to rush. A man could get his fingers broke real easy if the tapin' ain't done right."

Solinger just stared at him, squinting through the blue haze.

They could hear the ring announcer over the auditorium speakers. "Ladies and gentlemen, the winner, by a knockout in fifty-six seconds of the fifth round, Danny Dunnigan!"

"That Dunnigan, he's a good kid. I seen 'im fight before," Sam said.

Solinger glared at him.

"Uh, yeah," Sam said. He looked at Rocky. "Well, you just rest easy, kid. I'll get you took care of before you go into the ring. You don't worry none about that."

Rocky nodded.

"Hear that crowd out there?" Solinger asked after Sam left.

"Yeah," Rocky said. "Sounds like a big one."

"It *is* big. And the Gillette Cavalcade of Sports is here too. Your fight's goin' to be broadcast over the radio. It'll be heard all over America."

"Wow," Rocky said.

"Kid, there's an opportunity to make some money here. I mean some big money."

"Yeah, I know," Rocky replied. "And don't worry, Mr. Solinger. I'm going to win the fight. I know I can beat Frankie O'Brien. I feel it inside."

Solinger stuck the cigar back into the middle of his mouth and squinted again at Rocky. Then, slowly, he shook his head.

"Huh-uh, kid. You ain't goin' to beat him."

"Sure I can. I'm tellin' you, I feel it."

"No, you don't understand. You ain't goin' to beat him. Have you got that?"

"You mean, you don't think I can?"

"Listen to me, kid!" Solinger said, clearly agitated. "I said you ain't goin' to beat him. You're going down in the seventh round. It's all fixed."

Rocky gave a gasp of disbelief. "You want me to throw the fight?"

"It's not what I want, it's what I expect," Solinger said. "You heard me. This fight is in the can. I've already made the arrangements."

"No!" Rocky said, shaking his head vigorously. "I told you, I can beat this guy."

"And I'm telling you it doesn't matter whether you can beat him or not. You are going to take a dive in the seventh."

"No. I ain't takin' a dive. Not for you, not for anyone."

Solinger's grin was mirthless. "Oh yeah, you'll take the dive," he said. "That is, if you want to go on living, you'll do it."

Solinger left the dressing room then, and Sam came in at once to finish the taping. "You okay, kid?" he asked as he worked. "You feelin' okay?"

"Yeah," Rocky answered. "I'm feeling fine."

One of the event managers stuck his head into the dressing room.

"You're up next, Sarducci," he called.

Rocky hopped down from the table and stood there as Sam put his robe on him. The robe was white satin with his name sewn in red letters across the back. He left the dressing room, then hurried up the ramp until he reached the arena. Glancing across the arena, he saw Frankie O'Brien climb into the ring, then dance around a little, throwing punches. Frankie's robe was kelly green, and his name was in yellow.

"Okay, Rocky, into the ring," the event manager said. As Rocky hurried up the aisle, he heard the fans yelling at him.

"Get 'im, Rocky. You can do it!" someone called out.

"You're a bum, Sarducci! You always have been and always will be."

Rocky climbed into the ring and did a little dancing and punching himself before returning to his corner to take off his robe.

"Remember, Sarducci, seventh round," Solinger said, next to him. Rocky looked at him but didn't answer.

The ring announcer introduced both fighters. To Rocky, it appeared that the partisans in the crowd were about equally split. He glanced over toward the radio announcer and saw him speaking excitedly into the microphone. The referee called them to the center of the ring for instructions.

Rocky stared at O'Brien's face, wondering if his opponent knew that the fix was in.

"Don't make it look too easy, Sarducci," O'Brien said quietly as they touched gloves.

Rocky came out with the bell and threw three quick left jabs, surprising O'Brien with their sharpness.

"What are you doin'?" he asked.

"I ain't goin' down," Rocky said.

"What?"

"You heard me; I'm not goin' down. You're on your own."

By the time the third round started, O'Brien's corner had gotten word to Rocky's corner that Rocky wasn't going along with the fix.

"You cross me up on this kid, and you're dead. You hear that? You're a dead man," Solinger said angrily. "Look over there."

Rocky looked toward the front row and saw a couple of rough-looking men open their jackets just far enough for him to see that they were carrying guns.

Rocky charged to the middle of the ring at the opening of the third round. Dodging a left jab by O'Brien, he threw a roundhouse right just over the extended left arm, slamming into his opponent's jaw. O'Brien's mouthpiece flew out, sweat fanned away from his face, and Rocky saw his eyes rolling up in his sockets, even before he went down.

Rocky went to a neutral corner until the count and the announcement. Then, even as Solinger was yelling curses at him across the ring, he stepped through the ropes, then off the apron onto the press table.

"Hey, what are you doin'?" one of the sportswriters asked.

To the continuing cheers of the crowd, Rocky hurried to the back of the auditorium, then outside through one of the fire exits. He ran across the parking lot, then up an alley, shedding his boxing gloves along the way.

Three blocks from the auditorium, he came to a residential area where he saw clothes hanging on a line in the backyard of one of the houses. He took a pair of pants and a shirt from the clothesline and hurried on.

Rocky was running away from a fifteen-hundred-dollar purse, an enormous amount of money. But there was no way he could go back to claim it without encountering Solinger's goons. He couldn't even go back for his billfold or watch. He was flat broke in the middle of St. Louis, with no idea what to do next.

Rocky spent the night in a warehouse. He planned to go back to the auditorium the next day to get his money, but he changed his mind when he passed a newspaper stand and read the headlines:

BOXER SOUGHT FOR MURDER

Jay Solinger, 47, of Cicero, Illinois, was found dead shortly after the conclusion of the boxing match between Rocky Sarducci and Frankie O'Brien. Solinger was Rocky Sarducci's manager, and police theorize that the boxer and his manager got into an argument over the split of the purse.

Turning away from the newspaper stand, Rocky saw a poster on the front wall of a building. It showed a sailor smiling broadly as he beheld the beauty of some tropical island. Behind him was a battleship. "JOIN THE NAVY AND SEE THE WORLD," the poster read.

A sign over the door of the building indicated that this was a recruiting office for the U.S. Navy. Rocky went inside.

"Greetings, young man," a sailor said. "What can I do for you?"

"My name is Tony Jarvis," he told the recruiter. He smiled. "And I would like to join the navy and see the world."

Honolulu, Hawaii
Friday, December 5, 1941

Since enlisting, Tony had tried hard to forget about Rocky Sarducci, and had nearly done so when he happened to see an article in *Ring Magazine*. The writer suggested that Rocky had what it took to be a champion, and lamented the fact that the former boxer had apparently gone bad. According to the article, the real murderer of Jay Solinger had been found, but Sarducci was still being sought for alleged involvement in fight fixing.

Hawaii was a lifetime removed from the seamy world he had known back on the mainland. He was certain he was safe enough here to risk fighting again, but after winning the interservice championship last fall, a civilian boxing promoter approached Tony and suggested that if he would take his discharge when it came up, he could make a lot of money boxing.

"You remind me a lot of a kid I saw fight once back in Chicago, by the name of Rocky Sarducci."

Tony didn't know if it was mere coincidence, or if the promoter knew who he was and was just stringing him along. He decided not to stick around to find out, and resolved then and there that he would not box again.

As he walked down the street listening to the spill of jukebox music, he honed in on the wailing clarinet of Benny Goodman—not so much because he was a Benny Goodman fan, but because the music was coming from the Wet Mouse Bar, and that was where he was headed. The Wet Mouse was always the first place Tony headed when he got liberty and the last place he visited before returning to his ship. It was a regular hangout for sailors when the fleet was in, because the bartender was a retired boatswain's mate who'd rather handle a disturbance himself than call the shore patrol. And if his handling was sometimes a little rough, it was excused, because almost everyone would rather have a small bump on the head than spend two weeks in the brig.

Rosie McCain was the other reason Tony came to the Wet Mouse. Rosie was a bar girl, and though her smile and company was for anyone who could afford the price of the drinks she was hustling, Tony was convinced that he had the inside track with her. Smiling broadly, Tony pushed his way into the bar. His smile faded when he saw Rosie sitting with Muley.

Saturday, December 6, 1941

Jerry and Dickey were having breakfast in the hotel restaurant when one of the waiters told Jerry that he was wanted at the reception desk.

"I'm Lieutenant Cornelison," he said to the receptionist.

"Yes, sir, Mr. Cornelison," the man said. He pointed to an overstuffed chair near a potted palm. Beside the chair was a small table, and on the table, a telephone. "You have a telephone call. You can take it over there."

Jerry walked over and picked up the phone. "This is Cornelison."

"Mr. Cornelison, this is Larry."

Ensign Larry Martin was one of the other officers of the *Turner*, and was acting as Officer of the Deck.

"What's up, Larry?"

Larry sighed. "Seems there's been a little disturbance. The Honolulu police are holding two of our crew. Since you're already downtown, Captain Poppell wants you to go bail them out."

"Don't tell me. One of them is Jarvis, right?"

"You don't expect to win a prize for guessing that, do you?"

Jerry chuckled. "I guess not. Who's the other one? Muley?"

"Now this one will surprise you. It's Leon Jackson."

"What? You mean Choirboy?"

Leon "Choirboy" Jackson was one of two mess stewards on the crew of *Turner*.

"The same," Larry said.

"But Choirboy has never been in trouble. He's practically the unofficial chaplain of the ship."

"I know. Curious, isn't it? In fact, if I wasn't OOD right now, I'd volunteer to go get them, just to find out what this is all about."

"All right, I'm nearly finished with breakfast anyway. Tell the captain I'll take care of it."

"Aye, aye, sir."

"Choirboy?" Dickey asked, chuckling as they walked to the police station. "Who would've thought it?"

Choirboy was known as a very religious and highly moral young man. He read the Bible all the time and could quote chapter and verse on just about anything. He also had a reputation for honesty and had become an unofficial arbitrator, settling disputes for others on the boat. His decisions were so respected that even the losing parties never questioned them.

Jerry and Dickey climbed the foot-polished concrete steps and opened the weathered door at the top. A uniformed policeman, a rather large Hawaiian, sat behind the desk writing on a tablet. He did not look up as Jerry and Dickey approached, and the two officers stood quietly for a moment, waiting for some sign of recognition.

"Excuse me," Jerry said.

The desk sergeant held up his left hand as he continued to write. Jerry waited for another long moment before the policeman finally quit writing and looked up.

"What can I do for you?" he asked.

"We're from the *Turner*," Jerry said. "I understand you have two of our crewmen here."

"*Turner*," the sergeant repeated. He opened another book and began looking through it. As he did so, he began reading off a list of ship names, as if he were calling roll for the vessels in the harbor: "*Arizona, California, Nevada, Shaw, Vesta* . . . Ah, yes, here it is. *Turner*. Seaman First Tony Jarvis and Seaman Second Leon Jackson."

"What are they charged with?"

"Disorderly conduct," the sergeant replied. "It seems they got into a fight outside the Wet Mouse last night."

"With each other?" Jerry asked. "That doesn't sound very likely."

"No, not with each other. According to the report, the two of them took on just about half the crew of the *Gaffey* all by themselves. We have"—the sergeant counted the names—"seven men here from the *Gaffey*. Three of them needed medical attention."

"How do I go about getting them out?"

"There doesn't appear to be any property damage involved, so all you have to do is sign for them," the sergeant said. "I'll have them brought out."

As Jerry filled out the paperwork, the sergeant picked up a phone and dialed a number. "This is Kanakalawana. Bring prisoners Jarvis and Jackson up front. Yeah, couple of their officers is here signin' for them." He put the phone back down. "They'll be right out."

"Thanks," Jerry said, handing over the completed release form.

A few minutes later Tony and Choirboy were brought to the front. Both were in handcuffs, and their uniforms, so crisp and white when they left for liberty yesterday, were wrinkled and soiled. Jarvis had a look of defiant anger on his face. Jackson's expression was one of mortification.

"You want to keep them in cuffs?" the escorting policeman asked.

"These are navy handcuffs. You can just turn them over to the shore police when you're through with them."

"No," Jerry said. "No handcuffs."

"You sure?"

"No handcuffs."

With a shrug, the policeman removed the cuffs from the two prisoners. As soon as he did, Tony came to attention and saluted. Seeing Tony, Choirboy did the same thing. Jerry returned the salute.

"Let's go," Jerry said.

"Where we going, sir?"

"Back to the ship."

"Back to the ship? But I got nearly thirty-six hours left on my liberty," Tony complained.

"Which is plenty of time to get into trouble again, right?"

"No, sir. I don't plan to get in trouble again," he said as the four of them walked back down the concrete steps and stood on the sidewalk.

"I'm sure you didn't plan to get into trouble this time," Jerry said.

"No, sir, I sure didn't plan nothin' like this."

"What happened to your big romantic weekend with Rosie?"

"Yes, sir, well, that's what started the whole thing."

"Let me guess. Muley was there."

"Yes, sir, he was. And me 'n' Muley got into a quarrel over Rosie, when the next thing you know she was butterflying on both of us. I looked up and saw her with some sailor from the *Gaffey*."

"So you hit the sailor from the *Gaffey* for stealing your girl?"

"No, sir," Jarvis said. "I hit him on account of Choirboy."

"I was wondering how Choirboy was involved with this."

"Yes, sir. Well, while me 'n' Muley was arguin' about which one of us Rosie should choose, I just happened to look out in the street and seen Choirboy walkin' by. So I told Muley, 'Let's ask Choirboy what he thinks.' Muley said, 'Yeah, why not?' So Muley went outside with me, and I whistled for Choirboy to come over. Then I yelled for Rosie to come outside so Choirboy could tell her which one, between me 'n' Muley, she should choose. Well, Choirboy come and so did Rosie. And so did near 'bout everyone else in the bar."

"What happened then?"

"Well, nothin' happened then. I just asked Choirboy to tell Rosie which one of us he thought Rosie should choose. And that's all I done. Ain't that right, Choirboy? I mean, I didn't say or do nothin' else, did I?"

"That's all he did, sir," Choirboy replied.

"I figured ain't nobody goin' to argue with Choirboy," Tony interrupted. "I mean, heck, he settles arguments for us all the time."

"Let me guess," Dickey said. "He chose you, and Muley didn't go along with it."

Tony shook his head no. "No sir, he didn't choose me. He didn't choose Muley neither. He just told us a story about some king who was going to cut a baby in two and give half of him to one woman and the other half to another woman."

Dickey smiled. "Solomon."

"Yes, sir," Choirboy answered.

"So what happened?"

"Well, sir, that's when them sailors from the *Gaffey* started in on Choirboy. They was saying things like, 'What you lettin' a nigger decide for?' and 'Nigger, get out of here.' So that's when I hit one of them."

"Yes, sir, that's when he hit one of 'em all right," Choirboy said. "Knocked him clean out, too," he added with admiration.

"You mighty right I knocked him out. Choirboy, he may be colored and all, but he's one of us, you know what I mean, Mr. Cornelison? He's one of us."

"Yes, I know what you mean. And that explains your situation, but why were you in jail, Choirboy?" Jerry asked.

"Well, sir, after Jarvis hit the man from the *Gaffey*, a lot of those *Gaffey* men started piling into Jarvis. I don't hold with fighting, but I couldn't just stand by and see one of my own crewmen get beaten up. Especially after he took up for me the way he did. So I joined in."

Tony laughed. "And you shoulda seen the way ole Choirboy joined in, Mr. Cornelison. I mean, he cleaned their plows good. Why, he's purt' near as good a fighter as me."

"What about Muley? What happened to him?"

Tony laughed again. "Soon's the fightin' commenced, Muley took out running. And Rosie, she seen what a coward he was. So in the long run, it worked out all right."

"Rosie chose you?"

Tony cleared his throat. "Well, sort of. The police come around 'bout then, and they took me 'n' Choirboy off to jail. Last I seen of Rosie, she was blowin' me kisses as she was goin' back inside the bar. Course, I don't blame her none, 'cause there was nothin' else she could've done. That's why I need to get back, Mr. Cornelison. I mean, what if Muley is down there right now, tryin' to beat my time?"

"All right, you can continue your liberty," Jerry said. "But don't you think you should go back to the boat and get cleaned up again? The way you guys look now, you wouldn't get a block before the shore patrol would pick you up."

"I guess you're right, sir," Tony said. Looking up, he saw a bus. "Come on Choirboy, there's a bus. The quicker we get back to the boat, the quicker we can come back to town." With a quick salute, Tony and Choirboy ran across the street to catch the bus.

Dickey laughed as he watched the two young sailors go. "Now there's an unlikely pair if I ever saw one. One white, one colored, one the biggest troublemaker in the fleet, the other one a living example of the perfect sailor."

"Yes," Jerry replied. "But if I was ever in trouble, I'd be happy to look up and see either one of them coming to my aid."

Dickey nodded. "That's the truth."

Guam
Saturday morning, December 6, 1941

The rising sun slipped in through the window, filling the room with light and waking Sean, who, along with the crew and the other passengers of the Pan Am flight, was in the hotel on Guam. They had arrived late the night before and would continue their flight shortly after breakfast.

With takeoff not scheduled until nine, Sean decided to take an exploratory walk around the island. He was just starting toward a gun emplacement when a marine sergeant came over to him.

"Passengers aren't allowed down here." The sergeant spit a stream of tobacco juice, then wiped his mouth with the back of his hand.

"I'm sorry, Sergeant," Sean said, holding his hands out. "I don't mean any harm. I just wanted to have a look around. I'll go back to the hotel if I'm trespassing."

"Wait a minute!" the sergeant said, a broad grin spreading across his face. "I know who you are! I've seen your picture lots of times. You're that writer fella, ain't you? Either Hemingway or Hanifin, I'm not sure which."

"Hanifin, and guilty as charged."

"Yeah, I read one of your books once. *Becalmed.* That was a real good sea story. Was you really at sea when you was young?"

"Yes indeed."

"And it was on an old-timey sailing ship, wasn't it?"

"Well, it was a sailing ship, but don't confuse it with something Columbus came to America on. The windjammers were big ships with steel rigging and electric lights; they even had radio. The only difference was that they used canvas instead of engines for their propulsion power."

"I sure would like to have seen one of those things," the sergeant said.

"Well, they're all gone now, Sergeant. They've slipped back into history, tone and tint. Now, with the Pan Am Clipper, you can cross the entire Pacific in less than a week, and the Atlantic in a matter of hours."

"You a passenger on the Clipper?"

"Yes, I'm on my way back home from Hong Kong. I'm just waiting for the plane to take off."

"Yeah, well, I envy you that," the sergeant said. "Going home, I mean."

"Where is home for you?" Sean asked.

"Tyler, Texas. It's near three years since I was there last."

"How much longer before you can go back?"

"Oh, I won't never be goin' home," the sergeant responded in a cold, flat voice, so devoid of emotion that it was frightening. "None of us that's here will."

"What do you mean, none of you are going home?"

"Do you know how many men we have defending this island?" the sergeant asked. "Four hundred and twenty-seven. And that includes the military governor. After the Japs come, there ain't goin' to be no one left alive."

"And you think the Japanese are going to come?"

"You're a smart fella, Mr. Hanifin. What do you think?"

Sean stroked his beard. "I won't lie to you, Sergeant. I think you're right."

"Yeah, well, I was sort of hoping you wouldn't agree with me."

"Sarge! Sarge, the lieutenant wants the morning report," a private yelled.

"Excuse me, sir. I've got to get back to work." The sergeant yelled over his shoulder as he started away. "If you ever get to Tyler, Texas, tell 'em you seen ole Frank Tanner, and he sent his regards."

"I'll do that, Frank Tanner. Count on it," Sean answered. He started back toward the hotel.

McKinley Slayton looked up from the table as Sean came into the dining room. Sean drew himself a cup of coffee from the Silex, then walked over to sit across the table from the preacher.

"Did you enjoy your walk, Mr. Hanifin?" McKinley asked.

"I did."

"God has given us a beautiful morning to enjoy today."

"God gave us this morning, did he?"

"Yes, of course," McKinley replied. "Everything we have is from God."

"So then, that means God is as responsible for the evil as He is for the good. Is that what you're saying?"

McKinley did not respond for a moment.

"Surely this isn't a new concept, Reverend. Surely you have contemplated this very thing."

McKinley chuckled. "You are testing me," he said. "Why do you test me, Mr. Hanifin? Do you think I lack the conviction of my faith?"

Sean took a sip of his coffee before he answered. "Nothing like that, Reverend. That is, I'm not consciously testing you, though perhaps I am testing myself. Like you, I am a Christian. But I often have questions. I'm sure that makes me less of a Christian, and more of a skeptic."

"Not necessarily. One learns from questions. A static, never-questioning faith can but survive, whereas a dynamic, learning faith will thrive. As you know, the gospel is filled with accounts of Jesus responding to questions, some of which were mean-spirited. But in every case, those questions and Jesus' answers became the teaching points and building stones of our faith."

"I suppose that's true," Sean said. "So, in that spirit, I have another question for you. Do you believe you can talk to the dead?"

"Talk to the dead? No," McKinley replied. "Séances are merely a means of taking money from the gullible."

"I don't mean séances," Sean said. "I mean having a conversation with the dead, standing up face-to-face with them."

"I must confess that I'm not following you."

"These men," Sean answered, taking in the island with a wave of his hand. "The men who are here, defending this island. They are walking, sleeping, eating, and drinking, and you can go right up to one of them and talk to him. From all appearances, one might think they are alive. But they aren't alive, Reverend. They are dead, nearly every one of them."

McKinley shook his head. "I'm afraid I still don't understand."

"We have stumbled upon a rent in the fabric of time, my friend. God has allowed those of us who are merely passing through to have a moment to commune with history, because when the war begins nearly every American soldier, sailor, and marine you see here will be killed."

"I pray that you are wrong," McKinley said. "I pray that cool heads in the U.S. and Japanese governments will find a way out of this crisis."

"Ah, but therein is the rub, Reverend. There *are* no cool heads in the U.S. or the Japanese government. Your time would be better spent in praying for the salvation of the souls of these poor men."

"You can rest assured that I am doing so," McKinley promised.

"Your father and my father seem to be deeply involved in conversation," Diane said. She and Pat were also in the dining room, sitting across the table from each other, on the side of the room that was farthest away from Sean and McKinley.

"So it would appear," Pat said. "I wonder what they are talking about."

"Religion," Diane answered.

Pat chuckled. "Religion? Well now, that would be a conversation worth overhearing. My father never talks about religion."

"And my father never talks about anything else."

"Perhaps the two of us will give them something more to talk about," Pat said. He reached across the table and put his hand on top of hers.

The touch of Pat's fingers had a curious and rather disturbing effect. They felt cool, yet somehow, from the very point where his fingers touched her flesh, a heat began to spread through her body.

"I, uh, don't know what we could give them to talk about," Diane said.

"Our kiss perhaps?"

At Pat's words, Diane experienced a sudden, spinning, lightheadedness. What was happening to her? This was the way she had felt when Pat kissed her. Involuntarily she put her fingers to her lips, as if testing whether or not he was kissing her at this very moment.

"Are you all right?" Pat asked, but his words seemed to come through a fog.

"What?"

"You seemed to have a strange reaction for a moment. I just wondered if you were all right."

"Oh, uh, yes, I'm all right," she replied. "Do you think they saw us?"

"Saw us?"

"Kissing. Do you think your father and mine saw us when we kissed? Do you think anyone saw us?"

"I don't know. Why? Would it bother you terribly?"

"I wouldn't want people to think that I was engaging in a promiscuous activity solely for the momentary pleasure."

"I don't consider one kiss to be a promiscuous activity," Pat said.

"Oh, it isn't the number of kisses that determine whether or not the activity is promiscuous," Diane explained. "It is the intent behind the kiss."

"In other words, it would be better to have twenty kisses between two people who are constructing a meaningful relationship, than to have one kiss that offers only the pleasure of the moment."

"Why, yes," Diane replied.

Pat looked directly at Diane and smiled broadly. "Well, I'm glad you told me that. It gives me something to look forward to."

The jolt passed through Diane's body again, and she couldn't stop a little shiver from running through her.

"Are you cold?"

"I'm fine," Diane said. "Just a momentary chill is all."

At that moment Ken Cooley came into the dining room.

"Folks," he called. "I don't want to rush you, but we've got weather clearance and will be taking off in ten minutes. I'd advise to you check your rooms to make certain you don't leave anything behind."

"Do you need to go back to your room?" Pat asked.

"No, the valet took our things to the plane earlier. I'm all ready to go."

Pat stood and offered his arm. "Then please allow me to walk you to the boarding dock."

Noon, Saturday, December 6, 1941
on board the China Clipper *between Guam and Wake Island*

As the big flying boat was carrying a light passenger load, the rear-most cabin was completely empty. Taking advantage of that, Pat retreated to the rear cabin. Then, taking some sheet music from a small case, he began going over it. When the purser looked in, he saw only someone studying a sheet of paper. He had no idea that, in that quiet moment, Pat was directing an orchestra in his head, hearing every note from every instrument.

"Could I get you something, Mr. Hanifin?" Jason asked. "Coffee or tea?"

Pat looked up and smiled. "No, thank you, Mr. Peabody. I'm fine."

"Very good, sir."

Pat returned to the music and was halfway through the second movement when Diane came into the compartment.

"Am I disturbing you?" she asked.

"You could never be a disturbance," Pat said, smiling at her. He slipped the music back into its case. "Did you have a nice nap?"

"I suppose. It's hard to sleep with the motors making such a racket."

Pat chuckled. "It would be harder to sleep if they *stopped* making that racket."

"What—" Diane started, then laughed. "Yes, I see what you mean. Given the choice, I would rather have the racket."

"I thought you might. Won't you join me?" He patted the seat beside him. "Would you like something? I can summon the purser or call the stewardess."

"No, I'm fine. What were you doing when I came in?"

Pat removed the sheet of music and showed it to Diane. "I was conducting Mahler's *The Titan*."

"Oh. I knew you were a pianist. I didn't know you were a conductor, too."

"I am a conductor by training," Pat said. "But by occupation, I don't think you could even call me a pianist. I'm a piano player. I play popular music in a nightclub."

"Why?"

Pat chuckled. "Why what?"

"Why do you play popular music in a night club? I mean, if you are a conductor by training, why aren't you conducting an orchestra?"

"You don't just go to the Boston Philharmonic Orchestra and apply for the job," Pat replied.

"Well, then, where do conductors start?"

"Often they start in the orchestra itself, on the instrument with which they are most proficient."

"Then why don't you do that?"

"Because, I am sorry to say, I can make much more money playing in a nightclub."

"But you aren't satisfied with that, are you?"

"I consider the situation to be a temporary one," Pat said, though his answer didn't sound believable even to himself.

Suddenly, and unexpectedly, the airplane encountered a spot of turbulence, and the rough air threw Diane against Pat. Automatically he put his arm around her to stabilize her. It proved to be only a patch of rough air, and the airplane smoothed out, but Pat kept his arm around her, and they found themselves looking into each other's eyes until they were only a breath apart. Then Pat closed the distance between them with a kiss.

To Diane, the kiss was as soft and gentle as the fluttering of butterfly wings on her lips. And yet she felt a reaction to it that seemed all out of proportion to the event itself. She pulled away from him. "No," she said. "We shouldn't do this."

"I thought you liked it."

"I do like it," she said. "But maybe I like it too much."

"All right. I don't want to make you uncomfortable."

"I'm not uncomfortable," Diane said. "I'm just confused."

Pat took Diane's hand in hers. "Diane, I'm sorry. I don't normally throw myself at beautiful women like this. I'm not a rake. I don't want to get our relationship off to a bad start."

"I don't think ill of you," Diane replied. "It's just that this is all so new to me that I'm not sure how I should act." She smiled. "I know what. I'll just leave it up to you. I'm sure you have experience in—what was the word you used? Relationships? I'll just let you be my guide."

"You are putting me on my honor?" Pat asked.

"Yes, you might say that."

Pat exhaled a long, slow breath through pursed lips, then, smiling, he shook his head.

"Diane, I don't know if you are incredibly naïve or incredibly smart."

Diane smiled back at him. "The end result is the same, isn't it?"

5

Four hundred miles northwest of Hawaii
December 7, 1941

At 0230 on Sunday morning, the seventh of December, on board the Japanese carrier *Kaga*, Comdr. Yutaka Saito was awakened from a sound sleep. The fact that he woke up surprised him, because he didn't know he had gone to sleep. He sat up, rubbed his eyes, and looked around.

The compartment was filled with activity as the pilots began going through various rituals to prepare themselves for what lay ahead. All put on new uniforms, saved especially for this occasion, and most put on the *hachimaki* headbands, traditional white bands with the red sun of the Empire.

At breakfast many of the pilots had a small glass of ceremonial *sake*. After breakfast, they gathered in the ready room, where they got their preattack briefing. They were given the latest information on wind direction and velocity and were told exactly where the carriers would be after the attack, so that all the airplanes could be successfully recovered. They were cautioned against using their radios, lest the attack be discovered by an errant transmission. Then they were read a poem composed by Admiral Yamamoto. It was in the form of a *waka*, a poem of twenty-four syllables that, like haiku, depends on very strict construction and line length.

> *It is my sole wish*
> *to serve the Emperor as his shield.*
> *I will not spare*
> *my honor or my life.*

"Banzai!" someone shouted at the end of the reading, and others joined in, laughing and shouting. The pilots then hurried to the flight deck, where the planes and deck crews stood in silence.

When Saito reached his plane, he saw that his bombardier and machine gunner were already aboard. The engine was running, having been started by the crew chief, so all Saito had to do was buckle himself into his seat, then watch the flag at the top of the mast.

He had seen several of the other pilots at the Shinto shrine this morning, lighting incense sticks, holding their hands together, and bowing their heads as they prayed to their ancestors. He knew they were praying for a successful attack, asking their ancestors to guide their bombs into the ships and bases of the Americans.

As a Christian, he couldn't pray for help in killing others. But he was also a military man, and an adherent of the Code of the Samurai. That code, as well as his fierce loyalty and love for his country, was somewhat contradictory to his Christian faith. Only a person with a will and a discipline as strong as Saito's could keep such things in balance. And while his psyche was often in conflict, he felt that his soul was at peace. He had given some thought as to what kind of prayer he could pray at this moment. Now, as he waited for the flag to drop, he prayed aloud without fear of being overheard, the noise of scores of aircraft engines drowning out all other sound.

"O Lord, As I embark upon this dangerous adventure, I ask that You guide me along the paths of righteousness and honor. Protect my crew and sustain my soul. I offer this prayer in the name of Jesus. Amen."

Just as he mouthed the word *amen,* the flag dropped, and the first plane roared down the deck, blue flames streaming from the exhaust stacks before it lifted into the air. Saito's was the third plane to launch. When it was his time, he nodded toward his crew chief, then pushed the throttle ahead to full. Almost instantly the tail lifted and, like the two before it, the plane roared down the deck of the carrier until it reached the end. It dropped off, and the wings caught hold. As he climbed to altitude, Saito twisted around in his seat and looked back to see the ones taking off after him. Reaching the assigned altitude, he moved into formation with the others as they winged south-southeast toward a rendezvous with destiny.

Pearl Harbor
Sunday, December 7, 1941

Worship services were being held on the fantails of all the battleships. To accommodate those sailors who served on ships too small to have their own chaplain, a church launch made the rounds of all the vessels, collecting the men who wanted to attend one of the shipboard services.

Ensign Larry Martin, the OOD of the *Turner,* had authorized the raising of a pennant on the halyard of the destroyer indicating that there were people on board who wanted to be picked up this morning. Choirboy Jackson was one. Dressed in sparkling whites, he stood on the deck waiting for the launch to arrive.

From the deck of the *Turner,* Choirboy had only to look toward Ford Island to see all the other ships in the harbor. Secure in their moorings in the morning mist, the fleet ranged from battleships, cruisers, and tenders, to submarines, minesweepers, and destroyers. Only the absence of aircraft carriers prevented the entire Pacific armada from being accounted for.

It was a very peaceful morning, the kind of morning that made Choirboy feel good to be alive. From somewhere ashore he could hear a church bell ringing. The water of the bay was as smooth as glass and

Sunday-morning quiet. The church launches were already out on the bay, making their rounds. Their muffled engines made a quiet growl as they left small V-shaped wakes on the blue-green water. Most of the launches were taking sailors back to one of the battleships for the on-board services, but one of the launches was flying a green flag, indicating that it would be taking sailors ashore to attend civilian church services.

Choirboy could understand the attraction for going ashore for services. He had done so many times, and often friendly families would invite him over for a fried-chicken dinner. Today, however, Choirboy planned to attend worship service on board the *California* because his cousin was a mess steward on that vessel and last night had invited Choirboy to come over.

Choirboy thought about last night. After Mr. Cornelison got him out of jail yesterday morning, he had come back to the ship, changed his uniform, and gone back downtown to meet his cousin. He had reported back to *Turner* before 2200 hours. Muley Lewis had come back as well, but Tony Jarvis had not returned at all last night. Choirboy hoped his crewmate wasn't in trouble.

Choirboy knew that the girl Jarvis was so crazy about, Rosie McCain, wasn't good for him. Choirboy had seen her with other sailors—not just Muley from the *Turner*, but many others. He had seen her with soldiers from Fort Shafter as well, and he knew she would be nothing but trouble for Jarvis. But that was white-man-and-white-woman business, and even though Jarvis had fought for him last night, white-man-and-white-woman business was something Choirboy knew better than to mess with.

Moses Parker came up on deck to join him. Like Choirboy, Moses was a mess steward. He had two bunches of grapes with him, and he handed one to Choirboy.

"Where'd you get these?"

"Cookie said we could have them," Moses replied. "He put 'em out this morning, but we didn't hardly have nobody show up for breakfast."

"Yeah, most of 'em are ashore." Choirboy popped one of the grapes into his mouth. "Thanks."

"So, what about Jarvis? He one of 'em still gone?"

"Yes."

Moses chuckled. "That boy can get into more trouble than any six cotton pickers I ever know'd."

"That's the truth, all right. But he's a good man."

"How can you say he's a good man? He's always mouthing off to one person or another. That boy's got a chip on his shoulder the size of a two-by-four."

Choirboy thought of Jarvis fighting for him Friday night. "Because he is, that's all."

Moses walked over to the railing and spit a few grape seeds over the side. The sound of several aircraft engines reached them, and Choirboy raised his hand to shield his eyes against the sun.

"Look at all those planes," he said, pointing toward a large flight coming from the north.

"Woo-wee, that sure is a lot of 'em," Moses agreed. "'Minds me of a flight of geese headin' south."

"Man, wouldn't I like to be up in one of them, though?"

"Ha! A colored boy flyin' a airplane. That'll be the day."

"Wonder what kind of planes those are?"

"What do you mean? Planes is planes."

"No," Choirboy said. "I know they aren't navy planes, but they don't look like army planes either. They aren't P-36s or P-40s. Some of them don't even have their gear up."

"Gear up," Moses chuckled. "What's that, some kind of airplane talk?"

"Gear means wheels. Nearly all army and navy planes I know of raise their wheels when they're flying. Some of these airplanes have their wheels down."

The planes began peeling out of formation and heading toward the battleships.

"Look at that," Moses said. "What you think they're doing?"

"Looks like they're making a mock attack on battleship row," Choirboy said.

Suddenly a column of water shot up; then a big red ball of fire blossomed, enveloped almost immediately by rolling black smoke. A second later there was a loud boom, followed by an oil-scented pressure wave of hot air hitting them in the face.

"Man, what's goin' on?" Moses asked.

"Moses, that's real!" Choirboy said, pointing to the airplanes. "Those aren't our planes. That's how come I didn't recognize them. They're Jap planes! Look at that red ball on their wings!"

Three of the fighter planes turned and started toward the *Turner*. For a moment Choirboy stood there, watching them approach, fascinated by the little winking lights on the leading edges of the wings. Then he saw that the lights were detaching themselves from the wings and racing toward the ship. They were live tracer rounds . . . and they were coming right toward him!

Moses had come to the same conclusion. "They're shootin' at us! They—"

"Get down, Moses!" Choirboy shouted, diving for the deck just as a hail of bullets whizzed and popped over the top of the rail, clanging into the deck and the superstructure behind him. But even as he was shouting for Moses to get down, he was talking to a dead man, for Moses' sentence had been cut off by machine-gun bullets slamming into his chest.

The three planes pulled up out of their strafing run just over the top of the ship, so close that Choirboy could feel a blast of air from their prop-wash.

With the planes gone, he got up and ran to check on Moses. His friend was sprawled on his back, his white blouse red with blood, his eyes open, his face still set in an expression of surprise. His arms were thrown out to either side of his body, and the bunch of grapes he had been eating lay alongside his open hand.

Another plane came over, also shooting, though not quite as accurately as the first one.

There was a mounted .50-caliber machine gun in a nearby, unmanned gun well, and Choirboy ran to it. Jerking off the canvas cover, he opened the ammunition chest and threaded the belt. He closed the bolt and cleared the headspace; then, with the gun ready to use, swung it toward battleship row. There, one after another, he saw ships exploding in great, roaring balls of fire.

The OOD, Ensign Martin, was the most junior officer of the crew.

He stumbled out onto the bridge-deck, then looked around in confusion. Seeing the mess steward at the machine gun, he yelled at him.

"Jackson, get away from that gun!"

Choirboy saw a plane just coming out of a torpedo release, and he started firing at it, giving it a lead just the way he did when he was back home, shooting at dove on the wing. The line of tracer shells spit out from the barrel of his gun, and Choirboy moved the line up, hosing them toward the Japanese torpedo plane. The plane flew right through the tracer shells, then a little finger of flame licked up from the wing root. No more than a second later the plane exploded in a ball of fire, then tumbled from the sky.

Even as those shipmates who had been watching gave a frenzied cheer, Choirboy was already swinging his gun toward another target.

"Jackson, get away from that gun!" Martin yelled again.

"Leave him alone, mister! He's the only one doing anything right!" another voice shouted. The new voice was that of Captain Poppell.

On the *Arizona*, an enormous ball of fire and smoke whooshed more than five hundred feet into the air. There was a low, stomach-shaking boom, followed immediately by a concussion wave so powerful that it knocked Choirboy away from his gun. He was thrown down and hurled halfway across the deck, but managed to get up onto his hands and knees and crawl back toward it.

"Look out!" someone shouted, and Choirboy looked up to see a bomb falling from one of the high-level bombers, heading straight for the *Turner*. It came down in a perfect arc, and Choirboy could almost imagine that he was playing outfield in a baseball game, watching a long, lazy fly ball drift toward his position. It was as if he could reach up and catch it as it came in, and he followed the bomb down, almost mesmerized by it. It plunged right through the top of Mount Fifty-one, then exploded in a loud, fiery blast, killing everyone inside.

There was another, secondary explosion way down in the bowels of the ship as the bomb struck the powder magazine. The second explosion lifted the front half of *Turner* out of the water, raising it to about a thirty-degree angle before slamming it back down again.

The ship began an immediate roll to port, and Choirboy started climbing up the slanting deck. Below him he could hear the ship breaking up as the furnishings and heavy equipment tumbled to port. As the roll deepened, it became increasingly difficult to stay on the deck, so that by the time Choirboy reached the starboard railing, he had to throw one leg over to stay up. He looked around and saw the other sailors who were topside. Some of them had also made it to the starboard rail, but most were still trying. A few of the less fortunate were dumped into the sea. The uniforms of two of the sailors were on fire.

The *Turner* continued to roll, and as it turned over, Choirboy and the others who had made it to the starboard railing stood and walked with the roll, ending up standing on the bottom of a ship that had turned turtle. Now, completely out of the fight, the men of the late *Turner* could do nothing but sit on the bottom of their capsized ship and watch what was going on around them, having a front-row seat to a drama of immense dimensions.

Everywhere Choirboy looked he could see ships burning, listing, or sinking. Several oil smears were spreading out across the bay, as well as flotsam and jetsam . . . here a hatch cover, there a life preserver, pieces of wood from smashed launches, bits of clothing, some bottles and water-tight containers, and a flower lei.

The Royal Hawaiian Hotel in downtown Honolulu

Jerry and Dickey had been unable to find a movie they wanted to see, so they wound up going to a dance at the Honolulu Officers' Club. At the dance, Dickey met the daughter of an army colonel and made a date to take her out on a picnic the next weekend. The girl, whose name was Cynthia Roxbury, promised to find a friend for Jerry.

The dance didn't break up until one o'clock Sunday morning, so the two men were sleeping in when a distant, rumbling roar came in through the open windows of their room.

"Is that thunder?" Jerry asked sleepily.

"I don't know," Dickey answered, his voice just as groggy. "If it is, one of us needs to close the window."

"Your bed is closer," Jerry mumbled, turning over and fluffing his pillow.

"Yeah, I guess it is." He sat up, yawned, stretched, and ran his hand through a shock of unruly hair, then got out of bed and padded over to the window. Just as he reached up to pull the window down, he saw a huge flash of light, followed by a billow of smoke and flame.

A few seconds later, the sound of the explosion reached him. It was so loud that the windows shook.

"Holy cow!" Dickey said.

Jerry, who had nearly drifted back to sleep, sat up immediately.

"What *was* that?"

"I'm not sure," Dickey answered. "But I think a ship in the harbor just blew up."

"Blew up? What do you mean, blew up?"

"I don't know. Must've been a boiler or something."

"They're in anchor—they don't even have steam up," Jerry said. "How could a boiler explode?"

No sooner did he ask his question than there was another explosion, nearly as loud as the first. "That was no boiler explosion!" he said, jumping out of bed and hurrying over to the window.

Leaning out of the window so they could look back toward Pearl Harbor, they saw the airplanes peeling off and diving onto the ships. They also saw tracer rounds zipping up into the air after the planes, hitting one, setting fire to it, and causing it to go down.

"Jerry, what is this? What's going on?"

"It's an attack," Jerry answered, almost as if he couldn't believe the words he was speaking. "We're under attack!"

"Germans? You think the Germans are attacking us? How did they get here? Where did they come from?"

"I don't know who it is, but we'd better get back to the ship," Jerry said.

They dressed quickly and ran out into the hall. As luck would have it, the elevator had just stopped on their floor.

"Hold the elevator!" Jerry shouted, and the operator, a young Japanese man, held it for them.

There were half a dozen others on the elevator, also in uniform. One was a Marine enlisted man, four were sailors, and one was a full colonel in the Army.

"Colonel, who is attacking us?" Dickey asked.

"Japanese," the colonel replied.

"Japanese? Why are they attacking us? Did we have any idea this was about to happen?"

"We've been having peace talks with them," Jerry said. "I've read a little about it in the papers. In fact, I think they have envoys in Washington now. It seems odd that they would attack us while they're still talking to us, don't you think?"

"No, it isn't unusual at all, given the Japanese penchant for duplicity," the colonel replied. "The peace talks in Washington? A sham. The Japs were planning this all along. Maybe this will teach everyone an important lesson. You can't trust a Jap."

The young Japanese elevator operator stood facing the front of the elevator, saying nothing, showing no reaction to the colonel's tirade.

"Are you men going back to your ship?" the colonel asked.

"Yes, sir."

"I hope you have a ship left to go to. From what I could see through my window, nearly every battleship in the harbor has been hit."

"We're off the *Turner*," Jerry said. "It's a destroyer."

The elevator reached the ground floor, and when the operator opened the door, Jerry was shocked to see the lobby filled with people. They were crowded into every archway and alcove, so that it seemed impossible for one more body to fit into the mix. Everyone was yelling and waving, trying to get the attention of one of the harried desk clerks so they could check out.

"We'll never get out of here," Dickey said.

"We have to," Jerry replied. "I'm sure we'll sortie as soon as the crew is aboard."

"What was your room number?" the colonel asked.

"Seven twenty-seven," Dickey replied.

"Give me your key and the money," the colonel said, holding out his hand. "I'll check you out."

Jerry and Dickey looked at each other with a broad smile.

"Thank you, sir," Jerry said, handing over the key and the three dollars. "That's very kind of you."

"Well, army and navy, we're all in this together now. And it seems to me that getting a destroyer out on sortie is a little more important than my job of buildings and grounds at Ft. Shafter."

The next difficulty the young officers encountered was in getting a taxi to take them to Pearl Harbor.

"Are you crazy?" a driver shouted when they tried to engage his cab. "I ain't taking you to Pearl Harbor. In case you haven't noticed, Jap airplanes are bombing out there."

"You have to take us," Jerry said. "This is a military emergency!"

"Yeah? Well I took my discharge here on the island, and I ain't in the military no more."

"I'll double your fare," Dickey promised.

"I wouldn't do it for triple the fare."

"I'll give you one hundred dollars."

"What? Are you joking me?"

Dickey opened his billfold and took out a hundred-dollar bill. "Does this look like a joke?"

There was the sound of another explosion, and the driver shook his head, then pointed to the back seat. "All right. I must be crazy, but get in!" he yelled.

"Thanks."

They climbed into the back seat as the driver put the taxi into gear and drove west on Ala Moana. He used the horn almost as if it were a siren.

Up ahead, and just to the right of the street, there was an explosion, not a very large one, but big enough to get their attention. The driver slammed on his brakes.

"Keep going!" Jerry shouted.

"Didn't you see that? They're bombing the town!"

"No, they aren't," Jerry said. "There aren't any airplanes over the city."

"Then where did that bomb come from?" the driver asked.

"I don't think it was a bomb. More than likely, that was one of our own anti-aircraft shells returning to the ground," Jerry explained.

"Yeah? Well, it coulda hit us!" the driver said. "You may've given me a hundred dollars, but a hundred dollars means nothing to a dead man."

"Don't you think it would be harder to hit a moving target?" Dickey said.

"Yeah," the driver said, accelerating again. "Yeah, maybe you're right at that."

"Dickey, I'll pay you my fifty dollars on payday. I don't have that much right now."

"Forget it. I would've paid that much to get back even if you weren't with me. Far as I'm concerned, you're just along for the ride."

"Yes, but I hate to . . ."

"Jerry, I won't miss a hundred dollars, and you know it. Don't give it another thought."

"Who is doing this to us?" the cab driver shouted as he dodged a pedestrian running across the street. "Who is bombing us? The Germans?"

"The Japanese," Jerry said.

"The Japs? Why? I didn't even know they were mad at us!"

Two bicycles pulled out into the street in front of the taxi, and once again the driver leaned on his horn.

Because it was Sunday morning, traffic was comparatively light, but the few drivers on the road were driving fast and recklessly, some of them weaving back and forth as if such evasive action would prevent their cars from being targets.

The reaction of the citizens could be divided into two categories, those who were running in panic, and those whose curiosity had overcome their fear. The ones who belonged to the latter group were standing in the streets, on the roofs of the buildings, or on the lawns in the front of their houses, most with binoculars, many still in their pajamas or dressing gowns. All were looking toward the several columns of smoke that billowed up from Pearl Harbor and Hickam Field.

After a drive at breakneck speed, the cab slid to a stop at the gate at Pearl Harbor. A marine MP hurried out from his duty post to meet them.

"Now, there's a brave man," Dickey said. "Still doing his duty, even under attack."

As soon as the marine saw that there were navy officers in the car, he saluted and waved them through, then ran back to the perceived, but wholly illusory, safety of the gatehouse.

The driver drove through the base and had just passed the Pearl Harbor Officers' Club at Merry's Point when the glint of a Japanese plane caught Jerry's eye as it swooped toward them, firing its machine guns. Chips of concrete and dust jumped into the air in front of them until the bullets hit the front of the car.

The plane zoomed by overhead, leaving behind a car with a punctured radiator and several holes in the hood. Geysers of steam gushed from the radiator, but the driver managed to guide the car over to the side of the road.

"Anybody hurt?" Jerry asked.

They ran their hands over their bodies, looking for wounds.

"No!" Dickey said. He laughed giddily. "No, I'm not hurt!"

"How about you?" Jerry asked the driver.

"No, I'm not, but my car—"

"Let's get out of here!" Dickey said, pushing open the door.

"How could the bullets have missed all of us?" Jerry asked.

"I say we don't question it, just be thankful," Dickey said. "Come on, we'd better walk the rest of the way."

"Or run!" the driver added, as a second airplane swooped down on them.

They sprinted into a nearby stand of palm trees. More bullets slammed into the cab, and this time one of the tracer rounds found the fuel tank. The car went up with a whoosh, and by the time the Japanese plane had completed its strafing run, the taxi was engulfed in fire and smoke.

"Oh, no!" the driver shouted, putting his hands to the side of his head as he watched the Plymouth burn.

"How much do you think your car was worth?" Dickey asked.

"Three hundred dollars, at least."

Dickey pulled out a tablet and pencil and handed them to the driver.

"Write your name and address on this pad. I'll see to it that the navy sends you two hundred dollars."

"I said three hundred."

"I already gave you one hundred." Dickey argued halfheartedly, his attention on the docks.

"Yeah, but—"

"Never mind. I guess you have insurance."

"Wait, I'll do it." Quickly the driver wrote his name and address on the tablet, then handed it back to Dickey. "You'll get it to them right away?"

"Yes," Dickey promised.

Pearl Harbor was covered with a pall of smoke and reeked with the stench of burning oil. It looked as if every ship in the harbor was on fire, and over on Ford Island planes were burning furiously as flames leaped high into the air.

"Let's get to the ship," Jerry said, and leaving the cab driver standing under a tree watching his car burn, they ran toward their ship.

"You don't really think the navy is going to pay for that guy's car, do you?"

"I'm not even going to try," Dickey answered. "I'll send him the money. I just didn't want him to think I was an easy mark."

When they reached the dock, they started looking around for a boat to take them out to their ship. Jerry saw it first.

"Dickey!" he said, a pained expression on his face.

"What is it?"

Jerry pointed to the harbor. There, through the haze of smoke and fire, they saw the orange-colored keel of the capsized *Turner*. No more than thirty or thirty-five men were gathered in clusters on the floating hulk.

"That's . . . that's not very many, is it?" Dickey said.

"No. I wonder how many we lost."

"Maybe it's not as bad as it looks. The crew was on liberty; there couldn't have been that many on board. And some of them may have left since then."

"Look, there goes the *Nevada*," Jerry said, pointing to one of the battleships.

The *Nevada*, though struck in the bow by a torpedo, had not only managed to stay afloat, but was now getting under way. As it moved out into the harbor, however, the Japanese planes pounced on it like sharks in a feeding frenzy. The ship wasn't taking it passively; nearly every gun mount was manned and firing back. The guns put forth such a rate of fire that the *Nevada* was almost obscured by the smoke. The firing was effective, too, for two of the attacking planes were shot down.

"Look at those guns work!" Dickey said. "Isn't she something?"

"Dickey, she's not going to make it," Jerry said. "Look at her."

Fires were raging on her foredeck, one bomb detonated on her starboard gun battery, and another punched through the deck to set off a terrific explosion below, sending a wall of flame high into the air.

Despite all the damage, the ship continued through the channel, down by the bow, trailing a thick smear of oil, burning and smoking, but with the flag waving defiantly high up in her truck.

"You're right, she's not going to make it," Dickey said. "And if something as big as *Nevada* goes down, it'll keep the channel stopped up for days. No one will be able to get out."

"Yeah, you aren't the only one to figure that out," Jerry said. "Look over there."

Jerry pointed to an array of signal flags flying from the Naval District water tower. They were ordering the big ship to stay clear of the channel. The skipper of the *Nevada* saw the flags as well; he gave the order to nose toward shore. At that moment, two tugs braved the bombing, strafing, and torpedo-launching airplanes to hurry out and push. The *Nevada* ran aground at Saipio Point, just short of the channel. Her stern was caught up by the current, causing her to swing around, then come to a halt, dead in the water. She was struck by still more bombs, and fires raged on the foredeck and superstructure, but her crew continued to fight on, half of them against the fires, the other half at their stations, still shooting at the Japanese.

Sailors . . . dozens of them . . . scores of them . . . hundreds of them . . . oil-covered and burned, were swimming through the water or being pulled out of the bay. Launches, which at the time of the attack were carrying sailors to church services, were now braving enemy fire and bombs to conduct rescue operations. The church launches had been joined by nearly everything else that was buoyant.

In addition to the sailors who were swimming, others were floating in the bay, facedown and perfectly still. They were being recovered too, but with grappling hooks rather than hands.

One more wave of enemy planes roared low over the harbor, firing machine guns and dropping more bombs at the already-burning ships before pulling up and away through the black puffs of antiaircraft fire that chased them, for the most part unsuccessfully, across the sky. Finally the last of the Japanese planes flew away, and the sounds of explosions and gunfire stopped, replaced by the rush and roar of the many fires, the shouts of firefighters and rescue workers, and the low, wailing moans of the wounded.

"Well, this is what we trained for," Dickey said. "Ready or not, we're in the middle of a war. And not just any war, my friend. We've got a wide-open, blue-water, anchors-aweigh, down-to-the-sea in ships, naval war. The only problem is, we've no longer got a ship."

"Submarines," Jerry said.

"What?"

"My guess is, they are going to be building a lot of submarines now. And we are going to be reassigned. I'm putting in for submarines."

Dickey smiled. "Yeah," he said. "Yeah, why not?"

6

Saito had never felt a greater sense of elation, had never felt more alive, than when his plane touched down on the *Kaga*. Coming to a stop, he killed the engine, then jumped down from the plane. As he started toward the ready room, he saw them pushing his plane toward the elevator.

"No!" he said, calling back to them. "There is nothing wrong with the plane. Refuel and rearm, quickly, so we can go back."

"We are not going back," Hiro Amano said. Also a commander, Hiro was a friend and flight leader of one of the other elements.

"What? But of course we are going back! We have nearly destroyed their navy. One more attack and it will be done."

"No more attacks," Hiro said, and the expression in his voice showed that he was as upset about it as Saito. "Look." He pointed to the signal flags. They were set to preclude any more launches. "We are withdrawing."

"I am going to see Commander Fuchida," Saito said. "Maybe he does not understand. Maybe if I told him . . . "

"Saito," Hiro cautioned. "Do you think Fuchida does not want to go back? This isn't his choice. You will only hurt yourself by complaining to him."

"The carriers weren't there," Saito said. "We must get the carriers, or this has all been for nothing."

"I know," Hiro agreed.

"We did not find the carriers. We did not destroy the repair dock."

"I know," Hiro said.

Saito looked back at the deck and saw that they were making ready, in all respects, to withdraw as quickly as they could. With a sigh of frustration, Saito walked over to the base of the superstructure. Leaning against it, he folded his arms across his chest and watched as the deck men scurried about. The deck was awash with sound: the noise of engines, the voices of men shouting to one another, and the electronic crack of the loudspeakers giving orders and directions. Then, as the last plane was recovered, the men gathered to shout *"Banzai!"*

"They are cheering our great victory," Hiro said, coming over to stand beside Saito.

"It is a hollow victory. The Americans are like a tiger. If you attack a tiger with a stick, you should kill the tiger. For if you only wound him, you do nothing but make him angry."

"Why do you think so?"

"Hiro, you know that I attended university in the United States."

"Yes."

"I know the Americans. I know them very well. I have been a guest in the homes of Americans."

"Yes."

"I can tell you now that if we do not totally destroy the American fleet, if we do not strike them such a blow that they sue for peace now, then we have already lost the war."

Saito opened the hatch and went to his quarters below, but no matter where he went, he could not escape the cheers and *banzais* of the officers and men of the carrier.

Saito crawled into his bunk. He could not help but think his nation had made a great mistake today, and as he thought about it, a verse of

Scripture came to his mind. Pulling his Bible from his sea bag, he opened it to Luke 14:31: "Or what king, when he sets out to meet another king in battle, will not first sit down and consider whether he is strong enough with ten thousand men to encounter the one coming against him with twenty thousand?"

Wake Island

Wake Island is formed by three low-lying islets, which are actually part of the rim of an ancient volcano. The crater of the volcano is the bay, and in that bay, the great Clipper rocked gently, glistening in the early morning light.

A totally deserted island until its location made it a stepping-stone in the chain of islands that stretched from Manila to Hawaii, Wake has no indigenous fresh water. Pan Am remedied that problem by building a large water storage tank and bringing water in. They also built a huge fuel storage tank so that the Clippers might be refueled on their stops here. The island facilities included a hotel to house workmen, aircrews, and passengers, and though there was seldom more than one plane there at a time, the hotel was built to facilitate expansion.

The very thing that made Wake valuable to Pan Am also made it valuable to the United States government. As a result, Wake was defended by the U.S. Marine Corps. It bore even more of the look of a citadel than did Guam, for the defenses here were more obvious, standing out against the otherwise bleak, nearly flat background. Here were entrenchments, rolls of barbed wire, machine-gun bunkers, and light artillery emplacements.

Shortly after the *China Clipper* landed the night before, Captain Cooley informed the passengers that he intended to take off no later than eight o'clock the next morning. All expendables, to include fuel and oil, were taken on board; spark plugs were cleaned or replaced as needed; and the airplane was ready to go.

A few of the passengers utilized the hotel's room service to have their breakfasts in bed, but Sean Hanifin, always an early riser, was in the dining room when the pilot walked through.

"Good morning, Mr. Hanifin," Ken said. He looked around the room. "Your wife and son aren't joining you for breakfast?"

"Katie is having toast and coffee in the room. I didn't knock on Pat's door. He's a big boy; if he's hungry, he'll wake himself."

"Do you mind if I join you?"

"I would be honored," Sean replied. He waved his arm toward a chair. "Please."

Ken sat down, ordered scrambled eggs, and poured himself a cup of coffee. At that moment Maj. James Devereaux, commander of the marine battalion on Wake, came into the dining room. There was a worried expression on his face, and he looked around until he saw Ken and Sean. He came toward them.

"Major Devereaux, how are you this morning?"

"Captain, I need a word with you."

"Well, sit down, Major, and join us for breakfast," Ken said, pushing the chair out.

"I'm afraid I don't have time. We just got word that the Japanese have attacked Oahu."

"What?" Ken put his cup down so quickly that coffee splashed over the rim. "When?"

"This morning. Right now, in fact. For all I know the attack is still going on."

Ken shook his head. "I can't believe they're actually carrying out their threat. It's almost incomprehensible."

"Well, the situation has been tense," Sean said. "That was the purpose of the peace talks."

"Those Japs didn't want peace," Ken said angrily. "All they wanted was to keep us occupied while they sneaked up on us, the little cowards."

"We have to expect that they will be coming here soon," Devereux said. "Perhaps as early as today."

"Here? You expect the Japs to attack Wake?"

"Expect them to attack? Captain Cooley, I guarantee that they will attack. If it's a stepping-stone for us across the Pacific, then it is for the Japs as well," Devereux replied.

"Does Cooke know yet?" Ken asked, referring to Pan Am's airport manager, John B. Cooke.

"Yes, he knows."

Even as Devereux was answering the question, Ken saw Cooke come into the dining room, wringing his hands with worry.

"You've heard about Pearl Harbor?" the manager asked.

"Yes, Major Devereux was just telling us about it."

"I've spoken with company headquarters. They want you to remain on the ground until the situation in Hawaii stabilizes. They'll advise us when they consider it safe to leave."

"They will advise us when *they* consider it safe?" Ken repeated.

"Yes."

"I don't know that I like the idea of someone sitting in an office halfway around the world telling me when it's safe. I'll make my own decisions."

"Captain, if it's any help to you in making that decision," said Major Devereux, "I think I should tell you that, though I intend to hold out for as long as I can, I don't know how long that will be. I have limited manpower and resources."

"I'll get our people rounded up," Ken said. "We're going to leave as soon as we can. Mr. Hanifin, I need to see to the crew and the plane. Would you round up the passengers?"

"Yes, of course," Sean said.

"Thanks."

"I'll try and get through to headquarters to ask for permis—"

Ken had already started toward the door, but he stopped and turned back toward Cooke. His face tight with barely controlled anger, he pointed his finger at the station manager. "No, Cooke, you don't ask for permission, you tell them I'm leaving. Have you got that? You tell them."

"Right, I'll tell them."

Ken allowed himself to smile. "Thanks."

Outside, a rain began to fall.

"Captain Cooley, how many people can you get on that airplane?" Major Devereux asked.

"Around seventy."

"And how many passengers do you have?"

"Fourteen."

"So you could take, what . . . fifty-some more?"

"If we stripped her down to nothing but fuel, I might even be able to get a few more on board."

"Then, if you don't mind, I would like for you to take as many of the Pan Am staff with you as you can safely get aloft," Devereux said.

"I'll do that. I'll get the mechanics busy stripping us down."

"How long do you think that will take?"

"Let's shoot for one o'clock." He looked at Cooke. "Can you and your people be ready by then?"

"I think so."

"Know so," Ken said. "Oh, and you can carry nothing except the clothes on your back."

"I've got some very important papers that—"

"Burn them," Ken ordered.

"Burn them. Right."

Although the passengers were told to stay in their rooms until time to go, Diane couldn't. She was too upset by the fact that her native country and her adoptive country were at war. How could this be? How could men of reason and intelligence let things get this far?

With nervous energy spilling over, she left her room and the hotel and began wandering around the island. Several times she was challenged by one of the young marines and told to get back to the hotel, out of harm's way.

Out of harm's way, she thought. *If this island really were attacked, would there be any place that would be out of harm's way?*

While Major Devereux and his men worked feverishly on the defensive positions, the Pan Am mechanics and flight crew busied themselves by removing as much weight from the Clipper as they could. They took out the bulkheads between the compartments, tables from the salon, and equipment from the galley. Ken was just going over the inventory, trying to find some other things they could remove, when two young marine lieutenants reported to him.

"Captain Cooley?" one of them said. "I'm Lt. George Graves, this is Lt. Robert Conderman. With your permission, sir, we're going to fly escort for you from here to Midway."

"Do your fighter planes have that much range?" Ken asked.

Graves laughed. "No, sir, not really. When I say escort to Midway, I mean we'll take you as far as we can go before we have to turn back."

"That is, if you don't mind us tagging along," Conderman added.

"I'd love to have you tagging along. But bear in mind, I can't go any faster than 150 miles per hour."

"One hundred fifty? That's it?" Graves asked.

"Afraid so."

"Don't you ever want to get out and push?"

Ken chuckled. "From time to time I have considered the possibility, yes."

"Well, look at it this way. Throttled down that far, we might get more range," Conderman said.

"Yes, we might at that, and if—"

Graves's comment was cut short by the sound of the air-raid alarm.

"They're coming!" someone shouted, running into the tent. "The Japs are coming!"

Stepping outside, Ken looked out to sea and saw several planes emerging from the clouds at about fifteen hundred feet. They were twin-engine bombers, painted in a camouflage scheme with a red ball on the fuselage and wings.

"Let's go, Bob!" Graves yelled, and the two pilots sprinted hard toward their Wildcat fighters. Graves reached his, climbed up on the wing, and slid open the cockpit. He was just climbing in when a bomb scored a direct hit on his plane. It went up in a ball of fire, killing him instantly.

Conderman was cut down by machine-gun fire as he raced toward his plane, seconds before a bomb hit it, pinning him under the wreckage.

Many of the passengers were having their lunches when they heard the bombs exploding. For a moment they looked at each other as if questioning what it was, then a bomb hit so close that it shattered the windows and rattled the crockery.

"The Japanese!" someone yelled. "They're here!"

"Everyone outside! Find a place to take cover!"

With that shout of warning, everyone dashed out of the hotel and ran toward anything they thought might offer them some protection.

"Pat!" McKinley called. "Have you seen Diane?"

"You mean she isn't with you?"

"No. She's been too nervous and upset to stay in one place. She told me she was going for a walk, but that was an hour ago. I haven't seen her since."

"I'll find her," Pat promised.

Getting up from the comparative safety of a prepared trench, Pat started running across an open area. Overhead, the Japanese bombers continued their work, passing back and forth over the island with impunity, dropping bombs and firing machine guns at airplanes, vehicles, buildings, and people on the ground. The gunner in one of the planes spotted Pat running and opened up on him. A stream of bullets popped and whistled past his ear, chewing up the ground in front of him.

"Pat! Pat!" Katie screamed. "Get back here!"

Ignoring his mother's pleas, Pat continued to run, zigzagging back and forth as he did so.

"Pat! I'm over here!" someone shouted, and, looking ahead of him, he saw Diane. She had taken cover among some concrete pillars, which would have been good except for one thing. Perched on top of these pillars was a twenty-five-thousand-gallon fuel storage tank.

"Diane! Diane, get away from there!" Pat shouted, waving his arm to motion her on. "Hurry!"

Another plane passed overhead, and once again bullets whizzed by, tracking across the ground, kicking up puffs of dirt, and striking sparks against the rocks as they raced toward Diane. Some hit a pillar, sending off tiny, stinging shards of cement.

"You've got to get out of there!" Pat shouted. He pointed to the huge tank over her head.

Diane either didn't understand, or she was too frightened to react, because she stayed put, leaving Pat with no choice. He ran to her, put his arm around her, and pulled.

"You can't stay here!" he said.

At first Diane resisted him, but he was insistent. She left the false safety of the stone pillars for the frightening condition of being exposed to the strafing Japanese planes.

Running back across the open area in the same zigzag fashion in which he had crossed it, they made it back to the trench where the passengers, including Diane's father, had taken cover. McKinley embraced his daughter as she was returned to him.

At that moment, the gas storage tank went up with a huge roar, sending flames high into the air; at the same time, Pat looked toward the Clipper, where a huge geyser of water erupted no more than fifty feet in front of it. A hit would have stranded them; they still had a chance to escape.

As suddenly as it had begun, the attack ended and the Japanese planes, totally unscratched and unconcerned, headed leisurely back toward their base at Roi. Behind them lay smoking ruins and a stunned silence.

In an attack that lasted only seven minutes, their bombs and bullets had totally wrecked Pan Am's facilities. The hotel was burning, as were twenty-five thousand gallons of fuel. Several other buildings were burned as well, and four Wildcats were destroyed. Nine of Pan Am's sixty-six-man staff lay dead. In addition, Gordon Travers and Betty Bridges were slightly injured.

Miraculously, the Clipper itself was basically unscathed. There were a few bullet holes, but nothing critical had been hit. Ken and Gordon made a very thorough inspection of the plane, then smiled broadly at each other as they came to the realization that they would be able to take off.

At one-thirty on the afternoon of December 7, with seventy-three souls on board and without fighter escort, the giant flying boat, Pan American's *China Clipper*, took off from Wake, heading for Midway Island.

In order to accommodate the full passenger load, all of the luggage had been left behind. In addition, the bulkheads between the compartments were removed so that the cabin of the airplane was one long tube filled with passengers, in some cases putting four on the bench seats designed for three. Pat, Diane, McKinley, and one of the Pan Am employees were so seated. They were right across from Sean and Katie, as well as two other passengers, but neither Diane's father or Pat's parents showed any reaction to how close Pat and Diane were sitting to each other, or to the fact that the two young people were openly holding hands.

Pearl Harbor
Sunday afternoon, December 7, 1941

As the launch approached the harbor, Tony Jarvis stared in awe at the *Turner's* orange underbelly. The front half of the keel was submerged, but the back half was partially out of water, exposing the rudder and her two large screws. They drew alongside, then stopped.

Tony had answered the call for a volunteer who was small and athletic. He had no idea what was expected of him, but he figured he'd find out soon enough.

A rescue team, commanded by a chief petty officer, was on the work barge alongside the capsized vessel. The chief looked up when Tony stepped off the launch.

"You the volunteer?" he asked. "I'm Chief McCoy. Glad to have you here."

"The *Turner* was my ship."

"Really? Too bad. We lost a lot of ships today."

"Yeah."

"What's your name?"

"Jarvis. Tony Jarvis." Tony was unable to take his eyes off the ugly orange smear sticking up from the water. There were three men crouched on the keel, working with a cutting torch. Sparks were flying from the point of contact between the tip of the flame and the keel. A network of hoses and lines snaked their way out to the work crew, all of whom were wearing darkly shaded goggles.

"Tony Jarvis, you say? I saw a Tony Jarvis fight in the island smokers last winter. Would that be you?"

"Yeah, that was me."

"That was a great fight," McCoy said.

"Thanks." Tony nodded toward the ship. "The cap'n said you were looking for a volunteer . . . someone who wasn't too big, but who could take care of himself."

"That's right. I have to warn you, though, it could be dangerous. Very dangerous."

"Yeah, well, I didn't figure it would be a walk in the park. What do you need done?"

"It turns out that several of the crew are still alive."

Tony smiled broadly. "That's great!"

"Yeah. But they're going to need help to stay alive long enough for us to get them out of there. That's where you come in."

"I'll do whatever I can."

McCoy pointed to an open porthole in the side of the ship, visible even though it was about six feet below the surface. "Do you think you can get through that porthole?"

"I don't know."

"Are you willing to try?"

Tony thought for a moment. No harm in trying; if he couldn't get through, all he would have to do is come right back up.

"Yeah, sure, I'll give it a shot."

"Good. We've picked up tapping, in Morse code, from inside the ship, so we know there are at least twenty-three men still alive down there . . . maybe more."

"You want me to find them, try to lead them back through the hole?"

"No, nothing like that," McCoy said. "Most of them couldn't get through it. What we want you to do is take an air hose, a telephone line, and some battery-powered lights down to them. If they have air and light and can communicate with us, I think we can keep their spirits up long enough to allow us to get them out alive."

"How are you going to do that? Get them out, I mean."

McCoy pointed to the men working with the torch. "We're cutting through the bottom of the ship. But it's thick metal and a double hull. We figure it's going to take about thirty-six hours or so, but we can get through."

Tony looked out across the harbor. Some of the ships were still burning or smoking; others were blackened, twisted wreckage. Nearly all were in some stage of submersion, down by the bow, down by the stern, or listing hard to port or starboard. There were several parties working on the other vessels, trying to free trapped men.

Tony thought of his own situation. Had he been on board the *Turner* when the attack occurred and had he gone down with it, he would want someone to try to rescue him. And he would want it to be more than a halfhearted effort.

Thinking about what it would be like down there, the hopes and prayers he would be sending up, made up his mind. He'd go all out to accomplish the task, and he would put his own life on the line if that's what it took.

"Okay," Tony said. "Let's get going."

McCoy smiled at him. "Good man, Jarvis. Just give us a few minutes to get everything set up."

If anyone had asked, Tony would have said he was a Christian. But, like many other young sailors, he had become what the deacons at the orphanage called a backsliding Baptist. Too often he had put his faith on the back burner. Now though, he knew that he would not be able to do what was being asked of him without God's help. He prayed that God would not hold his personal mistakes against the poor men who were trapped below.

Dear Lord, Tony prayed, *I know I don't deserve Your blessing, but, in Jesus' name, I ask that You forgive me all my sins, and please help me get through to those men.*

Behind him an air compressor sputtered, then roared into life. A long, thin hose was brought to him. Air was rushing from the end of it.

"All right, here's the air hose, the telephone line, and a battery-powered light," McCoy said.

"Wait," Tony said. He stripped out of his blouse, then his shoes, socks, and trousers, so that he was wearing only his undershorts. "Chief, have you got any idea where the men are?"

"According to Lewis, they're in the after engine room. That would be right about there." He pointed to a place on the ship's hull.

"Lewis?" Tony said in a small voice.

"Yeah. He's a radio operator and knows code. Do you know him?"

Tony would never have thought of Muley Lewis as one of his buddies. But, as of this moment, Muley Lewis was not only his buddy, he was his brother, and Tony was more determined than ever to make this work.

"Yeah," he said. "Yeah, Muley is a friend of mine."

McCoy put his hand on Tony's shoulder. "Then maybe it's God's will that you're here. I hope we can get your friend out, and the rest of them, too."

He pointed to the porthole. "When you go inside, remember that everything is upside down . . . ladder-ways that go down are actually going up. Turn right as soon as you get through the opening . . . after about ten feet you'll see a ladder-way going down . . . up in this case. That will give you access to the engine deck. The engine deck is about half-flooded. The after engine room is where you'll find the survivors."

"Yes, sir."

"You're going to have a long swim underwater, so take a deep breath and stay calm. And, son, if it's any comfort to you, there'll be a lot of us out here praying for you."

"Thanks," Tony said. "That *is* a lot of comfort."

Tony attached the battery-powered light to his waist. Then he took the air hose and a telephone line with handset attached and, grasping them in a closed fist, took several deep breaths before he went under. About six feet down he found the porthole. Fortunately he didn't have to fool with trying to open it. He stuck the lines through, then the light, then one arm and one shoulder. It took him longer than he would have wanted to get his head worked through, but he finally did and then pulled his other arm and shoulders in. After that it was just a matter of wriggling the rest of his body through.

Once inside, Tony picked up the lines and started swimming toward the ladder-well. With his light turned on, he found his way fairly easily.

The door to the ladder-way was dogged shut, making it very difficult to open. He was running out of air, and he was about to give up when he saw the bubbles shooting from the air hose he was carrying. Letting the air in his lungs escape, he put the bubbling airline in his mouth. He swallowed salt water and oil as he did so, but he also managed to refill his lungs with air. At first, he thought about leaving the hose in his mouth, but the air pressure was too great.

Re-oxygenated, Tony swam up the down ladder-well until he broke out of the water and into a large pocket of trapped air. "I'm here!" he shouted, happily.

There was no response. Holding the light up, Tony looked around. This was an engine room all right, but it was the forward engine room. McCoy had said the men were in the after engine room.

Tony swam toward a dogged hatch and tapped on it. "Anyone in there?" he called. Not getting an answer, he tapped again. Still no response.

Tony felt a sinking sensation. Had they run out of air? That was a possibility, especially with twenty-three men trying to breathe, and the air pocket no larger than this one.

Praying not to find them all dead on the other side of the door, Tony opened it.

As soon as the dogs were released, the door was pushed open by a gushing cascade of water. A tidal wave swept over him, causing him to drop his light, telephone, and air hose.

How could that be? Why was that room flooded?

Suddenly Tony realized what he had done. He had gone forward, when he should have gone aft. This wasn't the after engine room; this was the machine room, and since the ship was down by the bow, the machine room and everything forward was flooded.

Now, with the forward engine room completely flooded, he faced a new problem. If he opened the door to the after engine room, what just happened here would happen there. Whatever air pocket was sustaining the men inside would be taken up by the onrush of water.

There was only one thing he could do. Swim back to the porthole, go back up, tell the rescue workers what he had done, and see if they had any ideas.

As Tony swam back, retracing the path he had used to come this far, he was angry with himself for doing such a foolish thing. Now the men might not be rescued at all.

Yutaka Saito was flight leader of a two-plane element. Though he had been in a torpedo plane for the initial attack on Pearl Harbor, he was now in a Zero and flying at twenty thousand feet, on oxygen, when he saw the huge flying boat headed east. The *China Clipper* was about ten thousand feet below, and a few miles south.

Even though it was an enemy plane, he couldn't help but admire it. It was beautiful and gigantic, an absolute marvel of aviation engineering.

"Commander, enemy plane," his wingman said, excitedly.

"I see it." Saito peeled off and started toward the flying boat, slipping down the long corridor of air at well over three hundred miles per hour. He caught up to the Clipper quickly, but because he was on its tail and behind the plane, he was sure he hadn't been seen. Looking to his right, he saw his wingman with him.

"Shall we shoot it down, sir?" the wingman asked. It was obvious by his tone of voice that he wanted to do just that.

"Do nothing," Saito said.

"Nothing? But, Commander, it is an enemy plane!"

"It is a plane that carries civilian passengers," Saito said. "We will not attack."

"What if it fires at us?" the wingman asked.

"If you are fired upon, you can return fire," Saito said. "But I know this airplane, and I know that it does not have guns."

While Saito stayed slightly above and behind the airliner, his wingman moved up alongside the plane and looked over toward the windows of the passenger compartment.

"Oh, my heavens!" Katie Hanifin said.

"What is it?" Sean asked. His head was leaning back against his seat, and he was trying to take a nap—with some difficulty, because every available seat was occupied.

"Isn't that a Japanese airplane right there?" Katie asked, pointing through the window. Pat, who was sitting with Diane across from his mother in a facing seat, was also next to the window. He looked outside and there, no more than sixty feet away and hanging just off the port wing, was a Zero. It was so close that Pat could see the pilot's face. For a moment, he could almost believe that their eyes met.

The Japanese pilot stared at him, his face completely devoid of expression. Then the fighter climbed above them.

By now, several others had seen it as well. "He's getting above us to make his attack!" someone shouted, and others screamed in fear.

"No, wait!" Pat said, standing up and lifting his hands over his head. "Hold it; don't panic! I don't think he plans to shoot us down!"

"How do you know?"

"Think about it! If he wanted to attack us, he would have fired long before now."

"Not if he just got here," someone said.

"Mr. Hanifin is right," McKinley said, also trying to calm the others. "I know the Japanese people, and I know their military. They are men of honor. I do not believe they would shoot down an unarmed passenger plane."

"Were the ones who attacked us at Wake men of honor?" someone asked.

"Yes, they dropped bombs on civilians there."

"No," McKinley said. "They dropped bombs on a military target where which there happened to be civilians. This airplane is not a military target, and I do not believe they will fire at us."

"And we're supposed to put our faith in what you believe?" one of the passengers asked.

"No," McKinley replied. "You are supposed to put your faith in God."

McKinley's response calmed the passengers to the degree that the screams and cries stopped, but the uneasy fear continued.

"I think your father is right," Pat said as he sat back down beside Diane. "And if you know any prayers, this might be a good time to say them."

Diane smiled at Pat. "Are you kidding?" she asked. "I haven't stopped praying since we left Wake Island." She squeezed Pat's hand more tightly.

The first time Ken saw the Japanese plane was when it suddenly appeared in front of him, diving down from a point above and behind the Clipper, then falling off on one wing.

"Whoa!" Mark shouted. "What was that?"

"That was a Zero," Ken answered.

"What does he want?"

"At this point, I think he just wants to look us over."

The second of the two Japanese planes moved in now, flying alongside the Clipper, but this one was parallel with the Clipper's flight deck. The pilot moved in very close.

"I don't like this," Mark said. "I don't like this at all."

"Well, if this had happened yesterday, before they attacked Pearl Harbor, I would be concerned too. They would have been worried that we would give them away. But the attack has already happened, so we aren't any danger to them. We're okay." Ken paused for a moment, then added, "I think."

"You think?"

"I think."

For a long moment the two planes flew side by side. Then Ken saluted the Japanese pilot.

Saito wasn't surprised by the salute. He had lived in America long enough to understand the American demeanor. It was obvious that the big plane was at Saito's mercy, for he could take it down with one easy burst of machine-gun fire. But it was equally obvious that the American pilot had no intention of begging for his life. The salute was a greeting between pilots, and a challenge to Saito to show a sense of humanity under the circumstances.

Saito smiled, then returned the pilot's salute.

"Commander Saito, what are we going to do?" the wingman asked.

"We are going back to the carrier," Saito replied. "We have learned what we need to learn."

"I don't understand. What have we learned?"

"That the Americans have no war planes in this sector," Saito replied.

"How do you know that?"

"If they did, they would not let a passenger plane fly without an escort."

Saito waved his wings, then fell off in a long, arcing dive. His wing mate went with him.

"Elliot, get a reading on them; see if you can figure out where they're heading," Ken said as he watched the two Japanese planes flying toward the northeast. "It might be a way of locating their fleet."

"That's the source of the radio signals we heard the other night, isn't it?" Elliot asked.

"Yes, I'm convinced of it."

"What would you gauge their speed to be, Skipper? About 250 knots?"

"I'd say that's a good guess."

"Okay, I'll plot a position for one hour, one and one-half hours, and two hours from here," Elliot said.

"Good. When you get it worked out, let me know and I'll call it in. Our people might like to have a pretty good estimate of the Japanese fleet's location."

Pearl Harbor

Now that Tony had inadvertently flooded the forward engine room, the rescue team had no choice but to try and pump it out. To accommodate that, Tony had to go back down into the bowels of the ship. His first act was to close and dog the watertight door between the forward engine room and the machine room. He also carried a two-inch hose in, to be used to pump out the water.

It took all afternoon for the pump to clear out enough water, then pump air back in, recreating the air bubble that would allow the door to the after engine room to be opened. By then it was dark, and rescue teams could be heard all across the harbor. Sparks flew from the torches that were being used to cut through the thick metal hulls.

As night fell, the rescuers turned on powerful work lights and found themselves facing the hazard of friendly fire. The rumor that Japanese parachutists had landed on Oahu made the nervous and trigger-happy guards shoot at anything that caught their attention—sounds, work lights, even sparks from the torches the rescuers were using. Because of that, some of the rescuers chose to work in the dark.

That's the decision McCoy and his men made after several bullets snapped by their heads as soon as they turned on the lights.

"Jarvis?" McCoy called. "Where is Jarvis?"

"I'm right here, Chief," Tony replied. He was drinking coffee and eating a ham sandwich. It was nearly ten o'clock at night now, and the sandwich was the first bite of food he had put in his mouth all day.

"Are you ready to give it another try?"

"Yeah, I'm ready," Tony said, draining the rest of his coffee.

"I know we've asked a lot of you today," McCoy said. "But right now, you're all we've got. You're all those men down there have."

"I know. I'll get through this time."

"God go with you, son."

Once again Tony went underwater to work his way through the port-hole. Coming up in the air bubble in the forward engine room, he swam over to the watertight door that separated the forward engine room from the after engine room. He tried to undog the door, but he couldn't do it. Then he asked for help from anyone on the other side. He began tapping on the bulkhead.

Dash-dash-dash dot-dash-dash-dot dot dash-dot dash-dot-dot dash-dash-dash dash-dash-dash dot-dash-dot. Morse code for "Open door."

When he got no response, he tapped the message again, and a third time before he heard the reply.

Dot-dash-dash dot-dot dot-dash-dot-dot dot-dash-dot-dot dash-dot-dot dash-dash-dash. "Will do."

"All right!" Tony said happily. They were still alive.

By tapping alongside the dog he was working on to show the men on the other side where to start, he was able to loosen the latches one by one. Then, with the final latch loosened, the door swung open. Tony held up the lamp and stared directly into the face of Muley Lewis.

"Hi, Muley," he said with a wide grin. "Rosie sent me."

Over Honolulu
Noon, Monday, December 8, 1941

Making its approach from the north, the *Clipper* passed over Pearl Harbor, then turned back for its final descent. Sean stared out in shock and dismay at the remnants of the once-proud Pacific fleet. The harbor was filled with wrecked ships, some of them upside down so that only their red-brown hull bottoms showed, others so low in the water that their decks were awash, and still others completely sunk so that only their superstructures were sticking up. Several were still burning, and a billowing cloud of oily black smoke covered the entire end of the island.

It was obvious that the navy hadn't been the only target. On Hickam Field were a dozen or more blackened hangars and buildings, while on the parking ramps, airplanes that had been aligned in long, neat rows to prevent sabotage were now long, carefully aligned piles of blackened rubble.

The *Clipper's* passengers watched in stunned silence as they descended into Pearl Harbor. The airplane touched down, sending up a sheet of spray on its initial contact with the water, then settling into its taxi run until it was met by a tug that pulled it into position and tied it down.

On every previous landing there had been an almost giddy conversation and laughter from passengers as they deplaned. This debarkation took place in absolute silence, as if they were at a funeral, viewing the remains.

7

Honolulu
December 8, 1941

T he *China Clipper* was taken over by the government to carry high-priority personnel. Those passengers who had been en route to the States on the *Clipper* were told they would be provided with first-class passage on the next ship returning to San Francisco on December 12. Until then, they would be put up in the finest suites in the Royal Hawaiian Hotel, compliments of Pan American Airways.

From where she was standing at the window of their suite, Katie Hanifin could see the *China Clipper* as it took off. She heard the door open and close behind her.

"Is that you, Sean?"

"Yes." He flopped down in a chair in the sitting room.

"The *Clipper* just took off. You can still see it if you'd like."

"No. If we aren't on it, it's of no interest to me."

"Were you able to get through?" Katie asked, abandoning her vantage point at the window.

Sean shook his head. "I'm afraid not. No telephone calls to the States without military authorization. And cablegrams are nearly as difficult. I stood in line for an hour until they told us to go home and come back tomorrow because they already had more traffic than they could handle for the next twenty-four hours."

"Well, how important is it to get hold of your publisher anyway?"

"I want them to know that I was there when Wake was attacked, and I'm here now, on the heels of the attack on Pearl Harbor," Sean said. "I want young Pendarrow to know there is going to be a book or two to come out of this war."

"And do you think he doesn't know that?"

"I don't know. Phil doesn't seem to have quite as good a grasp of the business as his father did."

"I'm sure every young man who moves into a business behind his father has to put up with the same prejudice," Katie said. "You said yourself that he has done a wonderful job with *Gossamer Wings*."

"Yes, he did. And it was his idea to send us on this little excursion. Hey, do you think he knew something and was just trying to get rid of me?"

"Sean!" Katie scolded.

Sean laughed. "Oh, by the way, you'll never guess who I met today."

"I've no way of telling."

"Young Dickey Traser."

"Who?"

"Don't you remember last year, when we went deep-sea fishing with Art Traser?"

"Traser. Would he be the man who has something to do with the railroad?"

Sean laughed. "*Something to do with* the railroad is hardly the term I would use. He *owns* 8 percent of all the track in the United States."

"I do remember that it was a fine, big boat."

"It was indeed," Sean said. "Anyway, his son, Dickey, is in the navy, stationed here in the islands. Dickey lost his ship in the attack."

"Oh, what a shame. I hope he is all right."

"He's fine. He was ashore when the attack came. He invited us to dinner tonight, and I accepted. I hope you don't mind. I told him that Pat was with us, and he said bring him along."

"No, of course I don't mind. By the way, where is Pat?"

"With the young Slayton girl. Where else?"

"I hope things aren't getting too serious between those two."

"Why do you say that?"

"They've only known each other a few days. And where can it lead? A few more days on board the ship back to the States, then they'll each go their own way."

"Who is to say that their own way won't be together?" Sean asked. "After all, things tend to happen much more quickly during wartime."

"Aye, that is true, I suppose. But there is the other thing to consider."

"The other thing? What other thing?"

"Their religion."

"What does that have to do with anything? From all I can tell, Diane Slayton is a fine Christian girl. Her father is a minister, after all."

"A Protestant minister," Katie reminded him.

"But Christian, nonetheless. And I daresay she is a better Christian than Pat has been for some time now."

"It has long been my hope that Pat would come back to the mother church."

"Maybe Diane will bring that about."

"I mean the one true church. 'Tis Catholic he was born, and Catholic I want him to be."

"Katie, if there is but one true God, then any church that recognizes His son is a true church."

"That's blasphemous, Sean Hanifin," Katie said in shock.

"No, darlin', 'tisn't blasphemous at all," Sean replied. "It is the brotherhood of Christ."

Pat had planned a sightseeing bike ride, but it turned out to be much less comprehensive than he'd hoped. He and Diane intended to see

Oahu, but armed military guards turned them back from dozens of places. Access was denied to any hill that would afford them an observation point from which they could view the city and the island. Nearly every inch of beach was pocked with foxholes, filled with soldiers, and bristling with machine guns and artillery. Only a very small portion of beach remained open for public use, and it was marked off by concertina wire and patrolled by armed soldiers.

Finally they bought a loaf of bread, some lunch meat, a jar of mustard, and two Coca-Colas from a small grocery store, then rode inland to Launani Valley. There they picnicked under a banyan tree.

"Pat, are we having a romance?" Diane asked.

Pat had just started to take a drink, and he coughed and pulled the bottle away from his lips to keep from choking.

"Are you all right?" Diane asked in concern.

"Uh, yes. Some soda went down wrong is all," Pat said. He cleared his throat. "You asked if we are having a romance?"

"Yes. I've read about romance in books, but I've never experienced it, nor have I known anyone who has. Unless, of course, I'm having one now. Am I?"

"Well, yes," Pat said. "I suppose you could call what we are having a romance."

Diane smiled broadly. "I *thought* so. Oh, this is so exciting."

Chuckling quietly, Pat pinched the bridge of his nose and shook his head. "Diane, you shouldn't say such things. Don't you know that an unscrupulous person could take advantage of your naïveté?"

"I'm sure he could," Diane replied. "But I'm equally sure *you* would not. Remember, I have put myself in your hands."

Pat sighed, then waved his finger. "Most men count on the woman to draw the line as to how far they can push the relationship, and they use that as an excuse to abandon their own responsibility. But you have put the ball entirely in my court."

"Yes," Diane agreed.

"Why is that?"

"Because I know you will do the right thing."

"You may be naïve, Diane, but you aren't dumb. You have put me on my honor, and you know I will not violate that."

"But your honor will allow another kiss, won't it?" Diane asked. "After all, we do have seventeen left."

"Seventeen kisses left?" Pat asked, now thoroughly confused.

"Don't you remember when we were talking about promiscuous behavior? We decided that twenty kisses between two people who are constructing a meaningful relationship was better than one kiss that offers only the pleasure of the moment. We've had three kisses, so that leaves us seventeen more."

"Let's make it sixteen," Pat said, pulling her to him.

His previous kisses had evoked curiosity, a sense of wonder, and—she had to admit—a degree of pleasure. But this kiss started where the others had left off. It was shocking and thrilling at the same time. Her blood felt as if it had changed to hot tea as the kiss went on, longer than she had ever imagined such a thing could last.

It was Pat who finally pulled away. For a moment they looked at each other, as if confused by what had just happened and unsure of where they were going. A shock of hair had fallen across Pat's face, and Diane pushed it back. Pat reached up to take her hand in his. He held it for a moment, then moved it to his lips and kissed it.

This was not going the way he had planned. Back in Hong Kong, when he learned that Diane was taking the *Clipper* back to the States, his only thought was that it would be pleasant to have an interesting and attractive young woman as a fellow passenger. He had enjoyed an active social life all through college, and it continued into his professional career. But he had never been around a woman who had the effect on him that Diane did.

He realized that he was very protective of her; in fact, his interest in her was more than just protective, it was proprietary. Was he falling in love with her? Could a man fall in love with a woman this quickly? He had never been in love, so he had no way to measure what he was experiencing now.

Suddenly an airplane appeared just over the Koolau Mountains. It nosed down, following the slope of the hills, then flattened out very low over the valley, heading straight toward them.

"Pat!" Diane said fearfully.

"It's not a Jap plane," Pat said quickly. "It's all right . . . I think."

She clung to him, and they watched as the airplane flashed by overhead, so low they could feel the blast of wind from its propeller. It pulled up at the far end of the valley, then disappeared over another range.

"Why did he do that?" Diane asked.

"Probably just checking us out," Pat replied.

He stood and helped Diane to her feet. "I think we should get back to the hotel."

The naval officers' club at Pearl Harbor

The Japanese had struck none of the officers' clubs during their attack on Pearl Harbor. In fact, the administration building at Hickam Air Force Base was not bombed because the Japanese thought it was an officers' club—the mistake arising from the fact that a few dances had been held there. Even the naval officers' club at Pearl Harbor, which was very close to the center of action, was undamaged.

Dickey was waiting in the entry foyer of the club when he saw the Hanifins come through the front door. He was surprised to see that there was an extra person, and quickly called to a club yeoman.

"I have a table for five. Traser. Please change it to six," he said quietly.

"Yes, sir, Mr. Traser," the yeoman replied.

Smiling, Dickey started toward his guests.

"I'm so glad you could come," he said. He nodded toward Katie. "Mrs. Hanifin, I'm Dickey Traser. We've never met, but I believe you met my parents during a fishing trip last year."

"Aye, and it was a lovely time we had, too."

"And you are Pat Hanifin," Dickey said, extending his hand.

"Yes," Pat said. "I hope you don't mind that I brought Miss Diane Slayton with me."

"What red-blooded American man could possibly object to sharing a dinner table with such an attractive young lady?" Dickey asked. "By all means, Miss Slayton, you are more than welcome." Out of the corner of his eye, Dickey saw the club yeoman coming back from the dining room, nodding his way.

"I have a table waiting for us," Dickey said.

As they approached the table, Jerry Cornelison, who had been waiting there, stood to greet them. Like Dickey and many other officers present in the dining room, Jerry was wearing his white uniform. He hurried around to hold the chair for Katie, while Pat held the chair for Diane.

During dinner they exchanged stories of their recent adventure. Sean told, in great and embellished detail, of their harrowing flight out of Wake Island, concluding with the tale of how Pat had saved Diane's life.

"Oh, that may be stretching the story a bit, Dad," Pat said.

"I'm a novelist; I get paid to stretch the story a bit."

The others laughed, but Diane spoke up. "Mr. Hanifin is right. Pat did save my life."

Jerry and Dickey shared the story of their mad dash by taxi back to their ship, only to find it floating upside down in the harbor.

"What about you, Pat?" Jerry asked. "Will you be joining up when you get back to New York?"

"Joining up? Joining what?"

Jerry and Dickey glanced at each other.

"Well, the navy or the army, I suppose," Jerry said. "You showed great courage and clarity of thought in the way you rescued Miss Slayton. Our country could use men like you."

"I don't know," Pat said. "I'm not one to rush into things. I have a good job that I enjoy and that pays well. What if this all blows over in a couple of months? Then I would be stuck in the military. If I'm drafted, I'll go willingly, but I'm not ready to volunteer just yet."

Midway through dinner a young lieutenant wearing the braid of an admiral's aide approached the table and came to attention.

"Excuse me, gentlemen," he said.

"Yes, mister, what is it?" Jerry asked.

"Admiral Kimmel sends his regards and wonders if, after your dinner, you and your party would join him for dessert and coffee."

"What?" Jerry asked in surprise. "The admiral has invited us to join him? Are you sure you have the right table?"

The officer looked at Sean. "You are Sean Hanifin, aren't you, sir?"

"I am."

"The admiral saw your name on the passenger manifest of the Pan Am Clipper. When he learned that you were having dinner in the club, he asked me to give you this message."

"Well, that restores my faith in gut instinct. I knew he wasn't interested in Dickey or me," Jerry said with a chuckle.

Sean looked across the table at his hosts. "We are your guests, so I leave it to you. Do we accept the admiral's invitation, or not?"

Dickey laughed. "It's probably not good form for a junior officer to reject an admiral's invitation."

"May I add, sir, that the admiral is a great fan of yours," the aide said to Sean.

"Well, as someone who is also a great admirer of Sean Hanifin, I would hate to see the admiral miss out on this opportunity," Jerry said. "So, Dickey, I guess that leaves it up to you."

"Oh, no," Dickey said, grinning. "There's no way I'm going to turn him down. I don't plan to spend this war at some supply depot in New Mexico."

Sean turned back to the admiral's aide. "Thank the admiral for his kind invitation, and tell him we would be pleased to join him."

"Very good, sir. Thank you."

"Does an admiral really have that much power?" Pat asked.

"That much power? What are you talking about?" Dickey asked.

"To send you to a supply depot in New Mexico."

Dickey laughed. "Pat, when you do come into the service, whatever branch it is, the first thing you need to learn is the concept of *powerbus maximus*."

"*Powerbus maximus?*"

"It means admirals and generals have more power than God," Jerry said.

"Oh, I hardly think so," Diane said.

"Diane's father is a minister," Pat explained. "So she's pretty much an expert on the power of God."

"Yes, well, I may have overstated the case a bit," Jerry said, laughing. "But be advised that admirals and generals are very powerful people."

Admiral Eric Kimmel's admiration of Sean Hanifin showed. He talked about several of Sean's books with remarkable detail and was fascinated by Sean's personal history, eliciting several stories about his experiences as a struggling writer.

Like many authors and artists in the early twenties, Sean had lived in Paris for a while. And to Admiral Kimmel's delight, Sean spoke of the early days when he, Katie, and little Pat had lived in a fourth-floor walk-up on the left bank of the Seine. Their flat consisted of two rooms with mattresses on the floor and a tiny brazier which, according to Sean, had a prodigious appetite for the tiny but costly lumps of coal.

"We lived near a saloon where men and women stayed drunk all the time, or at least when they could afford it," Sean said. "But we avoided it as much as we could."

"Sure'n you'll not be forgettin' the bakery and its wonderful smells, are you now, Sean?" Katie put in.

"Wonderful smells? They were maddening. They got our appetites raging, and money was so scarce that we often had to make do with yesterday's crust."

"Oh, but when we could buy them, those loaves were like a wee taste of heaven, they were."

"Oh, it all sounds so exciting," Diane said. She looked at Pat. "Can you remember living there?"

"I remember a little of it," Pat said. He smiled. "I remember the man with the monkey."

"There was an organ grinder who used to work the corner in front of our house," Katie said. "Sometimes he would let Pat give the monkey peanuts."

"I kept trying to talk him into stealing a few of the peanuts for us," Sean growled. "That blasted monkey ate better than we did."

The others laughed.

Jerry and Dickey had remained quiet during the discussion, partly because they were fascinated by what was being discussed, and partly because of military courtesy. They were a little surprised then, when Admiral Kimmel turned his attention to them.

"So tell me, gentlemen, how did your ship fare in the attack?"

"Not very well, I'm afraid, Admiral," Jerry replied. "We were with the *Turner*."

"Were either of you aboard?"

"No sir, we had just come in from a cruise, and she had a skeleton crew aboard."

"Thank God for that," Kimmel said. "I'm sure you two are anxious to get another destroyer as soon as possible."

"No, sir."

"No?" Kimmel raised his eyebrows. "I would have thought you would want another sea assignment right away."

"We do want a sea assignment, Admiral," Jerry said. "But both of us feel there is a better way to get into the war. A destroyer minesweeper is, by definition, a vessel delegated to be on the periphery of things."

"What type of assignment would satisfy you?" Kimmel asked.

"Submarines, sir."

"Submarines?"

"Yes, sir. Dickey, uh, that is, Mr. Traser, and I are both graduates from submarine school. But when we joined the fleet, there were too few submarines in service to give us a berth. I have a feeling that they are going to be turning out more submarines than we can count."

"I wouldn't doubt that," Kimmel answered. "Our fleet is so crippled now that submarines may be our only hope in the Pacific. So, are submarines to be your next assignment?"

"We hope so," Jerry said. "Since the attack, we've applied to be transferred."

"I'll do what I can do toward seeing those transfers go through."

Jerry and Dickey's faces lit up with wide smiles. "Thank you, Admiral," they said as one.

Kimmel cut them off with a wave of his hand. "I don't know how much weight my recommendation will carry right now."

"What do you mean, sir?"

"It seems I no longer have active command over the Pacific Fleet. I've been called back to Washington. General Short has been called back as well," he added, as if taking some comfort in the fact that he wasn't going down alone.

So the rumors are true, Jerry thought. He and Dickey had heard that Kimmel and Short would have to pay the price for the disaster. He felt that some response was called for but didn't know what would be appropriate.

"I'm sure the War Department has some very important assignment for you," Sean said. "With this war just starting, they aren't going to beach one of their most experienced officers."

"Yes, sir, I'm positive of that as well," Jerry said.

Kimmel smiled wanly. "Would that this table were making the decisions," he said. "No, I'm afraid I'm going to be forced into early retirement. The biggest sea war in the history of man, and I, a professional sailor, will be beached."

There was a period of awkward silence then, broken by Pat.

"What about Guam or Wake, Admiral? Are we going to relieve them?"

Kimmel shook his head. "I doubt it. We would have to cover any relief effort with carriers, and right now those carriers are the only thing standing between us and Japan."

Sean sighed. "If it's any consolation to you, Major Devereux had already figured that out. He told me personally that he didn't think he would be relieved."

"I'm interested, Mr. Hanifin. How was his morale? And the men, how were they?"

"Morale?" Pat asked. "We're leaving four hundred men to die on that island, and you ask about their morale?"

"They are marines, son," Admiral Kimmel said gently. "I don't expect you to understand it, but they are prepared to die."

"What about you two?" Pat asked Jerry and Dickey. "I just heard you volunteer for submarine duty. That's very dangerous, isn't it? Are you prepared to die as well?"

"If you stop and think about it, Mr. Hanifin, everyone should be prepared to die at any time," Jerry replied. "You're going back to New York, and I've seen the traffic in that city. You could get hit by a car while crossing the street."

"That may be true, but I'm not searching for it as you and Mr. Traser seem to be. All this talk about dying, and you were trying to recruit me a while ago?" Pat shook his head. "Well, while your white uniforms are very sharp looking, I think I will pass on the opportunity to wear one. Especially if it means serving in a submarine."

"I think you misunderstood me, and you have underestimated yourself," Jerry said. "I don't relish the idea of getting killed in the line of duty, but I will not let a fear of dying keep me from performing that duty. Just as you did not let fear of dying prevent you from pulling Miss Slayton away from that fuel storage tank."

Sean chuckled. "Son, if you were fencing with Mr. Cornelison, I believe he could now say *touché.*"

Pat smiled, then nodded. "You are a good man, Lieutenant Cornelison," he said. "I'm glad I came to this dinner tonight. Speaking as a civilian, it is reassuring to know that men like you, Lieutenant Traser, Major Devereux, and the brave marines with him are defending us."

"Hear, hear," Admiral Kimmel said, raising his glass in a toast.

Pearl Harbor
December 12, 1941

Pat had thought that Diane would be returning to the States on the same ship, but at the last minute, her father had given up their passage, saying he was sure there were people with a more urgent need to return. Pat and Diane spent as much time together as they could for the last few days of Pat's stay in Hawaii. Then, on the day of his departure, Diane came down to the docks to see him off. They were in the passengers' lounge, sitting together as they waited for the last call to board.

"We have four kisses left," Pat said. "Shall we use them all up?"

"Not all of them," Diane said. "I think we should keep a few in reserve, in a bank, as it were."

"Good idea. That way, we can cash them in anytime we want."

"As long as you don't go to another bank to cash them," Diane teased.

The ship's horn sounded, then an announcement was made over the speaker system in the lounge. "All persons holding passage for the *Luriline* are advised to board at once. The ship will get under way in exactly fifteen minutes. All passengers aboard, please." Pat and Diane kissed, then they kissed again, again, and again.

"Oh," Diane said. "Our kisses are all used up."

"Good," Pat said.

"Good?"

Pat smiled. "Now we can start making deposits." And he kissed her yet again.

There were hundreds of people on the deck of the ship, and many more hundreds on the pier below, yelling and waving at each other as the ship prepared to get under way. He felt it begin to move as the tugs pulled it away from the dock, and with the onset of movement, those ashore threw confetti and bunting streamers while the band played "Aloha Oe."

Pat's parents were already below deck in the cabin, but he'd stayed above, waving at Diane. The people on the pier grew smaller and smaller, but Pat remained where he was until he could no longer pick out Diane. But even though he couldn't see her, he was sure she was still there.

The ship moved forward through the channel, while behind them Pat saw the Royal Hawaiian Hotel gleaming in bright pink against the shore. In the distance, the mountains rose in lush, tropic greenness above the multi-colored houses and buildings of the city. Losing all sight of the pier now, they passed Moana Park, the Yacht Basin, Fort De Russey, and Waikiki. Diamond Head was slowly coming up on the bow.

Pat was wearing at least a half-dozen leis, ranging from colored paper to plumeria to white gardenias. He'd been told the Hawaiian legend, "Throw your lei overboard as you pass Diamond Head. If it floats ashore, you will return. If it comes toward the ship, you won't be coming back."

As they passed Diamond Head, scores of people stood at the rail, all anxious to test the legend. Pat threw all of his leis overboard. Some floated toward the ship, others toward shore. He chuckled. "So much for the legend," he said aloud.

"What do you mean?" A middle-aged man in a white suit had overheard Pat's comment.

"I threw my leis overboard," Pat said. "Some went in, some went out. How do you interpret that?"

"Easy," the man said. "It means you will be coming and going to Hawaii many times."

Pat laughed. "I guess that's one way to interpret it."

"It's true," the man insisted. "My first trip to the islands was in 1928. I threw several leis overboard as I left, and some of them floated ashore while others floated out to sea. Little did I know at the time that I would take a job that would require many visits to Hawaii. I'm returning home now after my fifteenth trip."

McKinley Slayton had been pulled from his church in Japan just in the nick of time as it turned out, but he had no church to go to in the States. Therefore it was easy for him to give up his passage by saying he had no urgent need to return. But there was another, unspoken truth as to why he wasn't anxious to go back. It had been so long since McKinley had lived in America that he wasn't quite sure he would be able to readjust. He had always been considered somewhat of an odd duck anyway, perhaps half a beat out of step with his peers. What if he didn't get a church when he returned? Worse, what if he got a church, and he didn't fit in?

His ministry in Japan had been perfect for him. The Japanese culture was so different from America's that no one saw anything odd about him. He was simply American. He wouldn't have that cultural divide to protect him when he went back to the States. He knew he was going to have to face it sometime, just not yet.

He found a solution to his dilemma when he had lunch with a college classmate who was now a navy chaplain. The friend informed him that with the rapid build-up in the armed forces, there was a need for chaplains. Through that same friend, McKinley applied for a position, was accepted, and subsequently was sworn in with the rank of Lieutenant Commander.

Diane was going through her own period of difficulty. She had never had a boyfriend before, not even when she was attending school in the Philippines with other Americans her own age. Now she had one, but he was far away. Sometimes at night, she would think of him and could almost feel the brush of his lips against hers. She missed him terribly, sometimes even to the point of feeling a heavy sadness. Was this a broken heart? She had read about broken hearts, both in American and Japanese novels. That emotion seemed to transcend national cultural difference, so it must be real. Could one suffer a broken heart from a relationship that had been fewer than two weeks in duration?

Diane also found it difficult to accept the fact that the United States, her native country, was at war with Japan, a country whose people she had loved her whole life. Strangely, she even felt a degree of guilt, as if by living in Japan she had somehow committed an act of betrayal against the U.S. Her father said that such a feeling was totally unjustified, and intellectually Diane knew that he was right. Still, she couldn't shake the feeling.

She was convinced that her father might have gone through the same period of self-doubt, though he would never admit it, and had resolved it by joining the navy. And in a belief that what was good for him would be good for her as well, Diane decided to find her own way to serve in the war effort. Besides, it might help her deal with missing Pat Hanifin.

There were many civilian jobs available and, because she could type, take dictation, and file, she was sure she would qualify. On the day her father reported for duty on board U.S.S. *Lexington*, Diane took a taxi to the Navy Office of Civil Employment.

"Fill out this form and take a seat," a navy yeoman told her, handing her a clipboard.

The yeoman went back to typing. The popping sounds of the key-strokes were interrupted frequently while, muttering under his breath, he attempted to correct his mistakes.

Diane sat where indicated, filled out the form rather quickly, then handed it back. For her address, she was able to list the apartment she and her father had taken just two days earlier. She made no mention of the time she had spent in Japan.

As Diane sat waiting and listening to the yeoman's painfully synco-pated typing, she looked around the office. A gaily decorated Christmas tree stood in the corner, its silver tinsel stirred by the breeze of a stand-mounted fan. The words *Merry Christmas*, formed by letters cut from alternating red and green construction paper, were taped on the wall just behind the tree.

A little bell tinkled over the door, and a bicycle messenger, a young Hawaiian, entered with a pouch. His messenger's uniform was topped off by a Santa Claus hat. The yeoman stopped typing long enough to take the pouch and sign the receipt, then the messenger left, not one word spoken between the two.

Diane had been waiting in the outer office for nearly half an hour when the phone rang. Since it had rung several times during her stay, she paid no attention to it until she heard the yeoman say, "Yes, sir, she's still here. Yes, sir."

Diane looked toward the yeoman hopefully.

"Miss Slayton?" he said. "Lieutenant Dancer will see you now."

"Thank you."

Diane put aside the magazine and went into the office. Lieutenant Dancer, the personnel officer in charge of civilian employment, was a slender young man whose thinning hair made him look older than his years. He looked over Diane's application form.

"You left your employment history blank," he said. "You've never worked?"

"Only for my father. He's a pastor. I typed out pew sheets, letters, and reports and also kept books for him."

"It would be good if you had some sort of job history."

"There are many churches who hire secretaries to do what I was doing," Diane said in her defense. "If I had been doing the same thing for any church other than my father's, I would have been paid."

"Why didn't your father pay you?"

"He didn't think it would look good for him to use church funds to pay a member of his own family. I agreed with him."

"But you can type, and you can take dictation?"

"Yes."

Dancer sighed, rubbed his cheek for a moment, then picked up a piece of paper and handed it to her. "All right, let me see you type this. You can use that typewriter."

"Okay." Diane took the paper from him and walked over to a small desk with a large Royal typewriter on top. She rolled two pieces of paper into the machine, hit the return lever, and looked down at the paper she was to type. She hesitated.

"What is it?" Dancer asked. "Why aren't you typing?"

"Is this a joke?"

"What do you mean, is it a joke? No, it's no joke. I want to see if you can type."

"I mean this paper. It says it is a list of translations into Japanese."

"Oh, I didn't realize I had given you that." He picked up another paper from his desk and took it over to her. "This is a test we give to our Japanese translators. Why would you think it was a joke?"

"Well, look at this line, for example. In English it reads, 'When two vehicles arrive at an intersection at the same time, give way to the vehicle on the right.'"

"That's standard traffic procedure," Dancer said.

Diane smiled. "Perhaps so, but in Japanese it reads, 'When two vehicles arrive at an intersection at the same time, both shall stop, and neither shall proceed until the other is gone.'"

"What? Are you sure?"

Diane laughed. "I'm sure."

"You read Japanese?"

"Yes."

"Just a minute." Dancer picked up the phone. "Tell Kuroshu to come in here for a moment," he said.

113

A moment later an elderly Asian man came in. "You sent for me, sir?"

"This is Miss Slayton," Dancer said. "Miss Slayton, this is George Kuroshu. Mr. Kurosho was born and raised here in the islands, but he is of Japanese descent and speaks the language."

"I am honored to meet you, Kuroshu-san," Diane said in Japanese.

The expression on Kuroshu's face reflected his surprise at hearing the language spoken so flawlessly by an American woman.

"How is it that you speak Japanese?" he asked, answering in Japanese.

"I have only recently arrived in the islands from Japan," Diane said. "I lived in Japan for many years."

"Hold it, hold it!" Dancer said, waving his hand back and forth. "I don't like it when people are talking in front of me and I have no idea what they are saying." He looked at Kuroshu. "I take it then, that Miss Slayton does understand Japanese?"

"Yes, sir," Kuroshu replied. "She seems quite fluent, in fact."

Dancer handed Kuroshu the list of translations that he had inadvertently given Diane. "Read this line."

Kuroshu looked at it, laughed, and handed it back to Dancer. "That is a very funny joke!"

"Joke? It's not a joke! It's part of a test that we got from the Secretary of Navy. There are thousands of these out."

"Oh. A thousand pardons then. I didn't know it wasn't a joke. I apologize."

"No, no, no, don't apologize. Don't you see, it's . . ." Frustrated, he stopped in midsentence, then continued. "It's not anything you did wrong." He ran his hand through his thinning hair and sighed. "All right, that'll be all. You can go now."

Without another word, Kuroshu bowed his head slightly toward Dancer, then toward Diane. He left, and there was a moment of silence before Dancer spoke again.

"It would be a waste of manpower to have you working as a clerk typist. If you don't mind, I'm going to recommend that you go where you'll be more useful."

"I'll be happy to work wherever you need me," Diane said.

8

New York
Christmas Eve, 1941

When John Henry Welsko asked Pat if he would like to go to church with him for Christmas Eve services, Pat demurred.

Pat had been christened as a baby and as a child attended parochial school. In those days he was also a regular at Mass, rarely missing a Sunday. But when he was seventeen, during a meeting of the church youth group, Pat got into an argument with a priest. Pat hadn't intended to be blasphemous, nor even argumentative. In fact he was enjoying a fascinating conversation that promised to peel back some of God's mystery, or at least open it up to a spirited and spiritual discussion.

But Father Landers didn't see it that way. The priest, who was in charge of the youth ministry for St. Francis Xavier Catholic Church, became angry and tried to change the subject. When Pat persisted with his questions, Father Landers, with a purple vein standing out on his temple, stood up and pointed to the door of the parish hall.

"Get out!" he shouted, spraying spittle as his voice cracked. "Get out of the church, and don't come back until you are right with God!"

It did not escape Pat's notice that Father Landers had said "the church," and not "this church." Pat had not set foot in a church of any denomination since that day.

John Henry had heard Pat's story before. "I'm sure the priest wasn't speaking for the entire Catholic church, Pat, and I'm positive he wasn't talking for all of Christianity. I mean, didn't Jesus welcome sinners, lepers, and tax collectors? Surely you don't think He would turn His back on an inquisitive seventeen-year-old, do you?"

Pat chuckled. "No, I guess not."

"You want to know what I think? I think you've been using that as a convenient excuse now for six years. Come on, Pat, it's Christmas Eve, and our country is at war. What better time would there be for you to go to church?"

"I don't know," Pat said. "You're what, Baptist? I'm Catholic! I'd probably feel very out of place."

John Henry laughed. "With your record, you'd feel out of place anywhere. But, maybe we can compromise."

"What do you mean, compromise?"

"We'll go to the Christmas Eve service at an Episcopal church. It's Protestant, but there's lots of liturgy, so you should feel right at home. Besides, I'm told they have a wonderful organist and a magnificent choir. You might enjoy the music."

St. Thomas Episcopal on Fifth Avenue was constructed in the high Gothic style with ornate stonework, both in the windows and in the small arches of the triforium. Inside, behind the chancel, the reredos was one of the largest in the world, and approaching it gave one the illusion of standing before the gates of heaven.

The visual impact on Pat was augmented by the music, an organ with tones so rich that they resonated within every part of his being. The men and boys' choir sounded as if they were angels sent to earth to bring some peace to the soul in these tumultuous times.

During the prayers of the people, blessings were invoked for "President Roosevelt and all the officers and men of the armed forces who are now in harm's way, defending the freedoms that we so enjoy."

A significant number of the more than one thousand worshipers were in uniform. During the service, Pat kept looking toward them, wondering if this would be their last Christmas. As he studied their earnest faces, he thought of where they would be going from here and how they would carry the battle to the enemy at sea, on land, and in the air.

Recalling a conversation he had had with Pauley Todaro last week, he thought of his own situation. The club owner told Pat that business was so good he was going to raise Pat's pay from $100 to $125 per week.

"Think about it," Pauley had said. "You'll be making as much money as a general."

"What?"

"That's right. I saw a pay scale for the armed forces in the newspaper last week, and I cut it out so I could show you." He laughed. "What do you think about that, my friend? All these high-and-mighty generals and admirals ordering men to battle get $500 a month. That's what I'll be paying you, just for tickling the ivories."

"How much does a major make?"

"A major? I don't know; let me see." Pauley took out a folded piece of paper from his billfold. "What do you care what a major makes, anyway? I told you, you'll be making as much as a general."

"The man who was commanding the troops on Wake Island was a major. I met him the day the war started, and I was quite impressed with him. Major Devereux knew he was facing certain annihilation, but he did it with courage and dignity."

"And he was a major, huh?" Pauley asked, as he unfolded the piece of paper to examine the pay scale. "Okay, here it is. Major Devereux is making $250 per month. Ha! The good major is out there on Wake Island, up to his bottom lip in Japs, and he's doing it for $250 per month. Half of what you make. What do you think about that?"

"I think I would have a hard time looking into the eyes of a hero like Major Devereux and telling him that I make twice as much money as he does," Pat replied.

"Pat?"

Snapping out of his reverie, Pat looked over at John Henry. "What?"

"The service is over."

The organist was playing the postlude as the parishioners filled the center and side aisles on their way out of the church.

"I was just, uh, listening to the organ," Pat said.

"It is beautiful, isn't it? It wasn't just the music though. You were a thousand miles away."

Pat nodded. "Yeah, I guess I was."

"Are you having second thoughts about what we did?"

Pat chuckled. "Second thoughts? No. It's a little late for second thoughts, wouldn't you say?"

New York
Christmas Day, 1941

There was no greater manifestation of the financial success of Sean Hanifin's literary career than his home just outside East Chatham. The large English Tudor house was located squarely in the middle of a fifteen-acre estate. On grounds that were liberally dotted with maple, pine, and holly trees, a meandering stream served the deer, fox, and other wild creatures that had free range of the property.

On Christmas morning, the house was filled with the aromas of nutmeg and cinnamon, fresh-baked bread, and ham. The glistening ham, decorated with pineapple rings and red cherries, sat in aromatic grandeur on top of the kitchen stove. Katie, who had just taken it from the oven, was getting dishes down from the china cupboard when Sean sneaked into the kitchen and, behind her back, started to pinch off a little piece of the meat.

"Don't you be for disturbing my ham now, for if you do, sure 'n' I'll be coming after you with m' shillelagh," Katie said, without turning around.

"Blast, woman, do you have eyes in the back of your head?"

"It isn't eyes I'm using, Sean Hanifin; 'tis nothing but the wits God gave me, for I know you."

"I wasn't going to take a very big piece."

"Aye, just a wee bit you say, and the next thing I know you'll be for makin' yourself a ham sandwich big enough to feed all of County Cork."

"Have some compassion, woman. I'm starving to death, and there's no telling what time Pat will get here."

Katie began setting the table. "Didn't his wire say he would be arriving on the ten o'clock train? Promise me now that when he gets here, the ham will be as lovely as it is now."

"I'll not be making another attempt," Sean promised.

"I'm glad he could come for Christmas," Katie said. "And I'm glad that he's bringing John Henry. Christmas should be spent with family and friends."

"I have a feeling this may be his last Christmas with us for a while."

"And why would you be for saying such a thing?"

"Katie, you don't expect Pat will just sit out this war, do you?"

Katie sighed and leaned against the counter. "I, I don't know what I expect." Tears sprang to her eyes, and she lifted the hem of her apron to wipe them.

"There is such a thing as the draft, you know," Sean reminded her. "And with the buildup in the military, I would be very surprised if he didn't have to go within the next few months."

"I know," Katie said. "Don't think for a moment this hasn't been on my mind. I'm grateful for every minute we have him, and I can't help but think of those poor boys we met at Wake and Guam. Somewhere they have mothers and fathers who are praying for them . . . as I am. 'Tis said the Lord doesn't give a body a burden that's too heavy to carry."

As it was Christmas Day, there were very few people at the depot, enabling Sean to park his Packard right up by the station platform. That was good because it was cold outside, and this way he could wait for the train in the relative warmth of his car.

The "ten o'clock" arrived at 10:07, rumbling into the station with its drive-wheels wreathed in drifting feathers of glowing white steam.

Squealing to a stop, the locomotive sat puffing and popping as the gearboxes cooled in the cold gray air. From the third car behind the engine, two young men stepped down onto the brick platform. Pat and John Henry were the only passengers to detrain at the East Chatham Station.

"I'll serve pumpkin pie and coffee in the living room," Katie offered after dinner.

"Can I have my pie with—"

"Extra brown sugar and cinnamon," Katie finished. "An' did you think you would have to remind your own mother of that, Patrick Hanifin? Didn't I raise you from the crib?"

Pat laughed. "I just didn't want you to forget."

The Christmas tree glistened with multicolored lights, shining ornaments, red and green satin cords, and hanging tinsel. With their pie and coffee, they moved to the living room where they sat around an open fire exchanging presents and listening to Christmas carols on the record player. Then, surrounded by piles of wrapping paper, colorful bows, and discarded boxes, they found a quiet moment. That was when Pat told them.

"I'll be reporting to the navy on Monday, January fifth," he said.

Katie gasped. "You got your draft notice?"

"No. I volunteered."

His mother wept quietly, but said nothing else.

"I didn't think you would wait for the draft," Sean said. "I am a little curious though. Since you didn't join up in that first mad rush after Pearl Harbor, what brought it on now?"

"If I told you, I don't think you would understand," Pat said. "I'm not sure that I do."

"Try me."

"I'm joining because I learned that as a nightclub piano player, I was making twice as much money as Major Devereux."

Sean was silent for a moment, then nodded his head and put his hand out to squeeze his son's shoulder. "I understand," he said. "And I've never been more proud of you in my life."

"John Henry, did you know he had joined?" Katie asked.

"Yes, ma'am," John Henry said. He grinned broadly. "I did too. We're going in together."

"And you report on the fifth of January?" Sean asked. "Where do you go?"

"Columbia University," Pat said.

"Columbia University? That seems like a strange place to report to join the navy."

"Not if you are going to midshipman school," Pat replied.

Navy V-7 School, Columbia University
April 4, 1942

Midshipman Pat Hanifin stood at the foot of his bunk awaiting inspection. Through the open window of his room came the sound of lower classmen going through the regimen of dismounted drill. The drill instructor's voice and the sound of the footfalls drumming against the macadam pavement in perfect syncopation floated in on the surprisingly warm air.

Although John Henry Welsko was in the same class as Pat, they didn't share a room. Room assignments had been made alphabetically, and Pat's three roommates were Paul Griffin, Tim Hawthorne, and Jack Hayes. Their college dormitory room had been built for two occupants, so the four men crowded it to the limits. The original beds were now stored in the basement, and in their place the Navy placed two sets of steel bunk beds.

Pat's bunk was a top one. The gray blanket that covered it was stretched so tightly that a quarter dropped from a distance of one foot would flip over. Pat knew this because he had remade his bed three times that morning in order to accomplish the feat. His spare blanket formed a dust cover over the pillow. His wall locker, like the other three, was open for inspection, the extra uniforms displayed with exactly one inch of the bar showing between the hangers as pre-scribed. On the floor beneath his bunk was a pair of shoes, the leather glistening from the painstakingly applied spit-polish shine. At the foot of the bunk, back to back, were the two footlockers belonging to the men who occupied the upper and lower bunks. The lids were open and the trays were set at an angle and lined with white towels that showed off, in a precise pattern, the never-used toilet articles: socks, handkerchief, extra belt and belt buckle that were kept spotless just for the inspection kit.

This was Saturday morning, and it was Pat's final weekend as a mid-shipman. Their training already completed, the midshipmen would be given a pass for the remainder of the weekend. They would return Monday, at which time they would be commissioned as ensigns. Before leaving, however, they had to pass this final inspection.

Lieutenant, junior grade Bryant stopped just in front of Pat. He studied Pat for a moment, looking for an infraction. When he seemed unable to find one, Pat breathed a bit easier. But his relief was premature, for just before Lt. (jg) Willie Bryant turned away, his eyes lit up.

"Midshipman Hanifin, how dare you insult your fellow officers-to-be and the United States Navy by standing your last inspection with your uniform in such a deplorable condition! What is that hanging from your pocket?"

"Permission to look, sir?"

"Permission granted," Bryant replied.

Shortly after Pat arrived at the midshipman school, Lieutenant Bryant told him that he had once flunked an English literature assign-ment in college because he couldn't successfully posit the values in Sean Hanifin's novel, *The Titus Papers*. "I can't get even with the author for that humiliation," Bryant informed Pat, "but I can take it out on his son, and mister, while you are here, I intend to make you rue the day your father ever wrote a word."

He had indeed made Pat's time as a midshipman miserable, but he hadn't been any harder on Pat than on anyone else, nor was he any harder than any other faculty officer. Pat realized that Bryant's threat wasn't anything personal; it was just a scare tactic, a part of the game, the hazing to which all midshipmen were subjected.

Pat glanced down at his shirt to see what the infraction was and noticed a tiny thread hanging from the button on his left pocket. That must be what Bryant was talking about.

"Well, Midshipman, do you see anything amiss?" Bryant wanted to know.

"Sir, there appears to be a thread hanging from the button on my shirt pocket."

"A thread? A thread? Mister, do you call *that hawser a thread?*"

Bryant leaned forward until his face was but a half-inch from Pat's, and Pat had the sudden, rather incongruous thought that he had never been that close to another human being's face without kissing it. He couldn't hold back the smile.

"Midshipman Hanifin, wipe that smile off your face!" Bryant sputtered.

Pat quit smiling.

"No, Midshipman, put the smile back!"

Pat forced the smile back onto his face.

"Now, wipe it off. Wipe it off, I say!"

Pat kept the smile frozen in place, then raised his right hand and stiffly moved it across his face. As he brought his hand down, the smile was gone.

Bryant's raised voice brought other tactical officers over to see what was going on.

"Is there a reason for that cable hanging from your pocket, Midshipman Hanifin?" Bryant asked.

"I have no reason, sir."

Now that the others saw what was going on, they were free to make their own creative contributions to the discourse.

"Are you aware, Midshipman, that the navy no longer depends upon sail?" one of them asked.

"Yes, sir, I am aware of that."

"And yet, you are clearly carrying a halyard around with you."

"Perhaps he intends to run up a flag," another suggested.

"Gentlemen, having attended gunnery school, I believe I can identify that as a lanyard," Bryant said, leaning forward to inspect the offending thread. "Yes, it is clearly a lanyard. Midshipmen Griffin, Hawthorne, and Hayes, stand to."

"Aye, aye sir," the three roommates answered.

"Griffin, you will be the spotter; Hawthorne, you will be the aimer; and Hayes, you the gunner. Once Griffin locates and identifies the target, Hawthorne will aim the gun, and Hayes will fire it. Do you understand your assignments, gentlemen?"

"Aye, aye, sir!" they answered as one.

Bryant turned to his fellow officers. "What caliber would you ascertain this gun to be, gentlemen?"

"I suggest we have him fire a few practice rounds," one of the other officers suggested. "Perhaps by listening to the sound of the reports, we can determine the caliber."

"I concur," Bryant said. "Midshipman Hanifin, raise your right arm in the semblance of a gun barrel, then give us a boom."

"Boom, sir!" Pat replied.

Bryant looked at the others. "What do you think?"

They shook their head. "A forty-millimeter at best," one of them said.

"Midshipman Griffin, have you identified the target?"

"I have, sir!" Griffin replied.

"What is the target?"

"Sir, the target is a Japanese cruiser of the *Wakaba* class, ten thousand ton displacement."

"A *Wakaba* class cruiser? Oh, my, a forty-millimeter will never do. Fire another round, Mr. Hanifin."

"Boom, sir!" Pat said, louder this time.

"Five-inch," one of the officers said.

"No, I make it an eight-inch."

"Do you think an eight-inch gun is sufficient for the job?"

"No, I think we should go to the very top. Sixteen-inch."

"Insufficient ordnance. Try again, Mr. Hanifin."

"*Boom, sir!*" Pat shouted.

"Close, but I'd say that's a fourteen-inch at best," one of the officers said, and the others agreed.

"Ordnance is still insufficient. One more time," Bryant ordered.

"BOOM, SIR!"

Bryant smiled. "Gentlemen, we are armed. Engage the target, Mr. Griffin."

"Sir, the target is a Japanese cruiser, *Wakaba* class, ten thousand ton displacement. Azimuth, zero eight five degrees. Range one-five, zero, zero, zero yards."

"Fifteen thousand yards? Mr. Hawthorne, the gun will require some elevation for that, do you not agree?"

"I agree, sir," Hawthorne replied.

"Very well, acquire the target and adjust the gun accordingly."

"Permission to return to my desk for a compass, sir?" Hawthorne asked.

"Very good, Midshipman, very good," Bryant said. "Permission granted."

Hawthorne moved quickly to his desk, took out a hand-held compass, then returned to Pat and, sighting along the arm, established the firing azimuth.

"Elevation, Mr. Hawthorne?"

"Aye, aye, sir," Hawthorne said. He started to lift Pat's arm.

"You can't bend that barrel, Mr. Hawthorne; it is constructed of case-hardened steel," Bryant said. "You will have to elevate the gun at its base."

Hawthorne put one hand on Pat's shoulder and the other in the middle of his back, causing Pat to bend backwards at the waist. When Pat was leaning back nearly forty-five degrees, Lieutenant, junior grade Bryant asked the other officers if they concurred with the gun setting. Each officer made his own adjustment, and in so doing, prolonged Pat's discomfort to the point that it was beginning to be painful.

"Gun is laid in, Mr. Hayes," Bryant said. "You may fire when ready."

"Aye, aye, sir," Hayes said. He reached up to the offending thread hanging from Pat's shirt button. The thread was so small that he couldn't grasp it with his thumb and forefinger, though he made several tries.

"Quickly, Mr. Hayes, quickly," Bryant ordered.

"Sir, I can't grasp the thr—," Hayes corrected himself quickly. "Uh, lanyard, sir."

"Improvise, Mr. Hayes. The Japanese ship is clearly getting away."

"Aye, aye, sir."

Hayes leaned over and managed to grab the tiny piece of thread between his teeth. Once he had the thread in his mouth, he jerked his head back. He raised his head up, with the thread in his teeth.

Pat was ready for it. Determined that they would not make him fire again for lack of sufficient ordnance, he put everything he had into it, bringing the sound up from deep inside. *"BOOM, SIR!"* Pat shouted at the top of his voice. The windows of the room actually rattled.

Bryant and the other faculty officers were surprised by the explosive sound, and Bryant actually jumped.

"Very good!" Bryant said, a big smile spreading across his face. "I guess it is true what they say about creative talent running in a family. Midshipman Hanifin's father is a gifted writer, and young Mr. Hanifin here is obviously a gifted actor."

Laughing over the sport they had enjoyed at the hands of the hapless midshipmen, the faculty officers left the room. Pat had not been given the order to secure from his uncomfortable, backward-leaning position, however, so he held it even after they were gone.

Fully fifteen seconds later, just as Pat had expected, Bryant stuck his head back around the door. From the expression on his face it was clear that he was surprised, and perhaps even a little disappointed, to see that Pat hadn't moved.

"You may secure from the firing position, Mr. Hanifin. Room, rest."

With the "rest" command, the men were free to stand down from inspection. They could now close their lockers, talk, sit on their foot lockers, lie on the beds, do anything they wanted within the confines of their room. They awaited only the general order of dismissal before they would get their last pass.

"Well now," Hayes said, laughing softly. "I must tell you, this is one I'll be telling my grandkids."

"Grandkids? What makes someone as ugly as you are think you'll ever get married and have grandkids?" Pat teased.

"I'm not waiting to tell my grandkids," Griffin said. "I plan to write home about it this very night." He laughed.

"You won't be able to write after I break your arm," Pat said. "A ten-thousand ton cruiser at fifteen thousand yards? Couldn't you have found a canoe at thirty feet?"

The men were still laughing when they heard the boatswain's call over the loudspeakers.

"Now secure from inspection. Liberty call. Liberty commences for all authorized personnel."

New York, The Emerald Club
Saturday, April 6

When Pat and John Henry showed up at the Emerald Club, all the employees greeted them warmly. Even Pauley Todaro, who had called them both crazy when they left, came out of his office to say hello.

"I have to say, you fellas look pretty sharp in your officers' uniforms."

"We aren't officers yet," John Henry replied. "We won't be until day after tomorrow."

"And I may not then, if Lieutenant, junior grade Bryant gets another shot at me," Pat said.

John Henry laughed. "You've put up with him this long, you'll get through."

"Say, would you like to play a couple of songs for old times' sake?"

"You pick up the dinner tab for John Henry and me, and you've got yourself a deal."

"They must not pay you fellas much if you're having to cadge for meals," Pauley said. "Sure, I'll pick up your tab." He laughed. "I was going to anyway."

"I was going to play, anyway," Pat replied, going to the piano.

He played a half-dozen songs in response to requests from those who remembered him. He also got requests and was warmly applauded by those who didn't remember, but who thought it patriotic to support a man in uniform. After he finished, he returned to his table, where he was surprised to see two naval officers sitting with John Henry. He came to attention.

"At ease, Mr. Hanifin," one of the officers said easily. "Don't you remember me?"

At first, Pat had seen nothing but naval officers; now he realized these were the same two officers he had met in Pearl Harbor.

"Yes, sir, you are Lt. Jerry Cornelison, and you are Lt. Dickey Traser," Pat said. "I take it you've met Midshipman John Henry Welsko."

"We have met," Jerry replied. He chuckled. "He was entertaining us with a rather amusing story about you imitating a sixteen-inch gun."

"Oh, it was amusing all right," Pat said in a tone of voice that clearly wasn't amused. His reaction caused them to laugh again.

"What are you doing in New York?" Pat asked. "The last time I saw you, you were in Pearl Harbor."

"We're just stopping by," Jerry said. "We're on our way to New London to pick a crew." He smiled broadly. "I've just been given command of *Angelfish*."

"*Angelfish?*"

"Officially, the SS-217. It's a new, Gato-class submarine, top of the line," Dickey said. "Jerry is the CO, I'm the XO."

"Well, congratulations. That's just what you wanted, isn't it?"

"It is," Jerry said. "Now, what about you?"

"We don't know," Pat replied. "We won't get our assignments until after we graduate."

"I can grease the skids for you," Jerry suggested. "I can put you on the fast track through an abbreviated, two-week course at submarine school. You'll be finished in time to report aboard *Angelfish* before we leave Mare Island."

"Why, I don't know, I—"

"I've already taken them up on their offer," John Henry said.

Pat looked at John Henry in surprise. "What? Why in heaven's name would you do that?"

"Look, Pat," John Henry said. "The way I see it, if I'm going to be in this war, then I want to be where I feel I can make a difference. I think submarines are the place. Besides, I think it would be exciting. Come on, Pat, you don't want to spend the entire war handing out blankets somewhere, do you?"

"No," Pat said. "If I'm going to be in the navy, I want to do something that counts. I've been thinking about flight school."

"That will take you almost a year," Jerry said. "With submarines, you'll be at sea a month from now."

"What about it, Mr. Hanifin?" Dickey asked.

"When you say 'at sea,' you mean, at sea in a submarine," Pat said.

"Yes," Dickey said.

"Do you remember when we had dinner together back at Pearl, and you told me that you and Mr. Traser wanted to serve on a submarine?"

"Yes, I remember."

"And do you remember my response?"

Dickey laughed. "I think you said something about how sharp-looking our white uniforms were, and how you wouldn't want to be on a submarine."

"Yes, I did say that. So, knowing that's how I felt, why would you ask me now?"

"Look, submarines aren't for everyone, I'll be the first to admit that," Jerry added. "That's why it's a volunteer force. But for those who do qualify, it is a place like no other. We are unique in all the services.

"And I asked you because I know that you have more gumption than you think you have. I also seem to recall that you said you had no interest in joining the navy in the first place. Yet here you are, less than forty-eight hours away from being commissioned."

"What do you say, Pat?" John Henry asked.

"I'll think about it."

Jerry shook his head. "I'm sorry, but you don't have time to think about it. If you want my help in getting this assignment, you have to make up your mind now. There is a two-week course starting Monday."

"We can't start Monday. Our commissioning is Monday morning at 0900."

"The commissioning ceremony is Monday," Jerry said. "But I can arrange for you to be sworn in as soon as you report for submarine school."

"You mean we won't even have time for leave?"

Jerry shook his head. "Not if you want to get into the next class at submarine school. And you'll have to be in that class in order to connect with *Angelfish* in time to deploy to Pearl Harbor. You do want to go back to Pearl Harbor, don't you, Mr. Hanifin?"

"What makes you think that?"

"That night we dined with you and your family at the Naval Officers' Club in Pearl Harbor, I seem to recall a very beautiful young woman with you."

"Miss Diane Slayton."

"I told them you and Diane have written each other just about every day," John Henry said.

"Trust me, Mr. Hanifin," Jerry said. "This is your best, and perhaps your only opportunity to see her again."

"All right, Mr. Cornelison, you've convinced me. Put me in for the submarine school."

"Yahoo!" John Henry said, so loudly that others in the club looked over toward their table.

Pat laughed quietly and shook his head. "I've gone mad," he said. "Quite mad, and it began when I gave up a five-hundred-dollar-a-month job to join the navy."

"You did *what?*" Jerry asked.

John Henry chuckled. "Pat was playing the piano here for five hundred dollars a month, and he chucked it all to join the navy."

"Now why would you do that?"

"Because I was making twice as much as the major who was in command on Wake Island."

Jerry shook his head. "Okay, you've convinced me, you are mad. But we can deal with that."

"You mean there would be a place for a madman on your submarine?" Pat asked.

Jerry laughed. "Madness is practically a prerequisite."

Pat saluted. "Permission to come aboard, sir."

Jerry returned the salute. "Permission granted."

9

McKenzie Pass, Oregon
April 22, 1942

Under a gray and threatening sky, a 1926 Pontiac labored toward the top of McKenzie Pass. Its forward progress had been reduced to that of a walk, and the noise of the straining engine and rattling fenders caused a rabbit to jump and bound quickly up the road, easily outdistancing the car. The road itself was narrow and rutted, bordered on one side by a mountain, and separated from the McKenzie River on the other by a deep ravine.

Ensigns Patrick Hanifin and John Henry Welsko had bought the car upon graduation from submarine school. They had no leave time coming, but they did have a ten-day delay en route before reporting to Mare Island and their new assignment aboard the submarine *Angelfish*. They decided to use that time to drive across the country rather than take a train. This wasn't a spur-of-the-moment idea; they had begun talking about driving to the Pacific Coast nearly a year ago, long before the war started.

Now the ten-day delay en route seemed to be the perfect time to follow through with the planned adventure; they realized that if they didn't do it now, they might never get another chance. They were taking with them a bottle of water from the Atlantic Ocean, and when they reached the Pacific, they planned to pour it into the sea.

They were warned before leaving Sisters, Oregon, that the road might be closed at McKenzie Pass. However, as they were inquiring about it, a traveling salesman said that he had just come through.

"You can still get through, but if you're going to do it, you better go now," the salesman said. "It looks like there's another snow coming, and after it hits, the pass will be closed until mid-May."

Now they wondered if they had made a mistake. The car was barely moving, and a light snow had begun.

"Maybe this wasn't too good an idea," John Henry suggested.

"Now you tell me," Pat replied with a chuckle as he steered around a rut in the road.

"What do you think? Are we going to make it through?"

"We don't have any choice," Pat said. "You heard what everyone said. If this storm breaks and we get snowed in here, they may not find us for a month."

The engine shuddered, knocked, and suddenly quit. Pat had to put on the brakes to keep from rolling backwards.

"What happened?" John Henry asked.

"I don't know." Pat pushed on the starter with his foot. It made a grinding noise, but the engine didn't catch.

"Now what?" John Henry asked.

"I'll hold the brake, you get out and find a rock or something to put behind a wheel," Pat replied.

John got out of the car, found a fairly good-sized rock, and wedged it in behind one of the back wheels. "Okay," he called.

Pat gingerly removed his foot from the brake. The car rolled back more tightly against the rock and held. Pat got out, opened the hood cowl, and stared at the engine.

"Do you know what you're looking at?" John Henry asked. It was bitterly cold, and he shifted from foot to foot and wrapped his arms around himself in an effort to keep warm.

"Not really," Pat admitted. Sighing, he closed the hood. "I wonder how far it is to Vida?"

"Twenty-five or thirty miles, I'd guess. Why? Are you thinking of walking it?"

"We may have to."

"Maybe someone will come along. We'd probably be better off staying in the car. At least it will protect us from the wind."

"Nobody is going to come along," Pat said. "You heard what that salesman said. Once the snow comes, this pass will be closed." He held out his hand and caught a few flakes. "Well, the snow has arrived, and you better believe that we are the only ones dumb enough to be up here." He let out a laugh.

"What are you laughing at?"

"Here I was worried about how dangerous submarine duty is, when it turns out I might die on top of a mountain in Oregon."

"We aren't going to die," John Henry said easily. "Someone is going to come rescue us."

"You actually think someone is going to come?"

"I just prayed that someone would."

"Well, good, good. Then we have nothing to worry about, do we?"

John Henry chuckled. "I'm glad the whole world isn't as cynical as you are."

Pat chuckled as well, and shook his head. "I'm sorry, John Henry," he said. "I don't mean to be cynical. But we are in a bit of a spot here."

It was mid-afternoon. The two had been stranded for nearly five hours and, while the threatened snowstorm had not yet materialized, it was getting colder. The car did help keep the wind off, but did nothing to hold back the bitter cold. They had opened their suitcases and put on extra shirts and sweaters.

"I'm hungry," John Henry said.

"Don't think about it," Pat replied.

"You mean, don't think about a big, juicy cheeseburger?"

"With french fries?"

"And fried onions?"

"And maybe a hot piece of apple pie with melted cheese," Pat said.

"Now who isn't thinking about it?"

"I'm not," Pat said. "I'm not thinking about any of that."

"I'm not thinking about it either."

They both laughed, then Pat said, "I don't know why we're laughing. We could starve to death."

"No, we won't starve," John Henry said. He shivered. "We'll freeze to death long before we starve to death."

"What do you mean, freeze to death? I thought you had the prayer fix in," Pat said.

"You know, it might not hurt for you to say a prayer as well," John Henry said.

Pat shook his head. "I'm not sure the Lord would listen to my prayers."

"What about Diane? Don't you think she is praying for you?"

"If she is, she would just be praying in general, not any specific prayer. I mean, how could she be praying for me to get off the top of this mountain? She doesn't even know I'm here."

"If she is praying in general, and you and I are praying specifically, then the Lord is bound to hear us."

"John Henry, how is it that you are such a religious man? Is that part of your Southern culture, or something?"

John Henry chuckled. "Yeah," he said. "You might say that."

Leaning his head back, John Henry closed his eyes to recall an event from his youth. A small smile played across his lips as he recalled the Rev. Marcus Luscom's Soul Salvation Traveling Cathedral.

Denbigh, Virginia
August 5, 1932

The old truck sat parked alongside Warwick Creek. A tall, bony man, dressed all in black, was using a coffeepot to carry water from the creek to the truck, where he would pour it into the radiator.

John Henry was twelve years old, and he was riding his horse back from town, having gone to the post office for his father.

"Are you broke down, mister?" John Henry asked, dismounting and walking over to the truck.

"I'm not broken down, brother," the man replied. "But Michael the Archangel is a little thirsty." He poured another pot of water into the radiator, and it snapped, popped, and gurgled as the water ran through the coils.

"Michael the Archangel?"

The man in black patted the fender of the truck. "That's what I call this noble steed." He smiled at John Henry and extended his hand. "The name is Luscom. Reverend Marcus Luscom. And you are?"

"John Henry," John Henry replied. "Uh, John Henry Welsko."

"Welsko. This, I believe, is the Welsko farm?" He took in the area with a wave of his arm.

"Yes, sir. It belongs to my father."

"I wonder if your father would allow me to erect a canvas cathedral here on these grounds?"

"A canvas cathedral?"

"A tent, my boy. A tent to keep God's children out of the sun when they come to the river to pray."

"Oh, I get it. You want to conduct a revival here."

"Not just a revival, brother. Reverend Marcus Luscom's Soul Salvation Traveling Cathedral. I am a messenger of the Lord and saver of lost souls."

"I could go ask my father if you could put up your tent."

"Cathedral, son, cathedral," Luscom corrected.

"Yes, sir, your cathedral," John Henry said. "I could go ask my father if it would be all right."

"This would be a perfect place," Luscom said. "It even has a river for baptism. I've always thought that baptism means more if it is done in one of God's own natural rivers."

John Henry laughed. "This isn't a river," he said. "This is a creek."

"Whatever it is, it is God's natural stream," Luscom said. "Tell your pa the Lord would look kindly on him if he would allow me to hold my revival here."

Mr. Welsko gave his permission, and every night for four nights John Henry came down to the canvas cathedral, where he sat on the front row and listened to the Reverend Luscom preach.

Luscom was a charismatic speaker and powerful preacher. He didn't stay behind the pulpit, but moved up and down the aisles, personally delivering the Lord's message to each individual. As word of the revival spread, attendance grew, until on the last night the field around the canvas cathedral was filled with cars, trucks, buggies, and wagons. Every folding chair was filled, but the sides of the tent were rolled up, and the overflow spread quilts to sit on the ground.

Luscom had a baptism every night. On the last night John Henry along with forty-seven others, walked down to the creek, where he allowed the Reverend Luscom to immerse him in the name of the Father, and the Son, and the Holy Ghost.

McKenzie Pass, Oregon
April 2, 1941

John Henry opened his eyes. He wasn't sure if he had been remembering or dreaming, but something had brought him back to the present.

"Do you hear something?" he asked.

Both men listened. The cold wind howled loudly as it swirled about the car.

"I don't hear anything," Pat said.

"I heard something," John Henry said. "I know I did."

"Maybe you just want to hear it so bad that . . . wait a minute!" Pat grinned broadly. "Wait a minute. I hear it too!"

Over the wind they could make out the unmistakable sound of an approaching engine. Looking up the road, they saw a Ford pickup cresting the hill.

"Get out! Get out of the car!" Pat said. "We've got to stop him!"

Both men jumped out of the car then stood in the middle of the road, waving desperately. When the truck drew even with them, it stopped, and an old, white-haired man rolled down the window.

"You boys look like you could use some help."

"Mister, truer words have never been spoken," Pat said. "You are heaven-sent."

The man smiled. "Indeed I am. What seems to be your problem?"

"Our car has broken down. I wonder if you could give us a lift into town?"

"Sure I can," the driver said. "But why don't we have a look at your car first? If we can get it running, you can drive yourselves into town. Besides, you'll need it to finish your journey."

"With this old pile of junk?" Pat said. "I'm afraid that's impossible."

"Well now, don't be so quick to sell this car short, son," the driver said. "Pontiacs are good cars. In fact, this is a 1926 model, the first year they were built. I used to work in the General Motors plant, in the Pontiac Division. I worked on this very model, in fact."

The old man got out of his truck and extended his hand. "My name is Kingsley, Charles Kingsley, but most folks around here call me Crackers. Let me have a look."

Crackers stepped over to the car and lifted the hood. Leaning over the fender, he stuck his head far down into the engine well.

"Yes, yes, here it is," he said. "The timing gear is broken."

"Timing gear? Is that something we can just take off and drive without?" John Henry asked.

Crackers shook his head. "No, you have to have a timing gear."

"Then we're skunked," Pat said.

"Not necessarily." He began walking back down the road.

"Where are you going?" Pat called to him. "What are you doing?"

Crackers just held up his finger, as if asking them to be patient. Then, about two hundred yards down the road, he stopped, stepped over to the edge, and looked down into a ravine. He made a motion with his arm, signaling Pat and John Henry to join him.

"Look there," Crackers said, pointing down into the ravine. It was about seventy-five feet deep, and there at the bottom, smashed against the rocks, was the rusting hulk of an old, once-brown but now rusting car. "That, my friends, is a 1927 Oakland! That's perfect!"

"What's perfect? That's an Oakland; this car is a Pontiac."

"It's perfect because in the early years, nearly all the parts between the Oakland and the Pontiac were interchangeable. The timing gear on that car down there isn't broken. I can use it to get you boys on the road again."

"Obviously, one of us is going to have to go down there for it," John Henry said.

"I'll go," Pat offered.

"Wait, before you start. I've got a rope in the truck."

Crackers walked to the truck and drove it back. He took out a rope and a wrench, and as John Henry tied the rope around Pat's waist, Crackers told Pat where to locate the timing gear and how to remove it.

"It shouldn't be too hard," he said. "Most of the time the workspace is restricted because of the radiator. If that's the case, just pull the radiator out of the way. We won't be needing it."

When the rope was secured Pat, clutching the wrench, started down toward the wrecked car, his descent assisted by John Henry, who was holding on to the rope above.

Pat saw that the car was lying on its left side. It was badly damaged from its tumble down into the ravine and was terribly rusted. There were also several bullet holes in the car.

"It's covered with bullet holes!" Pat shouted.

"I wouldn't doubt it. Old, abandoned cars are often shot at out here. I don't know why; they just seem to be targets," Crackers called down. "Do you see the timing gear?"

Pat peered into the engine well. The hood cowl was gone, as were most of the engine components: the carburetor, the starter, the generator. The radiator fan was broken and Pat pulled it away, then put his hand on the timing gear. He pushed and pulled against it, testing it. "Yes, here it is, and it's in one piece. How'd you know it would still be good?"

"I just had faith," Crackers replied. "Take it off and bring it up."

It took Pat a few minutes and a skinned knuckle to remove the gear, but it finally came free in his hand. Gingerly he pulled it up from the engine well.

"I've got it!" he shouted. "Listen, I'm going to tie it to the rope, and you can pull it up. Then send the rope back down for me."

"Will do," John Henry answered.

Once Crackers had the replacement part, it didn't take him too long to install and adjust the timing gear. Then, closing the hood, he stepped back from the car and looked over at Pat. "Get in and give her a try."

Pat slid behind the wheel, turned on the ignition, pushed in the clutch, and put his foot on the starter. The engine turned over a few times, then caught and began running smoothly.

"Great! Great!" Pat shouted enthusiastically. "What do we owe you?"

Crackers shook his head. "Why, you don't owe me anything, son. I did this as an act of Christian charity."

"I appreciate it, but I wish you would let us do something for you. After all, we did interrupt your trip."

"No, you didn't. I came up here to help you boys."

"What do you mean, you came up here to help us? How did you know we were here?"

"Now, don't tell me you weren't praying for help."

"Well, yes, we were, but . . . "

"Listen, I'd love to stay and talk with you boys, but the snow is beginning to come down for sure now. If we don't want to get trapped up here, we'd better get going right away."

Crackers agreed to follow them over the pass and on down into Vida. The drive was long and hazardous, the more so with the onset of both darkness and heavy snow. It was comforting though, to look in the rearview mirror and see the lights of Crackers' truck behind them. The vacuum-operated windshield wipers whooshed back and forth across the glass, barely keeping the snow pushed away.

"Did you hear what he said about coming up to help us?" Pat asked.

"Yes."

"Don't you find that rather strange?"

"Why would it be strange? We needed help," John Henry said.

"Yes, but how did he know we were up there? And how did he happen to come at just that time?"

"You could also ask how was it that he just happened to be retired from the Pontiac division, and how there just happened to be an old Oakland on the side of the road with a part that just happened to perfectly match what we needed," John Henry said.

"All right, I will ask," Pat said.

"And I'll answer. I prayed for a miracle, and God sent us one."

Pat laughed. "Come on; so what is Crackers, an angel or something?"

"No," John Henry replied easily. "He's a man, just like us. But, as they say, God works in mysterious ways."

"Right," Pat said.

"Look, we're coming into town," John Henry said. "There's a little café; pull in there. The least we can do is buy Crackers dinner."

Pat pulled off the road to stop in front of the café. John Henry turned in his seat to see if Crackers pulled in behind them, but the truck wasn't there.

"Where'd he go?" John asked.

"Crackers? He's right behind us."

"No, he's not."

"Sure he is, his headlights have been in my rearview mirror the whole time."

The two boys got out of the car and looked back down a road covered with snow. The pristine white was broken only by a single set of tire tracks.

"I don't understand this," Pat said. "He was right there."

"He must've turned off when we came into town."

"Turned off where?" Pat asked. "The river is on one side of us, the mountain on the other. There is only this one road."

"Maybe he stopped at a house," John Henry suggested. "Come on, let's get something to eat."

They went up onto the porch of the café, stamped their feet, then pushed the door open, their entry marked by a tinkling bell. A potbellied stove sat on one side of the room, glowing red from the burning, popping wood inside. The heat that radiated from it made the café warm and inviting.

A heavyset woman came from the back to greet them. The name tag on her dark gray dress read "Emma."

"Well, I sure didn't think I'd have any customers on a night like this," Emma said. "Coffee?"

"Yes, ma'am. And whatever you've got to eat."

"Oh, we'll find something for you, I'm sure," Emma said cheerfully. "You boys sailors?"

"Yes, ma'am," Pat answered.

"We don't see a lot of sailor boys in Vida."

"We're on the way to San Francisco."

"Little out of the way, ain't you?"

"We thought we'd have a little adventure en route," John Henry said. "But it's turned out to be more than we'd planned."

"I reckon so. You come through the pass, did you?"

"Yes, ma'am," John Henry answered.

"Well, you were lucky. That pass will likely be closed from now until late spring."

"Yes, ma'am, we truly were lucky," Pat said. "And believe me, it feels good in here."

"I'm sure it does, after being out in that. How about our Blue Plate Special? Roast beef, mashed potatoes and gravy, green peas, and biscuits. I just took fresh biscuits out of the oven."

"Sounds good," John Henry said, and Pat agreed.

As the boys waited for their meals, they looked around. It was typical of all the small-town cafés they had seen during their trek west—walls covered with calendars, Coca-Cola signs, menu boards, and photographs.

"Hey, John, look at this," Pat said, pointing to a picture on the wall. It was a photograph of Crackers.

John chuckled. "Well, at least we know we didn't imagine him."

Emma came back with their meals, and as she was putting the plates on the table, Pat pointed to the picture.

"You know this man?"

"Oh, yes," Emma said. "That's Charles Kingsley."

"Crackers?"

Emma smiled. "Yes, that's what his family and friends called him. Where did you know Crackers from? Oh, I bet it was Detroit, wasn't it?"

"No, I . . . "

"Bless his heart, he retired a few years ago," Emma continued, interrupting Pat. "He said all he wanted to do was come back here to live out the rest of his years. Then a logging truck lost its brakes and ran Crackers off the road, just on the other side of the pass. You can still see his car in the ravine. It's a brown Oakland."

"A brown Oakland. Then that was his car," Pat said.

"Yes. They don't make them anymore, but Crackers wouldn't give his up. He thought the world of it. Sweet old man."

"I agree," Pat said.

"Folks here were mighty sad when he was killed."

Pat had just started to take a drink of his coffee, and he jerked the cup away from his lips, spilling it.

"Oh, honey, is the coffee too hot?" Emma asked, wiping the spill from the table. "I'm sorry about that."

Pat felt his skin tingling. "Did you say he was killed?"

"Yes, when his car was run off the road. That's been, what, five years now, I think. Let me pour you another cup."

As Emma left, Pat and John stared at each other. Neither could say a word.

10

On board U.S.S. Lexington *in the southwest Pacific*
Sunday, May 3, 1942

As Lt. Comdr. McKinley Slayton (Chaplain's Corps), prepared for the Sunday-morning service on board U.S.S. *Lexington*, he considered the irony of his situation. For many years he had lived in Japan, ministering to the very people he was now at war with. And while he was taking no direct part in the war, at least to the degree that he wasn't shooting at Japanese, he was part of an American task force that was.

Up until now, Diane had been more involved with the war than he had been, working in naval intelligence, intercepting and translating Japanese war correspondence. *Lexington* had just completed one month of repairs back at Pearl Harbor, and Diane had told him, at least to the degree she could, the kind of work she was doing. She had also told him about Pat Hanifin, who would be arriving at Pearl Harbor soon, though not in time to see McKinley before he sailed.

McKinley would have liked to have seen the young man again,

especially since Diane and Pat had kept in touch with each other by mail over the last several months. What had started out as a casual friendship on the *China Clipper* had become much more serious. McKinley wasn't sure how he felt about such a serious relationship. Pat seemed like a nice enough young man, but he didn't have much of a religious base. And what religious background he did have was Roman Catholic.

McKinley didn't consider himself an anti-Papist. His best friend on *Lexington* was the Catholic chaplain, and McKinley was sure that there was no one with a more abiding faith than Father Than Kern. But he believed there were Catholics of faith, like Father Kern, and Catholics of birth, like Pat Hanifin. And often people like Pat depended upon the accident of their births to be all the salvation they needed. They were born Catholic, baptized into the faith as babies, and rarely made conscious decisions to believe in the Lord. On the other hand, Diane's faith was very important to her.

McKinley would never say anything to his daughter about his concerns. He knew her well enough to realize that the best way to encourage a relationship between them was to discourage it. Besides, didn't the Lord work in mysterious ways?

He heard the announcement over the ship's speaker system.

"Now church call, church call. Divine services will commence in five minutes. Protestant services will be held in the after bay of the hangar deck. Catholic mass in the forward bay of the hangar deck. The smoking lamp is out throughout the ship during divine services."

Bougainville, Pacific Islands
Thursday, May 7, 1942

Overhead, the white-hot sun beat down mercilessly, and waves of heat shimmered up from the trees. The lush growth of the jungle threatened to take back the base the Japanese had carved from it, and new growth could be seen almost daily.

At the edge of the jungle, just before the clearing, were two palm trees that supported a palm-frond roof. Beneath the shelter, sitting on a cut-down oil drum, Comdr. Yutaka Saito drank from a coconut shell and squinted out over the bay at the fleet of Vice Adm. Takeo Takagi.

There were ten ships in the fleet: two carriers, two heavy cruisers, and six destroyers. Saito was the air group commander on board the flagship and normally would be aboard right now, but the oppressive heat in the bowels of the ship had driven him ashore to seek a cooler place to sleep. Relief from the heat had been offset by attacks of swarming mosquitoes, and today Saito's body erupted with hundreds of bites, many of them scratched into open sores.

Bougainville, like many other southwest Pacific Islands, had seemed a lush paradise when they had first landed. There were beautiful wildflowers, snow-white sandy beaches, sparkling blue waters, and friendly natives who had welcomed them, not as conquerors, but as guests. But Saito and the other pilots were finely trained fighting men and rapidly grew bored with the dull routine and the lazy ways of the soldiers and sailors who operated in the rear areas and backwashes of the Japanese advance.

It was a lazy day for Saito. He had spent much of it napping, to make up for sleep lost during the night, when the mosquitoes had been so ruthless. When he wasn't sleeping, he was reading a book he had taken from the ship's library.

As he looked over the fleet, his eyes detected something just over the ships. It arrested his attention and caused him to put down his book. To a thousand other men in similar circumstances, nothing would have seemed unusual, but to Saito it was glaring. Within the shimmering heat waves, which made observers dizzy and altered their vision, there was a sharper, more focused heat wave coming from the ships. Though not showing smoke, their boilers were heating up. The ships were raising steam. They were about to get under way.

Saito stood and walked down toward the pier, still looking toward the ships with interest. He saw the senior commander ashore there and asked him about the fleet raising steam.

"Why do you ask such a question?" the captain replied. "I've received no word of movement. Surely Admiral Takagi would inform me if he intended to move his fleet."

"Are you sure you have no message?" Saito pointed toward the ships. "Look. Can't you see they are getting ready?"

"I see nothing. Don't you see the flags? They are showing harbor watch. Is that the message of a fleet preparing to get under way?"

"I feel I must return to my carrier at once," Saito said. He waved at a small harbor boat, and the operator headed toward the pier.

"I think you have been too many hours in the sun, Saito," the captain called. "If you were needed, you would have been summoned."

Saito ignored the captain and climbed down into the boat, then motioned for the operator to proceed at top speed to his carrier. He studied the ships as the boat cut across the harbor waters, and though all were still showing flags that indicated they were on harbor watch, he could not ignore the feeling that something was afoot. Finally they pulled up alongside the *Shokaku,* and Saito climbed the boarding ladder. The officer on watch saluted as Saito stepped aboard.

"Is Admiral Takagi on the bridge?" Saito asked.

"Yes, sir."

Saito hurried across the deck through the parked airplanes. For the most part, activity seemed as lazy as it had been on the day before. He climbed the outside ladder to the bridge, then stepped inside. Takagi, the fleet commander, and Admiral Hara, the carrier commander, were bending over a chart.

"Excuse me, Admiral Takagi," Saito said. "But are we getting under way?"

"How did you know?" Admiral Takagi asked in surprise. He looked sharply at Admiral Hara. "Have we made smoke?"

"No, Admiral," Hara replied.

"There is no smoke, Admiral," Saito said, taking the commander off the hook. "I could tell by the rising heat waves that the boilers were being fired."

Admiral Takagi laughed. "By the heat waves? Well, there is not much one can do about the heat waves, is there? Let us just hope that the island watchers who send messages to the Americans and Australians aren't as observant as you are, Commander."

"Then we are getting under way?"

"Yes," Takagi said. "We are proceeding at once to attack an American task force that has been spotted in the Coral Sea. Tell me, Commander, do you believe your men are capable of launching a night attack?"

"We can launch and recover at night. But if the American fleet is maintaining radio silence and light discipline, we may not find them."

"We won't be in a position to attack them before dusk," Takagi answered. "If we are to have any chance of success, it must be a surprise night attack."

"I will see to the arming of the aircraft," Saito said.

It was nearly an hour before anchors were weighed and the ships left. By that time all preparations had been made, and steam had been raised so that the ships slipped quickly and cleanly out of the harbor, leaving so swiftly that many of the shore-based personnel were startled on coming outside to notice the bay mysteriously empty.

Japanese long-range search planes had spotted the American fleet earlier, and now they were keeping the fleet under observation and reporting its location back to Admiral Takagi. Swiftly, the two opposing forces drew closer.

But it was the Americans who drew first blood, not from Admiral Takagi's fleet, but from a small carrier, the *Shoho*, which was running alone and unescorted. The pilots in the Japanese ready room heard the American attack commander call his victory back to the American fleet.

"Scratch one flattop."

The arrogance of the American pilots infuriated the Japanese, and they shouted and called out to Saito to lead them now so they could have revenge for the loss of the *Shoho*.

Finally, just before dusk, they were within striking distance of the American fleet, and Saito took off with twenty-six other planes to attack. They found nothing, just as Saito had feared, so with dwindling fuel, Saito ordered the squadron to return without having fired a shot.

As they flew back, Saito fretted over their failure. Perhaps if the

Japanese ships had radar, they could be guided toward their targets. Without radar, and with the Americans following absolute radio and light discipline, there was no way to . . . *What was that?*

Saito's windscreen was suddenly filled with two dark shadows, winking fire from the nose and wings. They were American fighters, attacking Saito's squadron from the darkness above! Even as Saito realized what was happening, two of the planes in his flight burst into flame. One flipped over on its back and blazed earthward like a comet, crashing into the sea far below. The other exploded in a brilliant white-orange ball of fire.

"Americans! Where did they come from?" Saito asked aloud. His was a squadron of torpedo bombers, scarcely a match for the American fighters.

"Saito-san, on our tail, on our tail!" his gunner suddenly shouted, and even as he opened fire, Saito stood his slow, clumsy plane on one wing, killing all the lift and letting it fall from the sky.

The plane fell several hundred feet, twisting and turning until Saito was able to kick it into a skid. This allowed the American to flash by, darker black than the black of the night, pinpointed by the tiny blue exhaust flame from the engine stacks and by the red glow of the night-lamps in the cockpit.

Saito kicked the rudder back and straightened the plane, then squeezed off a burst of machine-gun fire from the twin guns mounted on the nose. If he had been in a Zero, he could have followed the plane on down, hosing round after round into it until it blew up. But his craft was so slow by comparison with the American fighter that one quick burst was all he was able to manage before the enemy plane got away.

The Americans hit almost every target, and only the protective cloak of darkness prevented all of Saito's planes from being shot down. Finally, just when Saito calculated that his entire squadron was at the edge of fuel exhaustion, the Americans halted the attack and broke away. When Saito finally landed, he learned that nine of his twenty-six planes had been shot down. He feared that he would be relieved of his command for having lost so many, but Admiral Takagi knew the realities of warfare.

"Get some rest," he ordered Saito and his men. "We will launch another attack tomorrow."

On board the Japanese carrier Shokaku
Friday, May 8, 1942

The sun was high in the eastern sky when a scout plane returned to report that it had found the American carriers. Saito launched immediately afterward and circled above the fleet until the last plane was launched. In all there were seventy planes: nineteen Zeros and fifty-one torpedo and bomber planes. Let the Americans attack now! Let them come now and challenge him.

Saito took his squadron to twenty thousand feet and headed in the direction in which the war-operations room told him he would find the Americans. He pulled the oxygen mask to his face and tasted the rubber as he searched the distant horizon. Then he saw the Americans: two carriers and eight other ships. He wagged his wings until everyone saw him, then his formation got into position to launch the attack.

On board the American carrier U.S.S. Lexington
1100 Hours, May 8, 1942

McKinley was in the chaplains' office when the alert bell sounded.

"General quarters, general quarters! All hands man your battle stations! All hands man your battle stations!"

McKinley's battle station, as it was for all chaplains, was the ship's hospital, known as sick bay. Their primary job was to provide spiritual comfort to the wounded and dying, but their secondary job would be to assist, in any way possible, in caring for the injured.

"Anybody know what's goin' on topside?" one of the doctors asked.

"Yes, sir, we got Jap planes comin' toward us," a telephone talker said. It was his job to keep sick bay in touch with the rest of the ship.

The ship's anti-aircraft guns opened up and the shooting resonated loudly, almost as if the compartment were acting as a sounding board. Panic flickered across the faces of many.

"I don't like it down here," someone said.

"Would you rather be topside, with all the machine-gun fire and shrapnel?" another asked.

"No. I'd rather be—" His comment was interrupted by a loud explosion as a bomb went off close to the ship.

"Just a near-miss, folks," someone said.

"Charley, you didn't finish telling us where you would rather be."

"I'd rather be at the City Pig Café in Sikeston, Missouri," Charley said, and the others laughed.

Father Kern and the other two chaplains had arrived by now, and Kern drifted over to stand by McKinley.

"Glad you could make it," McKinley said. "I thought you might get cut off in another part of the ship when they closed all the watertight doors."

"I nearly did," Kern said. He chuckled. "I wish my old high-school track coach could've seen me leaping through the doors as they were coming shut. He would've made me his lead hurdler."

"It's getting hot in here," one of the other chaplains said.

"That's what happens when all the hatches are closed and the ventilators are shut off," a doctor responded. "Think about those poor guys down in the engine room."

"More bombs coming down!" the talker shouted. Almost on top of his shout, *Lexington* swung violently to starboard as it heeled over into a turn.

McKinley grabbed a stanchion to keep from falling. His mouth felt dry, his tongue, like a large bath towel, taking up all the moisture. When the ship came out of its turn, he walked over to the closest scuttlebutt to get a drink. The water was tepid and, amazingly, didn't even feel wet. When he rose up from the fountain, his mouth was as dry as it had been when he had leaned over.

He didn't get more than three steps away when a tremendous explosion roared through the ship. The shock was so great that it knocked him down, and even as he was falling he saw that several others were knocked down as well. Before he could regain his feet there was a second explosion, nearly as devastating as the first.

"Torpedo!" the telephone talker shouted over the excited shouts and screams of the men gathered nearby. "Torpedo hit, port side, amidship."

"Get ready for the wounded!" one of the doctors shouted.

There were three more sharp explosions, these from direct hits by bombs.

Within minutes the first of the wounded were brought into sick bay. Corpsmen started an immediate triage. Wounded were classified into three groups: those who could wait, those who could be saved if they were treated immediately, and those who were left to die because they were too badly wounded to be helped. Denying them care was a hard thing to do, but trying to save them would take precious time and resources away from those who could be saved. The chaplains had their own system of triage, and it was just the opposite: they went first to the dying.

The doctors, corpsmen, and chaplains tended to their duties, getting periodic reports from the telephone talker, who was transmitting information from the bridge.

"The Japs are gone," the talker finally reported.

"Well, we've got that to be thankful for, anyway," one of the doctors said.

The ship began to list to port, but damage control parties stopped the list at about seven degrees.

McKinley prayed with some of the dying and for those who couldn't pray because they were unconscious or in shock. Like the other chaplains, he went from man to man, praying over each regardless of whether he was Protestant, Catholic, or Jew. One young Catholic seaman asked McKinley to hear his confession. Looking up, McKinley saw that Father Kern was involved with one of the other wounded on the far side of the compartment.

"Son, Father Kern is busy right now. I am a Protestant chaplain. I'll get him over here as quickly as I can."

"I'm not sure I can wait," the wounded sailor said. "I need someone now. Please?"

"Then of course I will hear your confession, and I'll pray for you."

"Bless me, Father, for I have sinned," the young man intoned. He began his confession, speaking quietly, and McKinley leaned over to hear.

A moment later there was a huge explosion, this one as large or larger than the first.

"What was that?" somebody yelled. "I thought the Japs were gone."

McKinley looked over toward the talker and saw him nodding vigorously as he was listening. The talker's eyes grew wide.

"It's the aviation gasoline!" the talker shouted. "The fires are out of control, and the skipper has just ordered every one topside!"

"All right, walking wounded, out of here!" the chief medical officer shouted. "Everyone else, bear a hand. Help the ones who can't walk."

McKinley looked back at the sailor who had been giving his confession. The young man had died. "Lord, look kindly upon this brave young man, and receive him into your company of saints."

"Chaplains, go with the walking wounded," the chief medical officer ordered.

"Wouldn't we be of more help staying here with the others?" McKinley asked.

"No," the doctor said, shaking his head. "Some of the walking wounded are barely walking, and I can't waste any of my trained medical personnel with them. I'm going to need all of them to help me evacuate those who have to be carried."

"All right, walking wounded, this way," Chaplain Eddington called. Eddington, a commander, was the ship's senior chaplain. The wounded, many of whom had not yet been treated, stood and started up the ladder to the deck. Eddington sent Rabbi Friedman to lead the way, then told McKinley and Kern to work their way into the middle of the stream while he brought up the rear. They did not come into direct contact with the fire on the way up, but the smoke was so thick they could barely see, and by the time they stumbled out on deck, they were coughing and gasping for breath.

Just outside the hatch, sailors were directing the wounded away from the superstructure. Up here, smoke and flames were clearly visible, but because they were outside, there was no difficulty in breathing. A couple of the wounded stumbled, and one fell. McKinley helped him to his feet, then put the man's arm around his neck and half-walked, half-carried him over to a part of the deck that was the designated holding area for the wounded.

"The *Minneapolis* is coming alongside," an officer said to Eddington. "Admiral Fitch will be transferring his flag. We're going to send over the wounded as well, and you chaplains will be going with them."

"Are we abandoning ship, Mr. Keene?" Eddington asked.

"We have received no such order. So far, we are just transferring the flag and the wounded."

"Then why are you expelling us? We aren't part of the admiral's staff, and as you can clearly see, we aren't wounded."

"You're going," Keene said firmly.

At that moment, Admiral Fitch and his staff arrived. Eddington appealed to the admiral.

"Admiral Fitch, request permission for the chaplains to stay aboard."

Fitch held up his hand. "Commander Eddington, I don't get involved in the running of the ship. You know that. This is Mr. Keene's call."

Although Keene was just a lieutenant and Eddington a commander, Keene was an unrestricted line officer and had more authority under the circumstances.

Keene shook his head. "I'm sorry, Commander Eddington, but my orders are to evacuate the wounded and to use my own judgment as to who might be nonessential."

"I see. And are you telling me, Mr. Keene, that you consider God to be nonessential?"

At that moment there was another explosion, followed by a shock wave and blast of heat.

"What was that?" someone asked in a frightened voice.

"Munitions or fuel," Keene replied.

"I don't know about you, Mr. Keene," one old chief said. "But if many more of those things are going to happen, then I, for one, would like to have God with us for a while longer."

Keene smiled in surrender, then pointed to the place of the latest explosion. "Tell me, Chaplain, did you arrange that little blast for my benefit?"

"Well, it did get your attention, didn't it?" Eddington replied, returning the smile.

"Okay, you chaplains can stay a while longer. But if the situation gets any more critical, you're on your own."

"We are never on our own," Eddington replied.

For the next two hours damage-control teams conducted a losing battle against the flames, putting out one fire only to have another erupt, each more fierce than the previous one. The chaplains said prayers over the dead and dying, prayed with the wounded and frightened, and carried water to the men who were engaged in fighting the fires.

By 1700 hours Capt. Frederic Sherman was forced to abandon the bridge, now totally engulfed by fire. He and the officers and the men who had stayed with him climbed down the outside ladder, then ran across the deck to the starboard side to get away from the flames and smoke. Captain Sherman was met by Commander Seligman, the executive officer who had taken personal charge of the effort to save the ship.

"What does it look like down here, XO?"

"Captain, we're going to lose her," Seligman told him bluntly.

"No chance at all of saving her?" The captain's face, like the faces of everyone else on board, was blackened with smoke and soot.

"No chance, sir."

Sherman took off his helmet and ran his hand through his thinning hair, then nodded. "How long do you think we have?"

"I don't think we can stay aboard more than another hour."

"That bad, huh?"

"I'm afraid so, yes, sir."

"Very well. Abandon ship," the captain ordered.

"Aye, aye, sir," Seligman said. "Mr. Keene, get the word out, abandon ship."

Keene and two other officers, equipped with bullhorns, began moving through the sailors who were gathered on deck, issuing the order.

"All hands, abandon ship! Over the side! All hands, abandon ship."

"Commander Seligman, there's still a fire party down on the hangar deck," a telephone talker said.

"What?" Sherman asked in surprise. He looked at Seligman. "I thought I had ordered all personnel topside."

"We did order them up, Captain. I thought they had complied."

"Tell them to get up here, now," Sherman said to the telephone talker.

The talker tried to make contact, then shook his head. "I'm not getting through to them, Captain. The lines are down."

"You're going to have to go get them," Seligman said.

The telephone talker's eyes widened, and his face grew white. He looked toward the hatch that led down to the hangar deck. Smoke was pouring through the open hatch. "Sir, you want me to go down there?"

"No, belay that order," Seligman said quickly. "Do we have an OBA up here?" The oxygen breathing apparatus would allow someone to survive a smoke-filled environment.

"Yes, sir," the telephone talker answered. He took off his telephone headset and started toward the OBA.

"I won't order anyone down there," Seligman said. "I'll go myself."

"No, Commander, you won't go after them," Sherman said. "I won't risk losing my XO or anyone else on the chance that they might still be alive. I'm sure they are dead, or they would have complied with the order by now."

"How long since you last heard from them?" Seligman asked the talker.

"Just a couple of minutes ago, sir. Just before the line went dead. They said they were trying to come up, but that some debris was blocking them."

"Captain, if they were alive a couple of minutes ago, they may still be. We can't just leave them down there without at least trying."

"I'll go," McKinley said quickly, having overheard the conversation.

Both Sherman and Seligman looked at him in surprise. Sherman shook his head. "I appreciate the offer, Chaplain, but no."

"Why not?"

"For one thing, you aren't trained for this sort of thing. For another, you're too old."

"How much training does it take to go down a ladder, Captain? Besides, if anyone is still alive, but unable to make it out, they might appreciate a little spiritual comfort." McKinley took the OBA from the telephone talker. "How do you use this thing?"

"Just strap the mask on," the talker said, "and carry the oxygen bottle."

"Chaplain, you will not go down there," Sherman said again. "And that is an order."

"I'm sorry, Fred," McKinley said. "But I'm afraid that on this particular matter, I'm going to have to take my command from a higher authority. If you plan to stop me, you're going to have to use force." He started across the burning deck toward the hatch.

"Captain?" Seligman asked, uncertain as to whether he should order men to restrain the chaplain.

Sherman watched McKinley disappear into the smoke. "Let him go," Sherman said quietly. "And may God go with him."

"Yes, sir," Seligman replied. "I think that's pretty much a given."

Once through the hatch, McKinley put his hand on the railing, but jerked it back when he felt the intense heat. The ladder well, acting as a flue, was filled with smoke drawn from below, but the OBA worked perfectly. When he reached the hangar deck he kicked the door open and went inside.

The moment he stepped onto it he was hit with a blast of air far hotter than anything he'd experienced so far. His exposed skin turned instantly pink.

"Hello!" he shouted, but his voice was muffled by the OBA mask. He took the mask off and shouted again. "Hello! Anyone down here?"

Away from the flue effect, the smoke wasn't quite as thick, so he could function without the apparatus. Also, having survived the initial blast of super-heated air, his body acclimated to the elevated temperature enough to allow him to continue.

As he walked through the hangar he could see the overwhelming devastation. There were several twisted heaps of smoking metal, and it took him a moment to realize that they were all that was left of the parked airplanes. Others were burning, even as he picked his way across the rubble. In some parts of the deck he could see that fire had already melted through the steel, exposing large, gaping maws, with dangling beams and hanging wires that reached to the decks below.

"Hello!" he shouted again.

"Over here!" a frightened voice answered.

Quickly McKinley moved toward the sound until he came upon a large, collapsed beam and bulkhead. There were a few gaps and spaces, but no single place was large enough to allow even a small man to crawl through. He leaned over and looked through an opening to see the six-man fire-fighting detail. Two of the men were down, their wounds obviously serious. The other four were gathered around the two wounded. He recognized one of the men as Seaman Muley Lewis. Muley had achieved some degree of recognition in *Lexington* for having been trapped inside *Turner* when that destroyer rolled over after the Japanese attack on Pearl Harbor.

"Are you throwing a private party, Muley, or can anyone join?"

"Believe me, sir, we ain't havin' any fun," Muley replied. "You'd be better off finding your own party."

"Yeah, and when you find it, take us with you," one of the others said.

"You got a rescue team with you, Chaplain? You got somebody over there that can take down some of this wreckage so we can get out of here?" Muley asked.

"I'm afraid not, son. I'm all alone."

"What the . . .? Would you believe it? We're trapped down here and they send us a chaplain," one of the other sailors said angrily. "They may as well have sent us a Girl Scout."

"Well, actually, they didn't send me," McKinley answered. "I came on my own."

"Ease up, Goldman," Muley said resolutely. "Under the circumstances, I can't think of a better man to have. Chaplain, I ain't led all that good a life. But would you pray for me anyway?"

"Of course I will."

"Chaplain, I'm sorry about that remark. I'd appreciate a prayer also," Goldman said.

"Of course I'll pray."

"Just a quick one," Muley said. "Then you'd better get out of here while the getting is good."

Even as Muley said the words, a large piece of flaming wreckage crashed down behind the chaplain. Looking around, the chaplain realized that he was now trapped.

"There's no hurry, boys. Looks like I'm not going anywhere," McKinley said calmly. He stuck his hand through. "Let us pray."

Four hands joined his, and a moment later two more hands. McKinley started with the Twenty-third Psalm, and he was gratified to see that Goldman joined with the others in its recitation. Then he said the Lord's Prayer.

11

On board Angelfish *at sea,*
between Mare Island, California, and Hawaii
May 26, 1942

S tand by to dive!" Lt. Comdr. Jerry Cornelison ordered. "Clear the
bridge."

Ahhoooga! Ahhoooga! The Klaxon diving alarm sounded twice, followed by, "Dive! Dive!" over the 1MC, the boat's intercom system.

"Hatch is secured," the last lookout down said.

"Bleed air in the boat!" Lieutenant, junior grade Roberts said.

"Air holding, sir," Chief Persico said.

Compressed air roared into all the compartments. Watching the
barometer, Lt. (jg) Darrel Roberts, the diving officer, held up his right
hand, palm and fingers open. Abruptly, he clenched his fist and ordered,
"Secure the air!"

Roberts looked up at the hull opening indicator light panel, commonly
referred to as the "Christmas tree" because it had red lights to indicate
open and green to indicate closed.

"We have a green board, Captain," Roberts said.

"Five degree down angle, take her down to ninety feet," Jerry ordered. "One third ahead."

As air in the ballast tanks was displaced by water, the bow began to tilt downward. Roberts, standing behind the bow and stern planesmen at the diving station in the control room, adjusted the boat's trim by pumping water into the variable ballast tanks so that *Angelfish* would settle evenly fore and aft. The burble of water sluicing into the superstructure, then breaking over the decks and conning tower, drowned out the sound of venting and pumping. In the conning tower, Jerry walked the periscope around, announcing that both bow and stern were underwater. Gurgling around the conning tower gave way to the rush of water filling the bridge cavity and up the periscope shears.

Roberts adjusted the boat with more pumping and venting until he was satisfied with forward and after trim.

"All compartments report."

Tony Jarvis, on sonar, was also on the telephone. "Captain, all compartments report they are watertight."

With the compartments watertight, Jerry took the boat down to 250 feet. Pat, who was torpedo data computer (TDC) operator, stood in the control room with nothing specific to do now but ride the boat down. The hull popped and creaked under the pressure, but everything held.

"Take her down another 150 feet," Jerry ordered.

Although Pat and John Henry had made a few dives in their very abbreviated submarine school, neither of them had ever been this deep before.

Pat looked around the control room to see how the others were reacting. Each seemed to be concentrating on his job, and if any of them were frightened, none were showing it. He looked over toward Dickey, who was leaning against a stanchion with his arms folded across his chest. He was chewing on a rubber band, half of which was dangling from his mouth, and his face was an absolute study of nonconcern.

The creaks, groans, and clanks got louder as the pressure increased. Lieutenant Roberts called off the depth every 25 feet until they reached 650.

"Six five zero, sir," Roberts said.

"All compartments report," Jerry ordered.

Again Jarvis transmitted the compartment reports back to the captain. "All compartments holding, sir."

Jerry smiled, then patted the emblem of the boat. It decorated the submarine sail outside, and was reproduced on the after bulkhead of the control room. The artist was S1c. Tyler Hornsby who, before the war, had been an artist for Disney Studios. Nearly all boats had a pugnacious representation of the fish after which they were named. Some of the men had complained that *Angelfish* didn't lend itself to that kind of art and suggested they try and get the name changed. But that was before they saw the finished emblem.

Hornsby had painted a fish with a determined scowl. Standing on its back, holding reins in his left hand and a broadsword in his right, was the archangel Michael. Thunderbolts emanated from the tip of Michael's broadsword, and everyone agreed that, angel or no, this emblem well represented the fighting spirit of their boat.

Each of the officers and chiefs had a cup decorated with his own particular coat of arms. Pat's cup showed him peering through a periscope that rose from the top of a grand piano. On Jerry Cornelison's cup, he sported a football uniform and cradled a ball under his arm as he stiff-armed Tojo and ran through a field strewn with burning Japanese ships. Dickey Traser's cup showed him sitting on top of a railroad locomotive, holding a torpedo under each arm.

The idea of using Michael as the angel for their boat's emblem had come from the mess steward, Choirboy Jackson. Choirboy had become a genuine hero, awarded the Silver Star for shooting down a Japanese airplane on the day Pearl Harbor was attacked. As far as the rest of the crew was concerned, the fact that Jackson and Jarvis had gone to submarine school in order to become a part of the crew of *Angelfish* was a ringing endorsement of the captain and executive officer.

Even though all the officers and enlisted men of *Angelfish* had successfully completed submarine school, they all had to undergo "qualifications" as soon as they came on board—a series of written and performance tests administered by the XO and the chief of the boat.

During the rest of the voyage to Honolulu, Pat and John Henry, as well as the others who had not yet qualified, used every spare moment to learn as much as they could about *Angelfish*. They memorized facts until they sounded like walking encyclopedias: *Angelfish* was 311 feet long with a beam of 27 feet. The full load displacement was 1,810 tons, with a maximum draft of 17 feet, and from fore to aft there were nine watertight compartments.

The forward torpedo room had six twenty-one-inch torpedo tubes, with storage capacity for fourteen torpedoes. The sonar gear, escape trunk, and crew berthing facilities for fifteen men were located in this compartment. Here too, was a head for the officers.

Next came the forward battery compartment. The lower portion housed 126 rechargeable batteries. The upper portion held the sleeping quarters for the officers and chief petty officers. The ship's office and officers' shower were located on the starboard side of the passageway, and the officers' wardroom and serving pantry were located forward of the staterooms.

Continuing aft, the adjoining compartment was the control room. Here were the master gyro compass, periscope wells, steering stand, high-pressure air manifold, hydraulic manifold, six hundred-pound main ballast tank blowing manifold, bow and stern plane diving station, radio room, decoding equipment, and main ballast tank vent controls. Above the control room was the conning tower, where the TDC, radar stacks, periscopes, sonar equipment, gyro compass repeater, and various apparatus were located.

The conning tower was connected to the control room below, and the bridge topside, through watertight hatches. These two compartments, control room and conning tower, were the operations center of the ship.

Below the control room was the pump room, which housed the trim pump, used to transfer water from various tanks and control the trim of the boat. Under normal conditions, a one-degree dive angle was maintained by use of the trim pump and bow stern planes. The pump room also housed two air-conditioning compressors, a refrigeration compressor, low-pressure blowers, and a hydraulic pump for operating the rudder diving planes, periscopes, and ballast tank vent valves.

Beyond the control room was the after battery compartment. Below its main deck were another 126 battery cells. Above it were the galley, crew's mess, crew's quarters with bunks for thirty-five men, heads, showers, and a washing machine. Below decks were the ship's freezer and cold room. Enough provisions could be stored aboard ship for ninety days of operation, although fresh stores such as milk and vegetables would last only two weeks.

The crew's mess, with its four stainless-steel tables and eight benches, could accommodate thirty-two men at a time for meals. It was also a convenient place to study, play cards, write letters, and pass the time when not standing watch. At sea there was always a cribbage or pinochle game in progress. Fresh coffee, cold cuts, cheese, and homemade bread, biscuits, and rolls were available twenty-four hours a day. At mealtime the cooks used the compact galley to prepare steaks, roasts, chicken, ham, soups, cakes, pies, and desserts—some even topped with frozen strawberries and whipped cream. Pat had been told, time and again, that submarine crews enjoyed the best meals of any branch of any service, and the first few days at sea in *Angelfish* seemed to support that claim.

The next two compartments were the forward and after engine rooms, separated by a watertight bulkhead to prevent the spread of flooding. Each engine room contained two sixteen-cylinder, two-cycle GMC diesel engines, capable of producing 1,600 horsepower each at 750 RPM. The engines were connected to four air-cooled DC generators rated at 1,100 kilowatts and 415 volts. The forward engine room also housed two distillers for making fresh water from seawater at the rate of 5,500 gallons per week. An auxiliary eight-cylinder engine, with an output of 750 horsepower, was located below decks between the two main engine rooms. The auxiliary engine could be used for topping off batteries and for maintaining electrical current while in port.

Aft of the engine rooms was the maneuvering room, which housed the electrical controls, switches, rheostats, and control cubicle. In the control cubicle were levers for arranging the current flow from the four main diesel-powered generators to the four air-cooled main motors below deck. These motors were rated at 1,375 horsepower at 1,300 RPM, and were connected in pairs to reduction gears that drove the two propeller shafts. The reduction gears made a significant whine that could be heard throughout the boat when running submerged. On the surface, any combination of diesel engines could be used for propulsion or battery charging or both. The maneuvering room also had a crew's head, oxygen flasks, and a six-inch metal-working lathe.

The last compartment was the after torpedo room, which had four tubes in its after bulkhead, stowage for eight torpedoes, and sleeping and locker facilities for fifteen crewmen. The hydraulic steering rams were positioned on the port and starboard sides of the hull. This compartment also contained the stern diving plane tilting mechanism, external air salvage connections, and an escape trunk.

Pat and John Henry drilled each other several times on the questions they could expect on the qualifying tests. They also toured the boat from stem to stern, so that by the time they reached Pearl Harbor they knew and were known by everyone in the crew.

Pearl Harbor
Saturday, June 13, 1942

As the boat slipped into Pearl Harbor, Pat and John Henry were standing on the deck. The Royal Hawaiian rose in front of them, and Pat pointed out the window at the room that had been his when he was here last.

"I guess you're excited about seeing Diane again," John Henry said.

"Yes, very much so. Since her father was killed, I've been concerned about her. She has no one now. No relatives any closer than second cousins, and she's never met any of them."

"She has you," John Henry said.

The steady exchange of letters between Diane and Pat through midshipman school and submarine school had deepened their relationship. Of course, there was the chance that it had been an artificial growth, accelerated by the fact that it was easier to say things in writing than in person. But Pat was sure that that wasn't the case.

When he graduated, he could tell Diane only that he had received his orders. He couldn't tell her to what boat he had been assigned or where he would be going. Now he planned to surprise her by showing up in front of her desk.

But Pat was the one who was surprised. When *Angelfish* docked at Pearl, he thought at first that his eyes must be playing tricks on him. There was no way she could have known that he was arriving.

"I don't believe it," he said.

"You don't believe what?" John Henry asked.

Pat pointed to the pier. "That's her," he said. "That's Diane!"

Pat and John Henry were among those granted liberty as soon as the boat docked, so they approached Diane together.

"How did you know I was arriving today?" Pat asked, after Diane's welcoming kiss.

"What makes you think I came down here to meet you?" Diane replied, smiling broadly. "I meet all the sailors on all the ships."

He laughed and introduced John Henry.

"So you are John Henry. Pat has told me a lot about you," Diane said.

"Pat said you were one of the prettiest women he had ever seen, and I can certainly vouch for that," John Henry said. "I hope he wasn't as truthful about me. I'd rather people get to know all my idiosyncrasies from firsthand observation."

"He had nothing but the nicest things to say about you," Diane said. "How long is your liberty?"

"Three glorious days," Pat said. "We don't report back until Monday morning."

"That's very generous of your captain."

"What say we get a taxi and get away from here before someone changes his mind?" Pat suggested.

Diane smiled. "We don't need a taxi. I have a car."

"Wow," said Pat. "I'm impressed."

The car was a forest green, 1937 Ford convertible with brown leather seats. Pat whistled as they approached. "Hey, nice-looking car."

"It belonged to an army captain who was sent back to the States," Diane said.

Pat opened the door for her, then hurried around to the other side while John Henry climbed into the backseat.

"Radio too," Pat said. "Does it work?"

"Turn it on."

It took a moment for the tubes to warm up, then the car was filled with the rich, baritone of Vaughn Monroe singing "I've Got You Under My Skin."

"Wouldn't that be nice to listen to, with the top down, watching the moon over the ocean?" Pat asked.

"Hmm, sounds like I might be in the way here," John Henry said. "Why don't you folks drop me off at that pink hotel I've been hearing about?"

Diane laughed. "Well, in case you haven't noticed, there is no moon right now; it's the middle of the day. And I just managed to get off work long enough to meet you, so I'm afraid I'm going to have to get back."

"When will I get to see you?"

"If you don't have other plans, I'd like to have you both over to my apartment for dinner tonight."

"Both?" The tone of Pat's voice showed that he didn't find that idea particularly appealing. He flashed a warning look to John Henry.

"Oh, no, I definitely don't want to be in the way now," John Henry said.

Diane laughed. "Don't be silly. I have a friend who's dying to meet you. If she shows up at my apartment tonight and you aren't there, she is going to be very disappointed."

"You got John Henry a date?" Pat said. "Oh, well, that's different."

"I beg your pardon?" Diane asked.

"Uh, I mean, that's very nice of you," he said, recovering quickly. "What do you think of that, John Henry?"

"What does your friend look like?" John Henry asked.

"John Henry! I can't believe that you, always the Christian gentleman, would even ask a question like that," Pat said.

"Oh, uh, I just wanted to know so I would recognize her when I saw her," John Henry replied weakly.

"I'll help you pick her out. She'll be the one who isn't Diane."

Diane laughed. "I don't mind telling you about her. I think she is attractive. And she has a very nice personality," Diane said.

"A nice personality?" John Henry responded. "Well, a nice personality is, uh, nice," he said dispassionately.

"Don't worry, John Henry. You'll like her. I promise you will."

The dinner was memorable for two reasons. One was the shrimp tempura that Diane prepared as the entrée.

"I know that a Japanese dinner might not be in good taste right now," she said. "But there is a difference between good taste and tastes good. And in this case, the latter was the determining factor."

"It's delicious," Pat agreed.

The other reason the dinner was memorable was because it introduced John Henry Welsko to Carol Thompson. Carol was the daughter of an army colonel and a member of Diane's church. And Diane's assessment was correct; she did have a very nice personality. She was friendly, intelligent, and had a good sense of humor. In fact, her personality was such that John Henry was caught up by it even before he even realized that, with her dark eyes, olive complexion, high cheekbones, and full lips, she was also a very pretty girl.

Before the evening broke up, John Henry had made a date with Carol for the following day. It was good, Pat thought, that John Henry and Carol hit it off so well. That would give John Henry someone to spend the weekend with and, more importantly, allow him to be alone with Diane without feeling guilty about abandoning his friend.

Sunday was a special day. Diane had asked Pat to go to church with her, and though it wasn't how he had planned to spend his weekend ashore, he didn't want to miss any opportunity to be with her. And, because Carol attended the same church, there was no question but that John Henry would go as well. Diane and Carol picked them up in front of the hotel.

The first thing Pat and John Henry noticed when they pulled into the church parking lot was how many sailors were present. There were hundreds of them, including a large number of officers.

"What is this, a navy chapel?" Pat asked.

"No. It's a civilian church," Diane replied. "It's the church I always attend."

"Look at all the sailors. Are you sure you want to go here? We won't even be able to find a seat."

"We have reserved seating," Diane said.

Pat gave her a questioning look, but before he could say anything a sailor wearing a black Shore Patrol armband approached the car. Seeing Pat and John Henry he saluted; the two officers returned the salute.

"Are you Miss Slayton?" the sailor asked.

"Yes."

"I was told to look for you, ma'am." He pointed to the front of the church. "If you'll go up there, you'll find a parking place reserved for you."

"Thank you."

"What is this?" Pat asked as she drove through the crowded parking lot. "What's going on?"

"They are honoring my father today," Diane said proudly.

As they entered the church they were met by an usher, who escorted them down to the front pew. He removed the little felt rope that sealed it off and let them in. Pat was surprised to see, sitting in the same pew, an admiral and two captains. He hesitated for just a second.

"Go ahead, sir," the usher said.

The choir sang "The Navy Hymn," and Pat was surprised at how moved he was by the music. Then the vested civilian pastor addressed the congregation. By now the church was so filled that there were sailors standing along the walls.

"I want to welcome all our guests on this special day," the pastor said. "And I especially want to welcome Lt. Kenneth Kern, late of the U.S.S. *Lexington*. Father Kern was the Roman Catholic chaplain for the ship and a close friend of the man we are here to honor today, The Rev. Lt. McKinley Slayton. Father Kern."

Father Kern took the pulpit, delivering a homily in praise of McKinley Slayton's action. "Chaplain Slayton gave his last full measure of devotion to the six sailors trapped on the hangar deck of *Lexington*," he said. "Three of those men were Baptist, one was Catholic, one was Methodist, and one was Jewish. Not one among them was of Chaplain Slayton's particular denomination, but in those last terrible and yet wonderful moments, all were brothers, and all died in the loving embrace of prayer and God's love."

After the homily, Capt. Frederic Sherman went to the front of the church and he read a citation awarding McKinley Slayton the Navy Cross. Then he called Diane forward to accept the medal on behalf of her father.

"I think it is very appropriate that this particular medal be a cross," Captain Sherman said, "for this award commemorates not only Chaplain Slayton's military valor, but his commitment to his faith."

When Diane returned to her pew, she leaned into Pat, and he put his arm around her. They had experienced the beginnings of the war together and had been supporting each other ever since. He felt her tears on his shoulder, and indeed felt a lump in his own throat. But he also felt a pride that was greater than his ability to describe. He was proud to have known McKinley Slayton, even if only briefly, and he was proud now, to be here providing what comfort he could to his daughter.

It was dark by the time Diane took the two officers back to *Angelfish*. She stopped in a parking area that was as close to the pier as she could get. Carol, who was a nurse's aide, had to work that night, so she had been dropped off en route. As soon as they reached the pier, John Henry hopped over the side of the car from the backseat.

"I enjoyed being part of the group this weekend," John Henry said. "But I think you two could use a little time alone."

"I'll see you in a few minutes," Pat said. He waited until John Henry disappeared into the darkness. "Ahhh. Alone at last," he said, laughing.

"It wasn't so bad, was it?"

"No, I enjoyed the weekend. And I was particularly moved by the service honoring your father this morning. But that doesn't mean I want every weekend to be a group activity."

"I thought it might make things go easier for us if we weren't alone this first weekend."

"Why did you think that?"

"Pat, a lot of things have happened in my life over the last few months. Leaving Japan, getting into a war, meeting you, and losing my father. My letters to you became very, very important to me. I'm sure I got much more personal than I should have."

"I liked the fact that they were personal. And the letters were important to me as well."

"I think we should take some time to see where we really stand with each other," Diane said. "We can start building our relationship now, this weekend."

"What do you mean, start building it now? What about what we had before? Doesn't that mean anything?"

"What we had before was nothing more than a shipboard romance, and an abbreviated shipboard romance at that. Then we had an exchange of letters, mine growing somewhat desperate because I needed you to help me through my grief. I just want to make certain that what we think we feel for each other is real."

"What I feel is real," Pat insisted.

"I believe that what I feel is real too," Diane said. "And if it is, it will stand the test of time. I just want us to be sure, that's all. I want us to be very sure."

She turned her face toward Pat, and as she did the silver glow of the moon gave her skin the opalescence of a beautiful alabaster statue.

Pat moved his face closer to hers. "I'm sure," he said. "I am very sure."

Their lips touched, at first, as gently as a rose petal floating on a pond. But the kiss deepened, and they held it for what seemed an eternity. When they finally separated, they looked at each other, caught up in the wonder of the moment.

Pat chuckled. "If this is building a relationship, I think we just put in the foundation, walls, and roof."

"I don't know what I see in you. You're an absolute nut."

"If I can get liberty next weekend, I'll call you," Pat said.

"You won't be here next week. But I'll be waiting for you when you come back."

"I won't be here? What do you mean? Where will I be?"

She grinned and said, "Good-bye, Pat. Stay safe for me."

Pat got out of the car and waited until she had driven away before he started walking toward the pier. He had wanted to ask her what she knew that he didn't, but he knew she wouldn't be able to answer him. He was sure that, even in suggesting that he was about to leave, she had told him more than she should. That meant that he was honor-bound to say nothing about it to anyone else.

The OOD was standing at the brow, and they exchanged salutes as Pat approached.

"Permission to come aboard?" Pat asked.

"Permission granted."

Pat felt a sense of superiority. Not because he knew something that the others didn't know . . . but because he had taken the first solid steps toward building a relationship with the most wonderful woman he had ever met. He was still smiling when he reached the officers' stateroom.

The smile faded when he saw John Henry packing his sea bag. "John Henry, what is it? Where are you going?"

"I've been transferred, old buddy. I'm going over to *Bullshark*."

12

Pearl Harbor
Monday, June 15, 1942

When they were first introduced, the Mark 14s were supposed to have been the latest innovation in torpedo technology. They were the answer to warships with side armor so strong that not even a direct hit would sink them. But while the side armor had been greatly thickened, the keel was left relatively thin in order to save weight. The Mark 14 was designed to take advantage of that thin skin by passing just underneath the target and exploding against the ship's soft underbelly.

Early on, skippers began to have serious problems with the Mark 14. The first was that it ran a lot deeper than it was designed to, causing many misses as the torpedoes tracked true but passed too far under their targets. The simple expedient of adjusting the selected depth of the torpedo upward by twelve feet corrected that. Then a second problem arose with the magnetic exploders. They were erratic, exploding as soon as they encountered the magnetic field, long before they could really do any damage to the ship itself. That was caused by the uneven magnetic bubble surrounding the ship, which tended to flatten out the closer one came to the equator. That phenomenon had not been taken into consideration, indeed, had not even been known, when the torpedo was designed.

After many angry exchanges of letters between the submarine commanders and the Navy Bureau of Ordnance, the captains were finally given permission to remove the magnetic exploders.

Angelfish's sixteen Mark-14 torpedoes were without the offending exploders. Pat watched as the torpedoes were loaded into the boat, lowered gingerly by cranes through the open hatches that led to the forward and after torpedo rooms.

It took most of the morning to board the consumables. It was just after noon when Cornelison stepped onto the bridge to issue orders for moving out. Pat couldn't help but feel a sense of excitement at this, his first war patrol.

"Let go all lines, fore and aft," Jerry called.

"All lines away, sir!" the bosun's mate on deck called up.

"All back two-thirds."

The telephone talker transmitted his orders, and *Angelfish* began backing away from the pier.

"Port ahead two-thirds, starboard back one-third."

The sub lost its sternway and began twisting around toward the basin entrance.

"All ahead two-thirds."

Jerry kept the con as they gathered headway and proceeded briskly through the channel at two-thirds speed. *Bullshark* was departing at the same time, so the two boats were running together, with *Angelfish* in the lead. Pat stood on the bridge of the latter and John Henry on the bridge of the former, giving the friends an opportunity to wave at each other.

"I tried to keep Mr. Welsko," Jerry said when he saw the exchange. "He's a good officer. But *Bullshark* is short three officers, so there wasn't much I could do."

"I know, sir," Pat replied. "We've been lucky to stay together this long. And if we happen to be in port at the same time, we'll have opportunities to visit."

They passed the channel entrance buoys and headed out to open sea.

Angelfish was running on the surface at twenty knots. Pat was on the bridge as Officer of the Deck, and he was looking toward the horizon when the lookout called down.

"Aircraft off the port bow, sir, about thirty degrees from the horizon."

Pat turned in the direction indicated and raised his binoculars to his eyes. After a quick adjustment, the distant airplane came into focus. It was unmistakably an American PBY Catilina, the long-range twin-engine flying boat.

"It's okay," Pat said. "It's one of ours." Dropping the glasses, he turned to the telephone talker. "Report the sighting to Captain Cornelison."

"Aye, aye, sir." The talker gave the report, then nodded. "Sir, Cap'n wants to know if we have given the recognition signal?"

"Doing that, as soon as I check the SOI," Pat replied. In truth, from the moment he recognized the airplane as American, he had put it out of his mind, thinking it represented no danger. But Cornelison was right. He needed to get the recognition code from the signal operating instructions book, then flash that signal to the plane, since it would have a more difficult time identifying the submarine than they had in recognizing the plane.

"Here it is," Pat said. "Set signal lamp, three long, two short, two long."

"Aye, sir," the talker said, setting the signal light to flash continuously, automatically, once it was activated. The light began to flash.

"Report to captain that signals are being sent."

"Aye, aye, sir."

Pat watched the PBY approach, then saw it began to drop lower. He wasn't alarmed by the action, assuming the pilot either wanted to get a closer look at the signals, or, out of pure boredom from a long, routine flight, just wanted to buzz the sub.

The PBY continued its approach, dropping lower and lower. Then Pat saw two black objects falling from the plane.

"What?" Pat said loudly. "Those look like bombs."

As he focused on the two objects, he saw he was right. Then, as the

PBY turned, its right-side blister gun began shooting. Tracer rounds zipped down from the plane and popped in the water. The bombs continued to arc down.

"Clear the bridge!" Pat shouted. "Emergency dive!"

The bombs hit and exploded so close that water sprayed the boat.

"Dive, dive, dive."

Pat was the last one down and even as he was closing the dripping hatch, the deck pitched forward. He could hear the sounds of air, as if the boat were breathing, and he felt a tightness in his ears.

"Pressure in the boat!"

Not only could he feel the tilt of the deck, he also felt the boat slowing precipitously as it changed from surface running to underwater running. The boat continued down with pops, clanks, gurgles, and sloshes.

"You sure that was an American plane?" Cornelison asked.

"Aye, aye, sir. It was a PBY."

"Mr. Hanifin's right, sir. It was a PBY," one of the two lookouts said.

"Then why is the idiot bombing us? You signaled?"

"Yes, sir."

"If we've got idiots like this on our side, we don't have to worry about the Japs sinking us," Dickey said with a growl. "Our own people will do the job for them."

"Sonar, any sign of depth charges?" Jerry asked.

"No, sir," Jarvis replied.

"Mr. Traser, level off at 250 feet. Maintain heading of two-one-zero degrees."

"Aye, sir."

Pat walked over to the torpedo data computer, not because he expected to use it, but because it was his station. He looked around the control room at the Christmas tree of green lights and at the planesmen at their wheels. The two young sailors were intently studying the compass and depth gauge.

"Sonar, still no depth charges?"

"No depth charges, sir."

"Looks like we caught a break," Jerry said. "My guess is he's either out of depth charges or never had them in the first place. All he could do was drop a couple of bombs and take a chance."

"Yeah, well, we gave the identification signal. Why did the fool drop them in the first place?" Dickey asked.

Jerry was calmer now, with the danger past. "Either he didn't see our signal, he misunderstood it, or one of us was using the wrong SOI."

"If someone was using the wrong daily code, Captain, it wasn't us," Pat said, thinking it might be prudent to defend himself before the discussion went any further. "CinCPacFlt Fleet Signal Operating Instructions, 24 June 1942. Recognition signal three long, two short, two long."

"How much longer till sunset?" Jerry asked.

"Four hours, sixteen minutes," Dickey replied.

"We'll run submerged until then. Even if he doesn't come back looking for us, he may report us to someone else. Ahead one-half."

When *Angelfish* surfaced, Pat exited the boat even as the foaming seawater was still spilling from the forecastle. Lookouts in life jackets came up with him to take their places on the bridge. After half a day of running submerged, the cool night air was especially refreshing, and Pat couldn't help but feel a bit sorry for those who were still below. However, he knew that both the forward and after deck hatches would be open to allow fresh air throughout the boat, and that would help alleviate the stuffiness.

Overhead the sky was filled with a carpet of stars. One of the stewards came up through the forward hatch, carrying a pot. "Permission to jettison, sir?" Choirboy called.

"Permission granted," Pat said.

Choirboy walked to the edge and poured out the contents of the pot he was carrying. After that, he set the pot down and took a handkerchief from his pocket and wiped his face. He stood for a moment, looking out over the sea, then up toward the sky.

"Beautiful night, isn't it?" Pat said.

"Aye, sir, it is," Choirboy answered. "It makes a body want to sing praises to the Lord."

"I suppose so."

Choirboy looked up toward Pat. "Excuse me if I'm offending you, sir, but from the way you said that, it sounds like you don't give all that much thought to the Lord."

"I guess I just don't consider myself all that religious. My girl is, though. Her father was a pastor, a chaplain, actually. He went down with the *Lexington*."

"You'd be talking about Chaplain Slayton, sir?" Choirboy asked.

"Yes," Pat said in surprise. "Did you know him?"

"No, sir, but I sure know about him. He was a true warrior for the Lord."

"I suppose he was."

"You know, Mr. Hanifin, it's not my place to be preaching or anything, but religion can be a comforting thing."

"I'm sure that's true." Pat was leaning on the rail with his hands clasped in front of him. "In fact, once—"

Pat paused in midsentence. He was going to tell Choirboy about the experience he and John Henry had when their car broke down in the Cascade Mountains, but he held back, afraid of appearing foolish. He was sure there was a logical explanation for what happened . . . he just hadn't been able to figure out what it was.

"Yes, sir, you were saying?" Choirboy asked.

"Nothing," Pat answered. "I was just going to say that my friend John Henry is a religious man."

"I remember that about Mr. Welsko, what little time he was on the boat," Choirboy said. "Mr. Welsko is a fine Christian gentleman."

"What about you, Jackson? Have you always been as religious as you are now?"

"Yes, sir, I reckon I have been. My grandpappy and my pappy are both preachers. I suppose someday I'll be one too, but I wanted to see something beside my little corner of Georgia before I settled down. Still, I've always felt like I should tell other folks about the Lord. I've got a feeling lots of folks are going to be calling on Him over the next several months."

Pat chuckled. "So what you're saying is, we need to get on God's good side?"

"Oh, no need for that, sir," Choirboy said cheerfully. "God doesn't have a bad side."

"I guess that's right," Pat said.

The two men were quiet for a while, the only sound the rumble of the diesel engines and the rush of water past the keel.

"Look at all those stars. There are thousands of them, and they say there are millions and millions more that we can't see," Choirboy said.

"Ever wonder what's on the other side?"

"The other side of what, sir?"

"Well, the other side of the universe. I mean, millions and millions of stars, then what? Does the universe come to an edge, then quit? And if it does, what's on the other side of that edge? But one could also ask what is on the other side of life, I suppose." Pat chuckled. "Anyway, that was a rhetorical question, Jackson. I'm not expecting an answer."

"I reckon not, Mr. Hanifin, but I think the answer is the same in both cases. God is on the other side . . . of the universe, and of life."

The phone on the bridge buzzed, and Pat picked it up.

"Bridge."

"Pat, get a navigational fix, will you?" Captain Cornelison asked.

"Aye, aye, sir."

Pat put the phone down, then looked back toward Choirboy, but the steward's mate had already disappeared down the hatch.

August 9, 1942

It was a little after 0200 when Chief Persico shook Pat awake. "Cap'n's called everyone to battle stations, Mr. Hanifin."

"What?" Pat asked, coming up from a deep sleep.

Persico was grinning broadly, excitedly, in the red glare of the night lamps. "We've spotted a Jap ship."

It wasn't until then that Pat realized they were running silent, with ventilators off. There wasn't a breath of air stirring, and Pat's body was covered with a patina of sweat.

"Cap'n wants you in the conning tower right away," Persico said.

"Thanks. I'll be right there." He put on his shirt and pulled on his trousers, then slipped into his shoes and hurried to the tower. When he arrived, he saw everyone in position at their stations, exactly as they had done during practice runs. But this time it was for real, and the tension in the air was palpable.

"What's up?" he asked the executive officer.

"Our lookouts picked them up about an hour ago," Dickey answered. "We closed to five thousand yards before we submerged."

"Them?"

Dickey smiled. "Yeah, them. A whole fleet of Jap ships. Better get on the TDC, Pat. You've got work to do."

"Aye, aye, sir!" Pat said excitedly.

"Darrel, come to sixty-four feet," the CO ordered, speaking to the diving officer.

"Sixty-four feet, aye."

The boat tipped up, and the big, round gauge ticked off the depth.

Pat could hear a distant, swooshing sound. It took him a moment to realize what he was hearing—the cavitations of dozens of turning propellers.

"Up scope," Jerry said. As the scope started up, he bent down to meet it, draping his arms across the handles and putting his eyes to the viewer even before the periscope cleared the water. "Boys, this is it! A big, fat transport, escorted by two destroyers. Target angle on the port bow, zero two five. Down scope. Prepare bow tubes."

Sweat was running into Pat's eyes, and he wiped his forehead with the back of his hand.

"Captain, they're on an active search," Jarvis said, and almost as soon as he spoke the words, Pat heard the searching sonar.

Ping . . . PING!

From outside the boat the thrumming sound of heavy, slow-turning screws grew louder.

Ping . . . PING!

"Open outer doors, tubes one, two, three, and four."

"Up scope."

"Bearing, mark."

From the backside of the periscope, Dickey read the azimuth ring. "Bearing zero three zero degrees."

"Range, mark."

"Three thousand yards."

"Set," Pat said from his position at the TDC.

"Captain, enemy target course is two-seven-zero degrees. Speed is ten knots," Dickey said.

"I'm going to have a final look around," Jerry said, and he swept the periscope all the way around. All was clear except for the target and its escorting vessels.

"Range, mark."

"Two thousand yards."

Again Pat cranked in the range and confirmed it. "Set."

"Bearing, mark."

"Zero three zero."

"Set. Captain, we have a firing solution," Pat said.

"Very good, Mr. Hanifin. Fire one!"

Lieutenant Roberts repeated the firing order while slapping the palm of his hand against the red firing plunger.

In the forward torpedo room, another sailor stood watching the firing panel, ready for a manual launch should the electrical firing fail.

The electrical switch did not fail. Compressed air forced the water out of the tube and ejected the torpedo and its five-hundred-pound warhead. The turbine kicked in and the torpedo propeller whirled rapidly as the torpedo started its two-thousand-yard run at nearly fifty miles an hour.

Back in the control room, Darrel gave the report. "One fired electrically."

The same procedure was followed for three more shots, launching three more torpedoes. As the torpedoes were on their way, everyone in the boat could hear the torpedo motors whine, descending in Doppler effect as the four missiles sped toward their target.

"All torpedoes running hot, straight, and normal," Tony said.

"Time to impact of first torpedo, twenty-five seconds," Dickey said, looking at his watch. Everyone waited silently, looking at Dickey, who was timing the run. When it reached five seconds, he began counting down.

"Five, four, three, two, one." He brought his hand down sharply.

"Contact!" Tony Jarvis said from his sonar station. "I heard it hit!"

There was a brief cheer, then Jerry called for silence. "Where's the explosion?" he asked. "This isn't a training shot! Where is the explosion?"

"Another hit, sir," Tony said. "Still no explosion!"

"Scope up!"

Jerry got on the scope as soon as it was up and looked toward the target. It was still proceeding along its course, with no ill effects from the attack. But both destroyers were turning toward *Angelfish*.

"Down scope! Right full rudder. All ahead full. Take it down . . . deep!"

"Four degree down bubble," Roberts said.

"Belay that," Cornelison said quickly. "Eight degree down bubble. Flood negative! Rig for depth charges! Rig for silent running!"

The Japanese destroyers closed fast. As *Angelfish* passed 180 feet, four depth charges went off, so close that Pat could feel the boat pushed down and sideways. Topside on the boat, some piece of gear was torn away by the closeness of the charges, and as it tumbled across the deck, it sounded as if the boat was coming apart. They leveled off at four hundred feet, then ran slowly to the north, while overhead, the destroyers continued their hunt.

The Japanese were persistent, alternately pinging and listening, dropping depth charges, waiting patiently for the sound of a pump, a motor, the ring of something being dropped.

"All stop," Jerry ordered.

The noise of the electric motors and reduction gear stopped, and *Angelfish* lay dead quiet, the only sound now being those over which the men had no control, the occasional hull creak or a soft whir from the hydraulic system. Choirboy and the other steward came into the conning tower room. Barefooted, they moved as quietly as if they were gliding on air. Choirboy carried a large coffeepot, the other steward a tray of doughnuts. The officers and men smiled and nodded their thanks as the unexpected treat was passed out.

It had been just after 0230 when *Angelfish* launched its attack. At 0235 they made their emergency dive. It was now 0615, and they had lain quiet and unmoving for nearly four hours. The air conditioners and ventilators had been off all that time, and the temperature inside the boat was about 115 degrees. Jerry had long ago given the men permission to take off their shirts, and in the forward and after torpedo compartments many had removed their trousers as well and were wearing only their underwear.

"Sonar?" Jerry asked.

Jarvis listened over the headset as he made a sonar sweep.

"Nothing, sir," he replied.

"They're gone!" Roberts said.

"Maybe. There could be one still up there, waiting for us," Dickey said.

"Bring us to periscope depth, Mr. Roberts."

"Aye, aye, sir."

Slowly the boat rose toward the surface. When she reached sixty-four feet, the ascent stopped. Jerry made a motion with his thumb, and the periscope started up. As it did so, the noise of the periscope hoist motors and cable sheaves seemed unnaturally loud in the silent conning tower. Seawater trickled from the periscope's flax packing in the overhead, corkscrewed down the barrel, and made a puddle on the conning tower deck. Jerry paid no attention to it as he leaned into the eyepiece. Every man in the tower awaited his report.

Jerry walked the scope around twice, then snapped the handles up, a signal that it should be lowered. He smiled.

"They're gone," he said. "Surface the boat."

The welcome roar of high-pressure air blowing water out of the ballast tanks resounded through the entire boat. When she broke through the waves, the eastern sky was red with the rising sun. The air was cool and bracing, and *Angelfish* was ventilated with the engines. A battery charge was started, and a new course was laid in.

Pearl Harbor
September 10, 1942

A very dejected crew brought *Angelfish* back into port. There had been three target opportunities during their patrol. Three times they had set up the approach, closed to within two thousand yards, gotten a perfect firing solution, and launched their torpedoes. And yet not one Japanese ship had been sunk or damaged.

Jerry fired off an angry radio message as *Angelfish* came home, claiming that faulty torpedoes were the reason they had not sunk a ship. When the sub returned, he saw a shining black Buick with a star plate on the front bumper parked near the dock. Rear Admiral R. H. English's staff car. English was commander of all submarines in the Pacific.

His aide came aboard as soon as *Angelfish* docked. "The admiral's compliments, Captain, and he asks if you would join him?" the lieutenant said.

"Tell the admiral I would be happy to join him." Jerry saw another officer with the admiral as he and the aide approached the staff car.

"Who is that with the admiral?"

"That would be Captain Christie, sir. He's with BuOrd."

"Bureau of Ordnance, huh? Well, my message must have gotten through."

The admiral's aide chuckled. "Yes, sir, it did that, all right."

Jerry and the admiral's aide rode on the little jump seats that folded down from the back of the front seats. The admiral asked nothing substantive but carried on a polite conversation. How had the weather been? How was the food? Did they make their mail rendezvous on time?

"I know how important mail is to the men at sea," the admiral said.

"Yes sir, considering everything, we received the mail in a timely fashion," Jerry replied.

Captain Christie made the ride in silence, staring through the window as if unable or unwilling to look at Jerry.

Captain Willis, fleet commander, met them when they reached the headquarters. After an exchange of salutes, they went inside. The long hallway was flanked by doors with frosted glass windows. Gold-leaf lettering on the one leading to Admiral English's office read *ComSubPac*. A marine came to stiff attention and saluted as they approached. On the other side of the door was an outer office, manned by a lieutenant commander and three petty officers. The petty officers remained busy at their desks, but the commander stood as the officers entered.

"Billy, is the conference room empty?" Admiral English asked.

"Aye, aye, sir."

"Good, good. I'm going to be in there with these officers for a while. I don't want to be disturbed."

"Very good, sir," the lieutenant commander replied.

Jerry followed the admiral and the two captains into the conference room.

"Sit there, would you, Captain?" the admiral asked, pointing to a chair at one end of the table. He and the two captains went to the other end of the table, effectively creating a huge gulf between them.

Jerry couldn't get over the feeling of being an errant student, summoned to a high-school principal's office over some infraction.

"You are an Academy graduate, aren't you?" the admiral asked, when all were seated.

"Yes, sir, class of '36."

"Admiral, you may remember the Army-Navy game of 1935?" Captain Willis asked. "Army won by a score of 28 to 6."

English shuddered, then chuckled. "Now why would any navy man want to remember that game?"

"Jerry Cornelison scored our only touchdown," Willis said.

"Jerry Cornelison. Yes, I remember you now," the admiral said. "I listened to that game by short-wave radio from the army and navy officers' club in Manila. Up on the club wall we had a big green board, marked out like a football field, and we advanced the ball up and down the field to follow the play-by-play over the radio. Good for you, Captain. At least you kept us from being skunked." Admiral English cleared his throat. "Now, about this message you sent regarding the torpedoes. What was it you said? Something about a ram, I believe?"

"Yes, sir," Jerry said. "I suggested that the BuOrd get to work on a long battering ram that we could affix to the fronts of our subs. It's obvious they can't make torpedoes that will explode."

Captain Willis laughed, but English cut him off with a scowl. "Captain, I asked Captain Christie from the Navy Bureau of Ordnance to sit in on this debriefing. Suppose you tell him what happened."

"Nothing happened, sir. That's just it. We scored hit after hit, and the things wouldn't explode."

"This was your first combat patrol, wasn't it, Commander?" Christie asked.

Jerry noticed that, though Admiral English had extended him the courtesy of calling him Captain, in recognition of his role as commanding officer of a submarine, Christie insisted upon calling him by his rank.

"It was, sir."

"Do you not think it possible then, Commander, that, given the excitement of the first patrol and the inexperience of your crew, you may have just missed?"

"With every torpedo we fired?"

"Yes."

Jerry shook his head. "No sir. In the first place, experienced or not, I'll put my crew up against anyone's crew in technical expertise. Our firing solutions were perfect. And on top of that, sonar heard the torpedoes hitting the sides of the target ships."

"He heard what he expected to hear," Captain Christie said.

"I disagree, sir."

"The truth is, Commander Cornelison, there is nothing wrong with the exploders." Christie waved his hand. "I'll admit the magnetic exploders weren't as successful as we had hoped they would be. Personally, I still don't think there was anything wrong with them. I believe the problem was the inability of the captains to compensate for the magnetic anomalies. But the magnetic exploders have all been removed, so that what you have now is essentially the same thing you have always had, a contact detonator."

"There is something wrong with them," Jerry insisted.

"I'll tell you what is wrong with them, Commander," Christie said. "They are contact detonators. That means that they must make contact. In other words, you must hit your target in order for them to explode."

"I brought one torpedo back. I'd like for you to take a look at it."

Christie shook his head. "Why should I do that? There is nothing to see."

"All I'm asking is that you take a look at it," Jerry said again.

Christie started to reply again, but Admiral English held up his hand.

"I'd like to see it," he said. He looked at Jerry. "I'm going to be tied up until around 1600. Can you have it out of the boat by then?"

"Yes, sir, I'll be all ready for you by then."

"Good. We'll see you at four this afternoon."

13

B *ullshark* had returned from its own patrol, also unproductive, two days ahead of *Angelfish*. John Henry was on watch the first two nights *Bullshark* was in port, but he was on liberty now, and he and Pat took a room at the Royal Hawaiian. They arranged for Diane to bring Carol to the hotel at around three o'clock that afternoon.

As the two handsome young men in their white naval officers' uniforms rode the elevator down to the lobby, they were admired by a couple of high-school girls, who tittered to each other behind cupped hands. Reaching the lobby, the men glanced up at a clock and saw that they were at least a half hour early.

Pat chuckled. "Well, you can't say we are anxious or anything."

"It's just as easy to wait here as it is to go back to the room," John Henry said.

There was a grand piano in the lobby, and Pat walked over to it.

"Are you going to play something?" John Henry asked.

"I wouldn't want to disturb anyone."

John Henry laughed quietly. "Pat, believe me, your playing could never disturb anyone."

Pat put his hands on the keyboard, paused for a moment, and then the lyrical notes of Liszt's *A Faust Symphony* began to spill from the instrument. At first he played quietly, hesitantly, but as he got into it, he lost himself in the music, growing bolder and more expressive. By the time he reached the end of the number, the entire lobby was filled with the power of his music. People drifted over toward the piano, and by the time he was finished, quite a large crowd had gathered. Their applause was genuine and enthusiastic, starting even before the last echo had died.

Pat looked up, returning slowly to this time and place, and was surprised to see so many people gathered around him. He smiled sheepishly at their applause and nodded his head in appreciation.

"Thanks," he said. "Thank you very much."

"That was wonderful," someone said. "Won't you play something else?"

Looking around, Pat saw Diane and Carol standing near the man who had spoken.

"Thanks for the compliment," Pat said. "But I see that the people we're to meet are here."

As Pat and John Henry started toward the two women, there was another round of applause, which Pat acknowledged with a nod of his head.

"That was beautiful," Diane said.

"Thanks," Pat replied, and then, looking up, saw Chief Persico.

"Chief," Pat said in surprise. "What are you doing here?"

"Mr. Hanifin, maybe you'd better come back to the boat, sir. I think Cap'n Cornelison is about to kill himself."

"What?" both Pat and John Henry asked, reacting at the same time.

"He's plannin' something crazy," Persico said. "Mr. Traser, he tried to talk him out of it, but the cap'n says he's goin' to go through with it."

"I'll drive you there," Diane offered.

There was a crowd gathered around one of the slips of the submarine pen, but Pat noticed that they all seemed to be standing some distance back from the boat. Hopping out of the car, he ran over to see what was going on.

There, on the concrete dock alongside the submarine, stood Lt. Comdr. Jerry Cornelison. Suspended several feet over Jerry's head and held aloft by a large crane was a long, fully armed Mark-14 torpedo. It was hanging nose-down toward the concrete dock, several feet below. John Henry saw Lieutenant Roberts standing nearby.

"Darrel, you want to tell me what's going on here?" he asked.

"I think our brave and noble captain is about to prove a point," Darrel replied. He was silent for a moment. "Either that, or blow his head off. That thing is loaded with five hundred pounds of Torpex."

At that moment Admiral English's Buick came to a stop just behind the crowd. The admiral, Captain Willis, and Captain Christie got out of the staff car. Someone shouted "Attention!" and the crowd, mostly naval enlisted men, responded.

"What is this?" English asked. "What's going on?"

"Admiral," Jerry called to him. "Is Captain Christie with you?"

"Yes. Cornelison, what are you doing?"

"I'm about to give a demonstration, sir," Jerry answered. He was holding a button-activated switch in his hand. An electric cord ran from it to the top of the crane. "Here is your detonator, Captain Christie," Jerry shouted. He pushed the button, releasing the torpedo, which started down toward the concrete deck.

There was a quick gasp of surprise from the crowd, and several of them began pushing and shoving, trying to get out of the way.

Pat flinched and automatically wrapped his arms around Diane, putting himself between her and the point of impact.

The torpedo hit the concrete with a thud, bounced up, then fell back with a clang, rolling a few feet before it stopped.

"Cornelison, have you gone mad?" Christie shouted in anger and alarm.

"No, sir," Jerry replied. "I invited you down here to examine why the torpedoes didn't go off. I just wanted to give you something to look at, that's all."

"You should be brought up for court-martial!" Christie shouted.

"No, Captain," English said. "He should be commended for having the courage to force BuOrd into another look at these torpedoes."

"Admiral, with all due respect, sir, we've already gone over the torpedoes and determined that nothing is wrong with them."

"Really? Well, it seems to me Captain Cornelison has just proven that there *is* something wrong with them. And since the Bureau of Ordnance can't figure it out, I'll do the job myself."

Admiral English took personal charge of the investigation. He had dummy warheads filled with concrete, fitted them with exploders, and, borrowing an idea from Jerry Cornelison, dropped them ninety feet from a crane. When the warheads hit head-on, seven out of ten firing pins failed to work. The fact that three of them did work, however, highlighted the risk Jerry had taken with his dramatic experiment.

It proved to be a plain case of jamming. The firing pin was a mushroom piece of heavy steel, incapable of responding fast enough and traveling far enough to set off the primer cap on contact. The cure was simple. The torpedoes needed only a lighter-weight firing pin. The ideal metal for the pin turned out to be the tough steel in the propeller blades of Japanese planes shot down in their attack of December 7. Soon after the discovery of the problem, all the navy machine shops at Pearl Harbor were put to work turning out the new firing pins.

The first submarines to go out with the new firing pins showed immediate improvement. *Trigger* sank three ships, *Seahorse* got three, and *Haddock* got two. *Bullshark* also got two. *Angelfish* returned from its second patrol with no victories to claim. It wasn't that the torpedoes didn't work, or that they missed their targets; it was simply a matter of not having sighted any Japanese ships.

They sailed, in Dickey Traser's words, "from tedium, to monotony, to boredom, and back to tedium again."

Western Pacific
December 7, 1942

The first anniversary of the attack on Pearl Harbor did not pass without notice. By now the submarine had proven to be a very effective weapon in the Pacific, and some of the submarines had created pennants to fly from their periscopes, indicating the number and types of ships they had sunk. *Bullshark* had four tiny Japanese flags on its pennant. Three of the flags were white, with a red ball in the middle; those were for merchant ships. The fourth flag had not only the red ball, but red rays emanating from it. This was the Japanese battle standard, indicating that a warship had been sunk.

Angelfish still had not sunk a single ship. There had been the problem with duds on the first patrol, and not one enemy ship was spotted on the second. And, much to the crew's disappointment, they had been specifically barred from engaging the enemy during the third and fourth patrols because they were on standby as a downed-airman rescue vessel.

This was the fifth patrol. Everyone on board had high hopes because they had been sent to a spot where they were assured they would encounter some enemy shipping. It was their second week out, and they were cruising on the surface with lookouts aloft. Jerry was in the wardroom drinking coffee with Pat, who had just come off watch. Choirboy came in to refresh their cups.

"I'm beginning to think we'll never sink a ship," Jerry said to Pat, as he held his cup toward Choirboy.

"Pardon me for interrupting the conversation, Cap'n. I know I'm just a steward, and what I think probably don't matter. But the way I look at it, you've already sunk a lot of Jap ships. Every one that's been sunk by one of our submarines in the last four months is because of you."

"How do you figure that?"

"Well, think about it, sir. If you hadn't made them work on that torpedo, we'd still be out here throwing rocks."

Pat laughed. "Choirboy's got a point, Captain."

"Maybe so," Jerry agreed. "But still, I'd like for *Angelfish* to get one."

"Mr. Hanifin, if you don't mind, sir, I've got something for you," Choirboy said just before he withdrew.

"For me?"

"Yes, sir. I made it for you last night. If you've got just a minute, I'll bring it to you."

Pat looked at Jerry. "Do you know what he's talking about?"

Jerry shook his head. "I haven't the foggiest."

A moment later Choirboy returned, holding something behind his back. Smiling broadly, he handed Pat a carved wooden baton.

"What is that?" Jerry asked.

"It's a conductor's baton," Pat said, reaching for it. He held it up for a closer examination. "You made this?"

"Yes, sir. A week or so ago Cookie broke a wooden stirring spoon," Choirboy said. "He was going to throw it away, but I salvaged it."

Pat tapped the baton on the table a few times, then raised it and "conducted" for a few beats. He held it out and looked at it again.

"Choirboy, you did a great job. It has a wonderful balance."

"Thank you, sir," Choirboy said, beaming.

"But how did you know that I might want something like this?"

"I've seen you, Mr. Hanifin, when you didn't think anybody was watching. You'd be listenin' to that highbrow music on the record player and makin' out like you were the director."

Pat grinned sheepishly. "Thank you, Choirboy."

A voice came over the 1MC, interrupting their conversation. "Captain, lookouts have seen smoke!"

"I'm on my way," Jerry said, putting his cup down so quickly that some coffee splashed out. Automatically Choirboy wiped it up, even as the rest of the boat was galvanized into action.

Lieutenant Roberts had the watch. "Captain's on the bridge," he announced as Jerry came up.

"Where away?" Jerry asked.

"Forty degrees off the starboard bow," Roberts said.

Raising his binoculars, Jerry looked in the direction indicated. There, just over the horizon, a very thin, barely noticeable puff of smoke snaked through the air.

194

"You've got good eyes, Darrel," Jerry said.

"I didn't see it first, Captain. Seaman Hornsby did."

"Good job, Hornsby."

"Thank you, sir," Hornsby replied proudly.

"Let's hope it's a big, juicy target." Jerry picked up the phone. "Engine room, all ahead full."

At Jerry's command, the sound of the diesel engines grew from a muffled rumble to a louder thrum, and the speed of the boat increased precipitously. They continued on the surface at flank speed until the ship's superstructures could be seen.

"Clear the bridge!" Jerry ordered. He waited until the last man was off the bridge, then he dropped down inside and dogged the hatch shut. "Take her down to periscope depth." He looked at the others with a broad grin on his face. "I think we've hit pay dirt."

The boat continued at maximum underwater speed for several more minutes with Jerry taking several looks. "Two freighters," he said. "Five thousand tons each. Two destroyer escorts."

Pat stood by the torpedo data computer, excited at the prospect of getting another chance at an enemy ship. They worked out the targets' speed, bearing, and other essentials, feeding the information into the TDC. Jarvis reported echo ranging from the escorts, and even Pat could hear the faint, far-off pinging.

"Make ready forward torpedo tubes," Jerry ordered.

"Tubes ready, sir," Persico reported.

"Enemy course now?"

"Two six five," Dickey said.

"Using divided fire! Track angle to first target?"

"Port one zero six, one one zero, one one three."

"Second target?"

"One two five, one two nine, one three three."

"Gyro angles?"

"Three two eight, three two nine, three three oh, three three one, three three two, three three three."

"Match gyros forward!"

Jerry guided *Angelfish* into an attack position and fired three torpedoes at each of the two merchant ships. The boat shuddered as the torpedoes left the tubes, and they could hear the descending whine of the turbine drive props on the speeding missiles.

"All torpedoes running hot, fast, and normal," Chief Persico said.

Dickey Traser was timing the runs, and he started counting down. "Five, four, three, two, one."

For a moment there was nothing, and everyone in the conning tower looked at each other in disappointment, wondering if this was going to be a repeat of their first attack. But before anyone could speak, the sound of the first explosion reached them. It was followed almost immediately by a second, third, fourth, and fifth. They had launched six torpedoes, and there were five hits.

"Periscope up!" Jerry shouted. He had to shout to be heard over the cheers. In fact, the cheers were coming from the entire boat; everyone, from the forward torpedo room through the after torpedo room and to the galley, had heard the explosions.

Hooking his arms over the handles, Jerry rode the scope up. As soon as the water cleared away from the lens, he saw the results of their attack. From both freighters, flaming bits of debris were whirling through the air in every direction. The lead ship had collapsed in on itself, broken in two as bow and stern pointed up. The second ship went down by the stern, the shriek of collapsing bulkheads and rumble of crushed compartments giving off death throes. Within moments, all that was left of the two freighters were swirling domes of bubbles and drifting steam.

"Take a look, Dickey," Jerry said.

The XO put his eyes to the eyepiece. "Now, that is an awesome sight."

Jerry returned to the periscope. "1MC," he said, calling for the ship's public address system.

Dickey handed the microphone to him, and Jerry keyed the switch.

The sweating men in *Angelfish* could not see what was going on, but like a play-by-play announcer calling a football game, Jerry gave them an account of the double sinkings.

"Okay, fun's over. Down scope, flood negative, take us down," Jerry said, snapping the handles closed on the periscope.

Once again, the crew of *Angelfish* heard the sound of probing sonar. *Ping . . . PING!*

"Four hundred feet, Captain," Persico said.

"Level off at four hundred," Jerry said.

They could hear the throbbing sound of the Japanese destroyer as it passed directly overhead. Then they heard two clicks, as if steel balls had been dropped on the outside of the boat. Everyone knew that was the detonator, and they all braced for the explosion to follow.

The conning tower quivered as if *Angelfish* were the toy boat of some giant child who had picked it up to shake it. A few loose objects flew about, and water started gushing from one of the fittings.

"Get on that!" Jerry shouted.

Click, click!

Again, the men braced themselves.

The second explosion knocked out the lights and caused the boat to thrust upward several feet. Some of the men fell, and in the darkness one of them rolled against Pat's legs, bringing him down. An electric cable began swinging, emitting blue sparks. After a moment, the lights came back on.

"Jerry, he has our depth," Dickey said. "We need to go deeper!"

"All right, take her down to . . . no, belay that. Take her up to one hundred feet."

"One hundred feet, Captain?" Roberts asked.

"One hundred feet. I'm going to try and create a bubble that will confuse their ranging."

"Aye, aye, sir. One hundred feet," Roberts said.

As *Angelfish* started up, there were four more depth charges, but they were below where the boat was now, and though they were still loud, they were far enough away that the boat didn't react to them. The next volley was also too deep.

"You did it, sir," Roberts said. "They can't find us."

The pinging started again.

"They're moving away, sir!" Jarvis yelled excitedly.

"Which way are they headed?"

"Two five zero, sir."

"Take up a reverse azimuth. Steer zero seven zero," Jerry said. "Let's get out of here."

Angelfish stayed submerged until night. With Jarvis reporting no traffic on sonar, she surfaced to recharge the batteries and ventilate the boat. The galley rewarded the crew with fresh-baked apple pie.

Two weeks later, *Angelfish* rendezvoused with the destroyer *Patterson* as it came alongside to deliver mail and pick up outgoing mail. Pat was Officer of the Deck as the destroyer came alongside. Looking up at the bridge, he recognized the ensign on duty, Paul Griffin, his roommate from officer candidate school. Pat raised the bullhorn.

"Paul Griffin, how are you?" he called.

Griffin, who had been supervising the transfer, hadn't seen Pat. He looked around in surprise at being called by name, then smiled.

"Well, if it isn't old Sixteen-inch Boom, sir," Griffin shouted back to him. "How's it going with you?"

"Fine, fine," Pat replied. "What movie do you have?"

"Abbott and Costello in *Keep 'Em Flying*. What about you?"

"*King's Row* with Ronald Reagan and Ann Sheridan."

"Sounds good; send it over."

"What do you hear from Tim Hawthorne and Jack Hayes?" Pat asked, referring to the other two roommates.

The smile left Griffin's face. "You haven't heard? They were in *Barton*. Their ship went down at Guadalcanal last month, with 80 percent of her crew. Tim and Jack were both lost."

"Oh," Pat said. "No, I didn't know that."

"Yeah, well, we're losing a lot of good guys in this war," Paul said. "So you take care of yourself, you hear?"

"Yes, you too."

The bosun's call sounded in *Patterson*.

"Well, I guess we'll be going now," Paul called down to Pat. "Merry Christmas to you."

"Merry Christmas," Pat replied.

Somewhere in the South Pacific
December 24, 1942

It was just before sunset, and *Angelfish* was cruising on the surface with lookouts aloft. In the west the sun was spreading color through the heavens and painting a long smear of red and gold on the surface of the sea. Below decks, in the control room, stood a small Christmas tree. Strains of "O Little Town of Bethlehem" wafted throughout the boat by way of the 1MC. Pat was in the wardroom, drinking coffee.

Much of the crew was in the forward torpedo room, watching *Keep 'Em Flying*. Some were reading their mail. Pat had received ten letters, including three from his parents and six from Diane. The tenth was a notice from the superintendent of the apartment building where he had lived in New York.

There have been complaints that some of our tenants are making too much noise after hours. All tenants are advised to check their occupancy lease in which they will find it clearly stated that loud music, over-exuberant parties, and unruly conduct will be sufficient cause for eviction.

"You're too late," Pat said quietly, as he wadded the letter into a ball and threw it into the wastebasket. "The U.S. Navy already evicted me and put me on a submarine."

Pat rationed himself to reading no more than three letters per day, spreading out the joy of new mail.

This was the third day, and he was reading the last of his letters from Diane.

If my calculations are correct, you will be receiving this letter on or very near Christmas. Merry Christmas, though it's hard to understand how a Christmas could be merry in the cramped confines of a submarine, far at sea in the midst of a war.

I received three letters from you yesterday. Letters are a bittersweet thing. While they are fresh, and while I am actually reading them, it is almost as if I am with you, enjoying a conversation and watching your eyes sparkle with some of the devilment that always seems to be just beneath the surface. But when I finish the letter it is as if I have been awakened from a wonderful dream, torn away before I'm ready to leave. I look for you, but you are gone. It leaves me with a choking, lonely, tearful feeling.

But please don't get me wrong. Don't think for a moment that I want you to quit writing, because after the initial depression passes I can bask in the pleasure of knowing that the letters are still there, and I can read and reread them as often as I want. And, with each rereading, we are together again.

You asked in your last letter where I thought our relationship was going. In order to answer that, perhaps we should review where it has been. It has now been over a year since I was "rescued" in the lobby of the Royal Savoy Hotel in Hong Kong by the most handsome and certainly the nicest young man I have ever met. That began our relationship, though for much of this past year that relationship has been carried on via long distance.

Having grown up away from American culture, I am not sure how a "proper young woman" should answer your question, so I will just tell you what is in my heart. I love you, Pat Hanifin. And I believe you love me as well. My hope, then, is that someday I will be your wife. There. Have I shocked you, my darling? I confess to having shocked myself. I will close this letter now and wait anxiously for your response.

Love, Diane

"Yahoo!" Pat yelled loudly, then looked around sheepishly to see if anyone had heard him. If so, no one gave any indication.

He unbuttoned his shirt and put the letter next to his heart. It was almost as if he could feel her hand there. Then he picked up the last of the letters from his parents. The first half was in small but perfectly legible script. This, he knew, was from his mother.

I worry so about you, but I put my trust in the Lord to whom I pray every morning and every night to preserve your body and soul. Please be careful, Patrick, and come home safely to the mother who loves you so.

His father's half of the letter was in a larger, bolder script. Half of the letter was printed in block letters and half was written in longhand, often changing from block to cursive even in the same word.

Pan American World Airways System is buying full-page ads in national magazines, in which they are running a series of articles written by guest authors. The authors state their opinion of what sort of world we are fighting to create. They have included articles by the philosopher Dr. John Dewey; the Chinese Ambassador to the United States, Dr. Hu Shih; and most recently, The Most Reverend William Temple Cantuar, Archbishop of Canterbury. And now, they have invited me to submit my own vision of the world as I would want it to be after the war.

Outside of a world where there is no war, and where there is 100 percent literacy rate with everyone clamoring to buy my books, I don't know what to say (ha ha).

I will give it serious thought, though, because it is a serious subject, the more so because my own son is now in hazard. Stay safe, Patrick. It would break your mother's heart if anything should happen to you. Well, mine too, but I'd have to put on a brave front . . . and I'm getting too old for brave fronts.

Pat was just finishing his mail when Choirboy stepped into the wardroom carrying a coffeepot, which he extended toward Pat.

"Thank you," Pat said.

"Mr. Hanifin, you're the junior officer of the boat, aren't you, sir?" Choirboy asked as he poured a thin, richly aromatic, brown stream into Pat's decorated cup.

Pat chuckled. "Thanks for reminding me." He reached for a Pet milk can. He noticed dried evaporated milk around the two knife holes and scraped the yellow gunk away with his thumbnail, then added a bit of milk to his coffee.

"Yes, sir," Choirboy said. "Well, sir, the reason I mention it is because you being the junior officer of the boat also makes you the morale officer. So you're the one I need to talk to."

"Are you having a problem with your morale?"

"No sir, not exactly. It's just that some of the men have asked me if I would conduct a worship service for them in the forward torpedo room tonight. I mean, being as it's Christmas Eve and all."

"Why, I think that's a great idea, Choirboy. But why come to me? Do you need my permission or something? If so, you've got it."

"Thank you, sir. But, I'm wondering if it's proper."

"Proper? What do you mean, proper?"

"I'm a colored man, Mr. Hanifin. And there's only one other colored man on this boat. I don't know how proper it would be for me to be holding a worship service for a bunch of white men. Besides which, I'm not even an ordained minister."

"Choirboy, you know the Bible a lot better than I do, a lot better than anyone on this boat. So who am I to be quoting Scripture to you? But it seems to me I can remember something in the Bible about where two or three are gathered."

"Yes, sir," Choirboy answered. "Matthew 18:20, 'For where two or three are gathered in my name, there am I in the midst of them.'"

"No, you must be wrong. It must say where two or three *white* men are gathered in my name."

"No sir, it doesn't say anything about white or . . ." Choirboy stopped, then smiled at Pat. "Yes, sir, I see what you mean."

"Okay, so it says, 'For where two or three are gathered in my name, with an ordained minister, there am I in the midst of them.'"

Choirboy laughed. "No, sir. It doesn't say anything about being an ordained minister, either."

Pat put his hand on Choirboy's shoulder. "I'm glad we had this little talk," he said.

"Yes, sir. I am too."

"What time are you going to do this?"

"Some of the men want me to do it just before midnight. That way we can sort of welcome Christmas in."

"Good. I'll be there," Pat said.

"You, sir? An officer coming to a worship service I'm giving?"

This time Pat laughed. "Do we have to go through this again, Choirboy? Did I miss the part where it talks about commission and enlisted?"

"Sir, I'd be honored if you came."

Pat wasn't the only officer to attend. Every officer on the boat, with the exception of Dickey Traser, who was on the bridge as OOD, attended Choirboy's service. As Pat looked around at the others, he knew that all of them were remembering Christmases past. He thought of his own situation a year ago, when he and John Henry had attended a solemn mass at St. Thomas Episcopal Church. It had been an impressive and moving service, with music, candles, statuary, vested clergy, and acolytes. Yet he knew that this simple service, with its heartfelt words and prayers, would be one that he would remember for the rest of his life.

14

D iane received an answer to her bold letter. It was short and to the point.

I love you. Will you marry me?

Her return letter was even shorter and more to the point.

Yes!!!

She looked forward to the day *Angelfish* returned to port so she and Pat could begin making plans in person for their wedding. But that was not to be. *Angelfish* did not return to Pearl Harbor, but was relocated to the submarine base at Fremantle, Australia.

It was a bitter blow, but Diane reminded herself that this war had separated millions of people from the ones they loved. She had been fortunate to see Pat as often as she had. And she often saw reports involving *Angelfish*, which meant she was able to keep up with him more closely than most wives, fiancées, or girlfriends.

It was late Friday afternoon, and Diane was almost ready to go home when a clerk dropped the latest batch of intercepts on her desk.

"Sorry to give these to you so late on a Friday," he said, "but we just picked them up."

"That's okay," Diane said. "I've no place to go anyway."

She began reading through the intercepts. Most were routine traffic-managing messages, but one caught her attention immediately: *At eight o'clock on the morning of Sunday, April 18, Admiral Isoroku Yamamoto will inspect the units on Bougainville.* She hurried to Commander McIntyre's office.

Before the war, Nelson McIntyre had been a motion picture producer. In fact, he had produced *Becalmed*, a movie based upon Sean Hanifin's novel. Because of that, and because Diane was now engaged to Sean Hanifin's son, McIntyre felt an almost cosmic connection to his star interpreter.

As a producer, McIntyre believed in props, and his office reflected his Hollywood idea of a naval officer's decor. On his desk sat a polished brass casing from a forty-millimeter anti-aircraft shell. A brass plaque claimed that it was from a burst that brought down a Japanese attacker over Pearl Harbor on December 7, 1941. There was no way of validating it, but no one questioned him. A sextant also occupied a section of his desk, a coil of rope and an anchor decorated one corner of the room, and crossed signalman's flags hung on the wall.

Despite the rather elaborate ruse, McIntyre was in fact a very good intelligence officer. He had the ability to assimilate bits and pieces of information and put them together to form a coherent whole. When a senior officer commented about it, McIntyre laughed and said, "You should see some of the disjointed movie scripts I've had to work with."

Diane knew, even before she reached McIntyre's office, that the commander was in, because the door to his office was open and the air in the anteroom was perfumed with his expensive and aromatic pipe tobacco. She knocked at the open door, then stepped into his office.

"Commander McIntyre?"

"Yes, Diane, what is it?" He smiled up at her.

"You said you wanted to be informed on any message we intercepted about Yamamoto."

McIntyre read the message, then hit his fist on the desk. "Yes!" he said aloud. "Yes, this is it! This is what I've been looking for. Diane, you beautiful babe, if you weren't engaged, and if I weren't a married man, I would kiss you!"

Diane laughed. "I am engaged, Commander. But you aren't married."

"I'm not? That's right; Darla divorced me, didn't she? Well, no matter. This"—he held up the piece of paper—"is a great piece of information."

Henderson Field, Guadalcanal
2230 hrs, April 17, 1943

Army Air Force Capt. Ken Cooley lay on a canvas cot with his hands folded behind his head, watching the smoke from his cigarette gather in a little cloud just under the roof of the tent. Outside, rainfall drummed against the canvas, ran from the eaves, and trilled into a spreading puddle on the ground. Ken and the other pilots of the Army Air Corps' 339th Fighter Squadron had dug a small channel around the tent to keep the water from coming inside, and so far it seemed to be working.

Since Ken's job flying for Pan American Airways was considered critical, he could have deferred his enlistment. But he wanted to be closer to the war than flying cargo and personnel in the backwater areas of the Pacific.

He applied to have his reserve commission activated, and his first assignment was with the 70th Fighter Squadron on Fiji. There he trained with the P-39 for six months but saw no action. He began to think he would be better off flying for Pan Am. Then in October he was detached from the 70th and assigned to the 339th on Guadalcanal.

The 339th was bivouacked alongside the airstrip on an airfield built by the Japanese and taken over by the Americans. It was named Henderson Field to honor a marine pilot killed in the Battle of Midway.

Although the island had been wrested from the Japanese, there were still several holdouts in the black jungle that crowded down to the very perimeter of the field. That point was vividly brought home a couple of days earlier when one of the flight-line mechanics had been killed by a sniper's bullet.

Lt. Rex Barber stood at the flap of the tent looking out. "No sign of a letup in the rain yet," he said.

"Has Major Mitchell come back from his meeting with the navy brass?" Lieutenant McClanahan asked.

"No," Barber answered. "I don't know what the navy wants with us anyway."

"You know how it is. When the navy bites off more than they can chew, they send marines. And when it's too big for both of them combined, they come to the army," McClanahan said.

Lieutenant Canning put a record on his machine—Glenn Miller's "Serenade in Blue." "What do you say to a little music?"

"For crying out loud, Canning, is that the only record you've got?" Lieutenant Barber asked. "That's about the fifth time you've played it in the last two hours."

"I like this song," Canning said. "Help me out here, Ken. You like Miller too; you told me so."

"Yes, I like him."

"You ever meet Miller, Ken?" McClanahan asked.

"No."

"But you have met a lot of famous people, haven't you? I mean, only rich and famous people could actually afford to fly on those big Clippers," McClanahan insisted.

Ken laughed. "I suppose I've met a few of the rich and famous. But they were passengers; I was the pilot. It's not like we hung out together or anything."

"Still, that was some glamorous job you had. I worked in a drugstore," Canning said.

At the time of Ken's arrival, the island was still being contested, with the Japanese only six hundred feet from the airstrip. The situation was so critical that the mechanics removed machine guns from the airplanes to use as a last-ditch defense if necessary.

Despite the inferiority of the P-39 to the Japanese Zero, Ken not only survived several dogfights with the Japanese, he even managed to shoot down an enemy plane. Then, in January of 1943, the P-39s were replaced by twin-engine, twin-tailed P-38s. Every pilot in the squadron welcomed the replacement, for the Lightnings, as they were called, had a top speed of four hundred miles per hour.

They also had devastating firepower, mounting four .50-caliber machine guns and one twenty-millimeter cannon in the nose. This enabled the guns to fire straight ahead, rather than in the more common converging patterns of wing-mounted guns. That allowed for much greater accuracy up to a range of one thousand yards. Since moving to the P-38, Ken had shot down four more Zeros, becoming an ace in March of 1943.

"Here comes the major," Barber said.

Major John Henry Mitchell stepped into tent, then took off his rain-coat to pour off the water. He saw everyone looking at him anxiously and smiled.

"Okay, boys, listen up," he said. "We've got a big one."

Rabaul, Solomon Islands
0500 hours, Sunday, April 18, 1943

Yutaka Saito stood on the beach of Rabaul, looking out to sea. Today was Palm Sunday, though Saito was absolutely certain that he was the only one aware of that fact. Of all the airfields and bases he had visited since the beginning of the war, this was the most inhospitable. The landing strip shimmered with heat under a constant layer of dust. Nearby, a volcano rumbled and erupted often enough to blanket the area in thick, noxious smoke. Even the trees were naked of foliage. But for all its hostile environment and ugly scenery, Rabaul was the best place to be if one wanted to be in the midst of the war, for it was the headquarters of all Japanese naval and air operations in the southwest Pacific.

It was even more important now than it had been when first occupied, for if Japan was to hold on to everything it had captured, this island was the key. That wasn't just Saito's assessment; Admiral Yamamoto had said the same thing in early March after a convoy of Japanese transports was totally destroyed by American and Australian air attacks. The destruction of the convoy, which was carrying almost seven thousand troops to the base at Lae, New Guinea, represented one of Japan's most stunning losses of the war. From that day forth, Japanese planners no longer spoke of offense. Now, all plans were defensive. Even the emperor was aware of the change in policy, because Saito read the reports of the emperor's briefing concerning the Japanese decision to evacuate Guadalcanal.

"What do you plan to do next?" Emperor Hirohito had asked calmly.

"We intend to stop the enemy's westward movement," the warlords had replied.

Embodied in that one sentence, Saito knew, was the first official recognition of the turning tides of war.

It was a bitter pill to swallow. From the very beginning, he had known that Japan's only hope lay in a quick and decisive victory. But that opportunity had been lost the previous summer when the American and Japanese fleets clashed in the battle of Midway. Now, with the abandonment of Guadalcanal, the distant outposts that protected the Empire were beginning to crumble. If these perimeters of defense were pulled in to the degree that the Americans could begin long-range bomber flights over the main islands of Japan, there would no longer be any hope of winning.

"Ah, Saito, there you are," Admiral Yamamoto said, joining his officer on the beach. "Watching the sunrise, I see."

Saito came to attention. "Yes, Admiral. Perhaps it is the symbolism, but I always find the sunrise particularly inspiring."

"As do I," Yamamoto replied. "So, what do you think, Saito? Do I look impressive enough to instill confidence in our pilots?" Yamamoto, who was wearing dress whites replete with his numerous awards and decorations, struck a quick and comical pose.

Saito laughed. "Admiral, you would be impressive enough if you spoke in a fundoshi," he said, referring to the loin wrap the laborers often wore to combat the heat.

Yamamoto laughed a deep, rich laugh.

Saito not only respected Yamamoto as his commander, he liked him as a person. The admiral was a naval genius, widely traveled, and he greatly admired America. Like Saito, he had spent several years in the United States and he counted many Americans among his close personal friends. He spoke English fluently and often imitated various American dialects. He loved to entertain his friends with stories in which he assumed the role of a Southerner speaking with an exaggerated drawl, a hillbilly speaking with a flat twang, or a proper Bostonian. Though not a believer, Yamamoto had a respect for the Christian religion and did not exhibit any indication that he thought Saito was dishonoring his country or his culture by being a practicing Christian.

"I trust you are passing a peaceful Palm Sunday?" Yamamoto said.

"Yes, Admiral, thank you," Saito replied. He should have realized that if anyone else realized this was a Christian holiday, it would be Admiral Yamamoto.

"Are your wife and daughter well? Have you heard from them?"

"They are well, thank you."

"Pray to your Jesus that they, and all our people, stay well and safe."

"I believe they are safe. You have built a most formidable line of defense, Admiral," Saito said.

"Yes." Yamamoto was silent for a moment. "Defense," he finally said, quietly. "I have built a line of defense when we should have a line of offense." He sighed, then slapped his baton against the side of his pants. "But I have a plan, Saito. I have a magnificent plan. With a strengthened line of defense, we will be able to put together another offense, and you would be surprised at what will be my new target." He chuckled. "Yes, you would be surprised. But the most surprised of all will be the

Americans. I promise you, Saito, this will strike as great a blow against the Americans as did our attack on Pearl Harbor."

Saito was more than intrigued. He was excited, recapturing a glimmer of hope for a successful outcome of the war. "You have quickened my fighting spirit, Admiral," he said. "Tell me, please, what have you in mind."

Yamamoto turned toward Saito and raised his finger, wagging it back and forth slowly. "No, no," he said, smiling. "If I tell you now it will spoil the surprise. But keep your fighting spirit, for we will begin planning it as soon as I return from Bougainville. I'll tell you this, and this only: it will turn the tide of war. In fact, it will end the war. It will be the bargaining chip we need to cease all hostilities and to hold on to our gains." Yamamoto chuckled. "Now, what about my flight to Bougainville? Is everything arranged? I want to take off at precisely 6 A.M."

Saito smiled. Yamamoto's compulsive adherence to a time schedule was legendary throughout the Imperial Navy. "We'll leave on time, Admiral. I've made all the necessary arrangements: two bombers and six escorting Zeros. I will accompany you in your plane."

"Excellent, excellent. I could ask for no finer company."

Another officer approached them. He stopped and bowed to the admiral.

"Forgive my intrusion, Admiral, but the pilots are ready for your speech."

"Ah, yes, my speech," Yamamoto replied. "Yes, I suppose we must get it over with. I will tell them to go fly bravely, something they all do anyway, but for some reason it is expected that I should tell them to do so. You have heard my speech before, Saito, so you need not listen. I'm sure you have final preparations to make for our flight to Bougainville."

"Yes, sir," Saito said. "I shall go down to the airfield now."

When Admiral Yamamoto appeared at the airfield a few minutes before six, he had changed out of his dress-white uniform into the less conspicuous green fatigues. Just before he boarded the Mitsubishi bomber, he turned to Vice Adm. Jinichi Kusaka and handed him two scrolls.

"You will forgive my simple efforts at calligraphy," he said. "But here are two poems written by Emperor Meiji, which I have copied. Would you please give them to the commander of the Eighth Fleet with my compliments?"

"Yes, Admiral, it would be my privilege," Kusaka replied, bowing.

Saito waited until Admiral Yamamoto was on board and seated before he climbed aboard.

"You aren't flying, Saito?"

"No, Admiral. But our pilot is most skilled."

"I'm sure he is, or you would not have chosen him."

The pilot looked back into the cabin of the plane and, at a signal from Saito, started his engines. A few moments later, just as the bomber took off, Saito glanced at his watch. It was exactly 0600.

The small air fleet that Saito put together for the trip consisted of two bombers escorted by six fighters. The bombers flew at just over fifteen hundred meters while the six fighters hovered protectively overhead. In the clear, early-morning air, the flight was pleasantly smooth. Shortly after they took off, Saito glanced over and saw that the admiral was napping.

Saito was dozing himself when the copilot came back into the cabin and gently shook him awake. "Sir, we have Kahili airfield in sight."

"Thanks," Saito answered. In turn he gently awakened the admiral. As Yamamoto began buttoning his tunic, Saito looked through the window toward the lush, green island of Bougainville rising from the sea.

Their descent was long, slow, and gentle. Finally they passed over the coastline of Bougainville. Now, instead of water, they were flying over jungle.

With the U.S. Army Air Corps' 339th Fighter Squadron

Throughout the night, ground crews had fitted long-range tanks under the wings of the P-38s. By dawn eighteen airplanes were ready. Their mission was to intercept and shoot down the airplane carrying Admiral Yamamoto. After a breakfast of Spam, dried eggs, and coffee,

Maj. John Mitchell led a flight of sixteen airplanes, including Ken Cooley's, into the air.

They had been flying for two hours at an altitude of less than one hundred feet in order to avoid detection. Because the P-38 was designed for high-altitude flight, there were no coolers in the cockpit, and at this speed, they couldn't open the canopy. As a result, the sun beat down through the glass of the greenhouse, heating the interior to uncomfortable temperatures. They flew in absolute radio silence, depending upon Mitchell's navigation. When they reached Vella Lavella, they turned north.

Forty miles from Bougainville, they climbed to altitude. Ken breathed a prayer of thankfulness that the climb brought blessed coolness to the cockpit. Then, at 0934, Lt. Doug Canning broke radio silence. "Bogeys, eleven o'clock high," he called.

"Drop your tanks," Mitchell ordered.

Ken jettisoned his tank and saw the others rushing down as well.

Saito felt the bomber go into a steep dive, then pull out just over the very top of the jungle.

"What is it?" he called up to the flight deck. "What is going on?"

"Enemy planes!" the copilot answered.

The trees were a blur as they skimmed across them at well over two hundred miles per hour, flying so close to them that Saito felt he could almost stick his hand out and grab a branch. Flying low had decreased the bomber's space for maneuvering, but Saito knew that it also reduced the attack options of the enemy planes.

But it didn't work. The P-38s came crashing through, and suddenly Saito saw blood splattered all over the twisted metal and shattered glass. Both pilots were hit, and Saito saw them slumped in their seats. He got up and started forward, trying to get there in time to take over the controls, but even as he was working his way forward, the right wing and right engine were a mass of flames. It was no longer a functioning airplane; it was a piece of flaming debris, controlled only by gravity.

Saito thought of his wife, Hiroko, and his daughter, Miko. He recalled the magnificent sunrise he had seen that morning, and he knew God had sent it to him. "Thank you, Lord," he prayed. Just before the bomber crashed into the trees and exploded in a ball of fire, Saito smiled.

Before the two P-38s that had been in on the kill started back to their base, they did a victory barrel roll over the pillar of black smoke that rose from the funeral pyre of the crashed plane.

They had been about one hour on their return when Ken attempted to switch fuel tanks. "Foxfire Six, my fuel cross-feed is inoperative," he called. Foxfire Six was the flight leader, Major Mitchell.

"Have you tried manual?" Mitchell asked.

"Affirmative. It's no go."

"How much fuel do you have remaining in your useable tank?"

"I'm on fumes," Ken said.

"Call in your position. You are three niner seven four, grid able-easy."

"Roger, able easy, three niner seven four," Ken replied.

Had they used the regular longitudinal and latitude coordinates to pinpoint the position, the Japanese would be able to determine where he was. And though Ken wasn't the one who shot down Admiral Yamamoto, he had been a part of the mission. As far as the Japanese were concerned, it wouldn't matter whether he was the one of the "kill team" or not.

"Mayday, mayday, mayday. This is Foxfire Three, Foxfire Three. Does anyone read me?"

"Foxfire Three, this is Deep Ranger," a distinctly American voice replied. "Authenticate."

Checking his kneepad, Ken found the code he would need to authenticate his message. "Able, Charley, Zebra, niner, five, niner," he said.

"Baker, haystack, item, seven zero seven," Deep Ranger replied. "Goodnature." Deep Ranger had not only given the correct response, it had also indicated by the term *Goodnature* that it was a submarine. "What are your coordinates?"

"My coordinates are able easy, three niner seven four, able easy."

Jerry Cornelison was in the wardroom working on a report when Jarvis came to him with the message.

"Cap'n, we've got an American plane going down."

"Where?"

"Mr. Hanifin plotted his location. Looks like he's about forty miles north-west of us. Here's the heading, sir." Jarvis handed a piece of paper to Jerry.

Jerry took the phone receiver down from the wall mount. "Control room, come to course two eight three, all ahead full."

"Aye, aye, sir," Roberts replied.

"You going to bail out or try to ditch?" Mitchell asked.

"The sea is smooth. I think I'll ditch," Ken replied.

"You sure? It might be easier to bail out."

"I've never bailed out of a plane. On the other hand, I've made about five hundred water landings." He chuckled. "Of course, they were all in sea-planes."

"Yeah, that's right," Mitchell replied. "I guess if anyone can land on the water, you certainly should be able to. Okay, let's go through your checklist. Seat and shoulder harness tight?"

Ken tightened his belt and harness as tightly as he could get them. "Check."

"Life jacket on?"

"Check. And I've opened the access cover for the life raft."

"Emergency kit? Water, food, light, dye marker, flare gun? Your own personal can of Spam?"

Ken laughed, appreciating Mitchell's attempt to cheer him. "Check."

"How are you going in, with the canopy open or closed?"

Ken reached up and loosened the canopy, then slid it back. "Open," he answered.

"All right, good luck, and Godspeed," Mitchell said.

"I'm going to kill my engines," Ken said, pulling back on the fuel cut-off levers.

Both engines quit, and except for the rush of air, it was deathly quiet. He lowered the nose to maintain flying speed, then started a long, shallow descent toward the water. For a moment, he wasn't in the seat of a land-based P-38 fighter plane . . . he was once again in the left seat of a Boeing 314 Pan Am Clipper. The thought calmed him, and he set it down easily, skimming across the top of the water before settling down.

The plane glided through the water for a few feet, then stopped. It was still on the surface, but he had no idea how long it would stay afloat. Ken quickly loosened his seatbelt and shoulder harness, then climbed out onto the wing. Reaching behind the seat, he removed the emergency kit and life raft; pulled the inflation device; and launched the raft from the wing, doing so outside the engine nacelle so as not to be trapped in the space between the fuselage and tail. He stepped into the raft and paddled it away from the airplane, which slowly began to sink.

Only now was he aware of the sound of airplane engines, and when he looked around, he saw Mitchell diving toward him. Wagging his wings back and forth, Mitchell zoomed by overhead, then pulled up into a long, swooping climb. Ken waved at him and watched as he rejoined the other P-38s, who were still at altitude. They continued on in a southeasterly direction, growing smaller in the distance.

Ken had thought that one of the others might make a pass as well, but no one did. He understood why. The mission was over one thousand miles long, and every ounce of fuel was needed for them to make it back to Henderson. He watched and listened until he could no longer see or hear them.

Now, except for the slap of water against the side of his raft, it was absolutely quiet. He had never been more alone in his entire life. A terrible sense of foreboding came over him. Would the American submarine find him?

"Oh, God," he prayed, "let them find me before dark."

Late afternoon on the bridge of Angelfish

It was growing late in the day, and the search for the downed pilot was growing more critical with each passing moment. Ironically, however, as the sun grew less brilliant, the search became somewhat easier, due to the decreased brightness reflecting off the water. Of course, that situation would only last until the sun was down. Then the search would be infinitely more difficult, even if the downed pilot had a light.

The two men in the shears were Seamen Tinker and Hornsby. Pat was OOD, and Chief Persico was with him on the bridge. They were only twenty minutes into their watch, but already Pat's eyes were playing tricks on him from the strain of searching and the sun sparkles coming off the water. At least that condition was easing somewhat.

"Coffee to the bridge, sir?" Choirboy called up to the tower.

Pat nodded at Persico, and Persico called back down. "Aye, bring it up, Choirboy."

Choirboy climbed the ladder, carrying a coffeepot. The four men on watch had their cups with them, and he began filling them.

"That sun is going down awfully fast," Persico said, nodding toward the west. The bottom of the blood-red disc had just touched the horizon, and at the point of contact it created an illusion of the sun melting, spreading its crimson out onto the surface of the sea.

"I hope we find him before dark," Pat said.

"You will, sir," Choirboy said, as he poured the coffee. "I've been praying for that poor pilot. The Lord is going to lead us right to him."

"I wish I had your confidence."

"Confidence is easy if you've got faith," Choirboy replied.

"What happens to your faith if we don't find him?"

"Mr. Hanifin, raft in the water!" Tyler Hornsby shouted from his position in the shears.

Choirboy smiled knowingly as Pat stared at him in surprise. Then, recovering quickly, Pat called up to Hornsby.

"Where away?"

Hornsby pointed. "There, thirty degrees off the starboard quarter."

"Astern? Wow, we nearly went by him," Pat said. He began looking in the direction indicated by Hornsby, but he saw nothing. "You sure you saw him?"

"Wait for the next swell, sir," Hornsby said. "He's down in the trough now."

Pat continued to search the sea, then with the next wave he saw a tiny yellow dot come up to the crest, then slide back down into the trough again.

Pat laughed. "I see him! Thank God for those eyes of yours, Hornsby." Pat looked at Choirboy. "And I mean that literally," he said. "Thank God."

Pat leaned over to the push-to-talk button on the speaker. "Tell the captain we've got a sighting."

"Captain wants a heading, Mr. Hanifin," a metallic voice replied.

Pat took a reading off the bridge plotter. "Three three zero degrees," he said.

"Behind us, huh?" This time the voice on the speaker was Jerry's. "All right, we're coming about. Keep him in sight."

"Aye, aye, sir. Choirboy, maybe you'd better get below now."

"Mr. Hanifin, could I maybe say a little prayer of thanks before I go?"

"I should clear the bridge of all nonessential personnel," Pat replied.

"You sayin' the Lord's not essential?"

Pat stared for a moment at the innocent trust in the dark eyes of the steward. Then, with a smile, he relented. "Give us a prayer," he said. "The Lord can stay, but then you have to go below."

"Aye, aye, sir," Choirboy said. He bowed his head and closed his eyes. "Lord, whose voice the waters heard, we thank You for leadin' us to this very place on Your wide sea so that we could come to the aid of one of Your children. We thank You for the captain and crew who guide this boat and for the sharp eyes of Seaman Hornsby. We ask You to give us grace. We thank You also for the One who, through His goodness, we receive blessings, thy Son our Savior, Jesus Christ. Amen."

"Amen," the others on the bridge repeated.

It took fifteen minutes to come about and close the distance between them. As they approached the raft, the forward hatch opened, and two sailors came out onto the deck to help the downed pilot climb from the raft onto the boat. Pat watched from the bridge as the grateful pilot stood on the low, narrow deck and slipped out of his life preserver.

"Well, I'll be," Pat said aloud.

"What is it?" Persico asked.

"I know him." Pat leaned down to the speaker. "Captain, permission to leave the bridge for a few minutes?"

"Granted."

Pat climbed down through the conning tower into the control room. He was standing by as the downed pilot, on wobbly legs, was helped down the forward hatch access ladder.

"Captain Cooley, I believe?"

Ken turned toward the voice, then smiled broadly. "Pat Hanifin, isn't it?" he asked, extending his hand.

Pat shook his hand. "Yes. And I must say, I'm impressed that you would remember me, considering all the passengers you must have carried."

"Well, I did carry a lot of passengers. But only once did I manage to land in the middle of a war. That makes that flight a bit more memorable than the others."

"Yes, sir, I suppose it would. I see you've changed your Pan Am uniform for . . . wait a minute, that's not a naval aviator's uniform. That's army. What's an army aviator doing down in the middle of the ocean?"

Ken smiled and shook his head. "I'm not at liberty to tell you why I'm here," he said. "I'm just glad that *you* are."

"I am too. You want to come with me? I'm sure the captain will want to meet you."

"Yes, I'd like to meet him. I want to thank him." Ken looked around the torpedo room at the proud and happy faces of the crew. "I also want to thank you fellas. You're sort of an ugly looking bunch, but I have to tell you, a ship full of beautiful women would not look any better to me right now."

The crew laughed and applauded as Ken followed Pat toward his meeting with the captain.

15

On board Bullshark *in the South Pacific*
October 21, 1943

I t was 2330, and in the darkness *Bullshark* was running on the surface,
moving quietly and slowly toward a Japanese freighter. The freighter,
which had been hit by a torpedo they had fired earlier, had not gone
down but was now dead in the water off Oksu Island. She lay directly
in front of the sub, and because she could not proceed, there would be
no ship movement or computations required for the attack. This would
be a straight-on, zero-angle shot.

"Open bow doors one and two," Captain Berringer called down.

"Doors one and two open," John Henry said, relaying the report from
the torpedo room.

"Stand by below," Berringer said.

"Ready below, Captain," the XO called up.

"Fire one!"

John Henry hit the firing button.

"One fired electrically," he called.

"Fire two!"

John Henry hit the button again.

"Two fired electrically," he said.

"Number two has broached!" Captain Berringer suddenly shouted from the bridge. "She's coming back for us! All ahead full! Right full rudder!"

John Henry braced himself as the boat accelerated and started to turn. He could hear the high-pitched sound of the torpedo as it closed on them.

"Brace yourself!" Berringer shouted. "It's about to hit!"

The torpedo hit *Bullshark* amidships. John Henry was aware of a violent collision, followed by a blast of white heat. He never knew that the sub broke in two and went down, the forward and after halves separating.

John Henry died in the first seconds after impact. Not one member of *Bullshark's* crew was left alive to see the first of the two torpedoes just fired slam into the Japanese freighter.

Pearl Harbor
February 19, 1944

Commander Nelson McIntyre sucked on his pipe as he looked at the two documents Diane put before him. One document was written in Japanese and the other in English. He picked up the English version.

"And this is the translation?" he asked.

"Yes, sir. Of course, under the circumstances, I would expect you to have it translated by an independent source, since I wrote both the translation and the Japanese document. It's a letter I am writing to someone in Japan."

"A Jap? You're writing to a Jap?"

"Yes, sir, a Japanese woman who is my friend," Diane replied. "Her name is Miko Saito."

"That's right, you lived in Japan for a long time, didn't you?"

"Yes, sir."

"And just how do you plan to get this letter to her?"

"The Swiss have agreed to transmit personal letters between friends and relatives who are separated by their governments. There is an address that I can send it to. That is, if you grant approval."

His eyes skimmed down the paper. "You are telling her that your father was killed and commiserating with her over the death of her own father."

"Yes, sir."

"What happened to him?"

"Her father was on Admiral Yamamoto's staff. He was in Yamamoto's airplane when we shot it down."

"What?" McIntyre looked up quickly.

"So in a sense, you might say I am responsible for her father's death," Diane continued. "You can see then, why it is so important to me that I write to her, as one friend would to another under similar circumstances."

"Yes, I can see how you might take that personally," McIntyre said. He drummed his fingers on the desk as he thought about Diane's request. "But here is the question, Diane. Can you speak of her father's death without compromising the fact that you . . . we . . . are reading their private communications?"

Diane nodded. "Yes, sir. It has been nearly a year now since her father was killed. A few weeks ago his name appeared for the first time in the *Asahi Shimbun*."

"The what?"

"The *Asahi Shimbun*. That's Tokyo's largest newspaper.

"Did it say he was in Yamamoto's airplane?"

"No sir. All it said was that Comdr. Yutaka Saito had died bravely in battle for the Emperor. It gave no specific details, but then, it never does." She smiled. "I also want to tell Miko that I am getting married."

"You realize, don't you, that even if our censorship board passes it, and even if Switzerland transmits it, there is no guarantee that your friend will get this," McIntyre said, holding up the letter. "You also have the Japanese authorities to contend with."

"Yes, I know. But I feel that I must try. Neither Miko nor I started this war. Now we've both lost our fathers in it."

"All right. I'll run it by our censorship and intelligence people, along with my recommendation that they allow it to go through. If they give their approval, you can send it."

"Thank you," Diane said.

Yokohama, Japan
June 11, 1944

When the official car stopped in front of Hiroko Saito's home, she felt her heart leap to her throat. The last time such a car paid a visit it was to inform her that her husband had been killed. Why were they here now?

"Miko?" she called in a frightened voice.

Miko came to her mother's side and waited. In the small courtyard in front of the house a bell rang. Together Miko and her mother moved to the front door, and Miko slid it open.

Their fear turned to curiosity when they saw that one of the men was their postman, Hiro Amano. The man with him, though, was wearing the uniform of the national police.

"Miko Saito?" the policeman asked.

"I am Miko," she answered in surprise.

"You have a letter," the policeman said.

"I don't understand. Why would an officer of the prefect of police deliver a letter to me?"

The policeman nodded toward the postman, who pulled a letter from his pocket and handed it to Miko.

"Thank you, Amano-san," Miko said.

Amano bowed his head slightly in acknowledgement.

Miko took the letter and started to close the door, but the policeman stuck his hand out to stop her.

"Read the letter aloud," he said.

"Why do you ask me to read it aloud?"

"The letter is from an American. We are at war with America. I am sure you understand that such a thing makes our government suspicious."

Miko stared at the policeman for a moment, then she looked at the letter. A broad smile spread across her face.

"Mother, it is from Diane!" she said.

"Diane? No, it is from America," the policeman said.

"Diane is the name of my American friend," Miko explained. She looked at Amano. "Amano-san, remember the Reverend Slayton-san?"

"Ah, yes," Amano said. "He was a preacher in the American church here for many years. I brought many letters to him."

"So, you can see, this is just a letter between friends," Miko said to the policeman.

"I wish to hear you read it," the policeman said again.

Miko started to open the letter, then saw that it had already been opened. She looked accusingly at Amano.

"The authorities," he explained. "They have read the letter already."

"Then why must I read it again?" Miko asked.

"Read it," the policeman repeated.

Nodding, Miko drew a deep breath and began reading. "My dear friend Miko. I saw in the *Asahi Shimbun* that your father was killed. I express my deepest condolences to you and to your family. I regret to tell you that my father was also killed."

Miko looked up at her mother. "Reverend Slayton-san is dead," she said. "We must remember to say a prayer for him."

"Continue," the policeman ordered.

Miko returned to the letter. "I wish that wise men in both our countries could find a way to end this war so that no more good men will have to die.

"I also want to tell you that I am to be married. I wish only that there were no war so that you could share this happy event with me. Please write to me and tell me if you and your family are well.

"Your friend, Diane Slayton."

The policeman took the letter from Miko.

"Wait, what are you doing? That's my letter."

"You cannot keep it."

"But it is mine. Amano-san, you are the postman; do something," Miko demanded.

"I am very sorry," Amano said. "There is nothing I can do."

"If it weren't for Amano-san, you would not have seen the letter at all," the policeman said. "It was he who convinced my superiors to let him deliver it to you just long enough for you to read."

"I thank you for that," Miko said. "But may I just see it long enough to get the address?"

Amano shook his head. "Do not try to answer her," he warned. "I fear it will cause much trouble for you."

East Chatham, New York
August 7, 1944

Sean Hanifin stood at a window on the second floor looking out over the rolling, tree-studded hills. He had converted this part of his house—two rooms in the south wing—into a working area. One room was his library, with the walls covered by ceiling-to-floor bookcases. Two of the shelves contained books he had written. He also had two shelves of personally autographed books from writer friends and acquaintances, including F. Scott Fitzgerald, J. P. Priestly, and Ezra Pound.

Because Ezra Pound had remained in Italy and had written some pro-Fascist, anti-Semitic articles, there were many among Sean's friends and acquaintances who urged him to join them in denouncing the poet and burning his books. Sean had been quoted in news interviews, voicing his disagreement with Pound's views but refusing to take part in any book burning that would turn him into a Fascist to combat Fascism.

The second of the two rooms, and the one in which Sean was now standing, was his office. Here he had an oversized leather sofa on which he took frequent naps, a coffee table where he kept the pages of his manuscript-in-progress, a comfortable chair with footstool, a floor lamp, two desks—one of which was an antique rolltop—and three typewriters. On one wall was an original Monet; on another a painting by Norman Rockwell. He also had a framed certificate stating that Sean

Hanifin was the winner of the Pulitzer Prize Award for Fiction in 1936, for his novel *The Power and the Pride*.

While he was standing at the window, a deer came to the edge of the trees, stuck its nose out to sniff the air, then proceeded cautiously down to the stream and began to drink.

"Drink away, little deer," Sean said quietly. "Just be happy Hemingway isn't here. He'd shoot you."

Sean watched until the deer retreated back into the woods. Sighing, he returned to his typewriter. Although he had been asked almost two years ago to write an article giving his opinion on "the world after war," he had begged off until now, citing a book deadline. He wished that he had refused altogether, for the article was proving more difficult to write than he had thought. Picking up the pile of typed pages that lay beside his typewriter, he read some of what he had written.

Ask the man on the street if he is against war in principle, and he will answer that he is. Even though we know that this war must be fought, and is being won, the average John and Mary Doe will say that, in the abstract, war is an evil thing. Who can argue with that?

But ask if all the nations of the world should disarm. The answer to this question becomes a bit more complicated. While most favor disarming in principle, nearly all express the fear that disarmament might be unilateral. What if, they ask, the U.S. disarms and other countries do not? No one wants to leave America vulnerable to another Pearl Harbor.

Thus the door is open to experiment with an international organization. But wait. Such an idea was tried in the form of the League of Nations. Even now, with the world embroiled in war, the League has proven itself to be feeble.

The intent of the League was to provide a place for the belligerent nations to solve their differences before conditions reach the boiling point. And since we are now at war, many say there is no place for the League on today's stage.

Apologists for the League of Nations will explain that it was not designed to engage in war once war began. But Article 16 of the League's covenant does authorize the use of military force. There are many who believe that had military force been applied judiciously and promptly, we might never have reached our current condition. The League refused to use its teeth because the two nations that dominated it, Great Britain and France, had no will to invoke the article.

Now even the world body's most ardent supporters recognize that the League of Nations cannot be resurrected. An entirely new organization of nations will have to be formed. And success of this new organization will depend upon two things: American membership and, nearly as important, a willingness to use force when force is called for.

Some would say that civilization has no choice. In the end, if our world is to survive, we may require some means of accommodating the differences and settling the squabbles between nations. Nearly every war has produced some new invention that makes killing more efficient, and I don't believe this war is any different. Who knows what terrible new weapon will be devised by the evil ingenuity of man, bent upon killing his fellow man?

16

A ngelfish was submerged, heading north-northwest. Pat was off watch, lying in his bunk with his hands laced behind his head, thinking about Diane. It was now more than two years since he had seen her, but whenever he started feeling too sorry for himself, he had only to think about some of the other crewmen. Two of the men had three-year-old children they had never seen, and several more had not been home for their children's first steps or first words.

"Mr. Hanifin, Cap'n wants you in the conning tower," Tyler Hornsby called from just outside the door.

Pat glanced at his watch and saw that it was ten minutes until seven. He was supposed to have reported to duty at 0630, but was so deep in thought that he had lost track of time.

"Blast," he said under his breath. "Uh, yes, thank you, Hornsby, I'll be right there." Sitting up, he put his shoes on and moved quickly through

229

the long, narrow corridor to the control room, then up the ladder to the conning tower.

"Glad you could join us, Mr. Hanifin," Jerry said.

"Sorry, sir," Pat replied. "I didn't realize it was this late."

"Not only are you late, you are out of uniform."

"Sir?" Pat replied, looking down at himself.

"Commander Traser, would you see to it that this officer is in proper uniform?" Jerry asked.

"Yes, sir, it would be my privilege," Dickey said, frowning at Pat. Then his frown turned to a smile, and he stuck his hand into his pocket. "These are the bars I wore before I got this gold leaf on my collar," he said, holding out two sets of joined silver bars, the insignia of a full lieutenant. "I'd be honored if you would wear them, Lieutenant Hanifin."

"Yes, sir! It would be an honor to wear them."

"Darrel, help me get this fellow into proper uniform," Dickey said. Darrel, who was also a lieutenant, came over to assist Dickey in removing the single silver bar and replacing it with the new one.

"Now that you have joined us, Lieutenant, I can tell you that we may have found the invasion force," Jerry said. "You wouldn't want to miss out on that, would you?"

A Japanese task force consisting of troop transports and their escorts had been spotted by aircraft a few days earlier. There was some concern that it might be headed for Australia, and every submarine operating out of Fremantle had been put on alert to look for it.

"No sir, I most definitely would not want to miss out on that."

"Up periscope," Jerry said. Jerry looked through the scope for a moment, then pulled his eyes away. "Would the new lieutenant like to take a look?" he asked.

"Yes, sir, the new lieutenant would love to take a look!" Pat replied enthusiastically. Far in the distance he could see several columns of smoke, but the vessels emitting them were still hull-down.

"See anything?" Jerry asked.

"I see smoke, sir."

"Come to course zero nine zero, full speed ahead. Battle stations torpedo."

"Aye, aye, sir. Course zero nine zero, full speed ahead," Darrel repeated.

They maneuvered for nearly two hours to come to an intercept position. Jerry raised the periscope for another look and saw four transports with destroyer escorts on the flanks. He studied the biggest of the transports. It was covered with patches of rust at the waterline and painted a light gray color. He estimated it at about ten thousand tons. Checking the ONI book of classifications, he saw that it was in the *Kuniyama Maru* class. The next largest ship, of about sixty-five hundred tons, was of the *Heian Maru* class. He didn't check on the two smaller ones.

"We found them," he said. "Four transports, three destroyers. I'm going to try and take out the two largest ones. Target angle on the starboard bow, zero three zero. Down scope."

"Is it the invasion force?" Dickey asked.

"It is unless they have two convoys running around down here. Stand by bow tubes."

"Standing by, sir," Darrel replied.

"Open outer doors, tubes one, two, three, and four."

"Outer doors open," Darrel said.

From the backside of the periscope, Dickey read the azimuth ring. "Bearing zero-two-five degrees."

"Range, mark."

"Two thousand, five hundred yards."

"Set," Pat said from his position at the torpedo data computer.

"Captain, enemy target course is one-seven-zero degrees. Speed is ten knots," Dickey said.

"Range, mark."

"Two thousand yards."

Again Pat cranked in the range and confirmed it. "Set."

"Bearing, mark!" Jerry said.

Pat pressed a button that locked the last bearing of the enemy ship into the TDC. "Set!" he replied. "Captain, we have a firing solution."

"Fire one!" Jerry commanded.

Darrel hit the plunger that sent the first torpedo off with a jolting *whoosh*. The submarine shuddered as compressed air forced the missile out of the tube. Jerry fired six torpedoes from the bow tubes, four at the larger target, two at the smaller. He kept his eyes glued to the periscope, watching the wakes from the fast-running torpedoes as they streaked toward the Japanese ships.

"All torpedoes running hot, straight, and normal," Jarvis said.

Even without the aid of sonar equipment, Pat could hear the descending whine of the torpedo turbines as they sped toward their targets. Then, except for the subdued sound of ventilation blowers and hydraulics, there was only silence.

Dickey had been staring at his watch, holding his right hand up. He brought his hand down sharply. "Now!" he said.

"Dead hit!" Jerry said as he saw a large explosion at the waterline of the first target. Even without his visual, though, they would have known; everyone in the submarine heard the sound and felt the pressure wave.

More explosions followed the first one, and Jerry watched as a huge pillar of flame erupted from the second target. The ship began going straight down, her holds gutted and filling with water. He looked back toward the first target and saw steam escaping as she went down by the stern. He also saw two destroyers kicking up bow wakes as they came head-on toward the submarine.

Jerry slapped the handles up and backed away from the scope. "Take her down deep!" he called. "Flood negative! Rig for depth charge!"

Angelfish went deep as the destroyers passed overhead, their screws making a loud, thrumming sound that all in the boat could hear. For the next three hours, the destroyers dropped depth charges. Light bulbs shattered, loose gear scattered, pipes sprung leaks, and cork popped off the bulkheads. Not until night had fallen did the destroyers withdraw, and then Jerry waited for another full hour before he surfaced the boat.

Two days later they received a radio transmission from Fremantle, congratulating them on a job well done.

"Although it is now doubted that the Japanese had any intention of invading Australia," the message read, "the damage inflicted by our submarines against their convoy would certainly have changed their minds had they entertained such a thought."

Fremantle, Australia
Thanksgiving Day, November 23, 1944

When *Angelfish* put into port on the twenty-second of November, it was flying a battle flag from its upper shears displaying fourteen small Japanese flags. These Rising Suns surrounded the boat's emblem. The men were exceptionally proud of that emblem, and many had Hornsby draw smaller pictures of it for them. Some even had the emblem and words U.S.S. *Angelfish* tattooed on their bodies.

As *Angelfish* came into the Fremantle harbor, it was greeted by a huge hand-painted sign covering an entire wall of a warehouse near the docks: AUSTRALIA WISHES A HAPPY THANKSGIVING TO OUR AMERICAN FRIENDS.

The U.S. Navy went all out to ensure an enjoyable Thanksgiving dinner, shipping several thousand pounds of turkeys over in time for the celebration. In addition, the crew of *Angelfish* enjoyed a particular treat. Several months earlier Choirboy had written to the families of all the men, asking if there was any special dish that their loved ones liked for Thanksgiving. As a result, Lt. Comdr. Dickey Traser was served caviar and creamed cheese on toast points (his mother had even included a very special brand of caviar along with her letter). Pat was presented with a pumpkin pie, liberally dusted with extra brown sugar and cinnamon.

Tony Jarvis had developed a liking for cornbread and milk when he was in the orphanage, and he still enjoyed it. The cook made an entire pan of cornbread, just for Tony. Perhaps the most surprised of all was Jerry Cornelison. He had no family, but had once confided to Dickey that he remembered with fondness his mother's homemade noodles made with cheese, tomatoes, and jalapeño peppers. When Thanksgiving dinner was served, that dish was included.

The meal was as close to a family meal as one could get under the circumstances, and the men tasted each other's special dishes, swapped stories of Thanksgivings past and, inevitably, started talking about football. Some of the crew were avid football fans and had followed Jerry's collegiate career. They told the others of the gridiron exploits of their commanding officer. By the time the meal was finished and the stories told and re-told, Jerry Cornelison was a football player whose heroics loomed larger than those of Red Grange or anyone else who had ever played the game.

"Funny, isn't it, Captain, how they remember some things and not others? Like, who remembers your fumble on the goal line that cost us the game against Duke?" Dickey teased.

"Obviously, you do, you killjoy," Jerry replied. The others laughed.

After dinner, mail was delivered to the crew, and with their stomachs comfortably full, they lay around reading letters from home.

"Well, how about this?" Pat said aloud as he read his letter from Diane. "Diane is going to spend Christmas and New Year's in San Francisco."

"That'll be a nice trip for her," Darrel said.

"I suppose so. I'm just a little surprised, though. She doesn't know anyone there. I would think she would want to stay in Honolulu, where she has some friends."

"Now this is the captain speaking," the captain's voice announced over the 1MC. "Make ready in all respects to get under way."

"We just got here," someone said.

"I thought we would get at least forty-eight hours," another voice added.

"You might be interested in our destination," Jerry continued over the 1MC.

The groans and complaints stopped as everyone waited to hear his next words.

"We have just received orders directing *Angelfish* to undergo a refit. The refit, which will include the new, slower-running electric motors, will eliminate the need of the reduction gear. That will make us a much quieter running boat. We will also be getting the latest radar equipment."

"All right," someone said. "Bring 'em on. We'll kick some Jap tail now!" The unseen sailor's remark was met with laughter.

There was a pause, then Jerry added, almost as an afterthought, "Oh, by the way, you might also be interested to know that the refit will take place in San Francisco."

There was a moment of silence as everyone took in the meaning of the captain's announcement. Then, as it sank in, the cheering was loud and sustained.

Pat looked at the letter he was holding. Diane would be in San Francisco for Christmas and New Year's. And so would he.

At sea
December 26, 1944

Although Jerry made a valiant effort to get them back by Christmas Day, they wound up celebrating another Christmas at sea. But they were so close to the States, the men could look forward to belated Christmases at home.

At dawn on the twenty-sixth of December, *Angelfish* made a position report to the commander of the Western Sea Frontier. They were one hundred miles west of San Francisco Bay, having covered the distance from Australia in near-record time.

The submarine had a surface speed of twenty-two knots, and though they had passed through some areas where prudence might have dictated that they run submerged, Jerry had chosen to run the entire distance on the surface.

"The orders said return with all dispatch," Jerry said, "and I believe that running on the surface is the best way to proceed with all dispatch."

Jerry had no one in particular to hurry home to, so it was obvious that he was doing this for the men. As a result, every man on the crew performed at peak efficiency, often volunteering to work beyond their own watches in order that they may proceed with "all dispatch"—the crew's new catchphrase.

Jerry had given permission to anyone who was on the bridge to be able to issue the order for an emergency dive. But after two dives for friendly planes and one for a peculiar cloud formation, the bridge watch was asked to be a bit more positive with their identifications. There were no more dives after that.

For the last one hundred miles on into San Francisco Bay, however, the submarine faced more danger from American forces than it did from the Japanese. They were required to conform to a strict procedure in order to prevent attacks by friendly aircraft and ships. The operating procedure called for submarines to stay on the surface, maintain a speed of exactly fifteen knots, and follow a prescribed submarine route thirty miles south of the main east-west shipping lane to California.

By noon on December 26, they reached an assigned rendezvous point just off the Farallon Islands. There they were met by a Coast Guard cutter, flashing "welcome home" on its signal light. *Angelfish*, with her homeward-bound pennant flying proudly from the shears, fell in behind the cutter, following her through the channel by Seal Rocks Beach, then under Golden Gate Bridge. To their left lay the Marin headlands; to the right was the breathtakingly beautiful sight of the city of San Francisco.

As they sailed by Alcatraz, Pat stood on the bridge, looking toward the famous prison and wondering about the men inside. Could they see the war ships entering and leaving the bay? Even though they were criminals, did they have a sense of patriotism?

At North Point, they turned into the southbound ship traffic lane. Once they passed under the bay bridge, they angled just a bit to the right for a straight shot to the U.S. Naval dry docks at Hunters Point and the submarine berths at South Basin.

In addition to a navy band and a welcoming committee of naval officers, there were over a hundred people, most of them women, crowded onto the pier. The wives, parents, and sweethearts of the crew had all been notified that their loved ones would be arriving in San Francisco on or about this date.

The women fluttered handkerchiefs and waved and shouted names that could be heard only as distant, unintelligible yells. *Angelfish*, with its screws turning just fast enough to make headway against the current, maneuvered toward the pier. Jerry backed her down expertly as the line handlers, fore and aft, made her secure.

"All stop," Jerry ordered.

The rumbling sound of the diesel engines, a constant background sound for the last thirty days, fell silent. When the brow was put over, Pat was one of the first to disembark.

Standing at the foot of the walkway was Diane. She ran into his arms and they embraced and kissed, oblivious of anyone around them. Though most of the others, engaged in their own embraces, were equally oblivious of them.

San Francisco, California
December 27, 1944

Once *Angelfish* had been turned over for refit, the crew was dismissed. And because shore personnel maintained even the anchor watch, there was no need for anyone to remain aboard. Within minutes of docking, most of the men were signed out on the thirty-day leaves that would take them to their homes throughout the United States.

Very few remained in San Francisco, but those who did would have found hotel space at a premium had it not been for the Traser Hotel and the direct intervention of Dickey Traser's father. Although the source of J. Arthur Traser's rather considerable income was his railroad line, he also owned several hotels, including one in San Francisco. The crew of *Angelfish* was given priority there, with rooms allocated on the basis of one room per four enlisted, and one room per two officers. Crew members whose wives had come to meet them were granted private rooms regardless of rank.

At the moment, Jerry Cornelison and Dickey Traser were in the ballroom of the hotel. Although the hotel lobby was still festooned with Christmas decorations, the ballroom had been cleared of all vestiges of the holiday. The reason could be found on a large white card set on a tripod at the foot of the small flight of stairs that led down into the sunken ballroom. In beautiful calligraphy it announced:

Wedding of
Lieutenant Patrick Michael Hanifin, U.S. Navy
and
Diane Ashley Slayton
to take place at 9:00 A.M. on
Thursday, December 28, in the Year of Our Lord 1944

Vases of white carnations stood on every table, and garlands of flowers and greenery were draped across windowsills, fluted pillars, and balustrades that flanked the steps leading down into the ballroom.

"Wait," Dickey called, going over to the man supervising the decorations. "Those flowers won't do."

"Something wrong, Mr. Traser?" the supervisor asked. "I assure you, they are freshly cut."

"Perhaps, but this is a navy wedding. I want blue and gold carnations."

The supervisor chuckled. "Sir, there are no blue or gold carnations."

"Sure there are," Dickey replied. "Our dates used to wear them at navy football games. All you have to do is stick the stems down into blue ink. They'll color themselves. And yellow will pass for gold."

"Very well, sir," the supervisor said. "I'll take care of it."

As the supervisor began issuing instructions to dye the white carnations blue, Dickey walked back over to Jerry, then paused to survey the room. "So, what do you think?" he asked. "Will they like it?"

"Speaking as the bride's surrogate father, I think she will like it very much," Jerry said with a laugh. "And speaking as the groom's commanding officer, I say he'd better like it, or else."

Diane had asked Jerry to give her away, and Pat had asked Darrel Roberts to be his best man.

Dickey had taken it on himself to coordinate the wedding. The officers of *Angelfish* who hadn't gone home would provide an arch of crossed swords, under which the bride and groom would pass at the conclusion of the ceremony.

"I should go into the wedding planning business," Dickey said as he rubbed his hands together. "This is going to be one jim-dandy affair."

"Ha! I can see you as a professional wedding planner," Jerry said.

Dickey grinned and looked around. "By the way, have you seen Diane lately? I'd like to get her opinion on what I've planned."

"Why?" Jerry replied. "You haven't asked for anyone's opinion on anything else."

"I'd like hers, though."

"You don't want her opinion; you want her praise. And I'm sure you'll get it, but right now, I expect she has a few prewedding jitters. They say everyone gets them."

At that very moment Diane was in her room on the fourteenth floor of the hotel, sitting on a wide windowsill and looking out over the city of San Francisco. Father Kenneth Kern, the chaplain who had been her father's closest friend on board *Lexington*, was also now stationed in San Francisco. After arriving, she had looked him up and enlisted his aid in cutting through any red tape that might stand in the way of their getting married as soon as the submarine docked.

Father Kern was a godsend. He got immediate naval approval for the marriage, arranged for Pat to have his blood test processed immediately, and even managed to get the wedding license issued. All that remained for Pat to do when he arrived was to agree to the arrangements.

Though everything was set the day before *Angelfish* docked, Diane felt anxious, wondering if perhaps she had rushed things too quickly. Would Pat resent all that she had done to expedite the marriage? Would he prefer a few days to recuperate?

She needn't have worried.

Diane had wanted a quiet wedding in the navy chapel, but when Dickey found out about it, he insisted that they have a grand wedding in the hotel. "I'll take care of everything," he promised.

Diane had gone along with all of his plans, giving him full rein to make whatever arrangements he wanted. She was grateful to him and expressed that appreciation every chance she got. But sometimes when she was alone, she realized that having a big wedding was bittersweet. Most women had big weddings for their families and friends, but Diane had neither. As far as San Francisco was concerned, she was a stranger in a strange land.

There was a knock on her door, and when she opened it, she was surprised to see several young women standing there.

"May I help you?" she asked, certain that they must have the wrong room.

"Are you Diane Slayton?" The woman who asked had bright brown eyes and a mass of chestnut hair swept up on top of her head.

"Yes, I am," Diane answered cautiously.

"I'm Sally Traser, Dickey's sister," the woman said. "May we come in?"

"Yes, of course." Diane stepped back from the door.

"Come on, girls," Sally said as the girls came into the room, laughing and talking among themselves. Once inside, Sally leaned her head back out into the hall. "Okay, you can come in now."

A young woman with dark eyes, olive complexion, high cheekbones, and full lips stepped into the room, smiling broadly.

"Carol!" Diane squealed in delight. "What are you doing here?"

"You didn't think I was going to let you get married without me, did you?" Carol asked.

The two women embraced, at first in joy, then, as they thought about John Henry, in mutual comfort. Finally they separated, each with glistening eyes.

"I'm so glad you came," Diane said.

"Well, let's start the shower, shall we?" Sally asked. "Eddie, bring it in here," she called.

Two men wearing the uniforms of hotel employees came into the room, each pushing a cart. There were several packages on one, while on the other there was a silver teapot and little plates of petit fours, cookies, and mints.

"What . . . what is this? What's going on?" Diane asked.

"It's a shower," Sally replied, smiling sweetly. "A girl can't have a wedding without a shower, can she?"

"I . . . I don't know. I've never been to a shower. I'm not sure I even know what it is."

"Are you serious?" Sally asked in surprise.

"She didn't grow up in the States," Carol explained.

"That's right, Dickey said you grew up in Japan. Well, a shower is when friends of the bride have a party and give her presents to celebrate the wedding."

"Oh, how nice."

"Don't they have wedding showers in Japan?"

"In Japan, they have something called the *yunio*, but it is given to both the man and the woman. And the gifts are ritualistic. For example, the man is given a dried cuttlefish to ensure virility. The woman is given kelp for fertility, because the characters used for the word *kelp* can also be written to mean child-bearing woman."

"Well, honey, we don't have anything like that," Sally said. "But I did buy you some of the most beautiful lingerie you have ever seen. I mean, it is purely going to make Lieutenant Hanifin's eyes pop out."

The others laughed at Sally's comment, then rushed to present their own gifts.

"I'm sorry we weren't here for you earlier," Sally apologized, "but I didn't even find out about the wedding until this morning. I asked Dickey who was giving you a shower because I wanted to come, and he told me he didn't think you were having one. Well, honey, I said pish-posh to that. No girl should have a wedding without a shower, so I called together some of my friends and . . ." She threw her arms out wide and moved one foot forward. "Ta-da! I hope you don't think we're too forward."

"No, no, not at all. I'm glad you came," Diane said enthusiastically. "I can't remember when I have been so surprised."

"I assume that, since no one had planned a shower for you, you also have no bridesmaids."

"No, I don't."

"Well, being a bridesmaid isn't supposed to be a self-appointed position, so I can't presume to be one for you unless you would like me to."

"Yes, oh, yes, I truly would like that," Diane said enthusiastically.

"Then Carol shall be your maid of honor, and these eager souls and

I will be your bridesmaids," Sally said. She stood up. "Come girls, we have shopping to do. We must buy our bridesmaids' gowns, and we must have them ready by tomorrow."

"Oh, we'll never be able to get it done that fast," one of the other girls said.

"Sure we can," Sally replied with a little laugh.

"How?"

"I will just ask father to make it so," Sally answered simply.

Ballroom of the Traser Hotel
December 28, 1944

One by one the bridesmaids moved up the aisle to the front of the room. As best man, Darrel escorted Carol Thompson to the front, then took his place near Father Kern, who was already in position.

The organist began playing the wedding march, and all eyes in the crowded ballroom turned toward the back where they saw a radiantly beautiful Diane, calmly awaiting her cue. Jerry Cornelison stood beside her.

Together, moving in time to the majestic music, Diane and Jerry started up the long, narrow red carpet that stretched through the middle of the ballroom and up to the front where the chaplain and Pat Hanifin waited. The area above Pat's left breast pocket, bare when he went to sea, was now covered with a string of colorful medals.

There she is, Pat thought, *the most beautiful woman I have ever seen, and in just a few minutes she will be my wife.*

The music stopped as they reached the front of the room and, without further delay, Father Kern began the rite. When he asked for the ring, Darrel pulled it from his pocket, then stepped back.

The chaplain continued with the ceremony, calling God's blessing down upon them, charging them both with the responsibility of marriage. Finally he said, "Those whom God hath joined together, let no man put asunder. For as much as Pat and Diane have consented together in holy wedlock, and have witnessed the same before God and this company, and thereto have given and pledged their troth, each to the other, I pronounce that they are man and wife."

Kern looked at the two for a moment, then, smiling, he added, "A kiss is customary."

The audience applauded as Pat took Diane into his arms and kissed her. Then, to the music of Mendelssohn, they hurried back down the red carpet toward the rear of the room. Although Darrel Roberts was not the senior officer attending, he had been Pat's best man; thus it fell to him to issue the order.

"Present, swords!" he called.

As one, the officers raised their swords to form an arch, under which Lt. and Mrs. Patrick Hanifin began to pass. Midway the swords dropped to the horizontal, trapping them. Another kiss, and they were allowed to proceed.

17

Yosemite Valley
December 28, 1945

P at and Dianne honeymooned in the Ahwanee Hotel in Yosemite
Valley. The hotel, with its great granite façade, beamed ceilings,
and massive stone hearths, was the perfect location for a young warrior
to take his bride. Far from the sea and the *sturm und stiet* of war, it was
a haven of peace. After dinner they walked arm-in-arm through the
giant sequoias, inhaling the aroma of the pine needles and mingling
their breath in a cloud of white vapor as they exhaled. Then they
returned to the hotel, passed through the great lobby, and took the elevator to their third-floor room.

The room was exceptionally beautiful, with its rich fabrics, warm
woods, Indian motif, and panoramic view of Yosemite Falls. But the
appointments of the room, the view of the falls, and the beauty of the
valley paled into insignificance as Diane and Pat experienced the wonder of discovery in each other's arms on their wedding night.

Pat awoke once, and thinking for a moment that he was on *Angelfish,* wondered why he wasn't hearing the motors, reduction gear, blowers, and pumps. The moon shadows on the wall brought him back to this time and place, and he knew where he was. Looking through the window, he saw a giant pine, its branches limned by moonlight. When it answered a gentle breeze, the pine needles scattered slivers of silver through the night.

Diane lay beside him, her white silk nightgown almost luminescent. Her blonde hair was fanned across the pillow, and her lips appeared to curl into a soft smile as she slept. Pat reached down to put his hand on her hip and, through the sensual silk of her gown, felt the tactile difference between her pelvic bone and the flesh of her thigh. It was a simple thing and yet, incorporated in that innocent touch, was a sense of possession, belonging, and inclusion, a glue that made them one, now and forever.

East Chatham, New York
January 5, 1945

In the living room of the Hanifin house, "Mairzy Doats" was playing on the radio while a fire crackled in the fireplace. Sean was sitting in an easy chair, smoking a pipe and reading the newspaper, while Katie arranged flowers in a vase.

"Don't you think it would have been better for them to wait and get married here?" Katie asked. "I mean, why did they have to rush into it?"

"Rush into it? They waited for three years," Sean said. "I don't think they could have waited another day, let alone the time it would take for them to come here and get all the arrangements made."

"Still, I think it would have been better."

"And why would you think that?"

"They could've been married here, in our own church, by our own priest."

"They were married by a navy chaplain. I think that was more meaningful to them."

"But Pat should have been married in a Catholic church," Katie insisted.

"The chaplain was a Catholic priest."

"Aye, but only by coincidence. He married them because he was a friend of Diane's father," Katie said. "It wasn't a real Catholic wedding."

"It was real enough, Katie Hanifin, and you'll not be suggesting anything different to Pat."

"I'll not say a word about it."

"I would think you would be so happy for them."

"I am happy for them, and to be seeing Pat again. What time is it? Shouldn't we be getting down to the depot to meet them?"

Sean chuckled. "Going to the depot earlier isn't going to make the train arrive any sooner. We've got an hour yet."

Katie set the flowers on the coffee table, stepped back to examine them, then repositioned them.

"Would you be for tellin' me what you think about these flowers, Sean Hanifin?" she asked. "Do they look better here, or here?" She moved the vase from one place to the other.

"Either place is fine," Sean answered.

"Maybe they'd look better on the mantel," she said, taking the vase and carrying it over to the fireplace.

"Katie, for crying out loud, will you settle down?" Sean asked, exasperated.

"I can't help it," Katie said. "I'm longin' to hold my wee boy in my arms."

Sean chuckled. "He's hardly a wee boy anymore."

"He'll always be my wee boy," Katie insisted. "An' it's been so long."

"It's been just as long for me, but I'm not bouncing off the walls."

Katie fiddled with the flowers for another moment, then moved them back to the coffee table. "I think they look better here, where I had them in the first place. Don't you?"

"Yes," Sean agreed.

"What time is it? Sure'n it must be time to go now."

Sean sighed and put the newspaper down. "You'll be giving me no peace until we go, woman. I can see that now. All right, to the car with you."

Katie was no less anxious at the depot. Twice she got out of the car and walked over to look down the track for the train, each time allowing a cold blast of air into the car. Then, finally, they heard the whistle.

"Oh, it's here!" she said excitedly.

"We may as well wait in the car until it actually pulls in," Sean said. "It's cold outside."

"You can wait in the car if you want, Sean Hanifin, but when my son gets off that train I want to be the first thing he sees," Katie said, opening the door.

Sean watched her move across the platform to stand close to the track. Then, with a shrug of surrender, he got out of the car as well. He wouldn't admit it to Katie, but he was as excited as she was.

They stepped down from the train, a beautiful young woman in a green dress and a handsome young man in blue. Pat was leaner and more tanned than Sean remembered. There was little similarity between the self-confident, mature naval officer now embracing his mother and the nightclub piano player who had left them three years before.

Pat and Sean were upstairs in Sean's office suite. Pat was standing by one of the bookshelves, looking through the titles. Sean was sitting in his easy chair, smoking his pipe and looking through the page proofs he had recently gotten from his publisher. Diane and Katie had gone shopping— according to Sean, a necessary "bonding" ritual between the two women.

Pat put the book he was holding back on the shelf, then walked over to sit on the couch. "Do you still dislike working on page proofs as much as you used to?"

Sean looked up. "I dislike it intensely," he said. "It's like sweeping up after the job is done."

"What's the book?" Pat asked.

"*Dysmus*."

"*Dysmus?*" Pat echoed.

"The one they call the 'good thief,'" Sean said. "You know, when Jesus was crucified, how one of the thieves asked to be remembered in paradise?"

"Yes."

"That was Dysmus."

"How do we know that?"

"We aren't entirely sure, but we believe that was his name."

"Okay, so why are you writing about him? That's a little different from the things you normally do, isn't it?"

"I suppose it is," Sean agreed. "But the war has so dominated literature for the last few years that I wanted to get away from the horror and write about hope. So I chose to write about Dysmus."

"I'll be anxious to read it," Pat said.

"I hope you do." Sean emptied the bowl of his pipe and studied Pat for a moment. "Son, where do you stand on religion now?"

"What do you mean?"

"It's not a trick question. I know that years ago you had a run-in that made you turn your back on your faith. Your mother . . ." He paused for moment, then added, "and I as well, have been worrying about you. It is hard enough to realize that you could be killed in this war. It's even harder to think that your soul might be in peril."

"Have you ever heard the expression, 'There are no atheists in fox-holes'?" Pat asked.

"Yes, I have heard that."

"Well, there are no atheists in a submarine either. It's impossible to go through a depth-charge attack and not ask for God's help. I may not be quite the smells-and-bells liturgical Catholic mother would like. And I know she was disappointed that we weren't married in a Catholic church, but that doesn't mean that I have turned my back on Christ. John Henry Welsko was a good, God-fearing man, and there is no better Christian than Diane. I think they have been positive influences on my life."

"Diane is a fine Christian woman, I think even your mother would be first to admit that. And as for John Henry, I hope his family takes comfort in knowing that he was right with the Lord when he met his Maker."

"They are comforted by the fact that John Henry was a good Christian.

I wrote his parents after he was killed," Pat said. "I got a very nice letter back from them, thanking me for being his friend."

"Submarines don't have chaplains, do they?"

Pat chuckled. "They aren't supposed to, but ours does."

"You have a chaplain on *Angelfish?*" Sean asked in surprise.

"Well, not officially," Pat said. "But Choirboy will do in a pinch."

"And who is Choirboy?"

"His real name is Leon Jackson. He's a steward's mate, and one of the finest men I've ever known."

Calvary, Georgia
Sunday, January 7, 1945

The title of the Rev. Amos Jackson's sermon was "Dealing with Satan."

"I want to tell you about Satan," Reverend Jackson began in his singsong voice.

"Tell us, brother," the congregation replied.

"Satan ain't what you think he is."

"No, sir."

"You ain't going to find Satan with red skin, horns, and a pointed tail."

"No horns, no tail, no, sir."

"'Cause Satan, now, he don't look like that."

"No, he don't look like that."

"If he look like that, there wouldn't be no problem. You wouldn't want nothin' to do with someone who look like that," Amos Jackson said.

"Nothin' to do with someone who look like that."

"But the devil is very clever."

"Clever, yes, Lord, that devil clever."

"And the devil is sneaky."

"Sneaky, yes, Lord, that devil sneaky."

The good reverend was wound up now, and he grabbed the pulpit with both hands as he leaned forward and continued in a singsong fashion.

"He roams the streets like a roving lion, seeking whom he may devour."

"Like a lion, Lord, like a lion."

"And he can be as pretty as a good-lookin' woman."

"Yes, sir, a good-lookin' woman."

"And he can be as appealing as a big, fancy car."

"Yes, Lord, a big, fancy car."

"And he can be as temptin' as a dish of hand-cranked vanilla ice cream, smothered with Georgia peaches."

"Ice cream and peaches, yes, Lord."

"But don't you fall for any of his evil, sneaky ways." Now Jackson reached his high point, and he boomed out his admonition to the congregation. "GET THEE BEHIND ME, SATAN!"

The congregational response was loud and enthusiastic.

"We goin' put Satan behind. Yes, Lord, we goin' put him behind, amen!"

After painting all the ways a person could be tempted by Satan, Reverend Jackson then laid out the consequences of giving in to the temptation. By the time he was finished, his congregation had been squeezed through the emotional wringer, and there wasn't one among them who didn't make a personal resolve to change his or her ways for the better.

Following the sermon there was a potluck dinner in the church basement to welcome the reverend's son, Leon, home from the navy. In his dark-blue uniform, with its several bright campaign ribbons, Choirboy was the center of attention. Young boys crowded around him, pointing to various ribbons and asking him to explain what each particular award was for.

"Ladies and gentlemen, let us bow our heads and give thanks for this wonderful bounty that has been put before us," Amos said. "Leon, would you say the blessing?"

Choirboy gave the blessing and then, as the guest of honor, was accorded the privilege of being first in line. The food was good and plentiful, and the only problem he had was the fact that each of the ladies urged him to be sure and try *her* dish. He complied as much as he could and, as a result, his plate was practically spilling over by the time he took his seat.

Leon was no sooner seated than Daisy Chambers, daughter of the

251

principal of the George Washington Carver School for Colored Children, joined him. At first, Choirboy had a hard time remembering her. Then he realized that she had only been thirteen the last time he saw her; she was eighteen now, and had blossomed into a beautiful young woman.

"Are you ever afraid?" Daisy asked. "I mean, when you are out there in that submarine. Do you get scared?"

"Nah, Leon, he don't never get scared," a young boy answered. "Look at all them medals he's wearin'. You think somebody with all them medals ever gets scared?"

"I hate to disappoint you, Travis, but I do get scared," Choirboy said.

"You do?" Travis asked in disbelief.

"Of course I do. Any sane man would be afraid under the water with people dropping depth charges on him, trying to kill him."

"Not me, I wouldn't be afraid," Travis said boldly.

Daisy laughed. "You'd be the biggest scaredy-cat of them all, Travis. I remember the way you ran from Mrs. Simmons's dog last week."

"Yeah, well, that was a dog," Travis said. "And that's different from bein' scared of the Japs."

"How is it different?" Daisy asked.

"It's different 'cause dogs is dogs. I'm going to go get me some more ice cream 'fore it's all gone." Travis hurried over to the ice-cream freezer to stand in line with the other children.

"He's right, dogs are dogs," Choirboy said, laughing.

Choirboy and Daisy spent the rest of the afternoon together, and when Daisy's father started home later in the day, she asked if she could stay a while longer.

"How will you get home?" her father asked.

"I'll bring her home," Choirboy said. "I'll use Pop's car."

"All right. But be home at a reasonable hour."

"I will, Papa."

The afternoon stretched on, and as the parishioners left one by one, they came by to tell Choirboy how happy they were to see him and to let him know that he was always in their prayers.

"I appreciate that," Choirboy said. "I feel the presence of the Lord while I'm out there, and I know it's because so many good people back here are praying for me."

As it grew toward evening, Choirboy told Daisy about *Angelfish* and the men who served on her. "Have you ever heard of a man named Sean Hanifin?" he asked.

"Sean Hanifin? Yes, he's a writer."

"His son is on our boat."

"Really? What's he like?"

"He's very nice," Choirboy said. "All of the officers are nice. The chiefs too."

For the next hour, Choirboy entertained Daisy with humorous stories about things that happened on the submarine. He was careful not to be self-aggrandizing and said nothing about the terror of depth-charge attacks. For her part, Daisy explained that she had been accepted at Howard University and had plans to be a schoolteacher.

"You'll make a great schoolteacher," Choirboy said.

Daisy laughed. "How do you know?"

"Because I can tell you would be great at anything you did."

Just after sunset Choirboy's father approached them, handing Leon his car keys. "Son, it's got dark, so I spec' you best be gettin' Daisy on home now. Her daddy don't want her out too late."

"All right," Choirboy said. "Come on, I don't want to get your papa angry with me right off the bat. I might want to call on you again, if you don't mind."

"I'd love to have you call on me again, Leon."

The car was a 1937 Chevrolet, maroon, with gray wire wheels. Choirboy's father had kept it in good shape, especially considering the shortages caused by the war. But the tires were another matter, and halfway between the church and Daisy's house, one of them blew out.

"Oh," Daisy said. "Now what will we do?"

"If Pop's spare is up, it won't be any problem," Choirboy said, getting out and walking around to the back of the car. He opened the trunk, then groaned. There was a spare, but it had a huge oval worn spot in the tread. He wasn't sure it would even hold up long enough to get Daisy to her house, let alone get him back home. But he had no choice but to try, so he pulled out the tire and the jack and went to work.

Choirboy had just gotten the jack in place when a pickup truck loaded with high-school-aged white boys stopped behind him. They piled out of the truck.

"You need any help?" a redheaded boy asked.

Choirboy turned toward them. "No, thank you, it's just a flat tire."

"Wait a minute!" the boy said. He pointed to Choirboy. "You a colored boy. I thought you was a sailor. That's why we stopped to help."

"I am a sailor," Choirboy said.

"What about that, Lenny?" the redhead asked. "This here colored boy says he's a sailor. Same as your brother."

"No, he ain't the same as my brother," Lenny replied. "My brother's a real sailor. All colored boys can do in the navy is wash dishes and the like."

"Well, this here'n must'a done a lot more'n that. Look at all them medals he's wearin'."

Lenny shook his head. "There ain't no way a colored boy would get medals like that, lessen he stole 'em. You steal them medals, boy?"

Daisy got out of the car then. "I know you boys," she said. "Some of you, anyway." She pointed to the redhead. "You're Roy Carter," she said. "You're Lenny Mason, and you're Johnny Sanders. What are you doing here?"

"We stopped to offer our help," Roy said, his red hair glowing in the headlights. "But this here imposter said he didn't want it."

"What do you mean, imposter?"

"He's dressed up in a navy suit and wearin' all them medals. That makes him an imposter."

"No, he isn't. This is Leon Jackson. You know who Reverend Jackson is, don't you? This is his son," Daisy said.

"Yeah? Well, a preacher's son ought to know better than to pass himself off as somethin' he ain't. What do you say, boys? Shall we take them medals off of him?"

"Go away!" Daisy said, frightened now. "Go away and leave us alone!"

"Huh, uh," Lenny said, shaking his head. "There's too many good boys, good white boys, dyin' overseas to have some colored boy come around wearin' medals he ain't earned."

"Run, Daisy," Choirboy said quietly.

"No, I'm not going to leave you to these—"

"Run, Daisy!" Choirboy said more forcefully.

Daisy hesitated but a moment, then she turned and started running up the road.

"Let's get him!" Roy shouted, and all six rushed Choirboy at the same time.

Choirboy was holding the tire iron in his hand. It put him on more equal footing with all six of his attackers, but he knew that if he used it, even in self-defense, he could wind up in serious trouble. He dropped the tire iron and met Roy's charge with a left jab to the nose. Choirboy felt the nose go under his fist and saw blood gushing down Roy's face as he yelled in pain and anger. He knocked Lenny off his feet with a right cross and managed to get in one more punch before they grabbed him.

All six boys were football players and good-sized, strong young men. But Choirboy was also strong and athletic, and he continued to put up a fight until he suddenly saw stars and felt an explosion on the side of his head. As he dropped to his knees, he saw Roy toss the tire iron aside.

"Now hold him for me," Roy said.

Four of the boys, two on each side, grabbed Choirboy by the arms and pulled him to his feet.

"The first thing I'm going to do is take away these medals he's wearin'," Roy said. He reached out to Choirboy's chest and came away with a fistful of colorful ribbons. He tossed them aside. "And the next thing I'm goin' to do is teach this here colored boy a lesson that he ain't likely to forget." Drawing back his fist, he hit Choirboy in the face. Almost instantly, Choirboy felt his eye swelling shut.

"You ain't goin' to get all the fun," Lenny said. "Save some for me." Lenny took a punch as well.

Suddenly the explosive sound of a shotgun blast jarred the night. When the boys looked around, they saw that a car with a flashing red light had approached, unnoticed. Sheriff Harold Wallace was standing in front of the car, holding the butt of a smoking shotgun against his hip. Daisy was behind him.

"Let him go . . . now!" the sheriff demanded.

When the four boys let go, Choirboy nearly fell, but he regained his balance. He put his hand on the side of the car to steady himself.

"You boys get away from him."

When the boys stepped aside, Daisy hurried over to Choirboy and, using her handkerchief, began tending to the cuts on his face.

"Just what in the Sam Hill did you all think you were doin'?" Wallace asked.

"We was teachin' this here colored boy a lesson," Roy said. He whistled when he talked, because of his broken nose. A stream of blood flowed down his mouth and chin.

"Yeah, we was teachin' him a lesson," Lenny said, his left eye red and swollen shut.

"Looks to me like he was givin' out about as much as he was takin'," Wallace said. "But what I want to know is, why did you boys jump on him?"

"Can't you tell?" Lenny asked. "He's wearin' a sailor suit, which he prob'ly ain't supposed to be wearin', and medals, which I *know* he ain't supposed to be wearin'."

"How do you know?" Sheriff Wallace asked.

"Well, come on, Sheriff, he's colored!" Lenny said, as if that explained everything. "The only thing colored boys do in the navy is wash dishes. You don't get medals for washin' dishes."

"Girl, get those ribbons and bring 'em to me," Sheriff Wallace said.

Daisy did as he asked.

"You see this ribbon right here?" Wallace asked, pointing to one that was red, white, and blue. "This is the Silver Star. Leon got that medal for shooting down a Jap plane."

"What? I don't believe it," Lenny said. "My brother's in the navy. He never said nothing about no colored boys shootin' down an airplane, or getting a Silver Star."

"That's because your brother works in a supply depot in Nevada," the sheriff replied.

"What?" Johnny asked. All of the other boys looked at Lenny. "You said your brother was on a carrier."

"Well, he's goin' to be," Lenny said, defending himself weakly. He looked back at the sheriff. "Anyway, how do you know he shot down a Jap plane?"

"Because, you stupid idiots, it was in the newspaper. This here is Leon Jackson. He's on a submarine. I know a little about submarines, because my nephew is on one. It's the most dangerous job in the navy. And let me tell you something else. If a submarine goes down, everyone on board goes down with it, from the commanding officer to the lowest-ranking man on the boat. And it doesn't matter what color they are."

"You mean he's not just foolin'?" one of the other boys asked. "Them medals is for real?"

"They're real," Sheriff Wallace said. "Leon is a good man—and a genuine hero. If truth be told, we should be holdin' a parade for him." Wallace pointed to the pickup truck. "Now you boys get in that truck and get out of here before I throw you all in jail. You make me sick . . . all of you."

"Yes, sir," Roy said contritely. He headed for the truck, and the others followed. They drove off, and for a moment there was no sound except for the fading noise of the truck engine.

"Leon, you need a doctor?" the sheriff asked.

"No, sir," Choirboy said.

"You sure? I'll be glad to get one for you."

"I'll be all right. Thanks, Sheriff."

"Don't thank me, thank the girl. She flagged me down. Oh, and I'm sorry about those boys. We ain't all like that."

"I know, Sheriff," Choirboy said. "I know."

After he let the others off, Roy Carter went home and got his shotgun. Breaking it down, he slid two twelve-gauge double-aught buckshot cartridges into the barrels. He snapped it shut with a satisfying click, then carried the loaded gun back to the pickup truck.

"We'll just see how big a hero you are," Roy said under his breath.

Knowing that Leon Jackson would have to return by the same road he had been on, Roy drove to a spot near where the encounter had taken place. Turning off, he concealed the truck behind a row of shrubbery, then got out and waited.

"No nigra is goin' to bust my nose and get away with it."

He heard the sound of a car and, peering through the bushes, recognized it as the Chevrolet Leon had been driving. He slid the safety off, then put his fingers on both triggers.

Choirboy was whistling a little tune as he drove back home. Daisy had agreed to go on a date with him next Friday, and he was feeling pretty good about that. She had also promised to write him once he returned to duty. It would be nice to get a letter from a girl, especially someone as pretty as Daisy. He saw how the other men reacted when they got letters from their girls. Though his parents and a few members of his father's congregation had been loyal correspondents, he had never gotten a letter from a girl.

Suddenly he saw someone step out into the road. For a second he was afraid that whoever it was would dash in front of him, and he put on his brakes to avoid hitting him. Then he realized the person was one of the boys who had attacked him, and in the next instant he saw the shotgun pointing right at him. A huge flame pattern erupted from the twin muzzles, and the windshield exploded in front of Choirboy's face.

San Francisco
February 15, 1945

"They've got the murderer," Jerry said. "Think of it. You spend nearly four years fighting the Japanese, then you go home on leave and are killed by one of our own."

"Not one of my own," Pat said. "I wouldn't want to have anything to do with someone like that. I hope they put him away forever."

"Yes, well, he's still in high school. A star football player, they say. He's only seventeen, so I don't know what they are going to do with him."

"Seventeen," Pat repeated. "Jerry, we have boys no older than that dying in combat. He's old enough to be responsible for what he did."

"Yes, well, that's the way I look at it," Jerry agreed.

"What a thing to happen to someone like Choirboy," Pat lamented.

"They say he died instantly," Jerry said. "On the one hand, that's good, I suppose. But he didn't even have time to utter a quick prayer."

"We don't need to worry about that," Pat replied. "Choirboy's entire life was a prayer." He shook his head, then went into his stateroom, closed the door, and cried.

Angelfish stayed at Hunters Point for two months. Pat and Diane found a small house in Haight-Ashbury, and for a while they were able to live the life of a normal married couple. They often had guests for dinner, including Jerry and Dickey and, just as often, Dickey's sister, Sally.

Pat commuted daily to Hunters Point. Cables and hoses stretched from dockside to *Angelfish's* cluttered topsides. Bottles of acetylene and oxygen rolled around on deck, feeding torches that sputtered, sparked, and popped in the hands of men wearing coveralls and dark welding masks.

Below deck, pipes, valves, and wires hung from the overhead, while bars of sunlight slashed down into areas of the boat that had never seen sunlight. Old equipment was jerked out of the control room and conning tower to be replaced by new, upgraded electronic, computing, and communication gear. Periscopes were refurbished, and new radar and radio antennae put into place. New electric motors, which had no need of noisy reduction gear, were installed.

And while in port, the torpedo men went to school on the new Mark-18 torpedo. The Mark 18, unlike its predecessor, was battery powered.

Because the propeller was electrically driven, it would leave no telltale wake of bubbles to warn the enemy.

On the twenty-sixth of February, all work was completed, and Comdr. Jerry Cornelison received orders that would take them back to Fremantle. Diane had quit her naval job in Pearl Harbor so she could remain in San Francisco while work was being done on *Angelfish*. She loved the time they were together, and she loved the little house they had rented. Pat and Diane decided that she would remain there until the war ended. Her decision was made easier by the fact that she had made several friends—not only Sally, but also other navy wives.

Diane, Sally, and the other women came down to the dock to wave good-bye to the men of *Angelfish* as it nosed out of San Francisco Harbor.

Some of the men had not been aboard when she docked. And some of the men who had been aboard were no longer part of the crew. Twenty percent of her original crew, including Tony Jarvis, had been sent to New London, Connecticut, to teach school. Another 20 percent and been assigned to the new boat, *Blowfish*.

Dickey Traser was captain of *Blowfish*. His executive officer was Darrel Roberts. That left an opening for Lt. Patrick Hanifin to become XO of *Angelfish*.

18

Alamogordo, New Mexico
July 16, 1945

Trinity Site, the testing ground, was located in the middle of the desert in an area called *Jornada del Muerto*—Journey of Death. Dr. J. Robert Oppenheimer was passing out dark glasses to everyone.

"We're not going to be able to see anything through this," someone complained.

"Oh, but we will, my friend," Oppenheimer replied. "In fact, we are advised to look away from the initial blast, even with the glasses."

In the distance, he knew, stood a hundred-foot tower, though it was too far away and still too dark to be seen.

"Two minutes," Gen. Leslie Groves announced.

"Do you think we're safe here?" a witness asked.

"I think so," one of the scientists replied. "No one can guarantee it, of course. But then, as far as that goes, no one can guarantee that the world is safe. We have calculated that there is a one-in-a-million chance that once the chain reaction begins, it won't stop. It could split every atom on earth and turn this planet into so much cosmic dust."

"One in a million," the witness repeated slowly. "In the world of physics, one in a million may as well be even odds."

"I know. It's like shooting craps with God," the scientist agreed. "Let's just hope that He gives us a pass."

"Gentlemen, we now have one minute until detonation," General Groves said. "Everyone put on your goggles."

"Ten seconds! Everyone turn your back to the test site."

"Six . . . five . . . four . . . three . . . two . . . one . . . zero!"

At that instant, a light, more brilliant than any light ever before seen on the face of the earth, turned the predawn darkness into the sunniest afternoon, even through the dark glasses. Fed by a temperature of one hundred million degrees, the blast gave off a light that could have been seen from any planet in the solar system.

When the initial flash subsided, all the spectators turned back toward Trinity and lifted their dark goggles. A tremendous ball of fire began to grow, billowing larger and larger until some thought it would never stop. For a frightening moment it looked as if this really was the beginning of the chain reaction the scientist had spoken of. Perhaps the fireball would continue to grow, larger and larger, until the entire world was consumed.

Then, mercifully, it stopped growing and began changing colors, going from white to yellow to orange to red to deep purple. Finally it subsided, leaving behind a tremendous black cloud that formed into a gigantic mushroom.

Then there was silence. A long, long period of absolute . . . total . . . dead silence.

Finally it hit.

The shock wave and sound waves were traveling together. The concussion, even this far away, nearly knocked the witnesses over, and a whistling hurricane came up with sand thrown before a wind that had the searing heat of a blast furnace. Along with the concussion wave was a roar louder than anything anyone had ever heard, or could ever imagine, and they closed their eyes and prayed in fear, for it seemed as if they had tapped straight into the forces of hell itself.

When the blast finally cleared away, and the scientists could go to the site for a closer examination, the awesome power they had unleashed became even more graphic. The hundred-foot steel tower upon which the device had sat was completely vaporized. In addition, the explosion had left a twelve-hundred-foot-wide dish in the desert floor, formed of jade-green glass from the action of the heat on the sand.

As they stood on the site, Oppenheimer spoke, quoting the Bhagavad Gita. "I have become death," he said, "destroyer of worlds."

On board Angelfish, *near Kantori Saki, Japan*
August 1, 1945

It was four o'clock in the morning, still dark, and *Angelfish* was running on the surface five thousand yards from the beach. From the bridge, Pat spotted lights along the shore. Using his binoculars, he tried to make out what they were, but was unable to see them any more clearly. The fact that they were close to shore, and that the lights weren't moving, made him think that they might be buoy markers.

"Mr. Hanifin, enemy patrol boat," a sailor in the shears said.

Turning his binoculars in the direction indicated by the sailor, Pat saw what appeared to be blinking lights. Then he realized that something was passing in front of the shore lights. Finally the patrol boat appeared in silhouette. He could even see someone walking around on deck.

It was a dark night, and there was nothing behind the submarine that would put them in silhouette, so Pat was reasonably sure they hadn't been seen. Nevertheless, he held his breath until the boat passed by.

Angelfish stayed on the surface until it began to grow gray in the east. Then Jerry ordered the bridge cleared and took them down. They moved in to about two miles from shore, where they lay at periscope depth to wait for a target.

Pat went to breakfast, served by the new steward, Elroy Hayes.

"Cream and sugar with your coffee, sir?" Hayes asked.

"Just cream."

"Yes, sir, I shoulda remembered that. I'm sure Choirboy would have remembered it. Choirboy never forgot nothin'. He must'a been the greatest steward ever to serve in the U.S. Navy," Hayes added sarcastically.

Pat chuckled. "Are the men giving you a hard time, Elroy?"

"The old-timers are," Elroy admitted. "It's like they holdin' it against me 'cause I ain't him."

"Well, he was a very well-liked young man," Pat said. "And the crew misses him. On the other hand, I'm not sure even he could live up to the memory the crew has of him now. Just give them a little time, Elroy. Before you know it, they'll forget all about Choirboy and start singing your praises."

"You think so, sir? I sure be happy when that happens."

"XO to conning tower," a voice said over the 1MC.

Picking up his coffee, Pat hurried through the corridor toward the control room, then up the ladder to the conning tower.

Jerry was looking through the periscope. "Oh, yes," he said. "A nice, fat tanker. Bearing, mark."

Draining the rest of his coffee, Pat put his cup down, then read the azimuth ring. "Bearing zero-three-zero degrees."

"Range, mark."

"Three thousand yards."

In the forward torpedo room, the new Mark-18 electrically operated torpedoes were loaded. The talker called back to the conning tower, where the message was relayed to Jerry.

"Torpedoes loaded, sir."

"Very well," Jerry replied.

"Five degrees to go, Captain," Pat warned.

"Open outer doors."

"Outer doors open."

"Constant bearing, mark."

"Set."

Pat walked over to the torpedo firing console and held his hand over the firing buttons.

"Fire one!"

Pat hit the firing plunger, and they heard and felt the torpedo leave. The electrically driven prop on the torpedo made a descending whine as it sped invisibly through the water toward the tanker.

"One fired electrically," Pat said.

"Fire two," Jerry said.

Again Pat hit the plunger. This time, nothing happened.

"Electric malfunction," Pat said. "Torpedo being fired manually."

There was a sound of air being discharged, and a bump, but nothing more.

"Mr. Hanifin, torpedo room says the second torpedo just got hung up in the tube!" the talker said.

"Captain, we had a hang fire," Pat relayed to Jerry.

"Sonar, where is the first one?" Jerry asked.

"Running hot, true, and normal, sir!" sonar replied.

"Fifty-five seconds until target," Pat said.

"Pat, go to the forward torpedo room, see what's going on."

"Aye, aye, sir." Putting his hands and feet outside the ladder rails, Pat slid down to the control room, then started forward on the double, hurdling through the watertight doorways.

When he reached the forward torpedo room, he saw half a dozen anxious faces, including Chief Persico, who had come forward from his position in the control room.

In the distance they heard the explosion as the first torpedo slammed into the target. The men cheered.

"Is the torpedo still hung up?" Pat asked.

"Yes, sir," the chief torpedo man answered.

"Can you close the outer door?"

"No, sir. The torpedo is sticking out."

"Well, we're going to have to get it out of there," Pat said. "The Japs know we're here now, and we can't maneuver this way."

"What happened?" Persico asked. "Why didn't it fire?"

"I don't know, Chief. When it didn't fire electrically, I hit the manual button and the tank discharged, but somehow, the torpedo got jammed."

"Recharge the tank," Pat ordered.

265

Persico turned the air-valve handle. There was a blast of air, but the tank pressure gauge stayed at zero.

"Uh-oh. The tank isn't taking a recharge," the chief said.

Without compressed air, it would be impossible to fire the torpedo.

"Mr. Hanifin, if we keep going forward, the little spinner is going to arm the torpedo," Persico said. His face was drained of color. "If it gets armed and blows up in the tube, it will take the front third of the boat off."

"Let me have the phone," Pat said to the talker. "Put the captain on," he said into the mouthpiece.

"What have you got, Pat?" Jerry's voice asked.

"Captain, you're going to have to bring her to a dead stop, otherwise we might arm this thing."

"All right. Dead stop it is."

Pat handed the phone back to the talker. "Well, at least we can stop it from arming. Try to recharge the tank again."

Persico reached up to turn the air-valve handle. Again there was a blast of air, but the pressure gauge remained at zero.

"Maybe we really have pressure, but the gauge isn't working," one of the men suggested.

"All right, try to fire it," Pat ordered.

The chief torpedo man hit the firing button but again, nothing happened.

"What now, sir?" Persico asked.

"I want all of you out of here," Pat ordered. "Let me see what I can do."

"No sense in evacuating the compartment, sir. If that thing goes off, it's going to take the entire boat down."

"That's true, Chief, but I don't think it's going to go off. On the other hand, if something I do causes this breech door to open, it'll instantly flood the entire compartment. So I want everyone out. And close the watertight door."

"Aye, aye, sir," Persico said. "You heard the XO, everyone out of here."

The men hurried out, then closed and dogged the watertight door behind them. Pat pulled down the technical manual and started reading it, trying desperately to come up with a diagnosis and a solution.

"XO to the phone," Jerry's voice said over the 1MC.

Looking around the compartment, Pat saw the phone set the talker had left behind and put it on. "Yes, sir," he said.

"How are you coming, Pat?"

"Not good sir. The fish is jammed in the tube, and we can't get the air tank to hold a charge."

"Well, not to put any more pressure on you, but I thought you might like to know that there are a couple of destroyers up here looking for us. And I can't maneuver with a torpedo hung up in the tube."

"Yes, sir, I'll do what I can."

Pat went back to the manual, and saw that the discharge element was a one-way valve that is normally closed, but is sprung open when the trigger is operated. Then, when new air is introduced to recharge the tank, the valve should close again. For some reason, the valve was staying open.

Pat turned the handle again, letting air into the tank. He let it continue for several seconds, hoping the incoming air would force the valve closed and let the pressure build up. When nothing happened he closed the handle to keep from using up all the air.

Ping . . . PING!

The Japanese were conducting an active search.

Pat returned to the tech manual. "Come on, come on," he said aloud. "Surely this isn't the first time a torpedo ever hung up in the tube. Surely you have some suggestion for me."

Ping . . . PING!

He began searching for another option.

Click, click. BOOM!

The depth charge was close.

Dear Lord, Pat prayed silently, *I need help. I know I haven't been the Christian I should have been. I've been content to ride on the coattails of Diane and John Henry and even Choirboy. But they aren't here now, so I have to come to You on my own. Please don't let the crew suffer because of my unworthiness. Please, dear Lord, help me get them through this safely. And if I die, then, Lord, have mercy on my soul, and receive me into Your kingdom. In Jesus' name I pray. Amen.*

He began looking through the tech manual again.

"Mr. Hanifin?"

Pat looked up, but he saw no one.

"Mr. Hanifin?"

"Who's in here? This compartment is supposed to be cleared." Pat looked around, but saw no one. Then, from directly behind him, he heard the voice again.

"The Lord has heard your prayer, Mr. Hanifin. Everything will be all right now."

Pat spun toward the sound of the voice and gasped. "Choirboy?" He felt the hair standing up on the back of his neck and on his arms. Choirboy was standing before him, wearing steward's whites and smiling at him. Pat had never seen a more beatific smile.

Click, click. KABOOM!

The depth charge was much closer this time, so close that it caused the submarine to rock violently. The lights went out, and for a moment the torpedo room was in total darkness. Yet Choirboy was completely visible . . . as if illuminated by some inner glow.

The lights came back on.

"What are you doing here?" Pat finally asked.

"Didn't you just ask the Lord for help?" Choirboy asked.

"Yes, but . . ."

"Look at the pressure gauge," Choirboy said.

Pat looked at the pressure gauge and gasped. The pressure was up!

"Try it again, Mr. Hanifin. I believe it will work this time."

Pat pushed the firing button. There was a sudden whoosh of air as the torpedo fired. Then the water and air recycled as the outer door closed.

Pat grabbed the phone. "Captain, door is closed!" he shouted.

"It worked, Choirboy, it worked!" He turned back quickly, but the compartment was empty.

At that moment the watertight door opened, and the forward torpedo crew rushed back in, followed by Chief Persico. Even as they were entering the compartment, Pat felt the submarine making a very tight, evasive turn. Another depth charge went off, but this one was farther away than the first one. They were getting away.

"I don't know how you did it, Mr. Hanifin," Persico said. "But you sure pulled us out of the fire."

"Chief, were you looking through the window?" Pat asked.

"Yes, sir."

"Did you see anyone else in here?"

"Anyone else in here? No sir, I got everyone out."

Pat shook his head. "No, I don't mean any of the torpedo men. Did you see anyone else?"

"Sir, I was watching you every moment," Persico said. "Believe me, there was nobody left in here."

"I . . ." Pat started to tell Persico that Choirboy was here, that Choirboy had helped him. On the other hand, that was clearly impossible. He had to have been hallucinating.

There was another, very distant explosion. They were now well away from the Japanese destroyers.

Pat hurried back to the conning tower, receiving the cheers and accolades from the crew as he hurried through the passageway.

"Good job, Pat," Jerry said.

"Thanks."

A moment later, Persico came up to the conning tower. "What did you do, Mr. Hanifin? How did you make it work?"

"I'm not sure. One minute there was no pressure, the next minute there was. So when I saw the pressure was up, I just fired the torpedo manually. I guess the gauge is broken."

Persico shook his head. "No, sir, it ain't the gauge. It's the relief valve on the discharge tank that's broken. There's no way it can close to let pressure build up. We just checked it. It's in two or three pieces."

"Well, if that's the case, how did it fire?" Jerry asked.

"The Lord knows, Captain. I sure don't," Persico replied.

Pat reached for his coffee cup and saw that it was filled with steaming, creamed coffee.

"Looks like Elroy is catching on," Pat said as he took a drink.

"What do you mean?" Jerry asked.

Pat held out his cup. "I see he refilled my cup for me."

Jerry shook his head. "You must be mistaken. Elroy hasn't been up here since we started the attack."

"Choirboy!" Pat said quietly.

"Beg your pardon?" Jerry asked.

"Nothing," Pat said. Smiling, he closed his eyes and held the cup to his forehead, feeling the warmth of the coffee through the outside of the cup. He had prayed for deliverance, and he was delivered. Now he was offering a prayer of thanks.

Epilogue

Powerful searchlights sent their beams crisscrossing through the night sky as hundreds of people waited behind a red velvet rope in front of Mobile's Center for the Performing Arts. News personalities from all the local television stations were present, talking earnestly into hand-held microphones while the cameras sent their perfectly coiffured images back to the home base via the remote vans.

"Here they come!" someone called.

The announcement referred to two large chartered buses that were turning off Government Boulevard and pulling into the circular drive-way. With a hiss of air brakes and rattle of diesel engines, the buses stopped and began disgorging passengers to stretch and blink in the bright lights.

The arrivals looked around in curiosity at the unfamiliar surroundings and spoke quietly among themselves. This was the Tokyo Symphony Orchestra, its members a self-contained group relying on the familiarity

271

of their own company in a strange land. They were not on an American tour, but had come to Mobile for the express purpose of giving a concert to dedicate the new center. They hurried into the building and began setting up.

So far Alabama's governor, both U.S. senators, and a handful of congressmen had arrived. In addition, there were several dignitaries from the entertainment and business worlds. The official hostess for the event was Christine Lawler. She had earned the position by being on the center's planning commission. Tonight was the culmination of three years of hard work.

"You are sure they will be here?" the mayor asked again. It was at least the fourth time he had asked the question in the last five minutes.

Christine held up her cell phone. "I just spoke to them," she said. "They are in the car on their way, right now."

"This is really something," the mayor said. "Who would have ever thought that the Tokyo Symphony Orchestra would come to the States for just one performance, and that the performance would be in Mobile? And of course, we owe it all to Mr. Takamora."

Of all the business dignitaries present, Oshiri Takamora was the most notable. The Japanese billionaire was one of the most powerful names in the electronics business. His video cameras, VCRs, television sets, radios, and communication devices of all kinds dominated the world market, surviving even the recent downturn in the Japanese economy.

Mobile was an old and proud city, and yet never in its long and storied past had anything like this ever happened. The city fathers and the development commission for the Center for Performing Arts were very shocked when Oshiri Takamora, who had not even been solicited, made a private donation of twenty million dollars toward the completion of the project. Then he added to his generosity by arranging and paying for the visit of the Tokyo Symphony Orchestra. He had asked only one thing in return for his donation—that Christine Lawler's grandparents be present as his personal guests for the dedication.

"Takamora must be quite a fan of your grandfather's," the mayor continued. "I knew he was a good conductor, but I never knew he had a following as far away as Japan."

"I know it sounds as if I am bragging, but my grandfather wasn't just a good conductor. He was a *great* conductor. Arturo Toscanini said so himself," Christine said as she turned her head to the front of the portico.

A long, white Lincoln limousine pulled to a stop. One of the valets hurried out to the curb to open the door and help the passengers out. A dignified-looking man, thin, with white hair, and unself-conscious in a tuxedo, stepped from the back of the car and turned to help his wife exit. She wore a white pearl-studded dress, and the beauty of her youth was still obvious in her poised bearing. Though both were in their eighties, there was a vigor to their step and a vibrancy in their demeanor that would make the casual observer guess that they were much younger.

A scattering of applause greeted them, and when someone asked who these people were, Christine heard the response.

"That's Patrick Hanifin, one of the greatest symphony directors ever. Takamora is a big fan. That's why we got this building."

"Christine!" The regal-looking lady called as she waved her hand.

Smiling, Christine hurried over and kissed her, then she kissed her grandfather.

"Quite a turnout," he said, looking around at the crowd.

"Yes, it is," Christine said. "And it's all for you."

Her grandfather laughed. "Hardly for me," he said. "It's for the Tokyo Symphony."

The mayor came toward them. "Have you told them?"

"No," Christine answered.

"Told us what?" Pat Hanifin asked.

"Mr. Hanifin, Oshiri Takamora has asked that you and Mrs. Hanifin be his special guests for the concert. He wants you to join him and Mrs. Takamora in their box."

"Well, that's very generous of him."

"This way," the mayor said, leading them up the red carpet past the gathered crowd and through the double doors in the large, glassed front.

Inside the building they could hear the familiar sounds of an orchestra warming up: violins being tuned, brass and woodwinds riffing through the scales, and the timpani player making his final adjustments. The mayor led them around the carpeted hallway that encircled the auditorium, then into a large room that was actually a private box with oversized, comfortable chairs that enjoyed an unrestricted view of the stage. At the rear was a table of hors d'oeuvres. A window separated the box from the rest of the auditorium, but a network of speakers made certain that the occupants of the box would be able to hear every note played and every word spoken. The brand name on the speakers was, of course, Takamora.

"Mr. Takamora, your guests have arrived," the mayor said.

Oshiri Takamora smiled and extended his hand. "Mr. Patrick Hanifin," he said. "It is an honor to meet such a brilliant musician and conductor."

"The honor is all mine," Pat replied. He looked around the guest box and beyond to the auditorium. "This is a magnificent structure, Mr. Takamora, and we owe much of it to you. On behalf of the citizens of Mobile, I would like to thank you."

"You should thank my wife," Takamora said. "She wanted this to be her gift—a symbol of her affection for Mrs. Hanifin."

Pat's eyes squinted in confusion. "I beg your pardon? This is a gift from your wife to my wife?"

"Yes." Takamora turned and spoke in Japanese to someone whose back was turned. A small, gray-haired woman stood, then turned to face Pat, Diane, and Christine. A broad, happy smile was on her face.

"Oh!" Diane gasped and put her hand to her throat.

"Diane, what is it?" Pat asked in concern.

"Miko!" Diane said in a quiet voice. "Miko, is it really you?"

"I am pleased that you would recognize me after so many years," Miko said.

"How could I ever forget you?" Diane replied, embracing the friend she had not seen in over sixty years.

During the concert, by special request, the orchestra played "The Navy Hymn." In the strains of the hymn, Pat could hear the distant sound of motors and reduction gears, blowers and pumps, and the soft whisper of men standing watch. Closing his eyes, he saw once more McKinley Slayton, John Henry Welsko, Choirboy Jackson, Dickey Traser, Jerry Cornelison, Chief Persico, and Tony Jarvis, not as old men, but young and vibrant.

Wait, was that the 1MC calling him?

"XO to the conning tower."

About the Author

R obert Vaughan is a retired Chief Warrant Officer–3. He entered military service in 1953 as a member of the Missouri National Guard. Transferring to active duty, he attended the Aviation Maintenance in Fort Rucker, Alabama. After serving a tour of duty in Korea as crew chief on an H-19 helicopter, he returned to the Army Aviation flight school at Ft. Rucker, where he became a warrant officer.

After receiving his appointment to warrant officer, Robert was posted to the 101st Airborne Division at Ft. Campbell, Kentucky. His next assignment was the Seventh Cavalry in Germany, "Custer's Own." While in Germany he was historical officer for the Seventh Cavalry, and in that capacity, was custodian of the Custer memorabilia (such as Custer's field diaries, saber, hat, and so on). That assignment created a fascination with Custer, which eventually led to four published books.

From Germany, Robert went to Ft. Riley, Kansas, where he accompanied the 605th Transportation Company to Vietnam for the first of what would be three tours in Vietnam.

In Vietnam, he was a recovery officer (when an aircraft would go down, Robert would take a rigging crew to the site and rig it so it could be sling-loaded by helicopter, back to base; on several of these missions the crew would encounter intense and accurate enemy fire). Later, he would serve in the same job for the 56th Transportation Company. His last assignment in Vietnam was with the 110th Transportation Company, where he was chief of the Open Storage Depot. During his three years in Vietnam, he was awarded the Distinguished Flying Cross, the Air Medal with "V" device and thirty-five oak-leaf clusters, the Purple Heart, the Bronze Star, the Meritorious Service Medal, the Army Commendation Medal, and the Vietnamese Cross of Gallantry.

During his military service, Robert was selected by *Army Aviation Digest* as having written the "Best Article of the Year" for six consecutive years. He also wrote and produced several training films for use in the Aviation Maintenance Officers' Course. His last assignment was as Chief of the Aviation Maintenance Officers' Course.

As an author, Robert sold his first book when he was nineteen. Today, he has over thirty million books in print. Writing under thirty-five pseudonyms, he has hit the *New York Times* and *Publishers Weekly* bestseller lists twice: In 1981, *Love's Bold Journey* and *Love's Sweet Agony* each reached number one on both mass-market lists, with sales of 2.2 million each. His novel *Survival* won the 1994 Spur Award for best western novel, *The Power and the Pride* won the 1976 Porgie Award for best paperback original, and *Brandywine's War* was named by the Canadian University Symposium of Literature as the best iconoclastic novel to come from the Vietnam War. In the 1970s Vaughan was an on-air television personality with "Eyewitness Magazine" for WAVY-TV in Portsmouth, Virginia, and later, with a cooking show for "Phoenix at Mid-Day" on KPHO-TV in Phoenix, Arizona. He is also a popular speaker at several colleges and has appeared at numerous writers' conferences throughout the country. Each winter he runs the "Write on the Beach" writers' retreat in Gulf Shores, Alabama.

Robert lives on the beach of Gulf Shores, Alabama, with his wife, Ruth, and his dog, Charley. A lay eucharistic minister, Robert is a past warden and vestry member in the Episcopal Church. He is currently very active in the Holy Spirit Episcopal Church.

Touch the Face of God
A World War II Novel

Robert Vaughan

Explore the sweep and grandeur of World War II—along with those who fought it overseas and those who lived through it on the home front—at a time when faith in God was our national security.

"Oh, I have slipped the surly bonds of earth . . . Put out my hand, and touched the face of God" —John Gillespie Magee, Jr., a WWII airman who died in combat at the age of 19.

It has been called "The Last Good War" and those who fought it have been called "The Greatest Generation." They lived every day as if it were their last—loving, laughing, and trusting that God held their future.

In this moving novel, Lt. Mark White, a B-17 bomber pilot, meets Emily Hagan only weeks before he ships out to England. They fall in love through letters as each faces the war on separate sides of the Atlantic, but will the war and a misunderstanding tear them apart forever? Lt. Lee Arlington Grant has disappointed his military family by becoming a chaplain instead of a warrior. He hopes his service in the war will heal his rift with his father while he shares Christ with his fellow soldiers—especially Tom Canby.

This powerful story is about a man's love for a woman, the soldiers' love for their country, and the love of God for each of His children. Written by a decorated veteran of the Vietnam War, *Touch the Face of God* brings to life a time and a place that is quickly being forgotten.

ISBN: 0-7852-6627-5

Don't miss the next book by Robert Vaughan!

His Truth Is Marching On:
A World War II Novel

Available Spring 2004